Praise for *Po...*

D0339109

"An admirable job of bringi...
back to readers . ...
—*Richmond Tir...*

"The writing is so detailed, the descriptions of
mid-nineteenth-century New York so realistic . . .
A riveting, well-written, romantic story."
—*The News & Record* (Greensboro, North Carolina)

"May paints a detailed, relentlessly grim picture of a
pivotal year in Poe's life, set against the richly absorbing literary
society of nineteenth-century New York, which first
swooned over Poe and then shunned him."
—*Library Journal*

"Intriguing . . . [with] glimpses of colorful
pre–Civil War New York."
—*Publishers Weekly*

"The best word for *Poe & Fanny* is *mesmerizing*. John May's brilliant novel offers not only a sharply perceptive portrayal of
America's most striking literary figure but also a warm and generous
and highly dramatic appreciation of the wonderful Frances Osgood.
The knowing overview of antebellum New York society is a rich
bonus. I hung on every word of this brightly intuitive book."
—Fred Chappell, author of *Farewell, I'm Bound to Leave You*

"John May nails the gritty, lush details of Poe's rise and
fall in New York City's high society. An astounding debut
in historical fiction, *Poe & Fanny* is part literary history,
part heartbreaking love story."
—Julianna Baggott, author of *The Madam*

At age fifty, after years in business, **John May** began pursuing a writing career, returning to school and finally earning a master's in fiction
writing. This was followed by months researching what became *Poe &
Fanny*. Now sixty-two, he divides his time running his company and
working on a new novel. He lives in Greensboro, North Carolina.

Poe & Fanny

a novel by

John May

A PLUME BOOK

PLUME
Published by Penguin Group
Penguin Group (USA) Inc., 375 Hudson Street, New York, New York 10014, U.S.A.
Penguin Group (Canada), 10 Alcorn Avenue, Toronto, Ontario, Canada M4V 3B2
(a division of Pearson Penguin Canada Inc.)
Penguin Books Ltd, 80 Strand, London WC2R 0RL, England
Penguin Ireland, 25 St. Stephen's Green, Dublin 2, Ireland
(a division of Penguin Books Ltd.)
Penguin Group (Australia), 250 Camberwell Road, Camberwell, Victoria 3124,
Australia (a division of Pearson Australia Group Pty. Ltd.)
Penguin Books India Pvt. Ltd., 11 Community Centre, Panchsheel Park,
New Delhi – 110 017, India
Penguin Books (NZ), cnr Airborne and Rosedale Roads, Albany, Auckland 1310,
New Zealand (a division of Pearson New Zealand Ltd.)
Penguin Books (South Africa) (Pty.) Ltd., 24 Sturdee Avenue, Rosebank,
Johannesburg 2196, South Africa

Penguin Books Ltd., Registered Offices: 80 Strand, London WC2R 0RL, England

Published by Plume, a member of Penguin Group (USA) Inc. This is an authorized
reprint of a hardcover edition published by Algonquin Books of Chapel Hill. For information address Algonquin Books of Chapel Hill, Post Office Box 2225, Chapel Hill,
North Carolina 27515-2225.

First Plume Printing, July 2005
10 9 8 7 6 5 4 3 2 1

The Library of Congress has catalogued the Algonquin Books of Chapel Hill edition as
follows:

May, John, 1942–
    Poe & Fanny : a novel / by John May.
        p. cm.
    "A Shannon Ravenel book."
    ISBN 1-56512-427-8 (hc.)
    ISBN 0-452-28601-8 (pbk.)
    1. Poe, Edgar Allan, 1809–1849—Fiction.   2. Osgood, Frances Sargent
Locke, 1811–1850—Fiction.   3. New York (N.Y.)—Fiction.   4. Married
people—Fiction.   5. Women poets—Fiction.   6. Adultery—Fiction.
7. Authors—Fiction.   I. Title: Poe and Fanny.   II. Title.
PS3613.A95P64 2004
813'.6—dc22   2003070806

Printed in the United States of America

PUBLISHER'S NOTE
This is a work of fiction. Names, characters, places, and incidents are either the product of the
author's imagination or are used fictitiously, and any resemblance to actual persons, living or
dead, business establishments, events, or locales is entirely coincidental.

For Nancy Thorne Rouzer May

. . .

Ah, *if* the clarion tones of fame
  Shall ever ring for me,
They shall not drown—my *heart* shall hear
  The praise I won from thee!

—FRANCES SARGENT LOCKE OSGOOD

A U T H O R ' S   N O T E

All poetry in *Poe & Fanny* is genuine,
and an addendum at the end of the book
gives the full texts of all the poems
exchanged in print by Edgar Allan Poe
and Frances Sargent Locke Osgood.

POE FAMILY TREE

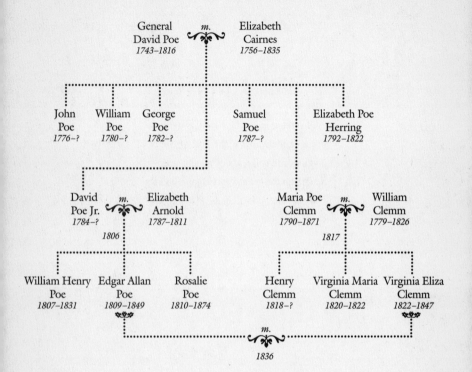

POE & FANNY

 Willis

---

New-York Mirror   Friday, December 27, 1844

THE END OF THE WORLD.—It is with a collective sigh of relief that New Yorkers anticipate the New Year, grateful that the world did not end as the Right Reverend William Miller of the Adventist Church in Chrystie Street prophesied.

For those unfamiliar with Mr. Miller, he apparently reckoned the apocalypse by way of an aptitude for the mathematical. From the Prophecy of the Book of Daniel and precise calculations of the intervals between epochs, he determined that the world would end in early December give or take a fortnight.

The effect was remarkable. My bootmaker, for example, reduced his prices reasoning that, if the world ends, what good is profit from the sale of footwear. But it seems that pinpointing the final conflagration requires more Art than Science; therefore, we of the *Mirror,* being as we are, disciples of the *Art* of Discourse, shall be so bold as to declare our own prophesy:—

THE WORLD WILL NOT END IN *1845.*

—not at least for the majority of mortals upon this earth. On the contrary, we predict that the new year will be the best ever—that notion consistent with our conviction that the march of time brings more good than ill.

W ILLIS SET HIS PEN in its cradle. Rising from his chair, he walked to one of the windows facing Ann Street and stared at the cold, overcast sky above St. Paul's. As it was nearly two o'clock, he decided to stop for lunch; the interval would allow his thoughts to wander. He had a knack for bringing a piece full circle despite its meanderings.

Noticing his reflection in the windowpane, he drew in his stomach and squared his shoulders. In three weeks, he would turn thirty-nine, though his reflection seemed as youthful as ever. He was clean-shaven, and a lock of brown hair that showed not a trace of gray fell across his forehead. Women had always found him attractive in a mischievous sort of way, not just for his looks, but also for his wit, which one critic, as he suddenly remembered, had recently called trifling—"the trifling wit of Nathaniel Parker Willis." Though he had ignored it at the time, the recollection irked him now. Who was lobbing missiles at him? He returned to his desk, considering a retort in his column. Appeal to my readers, he thought. He could cite the column—it was the *Star,* wasn't it?—and promote a shower of irate letters. At the corner of the partner's desk he shared with General Morris, he leafed through the stack of periodicals until he found the correct issue. Turning its pages, he dismissed the idea. He was being vain, and intuition told him not to reveal too much of himself. His readers adored his flirtatious style, and they didn't care that he was middle-aged, but vanity would disappoint. He flung the *Star* into the trash basket.

Trifling or not, Willis's wit attracted more readers than any other writer in America.

He walked to the coat rack, put on his gloves and seal-collared overcoat, deciding on the Astor House for lunch, a beefsteak and potatoes, steaming hot as befit the weather. Where was Morris? He should have returned from the printer's by now. Willis hated to dine alone.

"Hiram," he said, turning to Morris's assistant, who was hunched over a work table and wiping paste from his fingers. "Tell General Morris I'm at the Astor House."

Hiram Stoddard nodded as Willis looped a muffler around his neck. He fitted his beaver top hat snugly on his head to withstand the wind that would be blowing down Broadway; then he reached for his walking stick and descended the stairs.

Upon opening the door to the street, he encountered a small boy huddled in the doorway out of the wind, his arms hugging his knees for warmth. The boy wore an old woolen mackinaw with a yarn of faded purple shot through the pattern—a color so unexpected, it caught Willis's eye. Covering his feet was a bundle of magazines tied with string. Thinking to shoo him away, Willis noticed that the bundle hid bare feet.

"Afternoon, sir," the boy said in a shivery Irish accent, looking up with wary eyes. He was not more than five.

Just up Ann Street toward Broadway, another boy, an older brother by the look of him, hawked the same magazine the younger one used as a foot warmer. The brother wore an ill-fitting pair of men's boots.

"What's this?" Willis asked, tapping the bundle with his walking stick.

Pulling one of the magazines from under the twine, the boy handed it to Willis, who studied the masthead: *The Aristidean*, Vol. 1, No. 1. Who *was* Aristides, Willis wondered, Whig or Democrat? As he read, he tucked his cane under his arm and reached into his pocket; then, glancing down at the coins, he selected a shilling and thumbed it into the newsboy's palm, getting a strong whiff of him. No doubt the boy had never had a bath, and Willis suspected he lived in Five Points, which smelled of the cesspool on which it had been built.

"Go down to Grand Street," Willis said, "and get a pair of secondhand shoes. You can find a decent pair for a nickel." He saw by the look in the youngster's eyes that he could not come home with shoes unless he had permission first—not even secondhand shoes. "Does your brother share his boots with you?"

The boy nodded and turned back to the bundle covering his feet.

"Well, you can't stay here," Willis said. "Sorry, but this is a place of business." For his part Willis might have let him stay, but Morris would be furious. He watched the boy lift his bundle, cut him a surly glance, and trudge after his brother.

Another new magazine, Willis thought, following the two young hucksters toward Broadway. A deluge of print swamping the five hundred thousand residents of New York City, only a quarter of whom read with any hope of comprehension. Deciding this opinion was grossly unfair, he considered adding arrogance to vanity on his list of faults, and he chided himself. But it was ridiculous—a new magazine every week. How would he and Morris make a go of it with all these publications nibbling at their heels? At the corner of Ann and Park Row he heard a chorus of hucksters. "Here, sir, buy the *Herald*." "Have the *Express*, madam. Only a penny." The *Sun*, the *Tribune*, the *Star*, the *Mirror* . . . Newsboys besieged the crowd standing in line at the horsecar terminal. It was the best place in the city for selling newspapers, but the competition was intense.

Continuing his column in his head, Willis considered a second prediction for the new year, one regarding the number of new periodicals. He would predict a new one every week and the market already flooded, so flooded as to require a veritable Niagara of street urchins to provide distribution. Liking the word, *Niagara,* he began phrasing a sentence. Yes, he thought, that idea might work, and as he crossed through City Hall Park to avoid the mud and manure of the terminal, he smiled, thinking how grateful he was for this amazing gift of his—the parallel tracks on which his mind traveled, one experiencing life and the other describing it—and he recalled General Morris warning him to stop writing about the beautiful women he encountered on horsecars or at the theater, but Willis couldn't stop. Beautiful women were like a melody playing in his mind to which he added lyrics.

He crossed Broadway and climbed the steps to the Greek Revival front portico of the Astor House, the five-story hotel where he lived. Built by John Jacob Astor, the Astor was the finest hotel in New York. As he opened the door, he met two women just leaving.

"Anna!" one of them exclaimed. "It's Willis. Didn't I say you'd meet him if you came?"

"Fanny," Willis said, smiling, closing the door behind him and removing his hat.

Fanny offered her gloved hand, which Willis kissed, savoring its perfume.

"This is my sister, Anna," she said, reaching for her companion, "Anna Harrington. And this is the famous N. P. Willis—or should I say, the *infamous* Willis—adored by every woman in America."

Fanny stood just five feet tall, and, though in her early thirties, from a distance she could have passed for a girl in her teens. As bright and fresh as a shop window, she had dark brown, glossy hair and large, expectant eyes. She wore a scarf of purple satin neatly tucked beneath the collar of her gray woolen overcoat and, on her head, a bonnet tied under her chin with matching purple ribbons.

"Anna is from Albany," Fanny continued, tilting her head slightly to one side as if sharing a secret. There was nothing in the least artificial or affected in the gesture. It was as if she longed for Willis to believe that what she said could not be truer—Anna Harrington was indeed from Albany and nowhere else.

"I am a devoted reader, Mr. Willis," Anna said.

"It's Willis—everyone calls me Willis," he said, just as he had a thousand times, smiling and in his mind putting his admirer at her ease.

"Are you coming to Lynchie's tomorrow night?" Fanny asked, referring to Anne Lynch, whose Saturday night *conversaziones* at her home in Greenwich Village were a literary institution in New York City.

"Of course," Willis said, Fanny's petiteness making him feel taller than his six-foot frame. "But it's bitter cold. Stay and join me for lunch. I'll go up and get Mary, and we'll make a party of it."

"Thank you, but no," Fanny said. "We've lunched already. I'm taking Anna to Lynchie's. I want her to meet all my New York literary friends. Will you read something for her, Willis? Please! One of your pencilings. Don't let her to go back to Albany disappointed. Everyone there is so . . ." she broke off, almost out of breath, and turned to Anna as if Willis's presence alone were proof of her boasting and she wished to see her reaction. Then Fanny turned back to him and smiled. "We're on our way to Stewart's to buy Anna a pair of gloves."

"I saw Sam recently," Willis said as he reached to open the door for them. "Is he still in town?" By Fanny's reaction, he regretted the question. It was hard to know what to say. He knew she and Sam lived apart; in fact, Fanny and her two girls were the Willises' near neighbors; they lived just down the hall from the Willises' suite on the fifth floor. From this and things he had heard, Willis inferred that Fanny was somewhere between marriage and divorce, but divorce was still difficult and expensive in New York.

"No," she said. "Sam has gone to Baltimore and from there, south. He left yesterday. He will paint Mr. Elliot in Beaufort, then he's on to New Orleans. We shall not see him *encore une fois,*" she paused, searching for a couplet, "ere ripens red *la fraise du bois,*" and she seemed to revel in the triumph of her rhyme.

Through the frosted glass of the front door, Willis watched the two women descend the steps and turn up Broadway toward Stewart's. Shaking his head, he decided Sam Osgood must be a fool to abandon a woman so precious as Fanny and go traveling around the country painting portraits. She had the charming habit of turning conversation into verse—writing poetry was like breathing air to Fanny Osgood.

He turned toward the table d'hôte. Where was he? Ah, yes. Niagara. He took his favorite table beside one of the large windows overlooking Vesey Street and the snow-covered cemetery surrounding St. Paul's. After ordering a glass of claret, he unfolded his magazine.

The Aristidean. Thomas Dunn English, editor. Folly! Willis thought. Folly to go head-to-head with the *American Whig Review*—New York didn't need another Whig magazine. Folly to get embroiled in politics with elections far off—Polk, just elected, would not take office for another three months. And folly to give a magazine a name newsboys could not possibly pronounce. Without thinking, a tune began playing in Willis's mind, the lyrics breaking through into his consciousness.

> Don't you remember sweet Alice, Ben Bolt,—
> Sweet Alice whose hair was so brown,
> Who wept with delight when you gave her a smile,
> And trembled with fear at your frown?

He chuckled at the recollection. Dunn English had written it three years earlier. Morris had commissioned a sea chanty, but English composed a sentimental poem instead, a drippy trifle. They published it anyway, needing a filler, as Willis recalled. Later someone put it to music—a doleful German melody—and the thing took off like a Roman candle. Now it was sung at bachelor parties once everyone was in their cups. It occurred to Willis that he might use the *Aristidean* as proof of his prediction—the first of fifty-two new periodicals. What made it tempting was that English was something of a hothead.

Hearing his name called, he turned to see the printer's devil from his office. The maitre d' was pointing to Willis.

"General Morris wants you, sir," the boy said as he approached the table.

"What's the matter?" Willis asked.

"I'd rather not say. I was told to fetch you at once."

Willis stood, laid his napkin aside, and took up his overcoat. His first thought was his wife, Mary, who was six months pregnant. He stopped at the front desk to inquire; then, satisfied that Mary had not sent for him, he followed the young assistant back to his office.

At the top of the stairs, the door to *Mirror* office was flung open and standing in the doorway was Edgar Poe, unsteady, his top hat at an odd angle, his eyes glassy and unfocused.

"Mr. Poe seems to be in some distress," General Morris boomed as Willis approached the landing.

"Edgar?" Willis exclaimed. "What's the matter?"

"Willis!" Poe said in a slurred voice. "By God, Willis! I need a moment of your time."

Though Poe made every effort to stand erect and though his tie was straight and his mustache combed, his voice, his eyes, and the odd angle of his hat betrayed his condition.

"Willis," he said, as if the name consisted of but one syllable, "I'm in partnership with a fool and a damned fool at that."

Beyond Poe stood the full muster of the *New-York Mirror*. Hiram Stoddard, with his back to the door, seemed eager for an altercation, and beside Stoddard, big-eyed and nervous, was the printer's devil who had come to fetch Willis at the Astor. Beyond them two other clerks appeared to be enjoying the sport, but the commander of this army, Willis's partner, General George Pope Morris—short, stout, immovable—brandished his cane like a saber.

Willis decided on retreat. "Come, Edgar," he said, "I'll buy you lunch." Taking Poe's arm, he led him away. Poe was shorter and slighter than Willis, but anticipating the usual bellicosity that accompanies drunkenness, he guided Poe down the stairs with a firm hand.

"Briggs is a damn fool and an idiot," Poe said.

"We'll have oysters," Willis announced as they emerged onto Ann Street. He searched his mind for a suitable eating-house, one where Poe's condition would not be an embarrassment. Turning onto Fulton, they walked arm in arm toward the river. Faced with a freezing wind, Poe grew quiet; Willis hoped the wind would have a sobering effect. Poe's weakness for alcohol was rumored about, but in five months working for the *Mirror,* Willis had never seen him drunk. Now the smell of cheap wine was strong, and the odor of camphor rose from Poe's overcoat, a military relic, judging from the shadow of the corporal's stripes that had once adorned the sleeve. The cross streets were jammed with men from Wall Street going to lunch; a sea of bobbing top hats flowed all the way downtown. Poe drew curious attention when his hat blew off. Willis fetched it, placed it back on his head, and noticed pearls of perspiration on his forehead.

"Briggs is a damn fool," Poe repeated. His breath reeked. "The man's a greengrocer, for Christ's sake. Doesn't know publishing from parsnips."

"What happened?"

"It's Friday, is it not?" Poe shook his head. "The day every weekly in America goes on sale. Our first issue was due out, and where is it?" He stopped and turned to Willis, his hat about to fall off again. "The man belongs on Blackwell's Island."

Willis smiled, took Poe's arm again, and nudged him on. "What's the name again?"

"*Broadway Journal,*" Poe said, and he staggered into Willis, throwing them both off balance, and they nearly stumbled. Anyone seeing them would have thought them both drunk.

"That's a fine name," Willis said, thinking that at least it was one newsboys could pronounce.

"You think so?" Poe said. "Well, it's a damn rare one."

Willis chuckled to himself, thinking, This week the *Aristidean,* next week the *Broadway Journal.*

Two weeks earlier Poe had resigned his post as Willis's assistant to start a new literary journal with Charles Briggs, a former wholesale grocer, now a writer. Older than Willis, Briggs was not without ability, but he was also something of a stuffed shirt, a trait Willis invariably associated with Boston.

"Let's try this place?" Willis said, and he guided Poe into a tavern facing the wharfs, a place unknown to him, at the corner of John and Front Streets. Avoiding the patrons sitting at tables farther back, sailors mostly, Willis selected a corner of the bar near the front. He ordered coffee, oysters, and soda crackers as Poe took a stool and stared out the window across Front Street toward Burling Slip and the East River. A black-hulled China clipper, the *Bonaventure,* was moored in the slipway, the tip of its bowsprit almost touching a fourth-story window in the building across the street. The figurehead, a maiden shrouded in blue with one breast exposed to the cold, hovered twenty feet in the air. She held one hand aloft, seeming to bless the dock workers beneath her. Beyond the slip and as far up the river as one could see was a hive of ship's masts, sails, and spars, huge ships, their hulls three stories tall, their bowsprits towering above the mass of hawsers, dock lines, and barrel-laden drays thronging the wharf.

"So you missed your deadline?" Willis asked, hoping coffee and conversation would bring Poe around.

Poe explained that Briggs had selected an unsuitable printer. On learning this, he had suggested the printer used by the *Mirror*, the firm of John Douglas. "For in all of America," he declared, loud enough to draw the attention of other patrons, "who knows more about publishing than Morris and Willis?" And he praised their names such that Willis had to quiet him down. As it turned out, by the time Briggs and Poe had approached Mr. Douglas, it was too late to make the Friday deadline. They would have to delay their first issue for a week, and Poe would have to forgo a week's wages.

He rambled on. Willis ate two oysters, decided they were rancid, and lunched on soda crackers instead. Poe gorged, sucking the shells dry of their pearly liquid and stuffing crackers in his mouth as if he'd not eaten for a week. It's clear he wants to borrow money, Willis thought as he stared out the window, thinking also that the flood of new magazines might push up the price of printing. Maybe he should have a talk with John Douglas.

At last, his belly full, Poe lay his head on the bar and was soon sleeping. Willis tipped the proprietor to leave his companion undisturbed, then pulled the *Aristidean* from his pocket and started reading. It was an eight-pager and looked more like a newspaper than a magazine, thus qualifying for better postal rates. The brown newsprint was inferior, and typesetting and line spacing differed from article to article, giving it a patchwork appearance. Subscriptions were three dollars a year, pricy for a thing that looked so thrown-together. Single issues went for half a shilling.

The lead article, no doubt written by Dunn English, called for fresh perspectives in light of the sea changes transforming America at breathtaking speed—railroads, telegraphs, steamships, daguerreotypy, new and faster printing presses, modern waterworks. How would society cope? Willis suspected that the *Aristidean* was poised to provide the answers—at six and a quarter cents per copy.

He read the magazine through as Poe slept, snorting cracker crumbs that caught in the web of his mustache. Staring out at the clipper, Willis thought of his and Mary's plans to go to England in the spring after the baby came. Her parents were eager to see the new child and also their granddaughter, Imogen, the Willises' two-year-old. No doubt the second child would change their life; he would have to buy a house when they returned from abroad; therefore, the *New-York Mirror* needed to prosper.

Indeed, Mary longed to go home. She had even suggested that they live in

England, but Willis did not want to leave for good. There were changes afoot, and not only those noted by the *Aristidean*. Culture was changing and it all had to do with wealth. The subject fascinated him, and who in all America was a better chronicler of such things than he?

Poe stirred and rubbed his eyes. His forehead was red where it had pressed upon the bar. He wiped his mouth on the sleeve of his overcoat and looked up at Willis. "I should never have left the *Mirror*," he said.

"It will work out," Willis reassured him, hoping Poe would not ask for his old job back.

"I never worked for finer men than you and Morris. But the pay! Fifteen dollars a week for a man with a sick wife and a mother-in-law who wants everything just so. Now I'll have to move them into town. Briggs will never make it on his own."

"Perhaps I can help," Willis said, following an impulse. If this was going to cost him money, he may as well get something for it. "Did you intend to review Longfellow's Christmas gift book?" he asked. "We'd pay you ten dollars."

"Ten dollars," Poe said, spurning the sum.

Willis smiled. "Well, as you know, it's not our policy to pay contributors."

"Yes, I know," Poe said. He knew the drill. "'Pay comes in the form of seeing one's name in print.' Unfortunately, my landlord insists on the coin of the realm."

"And for that reason we will pay you ten dollars," Willis said, laughing and relieved that Poe seemed to be sobering up. "Do you have a copy? It's called *The Waif*. I'll get it for you."

"It's old stuff," Poe said, dismissing it and rising from his stool.

"I think you'll find that it contains some new pieces," Willis said, "and they may be . . . how shall I say . . . reminiscent?"

Poe eyed him suspiciously. "You want me to tomahawk the damn thing, don't you?"

"Well, I thought . . ." Willis paused, smiling. "In the past you've suspected the professor of borrowing from his fellow poets, and I thought perhaps you might perceive the same trend this time. If so, you might amplify on that theme. I remember one of your reviews—how did it go?—'the most barbarous class of literary robbery?'" He laughed out loud.

The idea was pure impulse. Controversy sold newspapers, and Willis could imagine a hailstorm of letters from Boston defending Longfellow. Had Poe not shown up in such a state of intoxication, the notion might never have occurred to him. Willis considered himself an exile from Boston: As a young magazinist fresh out of Yale, he had been attacked for his liberal ideas and expelled from the Park Street Congregational Church for missing communion and attending the theater. The rivalry between New York and Boston to be America's foremost city was a contest decided long ago, so far as Willis was concerned, but this fact did not seem so clear to Bostonians. At bottom, however, was his reluctance to dirty his own hands. He'd learned to avoid controversy and limited his reviews to works he could praise, leaving serious criticism to men who believed in its nobility—men like Poe.

As for Poe, he was perhaps too intoxicated to notice that Willis was quoting from a review written five years earlier, but Willis had always found Poe's reviews immensely entertaining. No one else could skewer a work as viciously and with such wit.

Poe brushed the crumbs from his overcoat as Willis paid the bill, and they left, heading up John Street toward Broadway.

"Shall I walk you to the terminal?" Willis said, thinking to ensure that Poe got safely home. "Next time you're in town, I'll have a copy of Longfellow's book waiting for you."

It was three-thirty. The gray sky had grown more ominous, and the cold wind persisted, now at their backs as they ascended the hill. When they reached the terminal, Willis searched for a Broadway line horsecar, steering Poe by the arm. "Do you have fare?" he asked.

"I was hoping you'd advance me for the Longfellow piece," Poe said. "You know I'm good for it, and I'm behind with my landlord."

"You'll go straight home?"

"You have my word," Poe said. "It's the end of the line for me, then a three-mile walk to put me right. I don't want my little wifey to think I've been backsliding."

Willis reached for his wallet and handed Poe a ten-dollar bill plus a shilling for fare. "Stop by next week," he said. "Longfellow's book will be waiting for you."

Poe climbed the steps at the back of the horsecar, holding tight to the rail, offering neither thanks nor good-bye.

As Willis walked back to his office, he felt a nagging irritation. The cheeriness of the morning had disappeared. Why this sour mood, he wondered. He'd been in such high spirits earlier. His column remained unfinished, but that wasn't it, and he recalled the word *Niagara* and the flood of new periodicals—his second prediction for 1845—the linchpin that would join the afternoon portion of his column with the morning portion. He pulled the folded copy of the *Aristidean* from his pocket and smoothed it flat, saving it for General Morris, who would want to see it, and just then he remembered the shoeless newsboy and the purple yarn shot through the plaid of his jacket, a color so unexpected on a street urchin, yet one so becoming to Fanny Osgood, those purple ribbons below her gray eyes. Was she not beautiful? And then Poe—drunk and broke. But it wasn't Poe or any of those other things that had dampened Willis's spirits. The culprit was that knife in his back—"the trifling wit of Nathaniel Parker Willis."

CHAPTER 2
🌿 Muddy 🌿

MARIA CLEMM LEFT THE Brennan farm at nine in the morning. High gray clouds hid the sun, but they were not so menacing as the day before, and the crust of ice on the trough showed evidence of melt. The stiff northeast wind that had been blowing for a week down the Hudson had moved around to the south.

She thought of herself not as stout, but *sturdy,* a sturdy fifty-four-year-old. She ascended the hill, staying in the center of the path and out of the icy ruts that carved a trail from Bloomingdale Road down to the farmhouse. A pain in her right hip bothered her, hurting most when she climbed stairs or hills. She tried to ignore it, certain nothing could be done, though she had never seen a doctor about it. It was a helpless kind of pain—dull, deep in the bone.

It was Tuesday, New Year's Eve.

She and her daughter, Sissy, had bathed the night before and washed their hair. Maria's white collar was clean and starched, and she wore a black dress that she wished she'd had time to sponge before she left. It showed signs of splatter along the hem. On her feet, hidden by her full-length skirt and coat, were black, ankle-high boots that buttoned up the side, and on her head she wore a black poke bonnet tied alongside her left cheek with a satin bow. In her gloved right hand she carried a carpetbag with the handle of an umbrella sticking out. The umbrella would provide protection against the weather or the wild dogs that roamed the outskirts of town.

When she reached Bloomingdale Road, she turned toward New York City, dodging the puddles and staying to the high side. The air smelled of juniper, and winter songbirds worked in the thickets beside the highway. Every so often she looked back, hoping for a carriage or a dray cart heading into town. She wanted a ride, she did, though she had a shilling for horsecar fare just in case. With payment for the piecework she carried in her bag, she would buy sewing thread and five yards of percale. Sissy wanted to embroider new pillowcases. If Maria was lucky and caught a ride, she could save the fare. If not, she would have to walk the three miles to the head of the Broadway line at Twenty-third Street and wait for a ride downtown.

Sissy had always called her Muddy, her baby way of saying "Mother." When Eddy Poe married Sissy nine years earlier, he started calling her Muddy, too. Now, though Sissy was only twenty-two and Eddy almost thirty-six, Muddy thought of them both as her children, and like any good mother, she did for them what she could, whatever was needed. Loving them so, she almost cherished the pain in her hip. She thanked God for bringing weather that was not so cold. If only He would send a brewery dray heading into town with a load of beer for the celebrations. Her bag was heavy. She had expected the road would be thick with truck farmers.

Eddy had not come home Friday night. Sissy worried herself sick. She told Muddy she had a premonition that he was hurt, mistreated in some way, so neither of them got much sleep. Muddy's fears of his whereabouts were not so innocent, but she kept them to herself. He arrived Saturday afternoon—broke, freezing wet, and reeking of vomit. Sissy locked herself in her room, which she always did when he was drunk. Muddy put him to bed in her room off the kitchen, and he'd been there two days, sleeping it off.

They were two weeks behind on their room and board, so Muddy was on her way to New York City to try and sell his new manuscript.

At supper last night, Eddy announced that they were moving into the city. Said he had no choice, that things weren't going so well at the new magazine. Sissy was upset, so after supper Muddy distracted her with some piecework sewing she was doing to help pay the Brennans. It was then that Sissy got the idea for new pillowcases. Won't it be fun, she said.

The last time they had embroidered pillowcases was three years earlier when they lived in Philadelphia. Eddy was working for Mr. Graham then, at *Graham's Lady's and Gentleman's Magazine*. Muddy had chosen an embroidery pattern from a page decoration in one of Eddy's poetry books, a twining vine of yellow rosebuds that she would stitch along the hem. As they worked, Sissy was singing when she was taken with a sudden and violent fit of coughing, and before she could catch her breath, Muddy noticed spots of blood on her handkerchief. After that, Muddy changed her mind to red rosebuds instead of yellow as if she could conceal her fears from the both of them. Had it been then that she realized Sissy would not have a long life? Had it been then, sitting with her sewing basket in her lap, when her hand reached for the yellow thread, then hesitated and took the red instead? Her own flesh and blood, so young, so fragile.

Stopping to rest, she set her bag on the ground and turned to look back. Black woodsmoke rising from the chimney of a farmhouse two fields away drifted north, and behind her, in the direction of the Brennan farm, Muddy could see Mount Tom, the outcrop of rock where Eddy sat for hours watching the river and doing his writing. It didn't seem like New Year's Eve. It was too quiet. She listened, certain some sound would let on that she was only two miles from town—a dog, a distant train, the whistle of a boat steaming up the Hudson toward Albany. But there was nothing, only the cheeping of the birds and the rustle of the wind through the firs that grew along the fencerows. She switched the bag to her left hand, held the brim of her bonnet with her right, and started off again.

With her gone, Muddy guessed, Eddy would be wanting Sissy to talk to him. She hadn't said a word to him since he got home on Saturday, and by now the silent treatment would be eating him alive. Sissy had been feeling better; country life was what she needed, but now he'd gone and gotten drunk, and they were moving again, and, as always, she'd grow worse.

To get her mind off these things, Muddy recalled a notion, one that was always a comfort, one that she often resorted to when nursing Eddy after one of his binges. It was that she would not undo anything that had happened, even if she could. Only Sissy's illness—she would undo that, of course. That was not a part of what gave her solace. It was Eddy. He couldn't keep house and home together. Every few months he dreamed up some new scheme only to be disappointed again. They always needed money. He moved from job to job, because every time, sooner or later, he took to drinking. He blamed everybody but himself. Sissy and Muddy went along with the make-believe, Sissy growing sicker, Muddy growing older. They packed everything up and moved again, just as they would now. For her part, she didn't mind living in town. She had spent most of her life living in Baltimore, right downtown. Town life was fine with her, but Sissy needed fresh air. Living on the river had been good for her lungs.

So once again Muddy recalled the choice she and Sissy had made ten years earlier. After Muddy's mother died and they lost her mother's pension, a distant cousin, Neilson Poe, offered to take them in. Neilson promised to adopt Sissy, who was twelve at the time, pay for her education, and introduce her to Baltimore society when the time came. He was a rich man; they would have had a comfortable life. Eddy had just gone back to Richmond after he'd lived with Muddy and Sissy in Baltimore for four years—four happy years. He had gotten a job with a new magazine in Richmond, and he begged them to come there instead of moving in with Neilson, promising to fulfill his pledge to marry Sissy when she came of age. Muddy had never taken that pledge seriously; after all, Eddy and Sissy were first cousins. It wasn't proper that they should marry, but Sissy took his pledge seriously. She worshiped the ground he walked on. His pleas were so pitiful, he was lonely without them, and in the end they could not deny him.

Had they done the right thing? Muddy always pondered this question after one of his sprees. Remembering those days in Baltimore with Sissy, a young and healthy girl, her whole life ahead of her, Muddy reconsidered Neilson Poe's offer, comparing it to Eddy's letter from Richmond begging them to come, promising everything good if they did. The answer swelled in her heart just as it always did. She could not have refused Eddy if she'd wanted to, and she hadn't missed Neilson Poe one stitch. Eddy might not have survived without her, being such a careless boy. It wasn't God's plan for Muddy to have a life of comfort. To care for Eddy and Sissy all her days—that was His plan for her. Wasn't Eddy the finest poet in America? And the finest storyteller, too? Thinking this, Muddy recalled some of her favorites, reciting them like a catechism: "The Fall of the House of Usher," "The Murders in the Rue Morgue," "The Mask of the Red Death," "The Pit and the Pendulum," "The Mystery of Marie Rogêt," "The Tell-Tale Heart," "The Gold Bug," "The Purloined Letter," "The Premature Burial." As he had composed them, he read them to her and Sissy; he relied on their opinion. That made Muddy feel she'd had a hand in their creation. And, too, there was never a moment—when Eddy was himself—that he would not suffer the tortures of Satan for the sake of his little Sissy. Maybe it had not been the wise choice, but in Muddy's heart she knew it was the right choice, the noble choice.

She recalled one particular night in Richmond, in Mrs. Yarrington's boardinghouse. She and Sissy had just come up from supper. As Muddy stoked the fire, Sissy went to the washstand and, with her back to Muddy, undressed and started sponging her chest and underarms. Muddy was describing how the other boarders had frowned on the two of them, Eddy and Sissy, for being so lovey-dovey at the supper table and how it wasn't proper—her being thirteen and Eddy, twenty-five. Then Sissy reminded her that she and Eddy were going to get married.

"You're too young to marry and that's that," Muddy told her. "And don't forget that he's your first cousin. There! That's two good reasons. Now hush up about it."

"Muddy," Sissy said, pulling her nightgown over her head, "if I have a daughter, I'm going to name her Maria after you and Eliza after Eddy's mama—Maria Eliza Poe. Now, ain't that the prettiest name you ever heard?"

Well, what could Muddy say? That it was a pretty name, but just not proper? Oh, it was a proper name all right, and maybe that's what took Muddy in—the thought of a grandbaby bouncing on her knee and named after her. She could just picture herself giving that little girl a bath, rubbing her with talcum powder and smelling her sweet baby skin, prying her arms from around her neck as she put her in the crib at night. Wasn't any talking Sissy out of it; she had her mind made up, and Muddy went along, holding fast to visions of that little girl—Maria Eliza. But it wasn't to be. Muddy learned to live without a lot of things, but giving up that dream was one of the hardest. She guessed it was even harder for Sissy, but after Sissy got sick in Philadelphia, Muddy knew better than to mention that name ever again.

A half mile from the end of the Broadway line, just outside town, Muddy came to a livery stable where she had once found a ride and where logic told her she might find another, but no one was stirring, so she walked on to Twenty-third Street and Madison Square to wait for the horsecar.

It was half past ten when she reached the office of the *New-York Mirror*, just as Hiram Stoddard was unlocking the door. Muddy asked if she could wait for Mr. Willis.

"Sorry," Stoddard said. "Mr. Willis is taking the week off, and so is General Morris."

"I'm here to pick up a book for Mr. Poe," Muddy said, studying the man, wondering if she should offer the manuscript she carried in her bag. She had strict instructions from Eddy regarding its sale.

Stoddard went to Willis's desk and fetched a brown paper parcel containing the Longfellow book. Returning to the counter, he handed it to Muddy and started writing something in a ledger. "Mrs. Poe, is it?"

"Clemm," she said.

"Clemm?"

"Yes. Mr. Poe is married to my daughter." Muddy didn't bother to tell him that her maiden name was Poe. Might confuse the young man, and anyway it was none of his business. She could have explained that Eddy was also her nephew, her brother's son. And, Muddy's husband, poor Mr. Clemm, had been dead for . . . She had to stop and think.

Stoddard wrote her name, misspelling it. As he turned the ledger toward her and handed her the pen, Muddy recalled that it was just two years after Sissy was born that Mr. Clemm passed. That would have been twenty years ago.

"I have a new poem that Eddy wrote," she said, signing the ledger. "It's called 'The Raven,' and it's a long one. He said Mr. Willis would pay twenty dollars for it." Her voice was determined. She was an old hand at this, and instinct told her to start by making demands, then work her way to begging.

Stoddard smiled. "Not today, Mrs. Clemm," he said, "and I daresay the *Mirror* wouldn't pay William Shakespeare twenty dollars for a poem if he brought it in here himself wearing a pair of striped britches."

Muddy stood her ground, staring at Stoddard from beneath the brim of her bonnet. She knew who Shakespeare was, of course, but she wasn't sure what striped britches had to do with it. "Maybe I'll take it to Mr. Willis's house," she said, deciding Stoddard lacked the authority.

"Be my guest," Stoddard said, putting the ledger away.

Muddy waited. "Well? Where might that be, young man?"

"I can't help you there," he said, smiling, looking high-and-mighty.

She waited a moment more, hoping the man's obstinance would thaw a bit. When it didn't, she took the book, stuck it in her carpetbag, and left.

From the *Mirror* she went to the office of the *Columbian,* then the *Knickerbocker,* then the *Democratic Review* and one or two others that might buy Eddy's poem. They were all within a five-block area between Nassau Street and Broadway. Eddy had told her where to go and in what order and who to ask for—and under no circumstances to accept less than fifteen dollars.

"Doesn't write that many poems, you know," she said to Mr. Duyckinck at the *Democratic Review* after waiting a half hour for him to return from lunch.

Duyckinck refused even after she dropped her price and offered to let him see the manuscript. He professed to like Eddy and admire his work, and he gave her two dollars on account, telling her to have Eddy bring it back in three weeks. Muddy took the money, being careful not to commit but agreeing to pass along the message.

By two o'clock she had exhausted her options. She delivered her piecework to the shop on Maiden Lane, receiving seventy-five cents for her labor, and she used some of it to purchase the materials for the pillowcases. Receiving a fresh bundle of piecework, she put everything in her carpetbag and walked back to Broadway. For a while she stood watching men working on the Trinity Church steeple. It was the highest thing she'd ever seen. After that, she walked to the terminal below City Hall Park.

The car was drawn by two horses, steam rising from their sweaty flanks like smoke curling off a pot of stew. With some difficulty owing to her hip, she climbed the high steps at the back and took a seat near the front. It was crowded, twelve or more folks, and the benches were hard and unpadded. She preferred to sit near the front of the car where it was warmer, though it smelled like a stable. Unlike Muddy, most passengers on the Broadway line tended to be on the stylish side. At half a shilling, it was beyond the reach of riffraff. Those folks had no business in the fine uptown neighborhoods anyway. Once settled, she rummaged in her bag for the lunch she'd packed and nibbled on brown bread and a slice of ham.

With all the traffic and stopping, it took an hour to cover the two miles from City Hall to Madison Square, the old Parade Ground. Then Muddy walked the three miles back to Patrick Brennan's farm. By the time she arrived it was five o'clock and growing dark.

She went straight to give Mrs. Brennan the two dollars plus the three shillings she had left from her piecework earnings; then she climbed the stairs to Sissy's room. Eddy was at his desk working, stiff and formal as he always was when feeling guilty. Muddy took off her coat and bonnet. Beneath her bonnet she wore a white widow's cap. She set her bag on a chair and took out Eddy's manuscript and the parcel containing Longfellow's book. Handing them to him, she told him about the two dollars, then turned to Sissy, who was lying on the bed, her eyes closed, her black hair covering much of her face and the pillow. She lay on the bed she shared with Eddy when times were good. When they weren't, she shared it with Muddy, and Eddy slept downstairs in Muddy's room off the kitchen. Eddy's overcoat served as a blanket. On the bed also, snuggled close to Sissy, was their tortoiseshell tabby, Catterina, her black-and-orange face resting on her paws. A woodfire burned low in the fireplace. Muddy added a stick of firewood from the hopper, then sat down on the edge of the bed. With her fingers, she brushed the hair from Sissy's face. "Did you eat a good lunch?" she asked, smiling.

Sissy opened her eyes and nodded.

"And did you talk to Eddy?"

Sissy frowned. Why does he do this, Muddy wondered? She turned and looked away, past Eddy and out the window at the evening sky and the palisades across the Hudson. Since they hadn't made up, Muddy would have to give things a little push. What could she say? Sissy didn't believe her promises anymore, promises that things would turn out well. But Eddy had been so good since they got to New York. All that previous summer and fall, he'd been on his best behavior. Claimed this was a new city, a new life, and a new Edgar Poe. Promised to join a temperance society and stay sober.

Muddy turned back to her daughter and resumed her caresses.

"He's been doing so well, Sis," she said, not caring that Eddy might overhear. "Think how bad he feels knowing he's disappointed you. He had such high hopes for this new magazine. And then something happened to ruin his dreams again. You mustn't blame him for wanting to forget. He'll make things right again. You wait and see. Mr. Willis is so fond of our Eddy. I know he is." And saying this, Muddy looked up to the ceiling and shook her head as if in wonder of the affection in which Willis held their angel boy. "Don't you see? Eddy can always go back to Mr. Willis if things don't work out."

Sissy closed her eyes tight. She wasn't ready to hear this, Muddy decided. Her cheek felt clammy; her skin was pale as candlewax.

"Let's go down and have some tea before supper," Muddy said. "You'll feel better and we can get warm by the fire. I'll show you what I bought. Oh, Sissy, you should have seen all the colors."

Muddy stood and took the materials from her bag. She laid the piecework aside and fetched the spools of floss she had purchased for embroidering the pillows.

Seeing this, Sissy sat up, letting Eddy's overcoat fall on Catterina, who squirmed out from under, jumped down, stretched and clawed the scatter rug in front of the fireplace. Sissy wore a white cotton dress with rows of pintucks on the bodice and a lace collar. Her eyes brightened at the sight of the colorful thread.

"Look!" Muddy said, holding up a spool of crimson.

Sissy took it in her hand and studied it. Then she dropped her hand to her lap and cupped the spool in both hands as if its weight were too much.

How will she ever find the strength to sew, Muddy wondered. It was Eddy making her so feeble. Eddy, losing control, making Sissy give up, become listless, weak as water. He was all she had to live for. The notion made Muddy angry. She would have a talk with him, she decided, and this time she'd tell him he was killing Sissy. But first they'd go down to tea.

Once Muddy had a notion, there was no stopping her. She knew Eddy better than anyone in the world did. Had she not nursed him when he was out of his head, heard his lunatic ravings? She'd heard dreadful words come out of his mouth. She never asked where he'd been when he failed to come home, nor did Sissy. Sometimes he told them, but mostly he didn't. Sometimes Muddy worried that he would wander into Five Points when he was drunk and get a knife in his ribs or come home sick and diseased.

"Do you want to go down for tea or start on the pillowcases?" Muddy asked.

"Tea, I think," Sissy said, reaching for her shawl and wrapping it around her shoulders.

Muddy took her arm and helped her stand.

"Sissy. Wait. Listen to this," Eddy said. "It's wonderful." He had opened the parcel and held the book Muddy had brought from Willis, the one by Mr. Longfellow.

Sissy and Muddy stopped and turned to him. He stood up, the book in his left hand, his thumb holding the pages open. He walked to the window and turned so that the fading light shone on the words, and standing straight as starch, his broad forehead held high, he read in his fine, clear voice.

The day is done, and the darkness
Falls from the wings of Night,
As a feather is wafted downward
From an eagle in his flight.

I see the lights of the village
Gleam through the rain and the mist,
And a feeling of sadness comes o'er me
That my soul cannot resist:

A feeling of sadness and longing,
That is not akin to pain,
And resembles sorrow only
As the mist resembles the rain.

He looked up at Sissy after reading these last two lines as if to emphasize their special beauty. Then he read on, stanza after stanza, holding Sissy and Muddy by the door, and Muddy thinking as he read what a wonderful gift was his. Maybe this would bring Sissy around.

And the night shall be filled with music,
And the cares, that infest the day,
Shall fold their tents like the Arabs,
And as silently steal away.

When he finished, he lowered the book, looked up, and smiled at them.

Sissy turned and left.

Eddy's face fell as he and Muddy stood there listening to Sissy's footsteps on the stairs. Muddy shook her head to indicate that he was expecting too much. She pushed the door to, then spoke in a low voice. "You're killing her." She paused, her words chilling. "Next time you reach for a drink of whiskey, remember that it is poison. And it's not your throat you're pouring it down; it's hers. You'll kill the both of you, and I'll end up in the poorhouse."

Eddy dropped his eyes to the floor. His lips, pursed together tight, betrayed penitence and anger. It was time to light the candles. Still Muddy stared at his dark silhouette against the window, his shoulders stooped, his head bowed. No more the proud posture, and Muddy worried she had gone too far.

"Promise me," she said.

A silent moment passed as Muddy waited for her answer. Eddy stared at the floorboards. She could not imagine what was in his mind. Was it as hard as all that?

"You have my word," he said at last, never looking up.

She left him there and descended the stairs to join Sissy by the fire.

 Eddy

The Broadway Journal   Saturday, January 4, 1845

PROSPECTUS

As will become apparent in this, our first issue, the *BROADWAY JOURNAL* will differ from other weekly periodicals now published in this city, as it will be made up entirely of Original Matter, consisting of Essays, Poetry, Tales, Criticisms on Art, Literature, Music, and the Theater, Domestic and Foreign Correspondence, and Literary and Scientific Intelligence.

EDDY HAD DREADED returning to the *Mirror* office after that day in December when he'd had so much to drink. Muddy kept harping on his shameful behavior, what with Willis being his best friend. If Willis were such a good friend, perhaps he could have explained some things to General Morris and the others—such as the fact that Eddy had been duped into a partnership with Briggs, who had proved incompetent, and the fact that Sissy suffered from consumption. Maybe they'd show a little compassion. Hadn't Eddy worked there five months without the slightest blemish on his record?

When he did return in mid-January to deliver his review of Longfellow's book, his reception was chilly: General Morris barely acknowledged him and Hiram Stoddard was downright hostile; but Willis welcomed him, motioning him to the chair beside his desk. While Willis read the review, Eddy stared out the window onto Ann Street, where the sun lit all but the lower stories of the buildings across the street. Except for the metal-to-metal clanking of the presses in the print shop on the floor below, the office was quiet. Eddy could sense the animosity, and though his memory of that day was sketchy, he recalled General Morris brandishing his cane and Stoddard asking if he should throw him out. How had things gotten so out of hand? He also remembered being in some tavern on the East River and Willis going on about Longfellow, but that was about all. The next day he had wakened on Bloomingdale Road, half frozen, lying in ditch water, his clothes wet and soiled. He had promised Muddy to swear off just to shut her up, but he'd keep his promise. Since arriving in New York eight months earlier, he hadn't touched the stuff. He could stop if he had to, and just then he recalled the day he swam the James River from the falls at Richmond to Warwick Park—six miles. He was fifteen years old and out to win a bet. Following in rowboats were his buddies, urging him to give up, but he didn't. He was a fine swimmer. Eddy could do whatever he set his mind to.

Willis seemed to enjoy the Longfellow piece. Eddy was proud of it. He formed his manuscripts into long scrolls by gluing the pages together lengthwise with dabs of tragacanth paste. When the paste was dry, he rolled it up, then pasted on a short length of ribbon—he preferred narrow, red ribbon—to form a tie. His chirography was excellent, a matter of great pride. He'd published essays on autography and considered himself the foremost authority in America. His manuscripts would do proud the world's greatest literary archive if there was such a thing, and there should be. The world treated its storytellers with shabby indifference.

"Mr. Poe, if I mistake not," Willis said, in a theatrical tone as if quoting Shakespeare. "If I mistake not, thou art calling Professor Longfellow a thief."

"Is that not what you had in mind?" Eddy whispered, not wanting to be overheard. Then he regretted saying it. Yes, he had, in fact, called Longfellow a thief in almost those words, but he would stand behind his review; not a syllable was inaccurate. It was true that Longfellow thought nothing of pilfering from his fellow poets.

"I suppose so." Willis smiled. "I thought you'd find similarities, but you're being rather hard on the professor, don't you think? You seem fond enough of the first piece; how does it begin? 'The day is done and the darkness falls.'"

"Yes. It's beautiful," Eddy said, "and I say so, do I not?" And he meant what he said. Despite Longfellow's foibles, Eddy thought him a fine poet. No doubt a line as simple as "The day is done and the darkness falls" had begun a hundred poems, yet it was still beautiful. Like a benediction, it was comforting—"The day is done and the darkness falls"—it was like being immersed in twilight. There was that awkward, extra syllable in the third iambic foot, a knot to be sure, but a poem without knots lacked ambition. It was the music that counted; the line reminded Eddy of his boyhood, of being called in to help Toby light the candles, smells of supper coming from the kitchen, his foster father, John Allan, arriving home from work, removing his boots in the front hall, and being greeted by his wife, Frances, as she descended the stairs.

Willis rerolled the manuscript. "I suppose you do, but you also say"—and he chuckled again—"that it contains a gross demerit; furthermore you imply that Longfellow doesn't know the difference between a dactyl and an anapest. And then you say"—Willis searched for the place—"that it is 'dexterously executed slip-shod-iness.'" With this he threw back his head and laughed with keen satisfaction. "It's really quite good, Edgar, but I confuse dactyls and anapests myself. You're very good at this. I rely on instinct, and probably Longfellow does, too, but not you. You understand the arrangement of verse like the set of a ship's sails—let one syllable be out of trim and the whole thing is blown off course. Where did you learn this?"

"It's simple mathematics," Eddy explained, flushed with the praise. "The parts must equal; otherwise, there is discord and the music of the thing becomes offensive." He stopped, warned by Willis's smile that his recital of an old lesson belabored the point. He glanced out the window at the building across the street, red brick with granite lintels above the windows. The regular courses of brick, the solid rectangularity of elements, the neat joints of mortar—they all spoke of order and stability. Lines of verse were no different. They contained a finite number of syllables, some stressed, some not, apparent to anyone who understood the forces of scansion.

The same held true for imagery, and Longfellow's metaphor deserved a demerit. Eddy would have been remiss for failing to expose it. He didn't hold with the sentiment of the day that overlooked the flaws in a work for no other reason than that the author was American. The metaphor, like the simile, was a simple mathematical equation, but not that simple! What could be more witless than to write that "the wings of night" were like the feathers of an eagle? Of course they were. They were both feathers, and feathers were like feathers. For that matter, clams were like clams, and turnips were like turnips.

"Still," Willis insisted, "you are rather unforgiving. Perhaps you should soften the blow."

Eddy relented. He took the scroll from Willis, unrolled it, and perused the first paragraph. Finding an appropriate place, he took Willis's pen, dipped it in the inkwell, and within parentheses, he inserted after Longfellow's name the words "a man who writes more and better than any man living." Then he handed the scroll back to Willis and laid the pen in its cradle.

Willis read it and laughed again. "Well," he said, "there's nothing like hyperbole."

An awkward silence followed. Eddy seized the initiative and leaned in toward Willis so as not to be overheard. "Can you pay me now?" he whispered.

The smile ebbed from Willis's face. "I have already," he said. "You don't remember. It was the day you were here. You said you needed the advance for your landlord."

"Yes, of course," Eddy said, and he stiffened. "I remember." But he didn't. He was not so much surprised as disappointed. He always asked for his money up front, since editors were notorious foot-draggers in paying for work once they had it in their pursy mitts. Unfortunately, the Brennans remained unpaid; they were owed fourteen dollars. Had Eddy been robbed? No wonder Sissy and Muddy were so upset.

"Come, I'll buy you lunch," Willis said, rising from his chair. "We'll go down to Delmonico's. The walk will do us good."

As they left, Eddy glanced at Hiram Stoddard. Their eyes locked, and during that instant, Stoddard sent a message. Perhaps a day will come, it said, perhaps it won't—but if it does, beware. The animosity depressed Eddy as he followed Willis down the stairs.

It was early for lunch, but the streets were a crush of pedestrians, hucksters, and carriages. On the way downtown Willis was hailed by passersby. Those same men tended to ignore Eddy. He didn't wear well with other men the way Willis did. Perhaps it was because he was so argumentative. But he felt passionately about things. Men want other men to be agreeable like Willis and Morris—they're happy together, dining out, laughing, sharing a brandy, smoking their cigars. Eddy had never fit in, never in his life. Why don't they like me? It was a question he had asked Jane Stanard when he was fifteen years old: "Why don't the other boys like me?" Jane had smiled her sympathetic smile, parting his hair with her fingers. "Because you are special," she had said. But he didn't feel special, not like Willis. Men noticed him; they saluted. "Ah,

Willis. Good morning. Fine day." But not Eddy. He could have been a huckster or street sweeper.

There were too few like Jane Stanard, and Eddy recalled her grave in Shockoe Hill, the cemetery in Richmond. One summer he had gone there almost every night. He could still smell the wet grass. He would lie on top of her grave and imagine her lying beneath him, facing him, separated by only a few feet of clay. He had met her when he was twelve and thought she was the most beautiful woman he'd ever seen. Then, of course, he did not call her Jane. She was Mrs. Stanard, as befit the mother of his best friend. She loved him; he was certain of it. They said she went mad, but they were wrong. She wasn't mad; she was lonely. Eddy had never seen such sublime loneliness. He was sixteen when she died.

At the corner of Nassau and Wall Streets, they dodged the pushcarts heaped with Saddle Rock and Cow Bay oysters—all you could eat for six cents. Eddy could have stopped there; he was famished. He had ten dollars in his pocket for a deposit on new rooms. That afternoon he planned to search for a boardinghouse where he, Sissy, and Muddy could live until moving day, the first of May, when he would look for an apartment. Of course, he would have to square things with the Brennans first, which meant selling the manuscript in his pocket now that he had nothing coming for the Longfellow piece.

They turned left off Broad onto Beaver Street. Despite the early hour, Delmonico's was crowded with men standing at the oyster bar, talking and eating, some drinking, some playing backgammon. The place smelled of wet fish and cigar smoke. Beyond the bar was a large fireplace with a sputtering, wet-log fire, and standing on each end of the massive mantle was a pair of taxidermist's beavers, erect on their hind legs, flashing buck-toothed grins at the patrons. Willis signaled for a table and, not liking the one chosen by the maitre d', suggested another farther from the crowd. Eddy took a seat opposite Willis, beneath the stuffed head of a bison mounted on the wall. Beyond Willis the two grisly beavers hunched on the mantle.

Willis ordered pork chops and coffee for the both of them.

"Willis," Eddy began, "I have a proposition." He cautioned himself not to go too fast. He had practiced what he would say and didn't want to rush it. Muddy had convinced him of Willis's high regard for him; the time had come to act. "The *Broadway Journal* has published its first two issues. Have you seen them?"

Willis nodded, his expression indicating he was unimpressed.

"Yes," Eddy agreed. "It has no national appeal. It won't even sell in Philadelphia. Briggs has no sense of what he's about, no focus."

Hoping Willis would disagree, which, sadly, he did not, Eddy considered the fact that he had been responsible for a majority of the pages in the first two issues. Truth was, his dissatisfaction stemmed more from money than content. He had taken a share of ownership in the enterprise in return for regular contributions at the reduced rate of one dollar per column. The result provided something he'd always wanted—a magazine of his own, if only partly his own—but the problem was income, and Eddy was only then beginning to see the disadvantages of his position. He had counted on freelancing to earn a living until such time as the *Broadway Journal* could provide full-time employment, but Briggs needed help now. There would be no time for freelance work, and since Eddy had to move his family into the city, why not start his own magazine?

"What I propose," he said to Willis, "is a new magazine—a true literary journal. Not this," and he pulled a folded copy of the first issue from his pocket and threw it to the side as if tossing it in the trash. It was a dramatic gesture he'd practiced sitting at his desk. "Politics! Where is the literature? There is one poem by James Russell Lowell—three stanzas, not a quarter of a column; two reviews, which I wrote; and the rest is politics. The second issue is no better. I suspect Briggs plans to turn the thing into an abolitionist rag. If he does, what good am I? I'm a writer, not a politician, and I can deliver subscriptions from all over the South, but who in the South is going to buy an antislavery magazine? I have a better idea. A monthly—one hundred and twenty-eight pages on the finest paper with high-quality engravings. The majority of pages will be devoted to original work, not just American writers as Briggs would have it. That's madness! The finest writers in this language are the English. It doesn't pain me to admit it. Why are so many people in this business such Anglophobes? You'd think we were still fighting the Revolution."

Something in Willis's manner told Eddy he was losing his prospect.

"In a year," Eddy vowed, talking fast and loud now, "I can deliver five thousand subscriptions at five dollars. In two years, ten thousand. When I joined the *Southern Literary Messenger,* they had seven hundred subscribers; a year later, fifty-five hundred. *Graham's* had five thousand when I became editor; eighteen months later, fifty thousand. Fifty thousand! I can publish the magazine I describe at a cost of thirty thousand a year, and I've estimated everything at the highest rate. Thirty thousand, Willis! In two years we can clear ten thousand apiece. I'll do the work, but I need a partner. Fifty-fifty. General Morris need not know; no one need know. All I need is two thousand seed money."

"Two thousand!" Willis made as if to whistle.

His reaction devastated Eddy. Blood rushed to his brain; his hands started shaking—the same uncontrollable rage that had surfaced whenever he argued with his foster father—and suddenly Willis took on the aspect of John Allan sitting across from Eddy at the dining room table back in Richmond, accusing him of being irresponsible, careless, and a spendthrift, just because he couldn't pay for his books. How could he pay for his books when the money his father gave him barely covered his rooms? Did John Allan want him to go to college or not?

"Poe. Poe!" It was Willis, not his father, reaching across the table and shaking his arm.

Eddy had lost control. His mouth was dry. He was ruining his chances, as always.

"I have a better idea," Willis argued. "Calm down and listen."

"It's true," Eddy persisted; he could not let go. "I did those things. It's the editor that makes or breaks a magazine. You know that better than anyone. It wasn't Graham. The man was an idiot. He gave discounts everywhere. What's more he charged only three dollars a subscription. Still, at fifty thousand, that's a lot of money, and he's a rich man today. But it was me, not Graham, who built it into a national magazine. I can deliver subscriptions better than any man in New York or Philadelphia—or Boston, for that matter."

"I believe you." Willis reached across the table and took Eddy's arm again. "I believe you. Calm down and listen to what I have to say."

Men at the bar turned to stare, disapproval in their eyes. From behind Willis the two beavers seemed to snicker at Eddy. He took a deep breath and started raking his mustache with his forefinger, a nervous habit to hide his mouth, convinced that anger and disappointment showed there. Willis smiled at him just then, his usual method for diffusing Eddy's excitability—not a word, just a pleasant, closed-mouthed smile until Eddy got the message, took his hand away and prepared to listen.

Once Eddy was himself again, Willis picked up the *Broadway Journal* from where it lay. "Somewhere . . . ," he said. "Here. Let me read this. The writer—Briggs?—is talking about international copyright. 'At the first session of the present Congress there were petitions, signed by some of the best men in the nation, presented to both houses, praying for an international copyright, received in silence, referred to a committee, and never heard of again.'" Willis looked up from the magazine.

Eddy shrugged, unable to shake off his disappointment.

"Obviously Briggs feels strongly about the copyright issue." Willis said.

"Of course," Eddy said. "We all do."

Willis laid the magazine back down and sat in silence for a moment. The waiter came and set their plates before them, piled high with pork chops, then refilled their mugs with coffee.

As Eddy was famished, he took his fork in one hand, knife in the other, not bothering to wait for Willis, and began ripping into the chops, stuffing chunks of meat in his mouth. Beads of grease glistened in his mustache. Willis joined the repast. When the edge of Eddy's appetite was blunted, he paused to add something he'd forgotten. "I want to call it *The Stylus*."

Willis stared at him for a moment. "Your new magazine, you mean? Listen, Edgar. I'm going to London in the spring. Mary and I are expecting a child in March, and once she's well enough, we sail for England."

The news was tantamount to rejection. The prospect of Willis's leaving New York left Eddy feeling adrift.

"Would Briggs accept you as coeditor of the *Broadway Journal*?" Willis asked.

Eddy was not listening. Dwelling on rejection, he glared at the sneering beavers.

"Cheer up, Edgar," Willis said. "I know it's not what you want. You want two thousand dollars to invent a new magazine. I don't have two thousand for such a venture. My money is tied up in the *Mirror*, and with a new magazine appearing every week, it would be folly. We should all have our money in railroad shares. As much as I like you, and as much as I believe you can do what you say, I can't afford the risk. For Christ's sake, I've got a child on the way! Try and understand."

"Did I not prove myself in five months as your assistant?" Eddy asked.

"Hear me out." Willis set his fork down, wiped his mouth, and pushed his plate away. "We all agree that the lack of an international copyright law is robbing us. Your work is published abroad, is it not? Your 'Rue Morgue' was quite popular in Paris. Were you paid for it? Of course not. I'll wager they didn't even give you credit for writing it."

Eddy did not answer; his thoughts were elsewhere. He had never had the luxury to worry about the copyright issue.

"There will be no such law," Willis continued, poking a forefinger on the table, "until England demands it. Briggs is right; there *were* petitions, accompanied by cases of brandy for the key legislators, but our government has neither the clout nor the inclination. The only way to bring about such a law is to exploit the lack of one."

Eddy stopped eating, fork in hand, and stared at Willis over a slice of pork fat.

"I'm going to London," Willis said, and shrugged as if his proposition were obvious, "and you have a magazine."

The rest came fully formed into Eddy's mind. Willis would send original work by England's finest writers, hot off the press. Carried by steamship, such work could appear in the pages of the *Broadway Journal* in three weeks. Pirating literary work was commonly done on both sides of the Atlantic, but not by someone as well connected as Willis. With original works from England, the magazine would truly become a literary journal, and not having to pay contributors would yield enough money for another salary—Eddy's. No doubt General Morris would never agree to such a thing at the *Mirror*; therefore, Willis would expect a commission.

"I'll have it on the boat before the ink is dry," he added. "Briggs must not know."

Eddy considered what was being proposed. On one hand, Willis was successful and immensely popular, and being in partnership with a man of his stature was exciting. On the other hand, there was something in the idea that seemed unethical, even disloyal. It was true that he was not paid for his "Murders in the Rue Morgue" published in Paris—the translator took the credit and the money—but every good writer in America had been cheated in much the same way.

"You mustn't peddle the work I send you," Willis added. "It goes in your magazine or nowhere. Too many questions otherwise. I hear Briggs shares an office with Dunn English?"

Eddy nodded. Both magazines, the *Aristidean* and the *Broadway Journal,* worked out of a ratty third-floor office at 153 Broadway, three blocks north of Trinity Church.

"English must not know, either," Willis said. "I'll post the manuscripts to you personally, but you can say nothing about how you got them. And don't do a monthly. People want weeklies, and a hundred and twenty-eight pages is too big. Perhaps something over thirty; I'll leave the details to you. Change the name to the *Stylus* if you like, but think about how newsboys would pronounce the name. At any rate, send me copies by return packet along with, shall we say, a dollar a page? I'll have expenses."

Not waiting for an answer, Willis turned in his chair to find their waiter. "Check," he shouted, then turned back to Eddy. "Not even Mrs. Clemm can know, or your wife. Agreed?"

Eddy hesitated. Willis waited patiently for his answer as he paid the bill, leaving a generous tip.

"As you know," Willis said, "I have many friends in England. Not just writers—publishers, printers. I have access to work even before the booksellers. Needless to say, they would see my head on a pikestaff if they knew what I was about. Believe me, the furor will echo in parliament. We'll have an international copyright law before Polk leaves office," he said, then leaned in close to speak confidentially. "Don't get me wrong, Edgar. I don't pretend to be noble. You've been to Washington; you know how things get done. It won't sting if there's no profit in it. In the end every writer on both sides of the Atlantic will thank us, and you'll have the national literary magazine you've been dreaming of." He extended his hand. "Shake on it?"

Eddy stared at Willis's hand for an instant. He still felt uneasy, but his own national magazine! He imagined original works by Charles Dickens and Alfred, Lord Tennyson, the finest writers in the world, alongside his own. What a vision. It would best *Godey's Lady's Book* and *Graham's Lady's and Gentleman's Magazine,* the two most popular monthlies in the country, and Eddy would become as rich as Louis Godey and George Graham. And his partner would be Willis, the best friend he had in the world, a man respected all over America. They shook on it.

"Come," Willis said. "We'll have a stroll through Battery Park on our way back. It will aid the digestion, and it's a fine day. The bonnets will be out. Mary's as big as a cow, and I've almost forgotten what a tight waist and a well-carved bosom look like."

Walking down Beaver Street toward Bowling Green, Eddy pulled the manuscript from his pocket. "I have a new poem," he said, and unflattened the scroll. "It's called 'The Raven.' It's my best yet." And he handed it to Willis, who smiled as if he were perceiving their new partnership already being used to his disadvantage.

As they walked, Willis read Eddy's new poem, and his appreciation of it showed in his eyes. Eddy had worked on it for months, revising, reading it aloud to Sissy and Muddy, polishing it to the perfection of a prism. Then one late night he had achieved a significant breakthrough. Sissy was asleep, and Catterina kept jumping up on the desk, demanding to be petted and shedding her fur into the wet ink. Thanks to that night, it was better now than when Muddy had tried to peddle it on New Year's Eve. The breakthrough came as such things come—gifts from heaven. Longfellow's poem came back to him—"a feather is wafted downward / From an eagle in his flight"—and he recited it to himself while Willis read. He had recited it many times, standing on Mount Tom, addressing the wind and the river as if he stood on center stage at Castle Garden addressing the Upper Ten, as Willis called New York City's ten thousand wealthiest inhabitants.

"Poe, this is wonderful," Willis said, and he read on. When they reached the park, he looked about for a bench, sat down, and continued reading, seeming to have forgotten about the bonnets. When he finished, he scrolled back to the beginning and skimmed it again. From time to time he shook his head as if amazed. "I'll pay fifteen dollars for it on the spot."

"I've sold it already," Eddy said. "To Colton at the *American Review* for the February issue." Earlier that same morning he had received the ten-dollar bill he carried in his pocket from Charles Colton, but he had intended all along to sell the poem to Willis also, certain he could get another ten. Twenty dollars was three weeks' room and board at the Brennans', and more than Eddy had ever been paid for a poem. The *American Review* was a monthly and usually appeared the Monday or Tuesday before the first of the month. The February issue would go on sale in late January, the 27th or 28th, but the post would delay its appearance for a day or two. "As you know," he explained, "it's the policy of the *Review* to publish only anonymous works." He paused, hoping Willis would understand what was being proposed. "The Raven" was good enough to sell twice.

"Very well," Willis said, laughing. "I'll pay you ten dollars for your name. When can I publish it?"

"The twenty-ninth," Eddy said.

"Done," Willis agreed. "And I'll review it—favorably, of course. And may I say that I'm copying it 'in advance of publication,' since Colton has it for February?"

Eddy agreed. Colton would be miffed, but Eddy needed the money. Now he could pay the Brennans and move Sissy and Muddy into town.

Willis stood, motioning for them to stroll on down to the Battery and watch the ships. With each step, he tapped his walking stick on the brick path. They were an odd pair—Willis tall and a perfect cut of fashion in his ten-button, double-breasted overcoat, top hat glistening in the sun, Eddy shorter, his shoulders bearing the slope of misfortune, and his unpressed suit showing wear at the seams. He never carried a walking stick, considering the habit a silly affectation of the Upper Ten, and his top hat was as dull as buggy harness.

Chapter 4

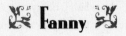 Fanny

New York Daily Tribune   Tuesday, January 28, 1845

MUSICAL INTELLIGENCE
>━◆>━◦━<◆━<

THIS THURSDAY at the Park Theatre at eight, internationally acclaimed violinist, Ole Bull, performing for the first time ever a new Original composition,—"Niagara."

LATE ON TUESDAY afternoon, the iron cast of the sky gave way to snow. Horsecars spilled their passengers at the City Hall terminal and headed for the barn, their drivers hunched under oilskins. Hucksters and pushcart vendors abandoned the streets, and shopkeepers pulled their shades and hurried home. The steamship *Wellington* dropped anchor in the bay rather than risk a mooring. Sailors on ships anchored in the offing sought the shelter of the fo'c'sle to smoke their pipes and keep warm huddled around the brazier. Snow piled up on the canvas sails furled beneath the yards; it iced the limbs of the trees in City Hall Park, the wrought-iron fences, and the gaslights lining Broadway; it banked on stoops, window ledges, and pediments. But for black chimney smoke, the city grew white and still as evening turned to night.

Snow continued all that night and into the next day. The wind picked up and blew a fine blizzard; it shut the city down. News spread throughout the Astor House hotel that the ferry between New York and Brooklyn had stopped running and that shops and countinghouses would remain shuttered.

Inside the hotel, a skeleton staff had drawn drapes in all the public rooms, cutting the cold that found its way through cracks. They stoked fires and lit candles to augment the gaslights, which burned dim due to water freezing in the gasometers; they strained to provide the luxuries of America's finest hotel. The second-floor ladies' dining room, which on this day became the nursery for every child in residence, was considered the best in the city. Its specialty was desserts: frosted cakes of every description—chocolate, vanilla, caramel, their icing topped with lovebirds or angels or castles; baskets of sugar eggs and cookies; dishes of fruit; and French crèmes and pastries. A procession of such dainties appeared from the kitchen, and by midafternoon, with lunch being served also, the room was as warm and festive as a Christmas Eve, men, women, and children overflowing into the ladies' parlor, the rules prohibiting spirits in that part of the hotel suspended because of the storm.

On Thursday morning the drapes were opened to reveal a magnificent prospect—City Hall Park beneath two feet of snow, the Croton fountain frozen solid, its jet of water a stalagmite of creamy ice. The iced branches of the trees in the park glittered in full sunlight, blinding to the eyes, and one by one the sleighs appeared, bringing the city back to life.

In a swoosh of satin and crinoline, Fanny Osgood appeared on the landing of the stairs that descended to the main lobby from the rooms above. Surveying it, she imagined Ned walking through the front door, searching for her. She wanted him to see her, but she wanted him to see her from a distance first—nothing abrupt and awkward as if she'd been waiting beside the door, tapping her toe. Nor did she want to be too much in the way of people coming and going, though she had made no secret of her separation from Sam. There was no sense in feeding the rumor mill needlessly, so she selected an ottoman surrounding one of the columns at the far end of the lobby. The red brocade slipcover would set off her blue dress. Before leaving her perch on the landing, she glanced down at the neckline of her dress pinned with double rows of shirred, ecru lace that served to augment her modest bosom. In light of the blizzard, the low neckline was a bit obvious, and her corset pinched her underarms, but she would show as much bosom as possible, suffering goose bumps if she must.

She descended the stairs and crossed to the ottoman, laid her cape beside her, and fluffed her skirts, watching the door and hoping he would not arrive just yet. She had to sit sideways on the edge, or her feet would not touch the floor. That the world was made for taller people was an absolute pox. Finding the right pattern for a dress, for example, proved to be a veritable treasure hunt. Patterns inevitably required alteration, and taking in the bodice and removing one of the flounces from this particular one had not worked out as

Fanny had hoped. It made her look like a dwarf, she thought, chopped off at the knees, so she fluffed her skirts again and resolved to put on her cape as soon as she stood. Her wool stockings made her legs itch.

She wore expensive perfume, a gift from Ned, a scent that was not to her liking. She and her daughters had indulged themselves during the storm. There was nothing so luxurious as a hot bath on snowy winter days, and Fanny was thankful that the Astor House piped hot water to the sky chambers, as Willis called the top-floor rooms. Her girls—Lily, eight, willful, and starting to be quite independent, and May, five and already composing her own precious verses—were doubtless driving the nurse mad. During the storm, when not in the bath or the ladies' dining room, the three of them sat on the floor of their room playing all fours, Lily's favorite card game. Fanny was happy at last to be free of them for a day and resolved to not give them another thought. Everything was ready, so Ned could arrive, and she nodded toward the door as if to cue him.

When he did not appear, her gaze wandered the lobby. Fanny loved the Astor House; its luxury was positively decadent—the thick red-and-gold carpets, the crystal chandeliers, the waiters' blue-and-gold uniforms that made them look like naval officers, the brass constantly being polished (she could almost smell the ammonia), the waxy gloss of the furniture, the towering arrangement of fresh flowers that always stood, regardless of the season, on the round mahogany table just inside the front door, the English seascapes in thick gilt frames (though the one to her left, the one of the breakwater at Lyme Regis, needed straightening just then)—and, above all, she loved the hot baths. Climbing stairs to her room in heavy skirts was torture for a woman with short legs, but sky chamber rooms were all she could afford. The richest, most eligible bachelors in New York preferred the Astor. Practical considerations were such a burden.

Meeting Ned Thomas just before Christmas at a party at Edith and John Bartletts' had proven most fortuitous. Wealthy and handsome, he seemed to adore her, never paying a call without bringing a gift—a book, a trinket, perfume. Her love of poetry amused him. He thought it frivolous, and that was disappointing, but a small price to pay for the attentions of such a man. For a Christmas present, he had given her an expensive bracelet. Despite his being a prosperous hardware importer—her pet term for him was "ironmonger"—

she considered the bracelet wildly extravagant. She sold it before deciding that their relationship might blossom, and now she would have to confess that she'd lost it. Where was he?

He entered just then and removed his hat. Without thinking, as soon as she caught his eye, she tilted her head in a flirting, girlish way that her friends often teased her about. He smiled and walked toward her, a newspaper under his arm, his eyes scanning the lobby. How old was he? Forty? Not more than forty-five. He wore no beard, and his prominent jaw and chin exuded confidence. He was not as tall as Sam, but he had meat on his bones. She liked his not being gaunt and pale like Sam, though there had been a time when those were the very qualities in her husband's appearance that had appealed to her—a passionate artist's indifference to anything but his art.

Ned wore a suit of the latest style, and his pant legs held a well-set crease. Oh, that crease, she thought; it says so much.

"Have you seen the *Mirror*?" he asked as he approached.

"No," Fanny said, surprised, "I've been snowbound for two days," and she held up her hand to be kissed, thinking this was a strange way to greet a paramour. Was that what she was? No, of course not, but what a bully word—paramour. "Is that all you have to say?"

Ned laughed. "You look lovely, Fanny. Truly lovely."

She tried to blush, wondering if he meant it.

"Then you haven't seen the poem," he said. "It's called 'The Raven.' It's remarkable—even for a poem. Everyone is talking about it."

Fanny took the newspaper and began reading. There were smudges of ink where the newsprint had gotten wet, but every word foretold the next with such urgency that the smears concealed nothing.

"I have a sleigh and driver waiting," Ned said. "Can't you read it later?"

She raised her hand to silence him, then continued reading. The sorrow of the protagonist was beautiful and compelling, but it was not the sentiment of the poem that gripped her, that made her feel empty inside. It was the genius that the words proclaimed and the dread notion that she would never write a poem to rival this. In her heart Fanny had always felt that she personified the elements of poetry more than anyone on earth. How was it possible that she would never write so magnificent a poem? If one thought in rhyme, if one heard an iambic foot in the beat of a heart—as she did—there could be no limit, no gravitational pull, no water's edge. But here was genius eclipsing her as if she were mere mortal.

She read it through while Ned waited. She could not stop, though it was long and he seemed impatient. When she reached the end, she dropped the paper to her lap, wishing she could be away, alone in her room to sleep and dream. Dreams would be a welcomed refuge. Ned sensed her emotion, though no doubt he misread it, but he waited patiently until Fanny composed herself and looked up at him, forcing a smile.

"Do you know this man, Poe?" he asked. "They say he's penniless and drinks like a sailor."

Fanny shook her head and looked down at the paper again to scan Willis's review: "We think this poem unsurpassed for subtly, ingenuity, and imagination. It will stick to the memory of everyone who reads it." He was right. Damn him; he was right.

As Ned sat down beside her on the ottoman, she began rearranging her skirts, then stopped, not wanting him too close. Not here.

"You should meet him," he said. "This poem will make him famous."

"He's already famous," Fanny said. "If you read more, you would know that. His tales are amazing. He's married, I think, and lives outside the city somewhere. Before he came here, he lived in Philadelphia. He was editor of *Graham's* there and published one of my poems. As a critic, he is thought to be quite vicious. They say he writes with a tomahawk."

This made Ned laugh. "I like him better for that."

"He works for Willis now," she added.

"'Namby-Pamby' Willis?"

"Careful, Ned," Fanny warned at the mention of one of Willis's less flattering nicknames. "Willis is a dear friend, and you might meet him someday if you don't incur my displeasure first." As she said this, she thought that Ned was, in fact, not so pleasing as before. The crease in his trousers spoke of money, nothing more.

"Your literary friends are not my type," he whispered, "and what I find irresistible about you, my dear Fanny, has not the slightest thing to do with poetry."

Again Fanny forced a smile but ignored his flirting; her heart was no longer in the effort.

"Well," he said, changing the subject, "despite the blizzard, Ole Bull will perform tonight as scheduled, and at your behest I have obtained the four most expensive seats in the whole of the Park Theater—a stage box belonging to Astor himself. It seems J. J. is out of town, no doubt on his yacht somewhere in the tropics."

Her spirits rose with this news, and Ned was reinstated.

"I had a devil of a time finding a sleigh," he continued. "The sun is out, but it's very cold. We can bundle up or send the driver out to Turtle Bay to fetch your friend."

"No, I want to go," Fanny said. "I've been shut in for two days, and I've already hired a nurse for the girls. And we should hurry; Margaret is apt to think the whole thing canceled."

Fanny went to the concierge's desk to compose a note to Anne Lynch, informing her of Ned's news about the concert and that, therefore, Margaret Fuller would be spending the night with Anne. Then she bundled up in her cape, gloves, bonnet, and muff and descended the steps with Ned to the sleigh awaiting them at the curb. To be out of the wind, they sat behind the driver, a man with a poorly set broken nose who seemed quite put out by the prospect of a long day in the cold. He spread blankets smelling of oats across their laps and drove up Broadway. Other sleighs had carved ruts in the snow, and the ride was skating on ice compared to the usual bump of carriage wheels over rough cobbles. Fanny snuggled close to Ned, removed a hand from her muff, and placed it on one of his. He responded by putting an arm around her. He was as lotioned as a lily, and Fanny expected he would kiss her once they left the city. It would be their first kiss.

When they reached Union Square, the driver turned right onto Fourteenth Street. Sam's studio was nearby, and without thinking, Fanny pulled up the hood of her cape. It was not necessary to hide, of course; their marriage was over and he was gone. She imagined him at his easel, the same sad, hungry look on his face. It was now the look of failure, though when she met him, it had been the look of a man crazed by his art. As a young woman sitting for her portrait, she had wanted him to kiss her instead of paint her. Her father would have killed him, but Sam kissed her anyway. They were married soon after and left Boston for London, where he studied to become a great artist, but it was portraits that paid the rent, and portrait painting seduced him. He kissed other subjects, too—at least one, the daughter of a baronet who posed nude for him. Fanny had walked in on them. Fidelity was something Sam could not give; in a way, he had always been a stranger. When they returned to New York after Fanny's father died, they did so with an understanding. Fanny had felt betrayed, but she had cured her bitterness through poetry, and just then she wondered how many poems she had written in which she gave vent to all those hurt feelings—dozens of them. But writing about it had helped, and now, though she pitied Sam, for her daughters' sake she worked hard to keep him in their lives and maintain their affection for him. They stayed with relatives or friends or at the Astor House, and Sam traveled or kept to his studio on Sixteenth Street. No doubt he considered separation a blessing.

She had kissed other men since then. A few. And she always wondered, as she kissed them, How will it turn out, or Why doesn't he bathe and clean his teeth, or Why must I have a husband? Men didn't have to have a wife. There were brothels not two blocks from the Astor House, some with furnishings to rival anything in the uptown mansions. And there were prostitutes at every theater in New York City, every night of the week, and wearing gowns and jewels every bit as expensive as those worn by women of the Upper Ten. The double standard was so unfair.

But Ned was different. He had the stuff of lover and husband, and she believed that she could love him. He could afford her divorce—Sam could not. If he proposed, he would have to meet Sam. Perhaps he would even sit for a portrait, and Fanny wondered how that might go. It might go well, she thought, and she realized how much she wanted Sam to be content, too. She no longer loved him, but she cared deeply for him.

At Third Avenue they turned north again. Traffic thinned, then disappeared altogether at the city limits at Twenty-third Street. Thereafter the avenue narrowed into old Eastern Post Road, the meandering country road that ran the length of Manhattan Island to the Bronx River ferry. Here the ruts disappeared and the ride was so smooth that the sound of harness bells all but ceased. Ned placed two fingers beneath her chin and lifted her face. She smiled, knowing what was coming. He returned the smile and teased her for an instant. Go ahead, she thought, get it over. Then he kissed her, and she closed her eyes to give in to the taste and feel of him, but she couldn't get out of her mind the fact that he was kissing her. It was as if she were spying from a distance, disgusted in a way. As a girl, she hadn't thought while being kissed, but now the whole thing had become mental—and she had looked so forward to being kissed.

When the kiss ended, she clung to him. Holding his lapel, she pressed close to his chest, her hood concealing her eyes and her grip preventing another kiss. She might chide herself later for this, but for the moment she let him think she was overcome by emotion. For a while she counted the fence posts, then lost her thoughts in the fields and tall brown grass that rose above the snow. A rabbit, spooked by the whistling runners, ran off in search of new cover, and Fanny found herself thinking about "The Raven."

Nevermore. She mouthed the word. What an awful and perfect refrain. Who was this man who always wrote with such despair, and what was it about despairing passion that she found so irresistible?

"Nevermore," she blurted, without thinking, needing to hear the sound of the word.

Ned laughed. "Was it that bad?"

Realizing that he meant the kiss, Fanny looked up at him and smiled, and she let him kiss her again, forcing passion into it.

"I was thinking of Poe's poem," she said, when it was over, and after a moment's silence asked, "Do you still have the newspaper? Margaret must see it; she'll want to review it."

"Yes," Ned said, exasperated. "I suppose that's all I'll hear about. I must have been mad, offering to take three scribbling women to dinner and a concert."

Fanny turned away, ignoring his comment. "Lynchie will have read it," she said, thinking out loud. "She'll invite him to one of her *soirées*."

"I hope you'll spare me that," Ned said. "What goes on at those parties of hers?"

Fanny liked that he did not pretend for her sake. "You won't try to change me, will you, Ned? Turn me into a lady of fashion, fretting over teacups and thank-you notes?"

He laughed but did not answer.

Was it a lover he wanted? Was that why he laughed? She would be a wife to him or nothing at all. She had her reputation to consider, and Lily and May's education. She would not be a paramour.

"I don't think it's in my power to change you, Fanny," Ned said, at last.

She gave him the benefit of the doubt; then, realizing they were nearing their destination, she looked up at the driver. "Do you know the turn for Turtle Bay? Is it far?"

"Half a mile," the driver said, in a thick German accent.

She looked back at Ned, smiled, and decided it best to kiss him again, since it would be their last opportunity of the day. She kissed him long and hard, a kiss meant to keep him coming back.

When they made their turn, Fanny noticed from ruts in the snow that a sleigh had traveled the road before them. "Do you know Horace Greeley?" she asked. "He must have gone into the city this morning. He's a farmer, you know, not just a newspaperman. I like that about him. He brought Margaret here from Boston to be his music and literary critic, and she lives out here with Horace and his wife, Mary." Fanny didn't add that Margaret Fuller was rumored also to be Horace Greeley's mistress; she didn't believe the rumors. "From her bedroom window she can see the lunatic asylum on Blackwell's Island. She went there to interview the inmates and wrote about them. She's amazing. It would be best not to mention her new book; she's very sensitive about it."

"What book?" Ned asked, teasing her. Fanny had already explained.

"If you read it, you might understand me better."

"Three scribbling women!" Ned sighed, shaking his head. "Three women who want the vote and take jobs from men and wear pants, no doubt. Such are my dinner guests."

"Call me a scribbling woman one more time, you ironmonger, and you can forget the kisses," and with this she glared at him to underscore her resolve.

He smiled as if he thought she was joking, but she wasn't. At that instant the driver reined in his horse in front of the Greeley farmhouse.

The serving girl led them into the parlor, where they waited for Margaret. She appeared moments later, surprised to see them. Tall and ungainly—she was as tall as Ned and a head taller than Fanny—her dark hair was braided and twisted into a bun at the top of her head, and her features were knotty and masculine. She wore a plain dress buttoned to the neck, in stark contrast to Fanny's, and she blushed when Fanny popped out of her cape in a show of bosom. Embarrassed by Margaret's apparent shock, Fanny decided she'd been indiscreet, but how could she please both Ned and Margaret?

"This is my friend Ned Thomas," Fanny announced. "He arrived this morning with news that Ole Bull will perform tonight as scheduled despite the snow. And he's reserved the best seats in the house, haven't you, Ned?"

Margaret's disdain for Ned Thomas was apparent in her eyes. The tickets not only failed to redeem him, they seemed to make things worse. Did Margaret think Fanny was selling herself for concert tickets? Fanny thought to say something more—that Ned was a businessman, proper, respectable, his intentions honorable—but still rankled by his "scribbling women" comment, she decided to let him suffer. Anyway, she would not be bullied by Margaret Fuller, who had the irritating habit of using her own independence as a measure of others.

Or, Fanny wondered, was Margaret jealous, being, as she was, a plain and shy spinster approaching her thirty-fifth birthday with no prospects? Fanny could not be Margaret Fuller; she had no desire to be.

To hide her discomfort, Margaret turned away to look out the window as if hoping to find more bad weather closing in, an excuse for not going. But there was no backing out; Ole Bull, the Norwegian violinist, had captivated New York City since arriving for his concert tour in October. He was big news; therefore, Margaret had a column to write.

Thinking she must do something to defuse the tension, Fanny began talking about the musician. "Did you know that Ole Bull lives in a suite at the Astor? He holds court every morning at ten. His entourage includes a secretary, blond and very handsome, who speaks not a word of English. All the women flirt with him but to no avail—the poor man hates New York. And he has a messenger who is forever flying out the door on some errand of life or death and a tailor whom we call Master of the Wardrobe. Every morning there are women waiting in the lobby for their audience, some very beautiful, and one wonders what goes on in those rooms upstairs. You should see him march through the lobby, wearing a flowing black cape, followed by his entourage and holding his violin case like a scepter. Everyone bows and scrapes as if he were the King of Norway."

A brief, awkward silence followed.

"I've read," Margaret at last said, her voice a Boston contralto, "that only Paganini is better."

"It was Maria who wrote that," Fanny said, suddenly remembering Maria Child. "Oh, Margaret, we forgot to invite Maria! What was I thinking?"

The comparison to Paganini had been made in one of the magazines by Maria Child, a popular freelance writer, and though Maria was older and seldom socialized with the other women writers of the city, she was much admired and respected. Her love of music—and Ole Bull in particular—was well known.

Having had a hand in the concert plans, Margaret shared Fanny's pangs of guilt for their mutual forgetfulness, and thankfully this overshadowed the tension of Ned's presence and the concert tickets and Fanny's *décolleté*.

Tea and sandwiches were served, and Margaret withdrew to dress and pack for the overnight at Lynchie's. Fanny and Ned sat facing each other on either side of the fireplace. He dozed, staring at the embers.

Fanny stood and walked to the window to look out on the snow-covered lawn that sloped down to the bank of sedge grass ringing Turtle Bay. Beyond the bay were the cold, steel-blue chop of the East River and Queen's County cropland on the other side. On the river a single sailboat beat hard to windward, looking tossed and bitter cold.

How sad that this will disappear, Fanny thought. So quiet and peaceful. It reminded her of her childhood: the dying embers, the winter day, a long afternoon of reading in the window seat and watching the sky. In a few short years the city would arrive. The grid of streets had been surveyed and marked more than twenty years before, and no doubt the Greeley farmhouse stood in the middle of some new intersection.

Fanny looked back at Ned, grateful that he could sit with her in silence, grateful that he chose to ignore the tension between her and Margaret. Did he understand? Probably not. At the Park that night, he would have to sit behind her in the box, and he mustn't touch her. She would avoid his eyes, but they would be noticed, and Fanny would be coy and evasive when asked about him, but sooner or later tongues would wag. She and Ned would be linked, and Sam might hear. Ned would have to propose then or be gone.

Staring at him, she wondered which it would be. Perhaps she was not so desperate after all, so desperate as to orchestrate the thing, and she resolved to confess that she'd sold the bracelet, not lost it, and see what happened. There were times when she simply didn't care, when the effort of maintaining respectability was too much trouble, times when she would prefer to live *par amour*.

When Margaret was ready, they sped back to town—smooth runners gliding through snow, the afternoon bitter cold, seagulls crying out overhead, harness bells jingling, the horse straining with the sleigh. Fanny and Margaret sat huddled behind the driver, shading their eyes from the bright, snow-reflected sunlight and reading Poe's "Raven" aloud, alternating verses, their voices affecting the forlorn lover. The poem captivated Margaret as it had Fanny. Laughing when they finished, Fanny imagined how Margaret's review in the *Tribune* might read on the following day: "Ole Bull's performance of his new violin concerto, 'Niagara'—eagerly awaited by his enthusiastic New York fans—the virtuoso second only to Paganini in all the world—must play second fiddle to a poem about a blackbird written by a penniless poet with a weakness for whiskey."

 Willis

New-York Mirror   Monday, February 10, 1845

MISS FULLER'S NEW BOOK.—There is much ado over a new book by Miss Margaret Fuller, *Woman in the Nineteenth Century*, recently published by Greeley & McElrath—the same Horace Greeley of the *New York Tribune* and, coincidentally, Miss Fuller's employer.

Regular readers of this column need no reminder of our sentiments regarding the new status of women in modern society. We applaud Miss Fuller for her Scholarship and for her dedication *à la cause feminique*.

We cannot resist noting, however, that Miss Fuller's support for woman's suffrage is not shared by her boss. Mr. Greeley's opposition to the vote for women has been publically trumpeted in the pages of the *Tribune,* the basis of his argument that—"the *worst sort of woman* will drive the *best sort* from the ballot-box." Implicit in this contention is the notion that the best and worst of the bonnet-set would divide along party lines, and we spent a most enjoyable afternoon wondering which sort would be Whig and which, Democrat?

Issues aside, however, we believe that women of Miss Fuller's sort could *not* be driven from the polls by a tribe of hollering Ojibwa, much less a pack of screaming molls. Furthermore, as our train of thought arrived at the station, we concluded that both sorts would likely agree on a majority of issues—annexation of Texas, amalgamation of Africans, &c., &c.

Therefore, we of the *Mirror* further conclude that the vote is unnecessary for women to achieve the goals espoused in *Woman in the Nineteenth Century*. This is not to say that we oppose such a privilege as suffrage being extended to the fairer sex—consistent with the policy of this magazine, we refrain from taking sides on matters of politics. We are merely expressing the opinion that most issues naturally unite women into a sisterhood that would, if effectively mobilized, speak with one voice—a very powerful voice—a voice that could deny the *worst sort of man* access to polite society. Such a fate would be the Ruination of even the most Powerful man among us.

SITTING AT HIS DESK, Willis read the column over again in light of a letter received just that morning from Maria Child. He had published the column a week earlier, and, though Maria wrote to thank him, her letter hinted that she was disappointed. She had suggested the column at a party at Anne Lynch's honoring Ole Bull, explaining to Willis that Margaret Fuller's *Woman in the Nineteenth Century* had been unfairly reviewed by the press and that Margaret, herself, had been chastised. Maria urged Willis to come to Margaret's defense. General Morris would dissolve their partnership were Willis to come out in favor of the vote for women, but how could he say no to Maria Child? Like a caring but exacting teacher, she had proven to be a steadfast friend back in Boston when he had got himself into so much trouble. Willis found himself, therefore, in a position of dancing on a high-wire, and the resulting column demonstrated remarkable agility, if he said so himself.

Maria's letter bothered him for another reason. For weeks Willis had been nagged by that "trifling wit" missile hurled at him from the *Star* back in December. Was he wasting his life writing trivial, chitchatty columns that reported the latest fashions, *la mode Manhattanesque*? More than one reader had suggested that he write something for posterity, implying that the product of his nib had thus far indeed been trifling. Now "The Raven" was driving home the point. Its publication was causing a sensation the like of which Willis had never seen. The poem was being reprinted in every newspaper and magazine in America, and, while Willis was happy for Poe, he felt a tinge of envy also. Poe's star was rising; he was being hailed as the greatest writer in America, a position to which Willis, himself, aspired.

He gazed out the window at St. Paul's steeple, returning his attention to the new column he was composing. It was to be one of his "Upper Ten" columns. Willis had coined the phrase to denote New York's ten thousand wealthiest and most fashionable citizens — that thin upper crust of the city's half million inhabitants. They were currently outdoing one another in the construction of new homes, sumptuous houses all up Broadway, north of City Hall to Madison Square, houses that rivaled anything in London's Mayfair. And they were importing everything French — perfume, dresses, crystal chandeliers, prettily uniformed maids, even titled husbands for their daughters. The current subject of debate among the Upper Ten, and that of Willis's new column, was where in the city to situate a driving park like London's Hyde

Park or Paris's Tuilleries Gardens, so they could hobnob *alfresco* in the comfort and privacy of their cabriolets and barouches. No doubt some suitable park would be set aside, with access guarded to keep out the riffraff from Five Points; otherwise, street urchins would invade, hawking everything from Jonathan apples to lily-white corn and turning it into a veritable grocery bazaar.

Willis did not number himself among the Upper Ten, as some supposed; nevertheless, they were the people about whom his readers wished to read. The new column would not come, however; his mood was wrong, and he decided to leave it for later.

He gazed at the other two letters in his mail basket. One was from Poe, just received and unopened, and the other from someone calling himself "H.," defending Longfellow in response to Poe's review of Longfellow's Christmas gift book. It was the very thing Willis hoped would ensue. H.'s letter charged Poe with confusing rhythm with meter. Poe's reaction had been predictably acrid, and his response to H. decidedly truculent. Willis published it, hoping for a hailstorm of letters from Boston, but alas, here it was three weeks later and not a word, not a salvo. How disappointing! Particularly so since Morris, shifting his chew from one cheek to the other, had seemed delighted by the skirmish. Willis had intended to dub the debate "The Little Longfellow War," provided he could get the troops to muster and do battle. He was certain of Poe, always belligerent, ready to fight, but Longfellow's army was affecting a passive and nonviolent nobility—the very thing one would expect out of Boston. Willis would have to reignite hostilities, so he reached for Poe's letter.

Poe had written to say that his family was moving into a boardinghouse on Greenwich Street, the Morrisons'. As Willis found a brisk walk beneficial in clearing his mind, and since it was too early for lunch, he put on his coat, descended the stairs, and walked the six or seven blocks, hoping to find Poe at home. West of St. Paul's and down toward the Hudson River, the neighborhood declined. It was an old section of the city, full of tenements and once fashionable homes converted into boardinghouses, factories, and here and there, a brothel. Willis turned on Greenwich, just two blocks from the river, and found the Morrisons', an old brownstone with a porch, solid and clean. A serving girl showed him up to third-floor rooms. Mrs. Clemm answered the door, a broom in her hand.

"Why, it's Mr. Willis!" she said, seeming overjoyed at his coming. No doubt her broad smile reflected enthusiasm for a first visitor to new lodgings.

Willis had met Mrs. Clemm on several occasions. She often ran Poe's errands. The week before, she had returned the Longfellow book to his office.

The outer room smelled of mildew. Despite the cold, windows were raised for airing it out. There was little furniture: an unmade iron daybed, a simple writing table, and beside the fireplace, a ladder-back chair with a cane seat and an old tin coal scuttle. Crates and wooden trunks in the middle of the floor indicated that belongings were being put away—books, china, clothing. On the daybed was a stack of women's things, a white chemise on top that Mrs. Clemm hastened to put out of sight.

Poe emerged from the bedroom holding a claw hammer, his white shirt-sleeves rolled above his elbows. He was thin and pale but grinning and cheerful. He beckoned Willis in, and the two shook hands.

"This is my wife, Virginia," he said, when his wife appeared at the bedroom door.

Peeking from behind the doorjamb, Virginia smiled and blushed. In her arms she cradled a black-and-orange cat as if hiding behind it, embarrassed by the way she was dressed. She was frail but rather pretty, Willis thought. She said nothing and stared, smiling at him.

"We arrived Saturday," Poe said. "So we're still sorting out, as you can see. I've been hanging pictures." He disappeared into the bedroom and returned with an oval silhouette portrait in a wooden frame, the portrait of a man in military uniform. "This is my grandfather and Mrs. Clemm's father, General David Poe." There was an instant of silence as everyone turned with reverence to the portrait. "He was one of the heros of the Revolution and a great friend of the Marquis de Lafayette. At one time I had wanted to follow him into the military, but that life was not for me."

Poe laid the portrait on the daybed and pulled up the chair for Willis. "Muddy, tea for our guest?" he asked, placing the chair next to the writing table.

Mrs. Clemm curtsied and turned to go downstairs. Willis tried to refuse, but the Poes insisted. All the while, Virginia stood at the edge of the doorway to the bedroom.

Poe went on about the accommodations. The price was quite reasonable considering the central location; the landlady was a plump, chatty old girl determined to fatten Sissy up, so he said, and Willis assumed "Sissy" meant "Virginia." No fear of starving—for breakfast they had a mountain of buckwheat cakes, ham, veal cutlets, and maple syrup, elegant syrup, nice bread and butter, and buckets of strong coffee. Not even the Astor House served a finer breakfast.

Willis listened, distracted and fascinated by Poe's wife. She was very young and painfully bashful. Her eyes were dark; her coal-black hair was parted in the middle, braided, pulled back, and pinned. Her skin had an incandescent pallor, and there was a helpless vulnerability about her that was compelling. She wore a white cotton dress that told by its wrinkles that she had been lying down. No doubt she was consumptive, and this realization made Willis certain that Sissy was Lenore, the "fair and radiant maiden" of Poe's "Raven." But why "Lenore"? Was it just a name to rhyme with *nevermore*? He recalled the French word *le nord*, the north—the cold north; cold as the grave. Was that the connection and did she understand? Did she know he was writing about her death? Or did she believe some fiction in which she recovered and lived to pluck a baby from her nipple and bounce it on her knee, laughing at its toothless grin? No, there was no such fiction. She was Lenore and knew it. She had read the poem and grieved, perhaps as much for her husband, haunted by a bird the color of her hair, as for herself. When the time came, Willis resolved, he would buy her a linen dress; one so lovely must not be buried in cotton.

The vision of Virginia made him wonder if he was using Poe unfairly, putting him on the front line, so to speak. It was apparent that the Poes were as broke as bric-a-brac. Their humble possessions spilled out of trunks and boxes and littered the writing table and daybed: Mrs. Clemm's china; Poe's manuscripts, rolled and tied with ribbon; neatly folded clothing; a few treasured pieces of silver flatware; an array of small trinkets—bits of paste jewelry; studs and hairpins; a pincushion, thread, needles; souvenirs that told of travel; the miniature portrait of a loved one; military service medals; a broken toy that had comforted childhood, a tin soldier like the one Willis treasured, the last of a platoon of fusileers, the muzzle of its musket broken off. Stacked on the writing table were bundles of letters tied with ribbon, the ink gone brown with age. And there were books, though not so many as one would suppose. Willis knew for a fact that Mrs. Clemm sold Poe's books if he failed to keep up the rent. She would do it without his knowledge. More than once she got Poe in trouble when he couldn't return a borrowed book because Mrs. Clemm had peddled it to a bookseller who had sold it in turn. What could Willis do but offer the man work and pay him fairly?

"Poe," he said, after Mrs. Clemm returned with his tea and she and her daughter retreated to the bedroom to let the men conduct their business, "I want you to write a letter to the *Mirror*. I want you to be your own critic."

Poe's puzzled expression said that the Longfellow exchange was all but forgotten. He knew nothing of Willis's warlike scheming, thinking the whole thing happenstance. Poe was deadly serious—dour, even—on the subject of poetry, so Willis decided to play to that.

"I had hoped," he continued, "that a debate on the subject of poetry would ensue from your letter to H. You do remember H.'s letter, don't you?"

Poe nodded, seeming to search his mind for details.

"As you know, we published your response, but we've heard nothing more. Not a word, and it's been three weeks now. I want you to write a letter attacking your own response to H. Be your own worst critic. Can you help me out? We'll pay you, of course."

Poe appeared to consider the proposition, and Willis stood to leave.

"By the by," he said, pausing at the door, "a friend of mine wishes to meet you. Frances Osgood. She's a neighbor. She told me you published one of her poems in *Graham's*."

Poe smiled. He was flattered, enjoying his newfound fame. "Yes," he said, "I admire her work. There is a wonderful line from a long thing she did called 'Elfrida.' Medieval. It failed, but not for want of ambition. Asked by the king if she loves him, Elfrida answers, 'When but a child I saw thee in my dreams.'" Poe paused and laughed. "Did she love him or not? What a marvelous line! Only a woman could write that line. Mrs. Osgood is a fine poet."

"Do you see what I mean?" Willis said. "You and I, Poe. We enjoy talking about poets and poetry. That's why I thought a debate on the subject would be stimulating. People feel passionately about it, and you in particular. I think you must know more about poetry than any man in America." Making himself stop, he put a hand on Poe's shoulder. Did he really mean what he was saying, or was he negotiating? Poe was passionate and uncompromising, and Willis worried that he was exploiting that to Poe's detriment. No doubt the man had some idea where Willis was headed, but in that instant, Willis lost his taste for the thing.

He hastened away, making a feeble excuse: a luncheon engagement. The Little Longfellow War seemed to profane the Poes' poverty and the tragedy of Virginia's illness—"nameless here forevermore." "The Raven" would not stop playing in Willis's mind.

On his way back to the *Mirror* office, Willis noticed a sign swinging above the entrance to Barnum's American Museum. It advertised the display of a revolutionary new casket guaranteed to protect against premature burial. He decided to go in and have a look.

After paying his half-shilling, he entered the main hall. Children's laughter echoed off the walls and high ceiling. In a central spot facing the front entrance was one of Barnum's star attractions, the one that thrilled the children most, General Tom Thumb. He stood on a round platform painted to resemble a bass drum and chatted amiably with children who would have been a head taller were he standing on the floor. He was not dwarflike at all; his four-foot figure was perfectly proportioned. From a distance he appeared to be an average boy of six or seven, but close up the wrinkles around his eyes and mouth betrayed a man approaching middle age.

Farther on was a live display of Eskimos, a man, two women, and a small girl, all sniffling and sneezing with colds despite their furs and skins, which they displayed with dutiful lethargy. Their manner brought to mind the listlessness of caged animals. They did not speak. Perhaps they knew no English. They brought their crude implements forward for the children to touch and handle—stone tools, weapons made of bone, a kayak made from the skins of seals. The man was short and muscular, older than Willis, perhaps the father of one of the women. He handed Willis the kayak, confident that its weight would surprise, and indeed it did; it was lighter even than a saddle. The Eskimos stood beside a reproduction of the ice house in which they lived, an igloo that Barnum had constructed of wooden blocks painted white. A line of children waited to enter.

It being a Monday afternoon, the second floor was nearly empty of patrons, and here Willis found the grotesque appliance advertised on the signboard out front: a casket made of lead and etched with elaborate scrollwork that reminded him of the frescos decorating Turkish seraglios. A small beveled window no larger than the glass pane of a carriage lantern looked down on the wax figure of a man lying in the casket and wearing on the thumb of his right hand a metal ring, somewhat larger than a finger ring. Willis watched as a museum attendant demonstrated how, once the lid of the casket was closed and the assembly engaged, the slightest movement of the deceased's right hand triggered the assembly into action, and the lid of the coffin sprang open, freeing its occupant from a fate truly worse than death.

Premature burial was a common theme in Poe's tales. He had used it to great effect, but Willis couldn't help being amused by the gadget, and he got an idea for working it into his Upper Ten column. From the attendant, he learned the name of the inventor—a Mr. Giles of Utica, New York, a manufacturer of cannons for the navy. A card explained that the need for such a casket arose from certain medical conditions, including tetanus, asphyxia, and phrenitis, that could simulate death. "Dreadful mistakes have been reported," it said. Willis was certain that such reports were cleverly fabricated to sell elaborate and expensive caskets to the more gullible elements of the Upper Ten, and he concluded that this Mr. Giles must be every bit the impresario that P. T. Barnum was.

The gadget put Willis in mind of a gift he'd received two years earlier, a silver ring set with a bluish-green scarab of beryl emerald, a symbol of resurrection to the ancient Egyptians according to Mr. Tenney, jeweler to the Upper Ten whose shop was under the Astor. Etched with indecipherable pictographs, the ring had been taken from the finger of a mummy on display at Barnum's, which a team of phrenologists had partially unwrapped in order to learn more about the character of the ancient Egyptians by studying the bumps on their skull. Interestingly, so Willis was told, the phrenologists had discovered large bumps of acquisitiveness and perseverence, evidence of an inclination to acquire material possessions and a fixedness of purpose. Willis concluded that such a man, if transported to the present day, would have plied his trade on Wall Street and taken his summers in Saratoga Springs.

The ring was of bold but crude craftsmanship—Tenney could have taught Egyptian jewelers a thing or two—and it brought to mind the elaborate preparations made by pharaohs for the afterlife. Composing his column in his mind, Willis saw no reason why the inventor of such a casket should not expand his enterprise by adding other appurtenances and services that would provide for a more comfortable eternal repose. For instance, why should the receptacle that holds our last remains be so claustrophobic? It was understandable in England, perhaps—a small island nation where land was needed for agriculture; but America, with its vast inland prairie as useless as the sands of the Sahara, could accommodate thousands of pyramids the size of Cheops's. One could almost imagine great herds of buffalo grazing among all manner of geometric burial structures pockmarking the Great Plains. An ambitious young man like this Giles could develop a thriving business of shipping late lamented members of the Upper Ten west by train in their bescrolled vaults to be housed in the commodious splendor of Egyptian-style pyramids, obelisks, and sphinxes. He imagined railcars designed solely for the purpose, painted black, their windows draped with crepe, and crowds of teary-eyed mourners at every crossing between Hoboken and St. Louis.

Meanwhile, back in New York City, the ground thus rescued from the sexton would provide an excellent driving park for the Upper Ten in which to hobnob and display their fine equipage—the whole thing was such a capital arrangement that Willis envisioned Horace Greeley exhorting, "Go West, *Old* Man—Go West!"

Yes, it would do. Willis's column was complete in his mind. Call it trifling if you would; he was excited by it. Why should he write something so grave as to be worthy of posterity? Leaving Barnum's and deciding never to entertain such thoughts again, he began searching his mind for a suitable place to entertain his appetite.

CHAPTER 6

 Eddy

New York Sun   Friday, February 28, 1845

ANNOUNCEMENTS

TONIGHT at the New-York Historical Society Library Mr. Edgar A. Poe, author of "The Raven," will deliver a lecture, "The Poets & Poetry of America."

EDDY LOVED A HOAX, and during February the Little Longfellow War had developed into a fine one. He had never tomahawked himself and was surprised at how effortless the task proved to be—he was vicious. Others had faulted him for perceiving plagiarism everywhere, claiming his reviews were blind to all but this, so he attacked himself on that basis. He had always considered plagiarism an artist's greatest flaw. No sooner did a poem remind him of another than he was off to find the similarity of their words and, failing that, the similarity of their metrical structures and, failing that, the similarity of their ideas. Such an extreme position was blinding indeed, and now that he thought about it, he considered the possibility that the sin of plagiarism might even be forgivable. How many poems, he reasoned, could be written about lost love, for example, without a repetition of words and, much more, of ideas? "The Raven" might never have been conceived had Eddy strictly applied his critical principles. He'd have written a poem about steam-powered printing presses instead, and who would read that? What had inspired him to write was lost love, not printing presses. Lost love! The theme made him stop and think, and he wondered if, in his mind, he'd already put Sissy in her grave.

He had hastened to put that thought aside, focused on the blank page before him, and accused Edgar Poe of plagiarism, even citing instances of such. Remote though these citations were, they were convincing, and the result yielded greater kindness to Longfellow than Eddy had ever thought possible. The exercise proved cathartic, and his letter to the *Mirror*, the most enjoyable review he'd ever written.

Inspired by the blinded cyclops of Homer's *Odyssey*, he had signed his letter "Outis," Greek for "No Man." Perhaps his disguise would be guessed; in fact, he hoped it would. The thrill of a hoax was basking in its cleverness once it was unveiled. Willis paid him ten dollars and published it at once. True, he was stirring up controversy in order to sell newspapers, but there was more to it than that. As his assistant, Eddy had learned of Willis's animosity to Boston for having "banished him," as he called it. His bitterness ran deep, and to some extent Eddy shared those feelings. His own dislike for Boston had its genesis in the few months he had lived there after breaking with John Allan, the man who had raised him but refused to adopt him. Eighteen at the time, without a job and friendless, he chose Boston because it was the city of his birth, and he perceived his going there as a new beginning; but Boston proved cold and alien, and Eddy felt unwelcome. His southernness was shunned, and unable to find work, he had joined the army.

With part of the ten dollars Willis had paid him for his Outis letter, Eddy purchased a new collar and necktie to wear for a lecture he had been invited to deliver at the New-York Historical Society Library at the end of February. The evening of the lecture, he paced the parlor of their Greenwich Street rooms. He had not eaten; he was too nervous to eat. While Sissy and Muddy went down for supper, he remained upstairs, practicing his speech. From time to time he stopped to gesture in front of the window, explaining a point of keen insight to the windows of the buildings across the street. When Sissy and Muddy returned from dining, Muddy pressed his suit pants and sponged his coat. Wearing his new collar and necktie, he walked the dozen or so blocks.

Rows of chairs filled the library's main floor. They faced a temporary speaker's platform erected in front of the staircase that rose to the mezzanine. Two chairs faced the audience, and assuming one was for him, Eddy sat down to watch people arrive and to review his notes one last time.

To his astonishment, the person taking the seat next to him on the speakers' platform was none other than Gulian Verplanck. Being invited to address the library membership was an honor indeed, but to be introduced by Verplanck—tireless advocate for copyright protection, distinguished orator and statesman, scion of New Amsterdam's founding fathers—exceeded Eddy's wildest dreams. Verplanck plopped his bulk down, turned in his chair, and extended his hand.

"Poe," he said, smiling affably. Verplanck was in his late fifties. His thick gray hair, curling at the ears, had been brushed with the haste of someone too busy to be fastidious. He had dark blue eyes and thick, bushy, sharply arched eyebrows. His necktie was crooked, his cheeks as rosy as a Catholic schoolboy's, and his watery eyes and bespattered lapels told of a hearty supper washed down with plenty of claret.

Certain key phrases of his lecture replayed in Eddy's mind even as he shook hands with Verplanck, whose single-word greeting seemed to elevate their acquaintance to that of old friends. Until that moment, however, Verplanck had been more legend than flesh and blood.

"I've been looking forward to this," Verplanck said, his voice raspy. "You realize, of course, that everyone expects to hear 'The Raven.'"

Eddy stiffened. He had been asked to give a lecture, not a reading, and he had no copy of the poem. Wondering if he could recite it from memory, he felt his chest tighten. He had done it before from memory, but not in front of two hundred fifty people, not in the presence of Fitz-Greene Halleck, whom he recognized taking a chair in the second row between two fawning younger women. Yes, he knew "The Raven" by heart, but what if he stumbled? He could not help but recall a recitation before the Jefferson Society at the University of Virginia twenty years earlier. Quoting from Shakespeare's *Julius Caesar,* nervous and in too much haste, he had transposed two words of Marc Anthony's funeral speech, "Friends, Romans, countrymen, lend me your bones" instead of "ears." He was laughed off the stage and teased for a week by his classmates. Jefferson heard about it and invited members of the society up to Monticello the following Sunday. Between the main course and dessert, he made Eddy recite the speech again, and there was thunderous applause when he got it right.

"Let me make a suggestion," Verplanck said. "When you finish your lecture, accept their applause. Let it die down naturally, then, when the room is quiet, do the poem as an encore. Take it from an old politician, my boy, make them wait for what they came to hear. It'll bring down the house, and you, my young friend, will be the darling of every woman in New York. You'll have more invitations to supper than a stuffed capon. You'll end up reciting that poem in every drawing room in this city."

The notion thrilled Eddy. Verplanck put his arm around him, and drew him close again, his breath in Eddy's face, breath that smelled of roasted garlic and a Conestoga stogie.

"Look, son," Verplanck explained, "all a man needs is one royal flush, and you've got yours. You can ride that blackbird till the day you die," and he laughed out loud, slapping Eddy on the back.

At that moment the crowd began applauding as a man and woman walked to reserved seats in the center of the front row. The man was fifty, of medium height and balding, though he had ample and bushy side whiskers. He bowed to the crowd, turned, and took his seat. Once settled, he smiled at Verplanck.

Verplanck turned back to Eddy again.

"We had dinner together," he explained. "The Bryants and I. Do you know Cullen Bryant?"

"No," Eddy said, staring at Bryant in the front row. "I mean, we've not been formally introduced."

"I'll introduce you when it's over," Verplanck said. "We had dinner at the Bread and Cheese. He is very high on your work. Said 'The Raven' is our best poem yet."

Eddy swelled with pride at this news. Both sides of the Atlantic considered Cullen Bryant to be the finest poet in America. That Bryant thought "The Raven" "our best yet" was to place it above his own "Thanatopsis," long regarded the greatest poem ever written in America. And here he was, Edgar Poe—an orphan, a southerner, self-taught, in New York less than a year, wearing holey underwear and a broken gaiter, carrying a watch with a broken stem, and living on assistant editor's pay—sitting in front of a crowd that included Halleck and Bryant. He had been told Washington Irving would be there and Henry Dana, too. Willis arrived with Mary, who looked as if she might give birth that very night; they waved to him from the back of the house. Perhaps Horace Greeley was there, and General Morris and Duyckinck and Colton and Park Benjamin of the *New World,* and Fenno Hoffman, even Gilmore Simms from Charleston, who was said to be in the city on business. And all the women writers would be there, including Frances Osgood, for whom Eddy had a special gift in return for her kind wish to meet him. It might just be the greatest assemblage of literary celebrities in the history of New York City. It appeared that there would not be standing room when the crowd finally settled.

Eddy inhaled deeply to calm his nerves, and he hoped that Verplanck was right about "The Raven." He would accept every one of those invitations to recite, and he would buy a new suit and new gaiters and a new watch with a gold chain.

Verplanck stood and walked to the center of the platform as the crowd quieted. Eddy's heart pounded.

"Today," Verplanck began, smiling, confident, jovial, "I had a letter from a friend in England. He tells me that on the mantle in his library there sits a bronze bust of Pallas Athena."

The crowd was amused, and Verplanck smiled, triumphant.

"And now that my English friend has read 'The Raven,' he cannot bear to enter that room after dark. Were he to find a wayward crow perched upon that bust, no doubt he would die of apoplexy."

The crowd laughed and applauded.

"He tells me that all London is agog over 'The Raven,' that never has a poem been so much the topic of conversation. Those not reciting it are imitating it. Already variations on this work would fill no small volume—some humorous, some even more frightful than the one written by the man we have before us tonight," and Verplanck turned and motioned toward Eddy as the crowd applauded again.

"This is a great day for American literature," Verplanck continued. "Perhaps our greatest. Long have we strived to gain the respect of our forebears across the Atlantic. We have puffed the works of our native sons *shamelessly* in our valiant but fruitless efforts to gain entry into that exclusive club. But no more. Our apprenticeship is over. *We have arrived!* An American poem has all London agog, and I say it is a great, great day."

Applause erupted like the Croton water jets. Shouts of "Bravo!" and "Hooray!" were heard above the din. Gradually the crowd came to its feet as Verplanck, clapping with the rest, turned to Eddy. Should he stand? Should he take a bow? Even Bryant came to his feet.

Eddy did stand and took his bow, flushed and red, fever rising into his forehead, his heart swelling with the certainty that he had reached the supreme moment of his life.

Verplanck returned to his seat, and Eddy, taking this to be his cue, moved to center stage and waited for silence.

His prepared lecture seemed at odds with Verplanck's enthusiastic introduction, and he decided on the spot to omit the portion most critical of Longfellow, but he could not avoid Longfellow altogether.

He began by asserting that didacticism had no place in poetry. Moral lessons belonged in the pulpit, not in the poem, so he claimed. Saying this felt good. As he spoke, power over an audience charged him like a drug. Using Longfellow as a whipping boy, he so belabored the issue of misplaced didacticism that Cullen Bryant began fidgeting in his chair, making Eddy pull up short of his conclusion. Bryant sat not twenty feet away, clearly irked, scowling at Eddy.

Deciding he should move on, Eddy attacked the puffing system. He used as his example a new collection of poems by Princeton poet William F. Lord. The much ballyhooed new book—Longfellow was one of the major puffers—had been called "very remarkable," but Eddy disagreed. Lord's compositions, he maintained, were abominable, puffed for no other reason than that Lord was an American and was being repaid for having puffed others first. "The puffing system must end," he declared with too much emphasis. "It is recompense, pure and simple, by an exclusive club of old boys. If Mr. Lord's poems are remarkable, it is because of their conceit, impudence, and platitude. Good Lord," he said, and smiled, "from any further evidence of your stupidity, deliver us!"

He paused, expecting at least a bit of laughter. There was none, and just then Eddy realized that he was speaking to the old boys club.

Quickly he turned to the centerpiece of his lecture, *The Poets and Poetry of America*, a new anthology edited by Rufus Wilmot Griswold. Eddy knew "Gris," another member of the club whom he disliked, in part because Griswold was making more money as editor of *Graham's* in Philadelphia than Eddy had earned when he had the job. As Eddy had borrowed Griswold's title for his lecture, he could not avoid mentioning the anthology, though he suspected his comments would further alienate his audience. In contrast to the forceful delivery he had practiced in front of the window, he voiced his opinions with timidity. Professing to dislike anthologies, he accused Griswold's selections of being biased and political. Furthermore, he saw no reason why the literary community should accept the opinions of a mediocre poet with bloated ambition. With practiced sarcasm, he attacked Griswold's method of ranking poets not only on the beauty of their poetry but also the heft of their output, their age, their wealth and social rank, the number of their friends, their political affiliations, and no doubt even the style of their whiskers.

The mention of whiskers, another attempt at humor, seemed to be a pointed reference to Bryant's prominent muttonchops, though this was not Eddy's intention in the least. Impulsively he glanced at Bryant, an impulse that did not go unnoticed, and a silent audience watched as their eyes locked. Bryant stared back with cold and unforgiving eyes, and in those eyes Eddy saw his own foster father's disapproval as if John Allan stalked him still, ten years after his putrid remains had been shoveled into the mold. By the greatest effort of will, Eddy drew his eyes away from Bryant and searched his mind for ways to repair the damage he'd done. He could almost picture Bryant walking out, followed by Verplanck and his entire audience.

He improvised. Hoping to redeem himself, he heaped lavish praise on Griswold's top five, three of whom—Bryant, Dana, and Halleck—were in his audience. Then he moved on to a discussion of the women poets. Conveniently ignoring the fact that Griswold planned a separate anthology for the poetesses, he attacked Griswold for omitting them and expressed the belief that double standards existed in America where criticism of poetry by women was concerned.

"So long as our critics treat our women poets with such gentility," he said, "they will never write poetry to rival that of men." He went on to criticize the sentimental poetry that the periodicals of the day demanded from women. It seemed to be their special genre—they were the authors of sympathy and sweetness. But they should be encouraged, Eddy professed, to do more, and with this he introduced the work of Frances Sargent Locke Osgood as exemplifying the level of excellence that women poets were capable of achieving. This was his gift for her, and he imagined her thrill as he capped his lecture by reciting one of her poems.

At the end there was polite applause—less enthusiastic than Eddy had earlier imagined as he paced the boardinghouse parlor. He had wanted to be liked, to be well received, but he had said all the wrong things. Why did he always say the wrong things?

Following Verplanck's advice, he remained standing as the applause died away, then he began.

> Once upon a midnight dreary, while I pondered, weak and weary,
> Over many a quaint and curious volume of forgotten lore—
> While I nodded, nearly napping, suddenly there came a tapping,
> As of some one gently rapping, rapping at my chamber door—
> "'Tis some visitor," I muttered, "tapping at my chamber door—
> Only this and nothing more.

The room grew quiet, the library a perfect setting. On a table on the mezzanine, visible from the main floor, stood a bust of George Washington, and Eddy noticed more than one pair of eyes glancing up, as if they envisioned the raven perched there. Bryant's eyes grew large, his mouth drooping open as if Eddy were some ghastly apparition. "The Raven" held them spellbound, and he sensed that Verplanck was right, that his recitation of this poem would be in demand for as long as he lived. He could tour the world like Ole Bull. What a life! Sissy could have a cottage of her own in the country where the air would be fresh and healthful, and Muddy would have a proper kitchen with shelves for her mother's china, china she had lugged from one boardinghouse to another. And Eddy would have his magazine, and he would call it *Poe's Magazine,* giving it the benefit of his name, and it would be the finest literary journal in America *and* in England.

As he recited, he embraced his audience, especially the women, imagining that secretly they agreed with everything he had said. It was unexpected, this affinity with the women, and Eddy was surprised and grateful for it. It was the women Verplanck had referred to when he spoke of invitations to supper. It was the women who believed that poetry should be beautiful and not didactic. It was the women poets who wanted the freedom to write about things other than the cares of the heart. It was the women poets who detested the old boys club as much as Eddy did. He could see that now, and he could imagine all that they would bring him: chocolate cakes and featherbeds and respect— respect above all. To that end, especially for them, he recited flawlessly, verse after verse, pausing now and again, looking up, looking down and feeling the sharp edge of his stiff new collar. At the end he put his hand over his heart, tears in his eyes.

"Prophet!" said I, "thing of evil!—prophet still, if bird or devil!
By that Heaven that bends above us—by that God we both adore—
Tell this soul with sorrow laden if, within the distant Aidenn,
It shall clasp a sainted maiden whom the angels name Lenore—
Clasp a rare and radiant maiden whom the angels name Lenore."
　　Quoth the Raven "Nevermore."

. . . .

And the Raven, never flitting, still is sitting, *still* is sitting
On the pallid bust of Pallas just above my chamber door;
And his eyes have all the seeming of a demon's that is dreaming,
And the lamp-light o'er him streaming throws his shadow on the floor,
And my soul from out that shadow that lies floating on the floor
　　Shall be lifted—nevermore!

A moment's silence followed, and then an eruption of applause that startled Eddy, waking him from the grief that had been palpable as he recited. His audience came to its feet, still applauding, and before he knew it, Cullen Bryant was pumping his hand, his wife, Frances, beside him beaming with admiration. As suddenly, he found himself surrounded by a crush of women; some he knew, and those he didn't introduced themselves. Among them were the writers—Ann Stephens, Caroline Kirkland, Mary Hewitt, Margaret Fuller, Anne Lynch, Elizabeth Oakes Smith—and there was also Mary Willis and others.

"It's a miracle, Mr. Poe," Frances Bryant said.

Someone slapped him on the back; Verplanck clapped him on the shoulder; Gilmore Simms embraced him and, in his cultured Charleston accent, swore that in his entire life he had never witnessed a recital so captivating. Eddy smiled and nodded repeatedly as he accepted praise from all who came forward. For twenty minutes he stood there shaking hands, thanking people, agreeing to more invitations than he could fulfill in a month, and feeling for all the world like a member of the club. As the crowd began to thin, he felt Willis's arm around his shoulder.

"You did yourself proud tonight," Willis said, as he, Mary, and Eddy stood on the platform in the emptying hall. Two workmen took up chairs and another lowered the chandelier in order to douse the jets.

Eddy gathered his papers and his hat and overcoat. "I must have met every poet in New York tonight," he said, "except for Mrs. Osgood. Was she not here?"

"I did not see her," Willis said, "but she will be thrilled that you read one of her poems. I'll arrange an introduction soon."

Eddy smiled. "How can I ever thank you, Willis? You must have had a hand in this."

"I did nothing," Willis said. "It was the poem that did it. I hate to think how many times you will have to recite it now. You'll be singing for your supper from now till Christmas. I'll wager you'll be sick of 'The Raven' by then."

"I have another Outis letter for you," Eddy said, thinking Sissy and Muddy must eat, too.

As they left the hall, Eddy pulled up the lapels of his overcoat. At the curb, Willis hailed a brougham, not wanting Mary, in her condition, to have to walk the eight blocks back to the Astor.

"Can we drop you?" Willis offered.

"I prefer to walk," Eddy said, and thanked him.

"You're costing me a fortune with these letters," Willis said. "But it's working. I've had two more letters from Boston, all applauding Outis for his support of Longfellow."

By Mary's amused reaction, Eddy guessed she knew all about the hoax, and he wondered if she also knew about their scheme to pirate work from England. They said good night, and Eddy turned to walk back to Greenwich Street, wanting time to savor the crush of the crowd of well-wishers and thinking life would be different now. He had arrived. He had most certainly arrived.

CHAPTER 7

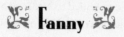 Fanny

Water-Cure Journal   March 7, 1845

BOOKS ON HEALTH
RECENTLY PUBLISHED BY
HARPER & BROTHERS, NEW YORK

———•◦•———

LECTURES ON ANATOMY
AND PHYSIOLOGY
BY MARY S. GOVE

Must your wives and daughters become Martyrs to French fashions
and the painful and Injurious practice of tight lacing? Illustrated with
anatomical engravings showing the Ill Effects to the rib cage, heart,
lungs, and other internal organs. 12mo. Price 37½¢.

FANNY GRIPPED THE EDGE of the washstand as the chambermaid
cinched the laces of her corset. May stood beside her, begging her
mother to take her along. Lily was in school, but May would not start until the
fall, and she did not want to be left alone upstairs.

"Tighter, Molly," Fanny said, "or we'll never get the buttons fastened."

The dress was another gift from Ned, made of pink damask with tiny covered buttons that ran from the back of her neck to a point below her waist. His
showering her with presents hinted of growing impatience, but as yet he had
not proposed. The dress was too tight, so Fanny had sent May for the chambermaid, and as Molly tightened the strings, Fanny expelled her breath and
glanced out the window. It was windy; probably cold; they could not go out,
of course. With May upstairs alone, they would have to stay in the hotel if
lunch were offered, and she would be miffed at Willis if it were not. He was
waiting downstairs with Mr. Poe.

Fanny had missed Poe's lecture at the New-York Historical Society Library. Truth was—and she saw no reason to reveal it—she had had four invitations to attend, but was already committed to Ned, and he hadn't wanted to go. Instead, they had dined at his hotel, the New York House. The next day in the Astor ladies' parlor, Willis thrilled her with the news that Poe had read one of her poems. That he had done so in the presence of *that* gathering was bully indeed. She implored Willis to ask Poe for a copy of the portion of his lecture that pertained to her and instructed him to explain that on the night of the lecture, she had been left waiting in the lobby, her card of admission in hand, until it was apparent that her escort had been detained, and she'd had no alternative but to retire to her room and read herself to sleep. Willis complied. He brought the copy, along with a handwritten and signed copy of the last two stanzas of "The Raven," saying he would bring Poe to the hotel the following Tuesday to meet her. But Poe had canceled, citing the press of business *contretemps*.

"He doesn't like the Astor," Willis had said, as if to explain, but a few days later, on Friday morning, Willis sent a note up to Fanny to say that he and Poe were in the lobby, and now she hurried to dress.

Molly struggled with the buttons as Fanny pinched her shoulder blades together and tried to empty her lungs of air, straining to help. When they finished, she was laced as tight as a buggy whip. Then, deciding she could not be seen in the lobby without it, Fanny put on her bonnet, also new, the fabric matching her dress. It had pink rosettes above the brim and a satin bow at the back, and she decided not to tie the ribbons under her chin, preferring to leave her throat exposed. She pushed wisps of hair up under the brim of her bonnet and pulled down curls around her ears. Instructing May not to leave the room, she bribed her with a promise that they could go out later. Repeating the instructions to Molly, she glanced at herself once more in the mirror, pinching her cheeks such that she might have raised blisters; then she draped a shawl over her shoulders and left.

The lobby was crowded. Fanny paused on the landing, searching for Willis. He was there with Poe, just inside the front door, leaning against the round table and half hidden by a towering arrangement of pink quince. Fanny recognized Poe from his likeness in *Graham's,* and her first thought was that he was all forehead. It was too broad for a face that was rather pointed and much too serious, perhaps even somber. Willis noticed her and straightened as Fanny arched her back, willing herself to be inches taller, and descended the staircase. At the bottom he accepted her hand and kissed her fingers, smiling and smug as if he saw through all her machinations.

"Fanny," he said, "may I present Edgar Poe."

"Mr. Poe," Fanny said, beaming and curtsying. "At long last." And she decided his forehead was not so large as it appeared from the landing. He smiled and nodded, seeming to be ill at ease. Was it his suit, she wondered, worn and nearly threadbare? Ned had been right; Mr. Poe was indeed penniless.

"Mrs. Osgood," he replied, looking her squarely in the eyes. His hair was dark, oily, and unwashed, but neatly brushed, and his face was clean, and after greeting her, he clinched his jaw with resolute pride.

Willis broke the ice with a story. It was not precisely true, but she let him tell it. "Fanny is a compulsive poet, Edgar," he said. "She has no restraint whatsoever. I'm convinced that even her thoughts are couplets and quatrains. There is a story about her. She and Anne Lynch were out for a day of shopping when Fanny discovered that she'd forgotten her purse. She instructed the driver to pull the carriage over, took out pencil and paper, composed four quick stanzas, popped into the *Knickerbocker*, and came out with a ten-dollar bill."

With this, Edgar turned to Fanny and smiled broadly, delighted by the story. His countenance changed totally, leaving Fanny bursting with pride. She liked him at once. The smile revealed straight white teeth, and any discomfort he might have felt appeared to evaporate. She knew then that they would become very good friends.

"In truth, Mr. Poe," she said, taking his arm and guiding him toward the stairs, "that's not the whole story, and I don't want you to expect too much of me. In the first place, it was not Anne Lynch. Anne is not a great shopper. It was Edith Bartlett, and Edith's husband, John, spread the rumor just to brag on me. You see, I had already composed the poem. I had worked on it for days, so I knew it by heart. And the ten dollars was payment not only for *that* poem but for two additional poems to be submitted later—poems I was yet to write. And, since I spent the entire ten dollars, you might say I ended the day in debt."

Hearing this, Edgar laughed out loud as they reached the second floor, and

Fanny led them into the ladies' parlor, deciding he was not in the least melancholy like his tales.

The parlor was quiet. A handful of women, enjoying their morning coffee, nodded as Fanny and her guests entered. She chose seats near one of the front windows that looked out on Broadway. Below them, men walking along the avenue held their top hats to keep them from blowing off, and flags flying in front of City Hall snapped in the wind, as did the white awnings of the shops on the street level, under the Astor.

Turning to Willis, Fanny said that she had seen Mary the day before and that it appeared her time was near. He agreed and talked about their upcoming trip to England. They would be gone six months, he explained. It would be his third trip abroad; amazing to consider, but the steamships had transformed the ordeal into a bona fide holiday. Fanny expressed envy, saying she missed London and hoped she would see it again someday. Then Willis drifted into recollection of his years in England, dropping names of important friends, Countess Blessington, Bulwer-Lytton, Dickens. He described how he and Mary had met there and how desperately Mary missed her home.

All the while, Edgar sat on the edge of his chair, listening and polite, and though Fanny's eyes focused on Willis, her thoughts centered on her new friend. His discomfort seemed to have returned, and she sensed that he was preoccupied, perhaps by something small—a delay, a toothache, one of the myriad everyday frustrations; or was it something bigger—a failing business, an unhappy marriage, fatal illness? Curious, she searched her mind for a way to draw him into the conversation until Willis did it for her.

"Edgar is no stranger to England," he said, "are you, Edgar?"

In a soft, careful tone, Edgar explained to Fanny that his family had sailed to England from Richmond when he was six years old and remained there for five years. He described the boarding school outside London where he had spent most of that time, his descriptions evoking draconian images that she recognized from his stories. The minute, incredibly vivid descriptions with which he colored his experiences captivated her; she could have listened to him for hours. Then suddenly he stopped, as if worried that he was talking too much. No wonder he writes, Fanny thought; the man was a born writer.

"I must get back," Willis said, at the pause, and he rose from his chair. "I have a column to write, and now that you've been properly introduced, no doubt you have much to talk about."

"Willis! Don't go," Fanny pleaded, fearing Edgar was not quite ready to be left alone with her. And what about lunch? It was obvious Edgar Poe could not afford the Astor dining room, and he would never accept an invitation from her.

But they *were* left alone and in circumstances that seemed almost too intimate. "You must call me Fanny," she said.

"And please call me Edgar. Fanny is a name that is dear to me. It was my mother's name—my foster mother, Frances Allan . . . everyone called her Fanny. My real parents died when I was two."

An orphan, Fanny thought, wondering where the tragedy of Edgar Poe would end. Attempting to change the subject, she thanked him for reading one of her poems the night of his lecture.

"I like that poem," he said, seeming to grow more comfortable with her every minute. "'The Spirit of the Dance.' It has an ethereal quality that few can do effectively. I think you're a fine poet."

"Do you really, Mr. Poe—Edgar, I mean? Or do you think I'm just another scribbling female?"

He smiled, amused by the term. No doubt he'd heard it many times; perhaps he'd even used it, but Fanny guessed he would not admit to that. Nevertheless, he shook his head with resolve. "No," he said, "I don't think that at all."

Staring at him, Fanny savored the sincerity in his voice. There was nothing artificial about Edgar Poe, no airs, no affectations. The surface of the man betrayed the depths there, too. Yes, she decided, they would become dear friends. Still, she wondered if he would give her brutal honesty when it came to her work. She wanted his brutal honesty.

"I dare say," she said to test him, "that you would never tomahawk a woman as you've done Longfellow."

The mention of Longfellow unsettled him, and Fanny regretted saying the name. "Mrs. Osgood," he said, "I would be run out of New York City on a rail were I to do such a thing. And my magazine—were it not for women, no magazine in America would survive."

"But I'm told that in your lecture you said men and women are held to different standards."

"And I believe they are," he said, "but I said many things that night that I should not have said. Thank God I had 'The Raven,' or it would have ended quite differently. If I want my magazine to succeed, I need to toe the mark, and that probably means leaving Longfellow in peace."

They stared at each other until Fanny had to look away. "It is sad to think," she said at last, "that the truth could do us in." She paused, then smiled again. "But let's not dwell on such things at our first meeting. Instead, I will congratulate you on the *Broadway Journal*. Willis tells me it's sure to succeed, and I intend to take a subscription."

"I hope you will do more than that," Edgar said. "Will you honor us with a submission, too?"

"How can I resist?" Fanny said, wondering if he intended to pay her. Much as she liked him, she was used to being paid for her work. It was how she made her living, at least in part. After all, in her mind she was an unmarried woman with two children to consider. But then she had second thoughts. By his reading her poem at his lecture, Edgar may have elevated her prestige, enabling her to ask more for her poems in the future, so she decided she owed him a poem in return, and she agreed, "On the condition that someday you will recite 'The Raven' for me, since I missed your lecture."

He promised, and Fanny resolved to begin working on a poem for him that very day.

"Do you know Anne Lynch?" she asked, and continued without waiting for a reply. "You will receive an invitation to a party at her house for Saturday week. She is my dearest friend. Everyone calls her Lynchie."

"I met her the night of my lecture," he said, "and I've heard about her parties."

"You will enjoy them," Fanny said, thinking how exciting it would be to hear him recite in front of Anne's fireplace. "They are not what you might imagine. It's always mostly writers, with a few artists and musicians thrown in. Ole Bull was there recently; he played for us. Writers read their latest compositions and sometimes things they would never dream of publishing. It's great fun. Will you come? And bring your wife? We're all eager to meet her."

Edgar stiffened again. "My wife is ill," he said. "She had an accident a few years ago. She was singing and burst a blood vessel. I'm afraid she's never fully recovered."

Fanny stared at him, wearing a sad smile. What little she knew—that he had been an orphan, that his stories revealed an obsession with death, that he struggled against poverty, that his wife was ill—all moved and fascinated her. And now he had written a poem so remarkable that half of America could quote portions of it. He sat before her straight and proud, excessively polite, asking nothing for all his misfortune. "You must be a very special man," she said, overcome with a feeling of compassion for him just then, "and you must think me very frivolous."

Her words alarmed him. Embarrassed, he started to speak, but Fanny stopped him.

"I want to be your friend." She swallowed and searched for words. "Your writing is astonishing, and you will find many people willing to help you if you let them."

He pursed his lips and looked away, and Fanny decided she was saying all the wrong things. "Perhaps my wife can attend," he said, ignoring her offer of help.

"Would she be uncomfortable?" Fanny asked, then regretted the question. "I shouldn't have asked that. Forgive me," she said, worried that she might frighten him away. Why so proud, she wondered? Was it her? Did he think her superficial—her expensive dress, her living at the Astor? He reminded her of Sam, gaunt, passionate, spurning life's niceties. "It's only that Anne's parties are not for everyone," she said, thinking about Ned's refusal to go and wondering how to say what was in her mind without seeming to be presumptuous. "Not everyone is a poet."

"Indeed not," he said, smiling again, seeming to understand the sincerity of her solicitudes, "but I will try to persuade her. She tires easily."

"Then you *will* go?"

He nodded.

"And recite 'The Raven?' Early in the evening, in the event that your wife cannot stay long. It will be the highlight of the party, and you promised to do it for me. I'll make the arrangements, and from now on you'll always be invited to Anne's. You'll meet everyone—all the most important people in this business. It might open doors," she said, wanting to stress that he should cultivate those contacts. Surely he knew that being gifted, that overcoming adversity, was not enough. One had also to work the system, corrupt as it might be, and be diplomatic, but it seemed to Fanny that Edgar Poe was no diplomat.

He took his watch from his pocket, then glanced up at the clock on the desk as if to verify the time. "I must go," he said.

They stood, and Fanny elected not to offer her hand to be kissed. She did not want to appear a silly fool; she wanted rather to be his equal, his professional equal, and she imagined long, rich hours of talking poetry with him, discussing all the great poets, hearing his thoughts about her work, learning from him.

As they descended to the lobby, Fanny wondered why he had checked his watch. It had no stem. At the bottom of the staircase they said good-bye, and Fanny watched him cross the lobby, looking both ways as if curious but also disdainful. He does hate the place, she thought. Isn't that marvelous?

All the next week Fanny pondered over what to submit to the *Broadway Journal*. She first decided to write a tribute to the poet of "The Raven," thinking Edgar's self-esteem could use a boost, but the thing did not go well. Her attempts sounded trite and reverential, and instinct told her that praise would make her appear all the more frivolous. So she tried her hand at a parody, something others were doing. Imitations of "The Raven" were appearing everywhere, and Fanny could not resist the exercise, confident she could best them all and laughing as she contrived long strings of gloomy adjectives all starting with the same letter. She made herself stop, deciding that the imitations must irritate him. The truth was that he hadn't seemed to warm to her, yet there was that brief instant when he let down his guard. It happened when Willis told the little story about her. Perhaps her mention of debt had made a connection, and she had liked Edgar ever so much just then. He obviously resented the Astor, and he concealed his poverty with heartrending pride like the broken watch he carried. She resolved to get him a new one, but how could she possibly explain to Ned why she needed a man's gold watch? The thought of what that favor might cost made her shudder, but she would tell him it was for a struggling young editor who would lose his job if he didn't get to work on time. Ned might suspect that it was Edgar Poe, and that might make him jealous, but what of it? Edgar would have a new watch, and it wouldn't hurt to remind Ned that he wasn't the only grape on the vine.

But Fanny decided positively that Edgar Poe would never fit in. It was impossible to imagine him in Anne Lynch's parlor like Irving or Bryant, content, growing old and portly, living off capital. Edgar Poe resembled more a fugitive, wary and on the run. When he looked at her, his gaze bored into her as if he needed to learn if she were friend or foe; he had a desperado's cunning for perceiving bare bones. He had stared at her just as Sam had stared at her when he first painted her, and she imagined that he saw things she couldn't see, herself, things she could not conceal, but also, by some daredevil desire, things she wanted revealed.

EDGAR PROVED HER WRONG.

He attended Anne Lynch's party a week later, accompanied by his wife. He was stiff and formal but also cordial and polite, shaking hands, smiling, and gracious in accepting praise as Anne led the couple from hall to parlor to dining room, making introductions. Fanny watched, fascinated, realizing that she had let her imagination run wild. He was putty in Lynchie's hands, angelic; one would have thought him a choirboy.

It was Willis who had started everyone calling Anne Lynch "Lynchie." She was younger than Fanny, not yet thirty, a spinster who had moved with her mother to New York City two years earlier from Providence by way of Philadelphia, and like Fanny, she possessed a disarming sweetness that belied her fortitude. She nursed her ailing mother, and every morning she caught the ferry to Brooklyn, where she taught English literature at an academy for young ladies. Her house in Greenwich Village was modest compared to the mansions lining Broadway, yet, despite her circumstances, Lynchie had established a salon of reputation unequaled in the city. Were she a man, she would have been an ambassador or the curator of a museum or the president of a university. Instead, she was a poet and a sculptor and a consummate tactician. She could charm a self-centered jackass into sugar pudding and did it nearly every Saturday night. She opened her home on Waverly Place to men and women of eminence: artists, musicians, writers, educators, clergymen, statesmen—even actors and actresses. Her walls were often festooned with the paintings of some new artist she was promoting. She served tea and broth, but allowed no spirits, no tobacco, no politics, and no sarcasm—indications all of low character, in her opinion. Musicians played and writers read. There was no evidence of a plan; Lynchie merely made quiet and polite suggestions to a select few, and the whole thing came together as if rehearsed. Before you knew it, amid the laughter and conversation, someone cleared his throat and the recitals began. It was masterful the way she brought it off. Fanny adored her; Anne was her best friend in the world. Everyone adored her. And it was said that many of the most important works of literature published in America had their first reading in Anne Lynch's parlor.

With the Poes in train, Anne approached the dining room and motioned to Fanny, calling her by name as if they'd never met. Anne knew better, of course; Fanny had convinced her to extend the invitation along with a request that Edgar recite "The Raven." When introduced, Edgar's smile conveyed his gratitude, but Fanny imagined more than gratitude there. She perceived affection and admiration, and she could not resist the impulse to tilt her head, conveying unmistakably that a bond linked the two of them already. Later, remembering the evening, she realized that it was as if many years bound them, as if all their poems had forged a trust, a sharing that had occurred though they had never met. Meeting had merely been the capstone of a long and close friendship. For what else is poetry, Fanny earnestly believed, but laying bare one's soul.

Becoming conscious of her gesture of intimacy, she turned to Virginia, smiling at her and thinking, Yes, your husband and I are going to become good friends, so I will be yours, too. Virginia's eyes had lit up at the mention of Fanny's name, showing that Edgar had told her details of their first meeting.

As Anne led Edgar away for more introductions, Fanny took Virginia's arm and guided her out of the dining room and to the sofa in front of the fireplace.

"Edgar has told me much about you," Fanny said as they sat down, "but he neglected to say how pretty you are."

By Virginia's reaction it was evident that Fanny's compliment provided much-needed support. Modest, her frailty apparent, she seemed nervous, almost frightened. She was much younger than Fanny expected, and simply dressed in stark contrast to most of the women present. Naturally she wore no corset, her condition prohibiting it, nor did she wear crinolines, and she seemed exceedingly self-conscious about her appearance.

"He bought me a new dress," Virginia said, reaching for her handkerchief, "with the money he earned from his lecture, but it can't compare with yours or all the others'. I must look very plain."

"Don't be silly," Fanny said, "and don't be taken in by the glitter. All eyes are on you and your husband. He's the talk of New York, you know. Did he tell you that I missed his lecture? And that he recit one of my poems?"

Virginia's eyes widened and she leaned in close to Fanny. "He was upset about the lecture," she whispered. "And he's nervous tonight. He thinks he may have offended some of the men and that he's not welcome."

"Of course he's welcome," Fanny said, thinking that explained Edgar's stiff formality.

"There are so many important people here," Virginia continued, looking around the parlor. "I hardly know what to say."

Fanny smiled and took her hand. "Everyone feels that way their first time at one of Lynchie's parties. You'll get on fine, and so will Edgar. You must call me Fanny."

"Be his friend, Fanny," Virginia said. "Eddy doesn't have many friends."

"Of course I will," she replied, and together they turned to watch Anne introduce Edgar to newly arrived guests. He was exceedingly self-conscious; it seemed he didn't know what to do with his hands, clasping them behind his back such that he could have been mistaken for the butler, had Lynchie the resources to employ one. Once the introductions were over and Anne abandoned him to finalize preparations for the recitals, he did not mingle but stood by the door to the front hall as if waiting to perform. Thankfully, Willis arrived and drew him into conversation, putting him at his ease. Fanny and Virginia stared, fascinated by their animated conversation, Fanny wishing desperately that she could hear what they said.

Willis made the introductions that night, and after a few minutes of consummate Willis wit and humor, he introduced Edgar. To everyone's surprise, as if on cue, the gaslights were dimmed as he moved to the fireplace. Fanny and Virginia sat just in front of him on the sofa, and others crowded into the parlor to hear. He paused before beginning, as if to draw forth the requisite state of mind, and his whole visage changed. His features softened, became more human, more vulnerable; his eyes saddened. After glancing down at his wife, he looked up, seeming to stare at some far-distant object. Then he began in a voice so soft that it was barely audible. He stood erect, the drama of his delivery giving great effect. Every word was singular and clear. Fanny had read the poem, of course, but hearing Edgar recite it was an altogether new experience. She surrendered to the emotion of his words, lost herself in their desolation, and with longing to console him, tears streamed down her cheeks. After many verses she pulled herself away from the words and focused on the man, the somber drabness of his black suit and tie, the careworn posture, the imperfections in his features, the mystery in his eyes. There was a certain grandeur in him that spoke of struggle and hardship, but also of knowledge and experience and, above all, of intelligence, perhaps even genius—the genius to write such a poem. Edgar Poe *was* the poem. While other poets spoke of morality or the beauty of nature, Edgar Poe bared his soul. He was head and shoulders above the rest, and that drew Fanny in; indeed, she imagined, it drew everyone in. It was such a performance that she guessed that these few moments would be forever remembered—this evening in mid-March of 1845 when the renowned poet, Edgar Poe, recited his "Raven" in Anne Lynch's parlor with the gaslights dimmed, the fire burning low in the fireplace, and the wind rattling the casements.

When he finished, there was deathly silence as if no one dared utter a sound, as if the slightest sound would mar a perfect work of art. Then, near the back of the room, someone started clapping, and applause swelled into a standing ovation, thrilling Fanny; she wanted to laugh with glee. She and Virginia rose from the sofa to stand with the rest. No actor in America or England—not Edwin Forrest, not William Macready—could have delivered a more moving soliloquy. Not only was Edgar Poe a great poet; he was a great actor. Women rushed forward to congratulate him, and from then on, during the remaining readings and for the rest of the evening, he was surrounded by a crowd of admirers. He reveled in this, a changed person. Perhaps he had been nervous before, perhaps he had worried about his reception in the aftermath of his lecture, but now he was relaxed and gracious. He smiled with ease, just as he had that morning at the Astor. He must smile more often, Fanny thought, for his smile radiated gentleness and appreciation.

Holding hands, Fanny and Virginia remained together on the sofa all evening. When it's over, Fanny imagined, listening to the final recital, when he comes for his wife, he will thank me and then I will congratulate him. But when it came time to leave, Anne fetched Virginia while Edgar continued receiving the congratulations of those departing. And it was Willis who came for Fanny. Edgar said not another word to her that night. She had wanted him to know that she arranged it all, but instead, it was Anne Lynch, not Fanny, who got credit for turning the tide for him, and she felt a pang of jealousy. Riding back to the Astor with Willis, she succumbed to disappointment. It had been Fanny who told Anne she must invite Edgar Poe and have him recite "The Raven," and Fanny who had persuaded him to go and to take his wife, and the result had been phenomenal—the most memorable recital ever at any of Lynchie's parties. But no one gave Fanny credit, and Edgar had not even wished her good night.

Lily was still awake when Fanny arrived, and with more impatience than was fair, Fanny coached her in unlacing her corset, then shooed her off to bed, fearing as she did that amid all the hoopla and adoration, Edgar would lump her in with all the other women—all the scribbling women who had fawned over him that night. Surely he was not like the rest of the men, with their inflated opinions of themselves. He hadn't seemed that way at first; he hadn't seemed that way as he recited. Would he even recognize her when they met again? Would fame seduce him, make him proud? Or would he be, as she hoped he would, her own new best friend?

CHAPTER 8

🌿 Eddy 🌿

The Broadway Journal   March 26, 1845

REVIEWS

"FASHION"
A NEW COMEDY BY MRS. MOWATT
Premiers tonight at 8 at the Park Theatre

Count de Jolimaitre	Mr. Crisp
Adam Trueman	Mr. Chippendale
Mr. Tiffany	Mr. Barry
Mrs. Tiffany	Mrs. Barry
T. Tennison Twinkle	De Walden

EDDY DECIDED THAT Thomas Dunn English, the irascible editor of the *Aristidean,* looked even more forlorn than usual as he arrived at work. Eddy sat at his desk in the one-room office that the two magazines, the *Broadway Journal* and the *Aristidean,* shared in order to split the rent and the cost of coal. Portly and balding, Charles Briggs sat with his back to the window that looked out on Broadway. He had a purple wen beside his nose that Eddy despised. In their three months as partners, Briggs and Eddy had come to co-exist in unfriendly silence. Eddy had just finished reading the manuscript of a new comedy, *Fashion,* due to open that night at the Park Theater. His name was on the free-list, and he was looking forward to the premier.

Instead of going to his own desk, English approached Eddy's.

"Willis's wife is dead," he said. "I've just come from the printer's where I heard. She died last night."

Eddy paused, placed his pen in its cradle, and put the cork back in the inkwell. Staring down at his papers, he recalled that Willis had said something the night of Anne Lynch's party, ten days earlier, about Mary being unwell.

Since he had seemed unconcerned, Eddy had thought little of it, deciding it may have been nothing more than an excuse for not braving the night.

"The child was born dead," English added. "A girl. I'm sorry. I thought you'd want to know." He turned, and went to his desk.

"You should go see him," Briggs said, eyeing Eddy.

He nodded, not looking up. He didn't need Briggs telling him what to do. He was sick of Briggs. The man was officious beyond belief.

But what of Mary Willis, Eddy wondered. How old was she? Thirty? Her father had been in the military, he recalled, Egypt and Waterloo, quite distinguished. Was he still alive? Poor man didn't know his daughter was dead; wouldn't know for three weeks. Perhaps Willis was composing the letter now: "Sir, It grieves me to inform you that your daughter is dead. She died in childbirth on Tuesday night, the twenty-fifth of March."

What must it be like to live for three weeks thinking one's daughter was alive? Thinking, She is nursing her new baby, recovering from the ordeal of childbirth, being pampered by a loving husband, having breakfast in bed, perhaps going for a carriage ride if the day is fine—and then to find that all those images were wrong. During the day, going about his tasks, when the poor man happens to think of her, when he wonders, Where is she now? What is she doing at this very moment? And he looks at his watch. Then the letter comes, and all those images vanish. All along, what he thought was a living, breathing, loving daughter was a lifeless corpse lying in the ground. How must it feel to be so cruelly deceived?

He closed his eyes and swallowed. When Sissy dies, he thought, there will be no one far away to grieve for her. No one deceived by thoughts of life when it is death that fills her day—only death and nothing more.

He pushed back his chair, fetched his coat and hat, and left without a word.

It was raining, and Eddy had no umbrella. He stayed beneath the awnings, dashing across the side streets, hurrying up Broadway to the Astor. There was a large crowd in the lobby, a measure of the man, Eddy thought, that there were so many waiting to express condolences. He saw Hiram Stoddard and grabbed his arm to pull him away from the crowd. "Stoddard, tell me what you know. Please," Eddy begged, putting their differences aside.

Stoddard hesitated as if trying to decide whether or not to be civil. Then he explained that Willis's wife had contracted scarlet fever. It had been diagnosed only two days earlier, and Willis had learned Monday night that the situation was grave and that the child would be lost. There had been no need to move her. She had given birth and died there at the Astor, lingering an hour or so after the birth. General Morris was at the undertaker's, and Willis was upstairs but wanted no company during the morning. He would receive them after lunch in the ladies' parlor on the second floor.

Eddy decided to wait. Stoddard drifted away, so Eddy wandered the crowd. He saw Fanny sitting on one of the ottomans, and she saw him, too, looked up, and smiled sadly. He turned away. Perhaps it was rude not to speak, but she was surrounded by other men, and he was in no mood for polite talk. Feeling uncomfortable, he walked outside and stood beneath the portico, out of the rain. For a while he watched the traffic in the street, thinking about Willis. It occurred to him that Willis was a happy man, or he had been. Strange that Eddy had never realized this before, but he didn't think of other men in terms of their happiness or sorrow but rather in terms of their success or failure, and now he pondered the difference. Thinking this, he listened to the rainwater dripping from the roof of the portico onto the pavement. The damp air smelled earthy. It smelled of spring.

Muddy was right. Willis was the best friend he had in the world. Willis lived a comfortable life, but he was not a rich man. Were he rich, he would never have returned to the city. He would have stayed in the country, stayed at Glenmary in the backwoods, writing his "Letters from Under the Bridge" and sending them off to Morris for publication. At Glenmary he had written about country life for those who lived in the city, and now he wrote about city life. Had financial problems not brought him back to New York, Eddy would never have known him, been his assistant, published his "Raven" in the *Mirror.*

Thinking he should go home and tell Sissy and Muddy, he quickly changed his mind, deciding he could not face Sissy just then, so he walked back to his office in the drizzling rain.

With difficulty he began his review of the new play. *Fashion* was a farce, a caricature of the Upper Ten. The author was a precocious young woman, Anna Cora Mowatt, twenty-six years old, the wife of a prominent attorney. Eddy was flattered that she had solicited his opinion by sending an advance copy of the manuscript; he had "The Raven" to thank for that. Had Mowatt been a man, he would have tomahawked the play. As it was, he compared it favorably to other American dramas, but marked it down as unremarkable. He suspected it would be a hit, despite his opinion.

Willis would have reveled in it, he thought, and sitting with him, watching his amusement, would have been most enjoyable. As Willis had pointed out in numerous of his pencilings, New York, for its size, was the most entertained city in the world. With six theaters, a circus, and two museums that offered dramatic performances, one could attend the theater every night of the week without seeing the same production twice. Eddy's name was on the free-list of every theater in town, and so long as he didn't tomahawk too many productions, he was welcome to attend as often as he liked, and he did, two or three nights a week. The Park was New York's finest. John Jacob Astor and John Beekman had spent a fortune creating a setting in which the wives of the Upper Ten, women who five years earlier refused to attend the theater, now felt comfortable, even pampered. The girls of the town still roamed the upper balcony—a surer drawing card than anything on stage—but the rowdies had been chased away by high prices and the pit swept clean and carpeted. By contrast, at Dinneford's Eddy had seen rats eating peanuts and orange peels in the aisles.

Eddy often bragged in print of being the son of an actress; he was proud of it. Eliza Poe had been famous in every seaport city from Boston to Charleston, and not just for her acting but also for her singing. Eddy had no memory of her, but he believed that he had inherited a bit of the theatrical from her and that he drew upon that inheritance when he recited.

His review consumed the rest of the afternoon. Rain continued, so he decided not to return to the Astor. He would see Willis later when they could be alone. At six Briggs and English went home for supper; Eddy finished what of his review he could write before seeing the play.

As evening came on, his stomach began to growl. He'd had nothing since breakfast. There was an eatery nearby, but he had little money. At the end of the month he was due to be paid for three replies to Outis letters, all published over Briggs's objections. Willis published his Outis letters in the *Mirror*, and Eddy rebutted them under his own name in the *Broadway Journal*. It was proving a profitable arrangement.

Officially Eddy was now coeditor with Briggs, so he had maneuvered himself into a position to pull off the pirating scheme Willis had proposed in January. But would Willis go to England now that Mary was dead?

At the eatery he bought a half loaf of bread and returned to his office to await the eight o'clock curtain. The coals had died, and the room was dark. Looking up Broadway, he could see the gas jets being lit in front of the theater, and straight ahead, he could see down Maiden Lane to the wharfs and the masts of the ships silhouetted against the night sky. The rain had stopped. Chimney smoke blew east toward Brooklyn, an offshore wind, a good night to weigh anchor and drop with the tide through the Narrows and past Fort Wadsworth.

Nibbling on his bread as if it were ship's biscuit, Eddy imagined running away. It was a familiar refuge, a fantasy to which he often escaped. Why such gloomy thoughts—the dreary day? the vision of ships' masts? Mary Willis's death? Go down to the wharf, he thought. Put himself in the way of the press gang, get knocked over the head and thrown down some stinking cargo hold, come to in the morning with a knot on his head, when the sun was high and the land stood far astern—no going back. Two, three years before the mast, see the Orient and Otaheite, endure the doldrums and the storms off Cape Horn. It was sore temptation.

The fantasy amused him, knowing its source was a night on the James River with Jack Mackenzie. They'd been home from college for the summer and had gone carousing in the taverns along the wharf. Sometime after midnight, as they staggered along the docks in an area called the Rocketts, Jack had spied a dory and decided on a fling. The wind was blowing upriver, but Jack was a fine sailor. They could beat downstream, he explained, then have a fine run home facing the lights of town with the sun coming up on their stern and no one the wiser. They slipped the mooring, and Jack raised the sail, took the tiller, and handed Eddy the main sheet. He trimmed the sail following Jack's instructions as they beat downstream against the tide and the wind, back and forth, shore to shore. The breeze was light, just enough to heel them over. The wind in their face was refreshing, but they were still as tipsy as their tender little boat.

A half hour later, on a starboard tack, giggling with exhilaration, Jack watching the eastern shore and their sail hiding the approaches, a shout came from downriver, and they turned to see the dark image of a hulk bearing down on them.

"My God!" Jack yelled. "Loose the sheet," and he pushed the tiller hard over.

The dory seemed to slow to a crawl; still the hulk bore down on them, kicking up a bow wave that could swamp their little boat. By the greatest luck—or perhaps the darkness played tricks on them, made it seem closer than it was—the hulk passed by their stern, not twenty feet away, its dark hull taller than their mast. Were it not for the direction of the wind, they would have never heard that warning shout. The great ship's wake propelled them away, and as they watched in relief, someone came to the stern rail, raised a balled fist, and yelled curses at them. Before the words were out of his mouth, the dory ran fast aground.

Jack dropped the sails and sat down facing Eddy, breathing hard, sober now. "Wish we had a drink," he said, and Eddy started laughing. "I know where we can get one—Miss Emma's. And we can get more than a drink if you've got two dollars left."

Eddy had laughed again; he was broke. Jack grabbed an oar from under the thwarts and pushed them off the bar. He raised sail again, and they hailed a broad reach back to town. It was a marvelous feeling, sailing upriver, having escaped death, or worse, the fury of their parents' rage. That hour-long sail up the James River was exhilarating, the wind at their back.

The memory of that night called to mind Eddy's voyage to England as a boy. His foster mother was sick during the entire passage, and her husband, John Allan, would bring her on deck only to have her blown back below. Eddy would sneak into the fo'c'sle and listen to the sailors spin their yarns. His *Arthur Gordon Pym* had its inspiration in that dingy room where shadows played on the walls like ghosts and the timbers creaked. Those men enjoyed a certain freedom that Eddy had envied ever since—no ambition, no responsibility; they stood their watch and followed their orders. What must it be like to rest the night swinging in a hammock with no rent to pay, no food to buy, no family counting on you?

In the light of these thoughts, New York seemed a dreary place that night. Remembering his review of *Fashion*, Eddy decided it was too critical. Why was he always so critical? Willis didn't seem to notice, but others did. He had been too hard on Longfellow and people despised him for it, and if they knew he'd done it for the money alone, they'd despise him even more. Eddy's opinion could be bought; he was corrupt and he knew it. But it wasn't just the money; it was also envy, envy of Longfellow's success. The old boys club could read him like a book, and they hated him. Sometimes he even hated himself. But what choice did he have? His salary barely covered his room and board.

At half past seven, putting these thoughts aside, he left the office, crossed Broadway, and walked up to the Park Theater. The crowd was thick and well dressed—more bonnets than Eddy had ever seen at a New York theater. He worried about finding a seat. As he descended the center aisle, he noticed Willis sitting in the pit. He was alone, and Eddy determined to sit with him, but halfway down, a hand reached out to him.

"Edgar."

He turned to see Fanny Osgood seated near the aisle.

"I saved you a seat," she said, indicating with her right hand the seat beside her.

Had she come alone? he wondered. Surely not. Yet there she was, sitting next to an empty seat. "I can't," Eddy said, eager to get to Willis before someone else did. As he turned away, he saw in her expression the offense he'd given.

Willis welcomed him, seeming to be relieved to have someone to talk to. His face was flushed; he'd been drinking.

"I'm so sorry about Mary," Eddy began. "I came to see you this morning, but there was such a crowd."

Willis waved him off; he didn't want to talk about it. He looked up and back at the chandelier. "It's going to be amazing," he said, "I couldn't miss it," and he turned back to Eddy, nervous and agitated. "How's your wife? And Mrs. Clemm? Are they well?"

Eddy nodded, regretting that Sissy and Muddy didn't know and thinking that he should have gone home for supper.

"It will be a packed house," Willis said, turning to study the crowd. He could not sit still, and his hands were shaking. "Look at the women, Poe. Look! Have you ever seen so many beautiful women in your life? And look there, in the stage box. It's Astor. And there," he said, pointing to people sitting in the front row of the first balcony. "It's the mayor and Mowatt. Where is Mowatt's wife? Probably backstage. They're next-door neighbors, you know, the Mowatts and Mayor Harper."

Eddy did not know, of course, but he followed Willis's gaze, looking back at the crowd sitting in the parterre circle. He searched for Fanny, wanting to catch her eye and show her that he was with Willis, thinking she would understand, but he could not find her.

Among the sea of faces, there were few Eddy knew, but by their dress it was apparent who they were—the flower of society, Willis's Upper Ten. In all his nights at the theater, he had never seen so many fashionable women. Directly behind the pit was a rail, and Eddy stared, half hidden by the posts, at wealth beyond his comprehension. He noticed Gulian Verplanck in a black cutaway, white waistcoat, and tie. In his lap his black top hat glistened in reflection of the gaslight sconces and the huge chandelier that lit the theater like a palace. Such formal black-and-white attire was the uniform for the men. Women, on the other hand, were every color of the spectrum—red and gold, emerald green and royal blue. Their silks and jewels mirrored the lights of the chandeliers such that they seemed to radiate an incandescence of their own, and they perfumed the air. Most astonishing of all, many of them were removing their bonnets. No wonder Willis was here. Customs were changing before their very eyes. How could New York's foremost chronicler of fashion miss this?

"Poe, look," Willis said. "The dandies have been exiled to the third tier, and they're crowding against the rail looking down at a sea of bosoms. Oh! what a sight that must be."

Indeed the third tier was all men, young men, not a woman among them, and Eddy wondered if the girls of the town would be admitted once the curtain lifted.

The stage itself rose four feet above the pit, and screens hiding the footlights rose another foot. Hiding the stage was a gold-fringed maroon curtain flanked by red-and-gold marble columns with gilt capitals. Fresco panels, also red and gold, encircled the theater, embellishing both balconies. It was the most magnificent structure in all of New York City, and the packed house portended something extraordinary. Willis had sensed it. It had lured him away from his grieving.

As the lights were turned down, a young man, an actor in makeup, dressed in a business suit, walked onto the stage in front of the curtain. Pretending to read a newspaper, he could have been a capitalist strolling down Wall Street, his top hat at a cocky angle.

"'*Fashion*, a Comedy,'" he announced, as if reading from his newspaper. "I'll go: but stay—" Then he turned to the audience.

> Now I read farther, 'tis a native play!
> Bah! Homemade calicoes are well enough,
> But homemade dramas *must* be stupid stuff.

The audience warmed with laughter. The actor had voiced a widespread notion, but there was bravado for putting it up front—a bold declaration.

> Had it the *London* stamp, 'twould do—but then,
> "*Fashion!*" What's here? "It never can succeed!
> "What! From a woman's pen? It takes a man
> "To write a comedy—no woman can."

Again there was laughter as the actor cut his eyes from his newspaper to the audience. A second gauntlet had been thrown down.

> Grant that *some* wit may grow on native soil,
> And Art's fair fabric rise from woman's toil,
> While we exhibit but to *reprehend*
> The social vices, 'tis for *you* to mend!

And he laughed, exiting stage right as the crowd applauded, and the curtain rose on the magnificent Broadway parlor of Mr. and Mrs. Tiffany.

Willis turned to Eddy and smiled, whiskey on his breath. "Let's see if they're still laughing when the curtain falls," he said.

They were. There was laughter from beginning to end. The caricatures that had seemed to Eddy obvious and heavy-handed on paper were far enough from reality to put a respectful distance between the characters in the play and those they satirized. Eddy's favorite was the poet, T. Tennison Twinkle, and his ridiculous poem, but he saw his own reflection in Twinkle and decided no one had been spared.

As the final curtain fell, there was an explosion of applause. Once the actors had taken their bows, there were calls for the author. When she did not appear at once, several of the men left their boxes and climbed on to the stage to search the wings. When at last she emerged carrying a bouquet of red roses—young, beautiful, one of their own—there were renewed cheers, and half the audience rushed the stage.

Willis grabbed Eddy's arm as they watched the commotion, and before the applause subsided, he turned to him. "Walk me home," he said. "I need a favor."

The weight of Willis's grief was suddenly apparent. Perhaps he had felt it his duty to attend the play, Eddy thought, but now he was anxious to be away. They made their way outside, Willis avoiding people he knew. They turned up Broadway. Willis was unsteady; he walked like a man unsure of where he was going. The Astor House was just up and across Broadway, a block and a half, but Eddy thought at first that Willis intended to go to his office, then, at the corner of Ann and Park Row, they crossed through the horsecar terminal to the Astor. A doorman held the door for them.

"Pat," Willis asked, "is the carriage ready?"

Eddy started to say something. He intended to walk home; he could not afford a carriage.

"All arranged, Mr. Willis," the doorman said.

Inside they made straight for the stairs. On the landing just above the lobby, Willis stopped and turned to Eddy. He was short of breath, his eyes intent, and his left hand shook as it touched the banister.

"I need you to take my daughter's nurse to Five Points," Willis said. "Her name is Harriet Jacobs. She came down from Boston when Mary's time came, to nurse Imogene and the new baby. She worked for us just after we moved back from Glenmary. She is a Negro, and cannot stay in the hotel overnight. I've imposed enough on the Astor. Last night was awkward . . . awful!" He broke off, shaking his head.

He stared down at the carpet for a moment. Eddy did not know what to say.

"My God, Poe," he continued. "I saw Mary this afternoon. She was so beautiful. So pale. Holding the child in her arms as if they were napping together, as if she had been nursing her and they had fallen asleep." He closed his eyes and swallowed, still leaning on the banister; then he looked back up at Eddy. "I suppose I'll have to find a house to rent. We had planned to go to England, but now . . ."

He grabbed Eddy's sleeve and pushed him toward the next flight of stairs.

"Imogen's confused," Willis continued. "She cries for her mother. Doesn't understand. How could she? She's only three. I can't leave her at home all day with a stranger, so I need Harriet." He stopped again and turned to Eddy. "She's a runaway." He searched Eddy's eyes as if trying to read his reaction. "You're from the South," he said. "Your family owned slaves."

Eddy nodded. What was Willis implying?

"Can I trust you, Edgar?" he asked.

Eddy was shocked. "Of course," he blurted, loud enough to be heard in the lobby below. "You know you can."

Willis put his forefinger to his lips to silence Eddy. "I know, I know," he said. "Forgive me, but I had to ask."

They turned and climbed stairs again.

"It means having someone to comfort my daughter while I'm at work," he said. "Someone she knows and loves. But it's dangerous here for Harriet. Mary and I met her two years ago, after she was smuggled into the city. She's quite remarkable—reads and writes, very intelligent, beautiful in that way of mulattos. She and Mary were devoted to each other, but her owners traced her here, and New York became too dangerous, so she went into hiding outside Boston. Her owners are from North Carolina. Apparently they fell on hard times and need the money she would bring. They hired a bounty hunter."

They ascended another flight of stairs, and at the next landing he stopped again. It seemed that Willis could not climb and talk at the same time. He was unsteady, and the higher they climbed, the softer his voice became, as if those who would kidnap Harriet Jacobs were lurking in the hallways above.

"They'll stop at nothing," he confided. "Deliver her alive, and they earn their bounty. Pat knows. The doorman. He can be trusted. I'll give you money for the carriage. See her safely to Five Points, then take the carriage home. If you think you're being followed, turn back. Take no chances, Edgar. Return here and bring her back upstairs."

Eddy nodded, and they ascended another flight of stairs. At the top, the pattern repeated itself. They were now on the fourth floor; the corridor was quiet and nearly dark, no one in earshot.

"One more thing," Willis said, whispering now. "Harriet walks with a limp. That's how they'll recognize her. She ran away from her owner and hid in the loft of her grandmother's house. Her grandmother had been manumitted, owned her own home. Harriet could not even stand upright, and the lack of exercise left her a cripple. It's a miracle she wasn't discovered. They would have whipped her to an inch of her life. She had two children taken from her and brought north, and she was determined to find them." He paused as if listening for some sound. "I would buy her freedom if I could, but they won't sell her running. That's their term for it. 'We won't sell her *running*,' they told me. 'Bring her back, and you can buy her proper.' I'd pay any price, but they won't hear of it. There's vengeance behind it."

Willis stared down the flights of stairs beneath them, anger in his eyes. He leaned against the baluster anchoring the next flight to steady himself.

"I'll be careful," Eddy said, to jar him from his reverie, but Eddy was nervous. He had no experience with such things.

"I know you will," Willis said, and turned to climb the last flight of stairs. Halfway up he stopped again. "Her owner made demands," he whispered. "You know what I mean. Harriet was fifteen. The man's wife found out and took it out on Harriet. Imagine! He's dead now, thank God, but the wife wants her back. It's more than money. She wants to punish Harriet, punish her for something her husband did."

They climbed the last few steps and turned down the hallway, stopping at Willis's door.

"I'll never forget this, Edgar. Never." And he motioned for Eddy to wait in the hall.

He stood there imagining dreadful apparitions lurking in the shadows, and he was defenseless. Why had Willis chosen him?

A minute later the door opened. Willis emerged with a woman dressed in a black, full-length hooded cape that must have belonged to Mary Willis. The hood concealed her face.

"I've explained who you are," Willis said.

Just then two eyes, frightened and determined, looked up at Eddy from under the hood. She said nothing, only stared at him, a gaze that would haunt him if he failed. Her eyes were pitiless, and there was grandeur in their ferocity, something Eddy had never seen in the eyes of a Negro—a willfulness that was horrific.

"When you leave the hotel," Willis explained, "let her take your arm. With your support, she can walk without limping. If she limps, they will know it's her."

Eddy nodded understanding, unable to look away from Harriet Jacobs's gaze. Willis took his arm, breaking the spell, and Eddy never saw her face again.

"I won't forget this, Edgar," he said again, and stuffed three dollars into Eddy's hand. "Pay the driver. I'll take care of Pat. Now go," he said, pushing him toward the stairs.

They descended side by side, Eddy holding one banister and Harriet Jacobs the other, her face hidden by the hood of her cape. He noticed the limp and decided his mission was too dangerous. He wanted to go back to learn from Willis more about the preparations, but Harriet hurried on ahead. Eddy willed himself to think. He must assume that they would be followed; why else would Willis instruct him to return if there was a problem? And why did he not tell Eddy to take some circuitous route to their destination? Then he realized that the bounty hunters knew Willis by sight, but not Harriet. They knew only that she limped.

These thoughts flashed through Eddy's mind in the time it took to descend one flight of stairs. On the next flight he considered the bounty hunter. He would be a man whose specialty was runaway slaves—strong, dangerous, well-armed. Eddy was no match for such a man. And he would be from the south, so he would have hired some confederate with local knowledge to spy and provide access to a network of rats willing to sell their souls for information.

He paused on the next landing. He was outmanned and had but three more flights of stairs to plot some clever stratagem. But Eddy was no detective; he only wrote about them, and he contrived his mysteries in reverse, solving them with hindsight. Now that forethought was needed, he found himself inadequate, possibly even spineless. Harriet Jacobs continued her descent, but Eddy could not move. Convinced that they would be followed, he felt a tightness in his chest. They would not kill her, he realized; they would kill him. She had value and he was in the way—just a hack writer who lacked the cleverness and creativity to effect her escape. They would kill him and leave him to bleed to death. He could picture it in his mind: the driver whipping his horse as Eddy watched them disappear into the night—watched from the gutter, dizzy from loss of blood. He closed his eyes, clutching the bannister, and pictured the face of his sister, Rose, her eyes big with fright. She was twelve. They had been to church; it was lunchtime. Her dress was light blue. When she stood to get down from the carriage, the horse bolted forward, throwing her out and against a picket fence. Before they could reach her, her face and dress were red with blood. She was unconscious, a deep gash in her forehead. As it turned out, she wasn't badly hurt, but Eddy had thought she was dead and he could not go near. Death was too frightening to approach.

Just then someone took his arm. He opened his eyes to find Harriet Jacobs pulling him down the stairs, her arm looped through his. On the landing above the lobby, he saw the crowd of playgoers returning from the Park Theater. He hesitated again, and again Harriet urged him forward, her face still covered. As they crossed the lobby, Eddy could feel the stares of those who parted to let them pass. Only once did he dare to look at them, and saw Fanny just turning to see him.

Only Harriet Jacobs's firm hold gave Eddy the courage to continue. The doorman opened the door for them and led them down the steps to the brougham. Eddy watched as Pat helped Harriet up into the carriage, then, motioning to Eddy to climb in beside her, he slapped twice on the lacquered side of the brougham as a signal to the driver, and the carriage jerked forward.

The rain had chilled the air, and inside, the carriage smelled of leather and horsehair. Beyond City Hall the streets grew darker and the traffic thinned, but there were other carriages behind and ahead of them, and Eddy did not dare turn and look through the narrow window in the rear of the brougham. They spoke not a word. The driver seemed to know the directions, and Eddy realized that he himself was just a prop, a set piece like the Ionic columns in the Tiffany parlor in the play. The plans were in place before he ever came on stage. The carriage made its turns, and Eddy played his part, thinking back at the trail of clues.

They delivered Harriet Jacobs to her destination; then the brougham carried Eddy back across Broadway toward Greenwich Street. He felt impotent despite having done what had been asked. He couldn't help but think that if escape had depended solely on him, Harriet Jacobs would be on her way back to North Carolina.

Was he indeed impotent, he wondered? He could not write. He had not written a poem or a story in months, not since "The Raven," and his criticism was uneven and bitter, not worth the paper it was printed on. In the back of the brougham, he faced what had been building for weeks—he had lost his ability to create. The only gift Edgar Poe had for the world was gone. Was "The Raven"—his greatest work—also his last? Night after night he had sat at his desk and nothing had come.

Perhaps it was the city and the pressures of a job. Or was it something else? Was there a finite number of poems and stories in Edgar Poe, and had he got them all out? He was only thirty-six, but Coleridge had flamed out at an even earlier age and spent the last half of his life writing criticism. No one remembered a word he wrote beyond the age of twenty-three. And Wordsworth, too. He was alive still, but his inkpot had been dry for thirty years.

At the Morrisons', Eddy stepped out of the carriage and paid the driver. From the street, he looked up to see that the candles were out, indicating that Sissy and Muddy were asleep. Rather than go up, he walked on along Greenwich Street to Chambers, turned left, and went down to the river. Water lapped the hulls of the ships moored along the wharf, and Eddy could hear singing and laughter coming from a nearby tavern. He walked on until he found an empty slip, where he turned to look out on the water.

Soon Sissy will die, he thought, and he felt emotion rise inside. If courage could save her, would he find it within him? He could vividly remember the last time they made love. She seemed only to endure it for his sake—suffer it, even—and it left her exhausted and depressed. And the last time he made advances, she turned her face to the wall and cried. When he tried to console her, she started coughing, and between her coughs and her sobs, she could not speak. He decided she was no longer up to it, but the truth was, he no longer desired her, and his lack of sexual desire for Sissy left him guilt-ridden. He was certain he still loved her, but for more than a year, he had not touched her. How could that be, he wondered, recalling how bright-eyed and precious she had once been, how girlish and natural. He remembered a particular night in Richmond. He and Sissy had been married four months, and she had just turned fourteen. She wanted to be a wife. Eddy sensed it, and even though he had promised Muddy to wait until she was sixteen, Sissy had no intention of waiting. She loved him to kiss her and let him all he wanted, and occasionally she slipped into his room, wearing nothing but a cotton nightgown, climbing into the bed with him where he read, whispering to him and giggling, putting her finger to her lips to shush him so Muddy would not come for her. He had ached to touch her, and one warm autumn night he put down his book and did. She let him, her eyes wide, lit by the light of the oil lamp, and held her breath as he slipped his hand under her gown.

Chapter 9

Willis

New-York Mirror   Monday, March 31, 1845

FASHION.— In a lecture delivered by this writer a year ago, we made the distinction that it is not *the fashions* that we review in this column, it is *Fashion!* Today we are moved to paraphrase this with an analogy current at the moment—it is not the *style* of the bonnet that we find newsworthy, it is the *Bonnet itself*.

Wednesday last, at the premier of *Fashion*—a new comedy written by the lovely Anna Cora Mowatt—New York's most fashionable citizens removed their bonnets upon taking their seats. While this was not universally the case, it was the prevalent one, and one of such significance that it cannot go unheralded.

Of late it has become the Fashion of the Upper Ten—*messieurs et mesdames*—to attend the theatre once or twice a week. In times past the theatre was an unsavory place for a lady—this, no doubt, stemming from that era in England when theatres stood amidst the bull-baiting arena and London's many stews. No self-respecting lady of that time would be caught dead in a public theatre and for good reason. More recently our own Puritan forefathers considered play-going an excommunicable offense.

Thanks to modern liberality and improvements made in the theatres of New York City by Astor and others, it has become quite acceptable for a lady of good repute to attend provided, of course, that her head should be covered. Not so any more. At the Park Theatre last Wednesday, the bonnets came off, and a sea of beautiful tresses appeared. Dandies in the upper gallery stared down in admiration and amazement.

The reason for this change, we believe, is that there is no need for a bonnet when all ladies in attendance are *Ladies*, and such was the case last Wednesday. The distinction that the bonnet provides was unnecessary, and so they came off in—what some might call—*shocking Fashion*. But we say, Hurrah! Hurrah for advances that have made public places more amenable to the fairer sex, and Bravo! to that *Dame Intrépide* with the courage to remove the first hat pin.

PS. Dear Reader, it is with a heavy heart that I report the recent death of my wife during childbirth. Sadly our newborn child died also. As a result of this tragedy in my life, I am taking a hiatus from this column in order to rest and spend time with my surviving daughter.

Don't think that I have abandoned you, my dearest friend. I find no greater pleasure in life than composing these pencilings to you, and I am certain that in time I will be inspired to write again, telling you all that I see and hear, and I shall return in the fall to resume this chair and our regular correspondence.

Very truly your Friend,
N. P. Willis

WILLIS HAD NEITHER the energy nor the inclination to write. General Morris understood and urged him to take time away from work, spend it with Imogen, and make his travel arrangements. The three of them, Willis, Imogen, and Harriet Jacobs, moved into a house on Bleeker Street. Harriet was a virtual prisoner there. More than once, Willis suspected the house was being watched. One slip and Harriet would be taken. But the same law that condoned the return of runaway slaves to their masters prohibited the breaking and entering of private residences for that purpose. Willis was confident, therefore, that so long as Harriet remained indoors, she was safe. She did not seem to share that confidence, and he assumed she lived in fear during her stay in New York City.

It became his habit to take a long walk in the mornings. He would dress after breakfast, put on his hat and coat, grab his walking stick, and ride the horsecar downtown. Rather than go to his office, he strolled down Broadway to Battery Park. He took to buying bags of safflower seed, and he sat for hours on the outside bastion of Castle Garden feeding the pigeons, watching ships in the bay, and feeling the cool breezes that he decided could be felt in New York only on the hilly battlements of the old fort. These mornings had a healing effect. Sitting there, he realized that he had been deeply in love with Mary. What he had felt when they first met was more profound than any feelings he had ever known for another human being—even including one to whom he had been engaged in Boston and whose love was denied him by the narrow, self-righteous, priggish, small mind of her guardian. That injury had ceased to fester only when he met Mary in England six years later.

Mary was ten years younger and so impressionable when they met that during their courtship Willis believed she worshiped him unreasonably. Perhaps more than anything, it was this adoration that he found captivating. It was a slender and transitory thing upon which to build a marriage, and he did not delude himself that Mary's devotion would always be so divine, but a man's self-esteem is terribly susceptible to such behavior. He found it charming and irresistible.

Willis felt guilty for viewing his love for Mary in such selfish terms. Instead he should have loved her first for her beauty—and she was beautiful—and for her other fine qualities, and he did love her for those attributes. Barely six months after their marriage, they had returned to America, and Willis bought two hundred acres on a small stream in upstate New York, a stream that ran down to the Owego River, which emptied in turn into the Susquehanna. There, on the frontier, fifty miles south of Lake Cayuga, he built a cottage and cleared fields. He named it Glenmary, in her honor. She accepted their rather primitive existence—primitive when compared to her life in England—without complaint. A man could ask no more of a wife than that she accept his circumstances.

Of all their days at Glenmary, there was one that Willis recalled with such joy that he thought of it often when he sat on the battlements of Castle Garden. Mary had decided that their mattress smelled moldy and sour, and she determined to wash the feathers. It was a day in early June when there was no threat of rain, when the air was clear and dry. With Willis's help, the mattress was got down from upstairs and brought into the kitchen, where Mary had already put their largest kettle on the stove and the water was just beginning to simmer. With the efficiency and nervous anticipation of one who had read the recipe but never cooked the dish, she went about her task while Willis watched in amusement, eating a breakfast of cold bread, jam, and coffee, since the cook—Mary—was otherwise employed. She brought sheets down to the porch to be laid out on the lawn. Once the feathers were washed, she planned to spread them on the sheets to dry in the sun.

"What if they blow away?" Willis asked, as he spread quince marmalade on his bread.

Mary looked at him with eyes that said she had not thought of that, but also in those eyes was an admonition that he should get out from underfoot and on about his business. This he did forthwith, it being a perfect day for sitting in the shade of the sycamore beside the bridge. Fetching notebook, pen, and ink, he adjourned to his outdoor study to compose some trifle to be sent off to Morris, and he left Mary alone in the kitchen ripping apart one corner of their mattress and preparing to spill white feathers into a hot, sudsy kettle that emitted a thick vapor of lavender. It would be an all-day job, she warned, so lunch would *not* be served until midafternoon, by which time all the feathers would be washed and laid out to dry.

Willis alternated sitting on his rock and taking walks. He stayed away from the house, as Mary was emphatic in her instructions. Around noon he walked clear to the banks of the Susquehanna, following the road for a ways and then a path that he knew well through the woods. It was one of those perfect days that come only in June. After a while he returned to his spot beside the bridge and resumed his mossy cushion. He uncorked his ink bottle, which sat atop a flat rock ledge at perfect writing level for his right hand—a proper secretary—in preparation to compose one of his "Letters from Under the Bridge."

In the stream below him, a venerable snapping turtle appeared, announcing himself with clouds of silt stirred from the creek bottom by flippers the size of Willis's hands. A frequent visitor, the turtle was as big as a barrel and had a long, sharp-pointed tail, and Willis imagined that its usual digs were downstream in the Owego. He supposed his beflippered friend wandered upstream in search of the tiny lobsters that were always scurrying across the bottom. In truth they were not lobsters at all, though, no bigger than large shrimp, they had all the accoutrements of lobsters. At any rate, the lumbering snapper appeared once or twice a week, stopping in a small pool under the bridge and eyeing Willis suspiciously. He could be a hundred years old, Willis thought, and he was king of this realm and never seemed happy to see an invader at its borders. With menace he stared as if Willis foreshadowed the invading Gothic hordes. How was a man to write in the presence of such royalty?

When Willis returned to the house at about three, his stomach growling for nourishment, he noticed one of their sheets lying on a patch of greensward between the kitchen garden and the cutting garden. There was not a breath of wind, and though the small array of feathers piled there did not threaten to blow away, they appeared to have suffered from their soaking. They seemed a meager amount for a double bed mattress, all goose feather and no down, whatever softness they'd provided washed away. Willis hoped they would re-cover before nightfall as he crossed the porch to go inside.

And there was Mary, her hair covered with down. She looked up at him in horror that he had discovered the mess of errant white feathers covering the kitchen. And just as she looked up, she was seized by a fit of sneezing. Two, three, four times she sneezed, putting her hand over her nose and mouth to try and stem the further spread of what was left of their mattress.

Frustrated and close to tears, Mary explained that when she tried to empty the feathers and downy fluff into the kettle, the steam rising from the water carried them up and away, making them impossible to corral. And the water was too hot for her to submerge the feathers handful by handful, so she'd had to let it cool, and it took forever. The task had proved slow and unpredictable. Half their mattress lay spread around the kitchen, some of it floating in midair as if the two of them had been pillow-fighting. The down defied sweeping.

The instant Willis started laughing, Mary started crying. In the frustration of well-laid plans gone awry, she could not share his amusement just then, so he took her in his arms, held her close, and plucked down from her hair. In the end her sobs turned to laughter, and the both of them got down on all fours and picked, piece by piece, downy feathers all afternoon. When at last they went to bed that night, their mattress had lost a third of its bulk. It proved so lumpy and unmanageable that Willis had to go for new feathers a day or two later.

There was nothing so heartbreaking as those little failed domestic efforts. Willis missed Mary most of all when he thought of her crying on his shoulder, her hair covered with white goose down.

Those were happy days. As a farmer Willis was a bumbling failure, but he didn't care. Between Mary's income from her father and what he made from his stories and articles, it was unnecessary that their little farm provide more than flowers for the table and enough buckwheat for his pancakes. They were quite alone in the early days except for a neighboring farmer's daughter, who helped Mary cook and clean and whose little brother Willis hired as a crow-scarer for a shilling a day. Deer ate half their corn, and crows the other half. Their heifer ate laundry off the line, and Willis's horse grew wild from lack of riding. And while the farm went to rack and ruin, he spent his mornings in his study or sitting on his mossy rock beside the stone bridge, listening to the stream run down to the Owego, composing lines too full of the joy to provide more than fugitive interest. It could not last, of course. That amount of happiness could never last for long.

In December of their fourth year, their first child, a daughter, was born dead. He and Mary had three children, all girls, but only Imogen survived. Sitting on a bench in Battery Park, Willis imagined what a fine old life would have been his, surrounded by his Mary and three daughters. He would have been spoiled beyond redemption, pampered and comforted, grown so portly and gouty that no amount of magnesia, no quantity of oatmeal poultices, could have cured him. But it was not to be.

Was it all a message? Things had always come so easily. By his writing, his name had become known all over America soon after he was graduated from Yale. He attracted money and women in whatever quantity he desired. He lived far beyond his income, spending a fortune on clothes; he commissioned the most expensive gig in all of Boston. It had a square top and was known all over town. People loved it or hated it—that was Boston for you. In the end the gig was seized by the sheriff to pay Willis's debts, but he learned no lessons from that, and afterward he had traveled Europe as if he were royalty. His grand tour would have been the envy of the Prince of Wales.

Perhaps, Willis thought, he was being challenged. Here in late mid-life, God was wringing his neck, declaring that the time had come to produce something lasting. The causes he had championed were trivial; he had not moved the world apace, yet he had more readers than any man in America. Perhaps he could move mountains, but instead he had reveled in fame, dodging controversy for the sake of fame, sacrificing moment for the esteem of his readers. Should he write more and scribble less?

Great writers have passion, and this notion brought him to Poe. Why Poe? Was it because he was a driven man, so certain, so careless of the opinions of others, so passionate, that though he might be wrong, he possessed a certain purity? A purity Willis lacked? On the surface this made no sense. Poe could be bought like any other man and was. Had Willis not spurred him to relentless drubbing of Longfellow—far beyond what was reasonable—for a mere twenty dollars? But, though Poe's public opinion could be bought, he was passionate in his private thoughts. It was his poverty that made him corrupt, made him berate Longfellow in print to a degree that he did not privately hold. Publicly Poe could be a scoundrel, but privately he had a certain purity. Willis was the opposite. Publicly he was respected—even loved—but privately he was corrupt. No passionate opinions of his turned men against him. He held none, or he beat them down. Was it self-esteem? Was he so bloated with ego that God was punishing him by taking all his precious girls?

Concluding that he was feeling sorry for himself, he put such thoughts out of his mind, reached into his bag of seeds to feed the birds, and watched the ships and the clouds in the sky. The budding trees and the earthy smell of greensward in the park served to rejuvenate his innate optimism, and Willis began to look to the future.

Strolling back uptown one day in early April, he decided not to go to England. Imogene needed Harriet, but so did her own children. She would never leave them to go abroad. England would have to wait. And Harriet was uncomfortable in New York City, so he would go to Boston to visit his sister, Louise, and her family and spend the summer there. Since the *Mirror* had published Poe's Outis letters defending Longfellow, Willis's reception in Boston might even be cordial. Perhaps he could do some traveling, too, and he considered Saratoga and Niagara Falls. He had an idea for a play, a parlor comedy in the spirit of *Fashion*. There was good money to be made in the theater now, and no one in America had more to say on the subject of fashion than N. P. Willis.

 Eddy

The Broadway Journal   Saturday, April 5, 1845

We might guess who is the fair author of the following lines—evidently disguised—but, though we are not satisfied with guessing and would give the world to know, we have judged it best to "let it be."

SO LET IT BE

Perhaps you think it right and just,
Since you are bound by nearere ties,
To greet me with that careless tone,
With those serene and silent eyes.

Violet Vane

"GIVING FLORIDA STATEHOOD is the stupidest thing I ever heard," Eddy said, as he entered the office, having just heard the news. "Next thing we know, women will have the vote."

Dunn English's eyes flashed, and Briggs glanced up from his papers. In truth it mattered little to Eddy whether women got the vote or not, but English and Briggs were devout Whigs, conservative to the core.

It was a sunny April morning, and Briggs had raised the windows and let the coals die. Outside, the Trinity Church bell tolled the hour: ten o'clock.

Eddy and Dunn English had become friends of a sort, thrown together as they were in the presence of Briggs, whom they both despised. They were like sailors on a whaling voyage, malcontents and fellow growlers. English had dark hair, a receding chin, and an oversize walrus mustache that made him appear a decade older than his twenty-six years. His eyes had the desperate intensity of someone eager for respect, an insecurity perhaps resulting from his patchwork career—medicine, mineralogy, law, carpentry, poetry, and politics, in that order. Now he was a magazinist. Eddy would profess to be for something merely because English was against it, and they argued constantly, driving Briggs to distraction. Briggs sat in front of the window in the sunlight, one ear cocked to listen, letting go deep sighs of exasperation.

The *Aristidean,* English's magazine, was a trivial thing. Too embarrassed to publish his own poetry, he had once tried to get Eddy to publish one of his poems in the *Broadway Journal.* Eddy refused on the ground that it was blatant plagiarism—he had cited Keats—and thought English would climb over his desk and punch him.

Before Eddy sat down, a street porter arrived with a letter for him. "Where did you fetch it?" he asked. Only his name appeared on the outside.

"The Astor, sir," the boy said, disappointed with his penny tip.

Eddy did not recognize the handwriting but, showing it to English, declared it to be that of a woman. "And I judge her to be a woman of certitude," he said aloud, studying the chirography. "Look at this *E.* No loops, no graceful curves. I would guess she is forceful, willful, perhaps even angry."

"Read whatever you want in your autographs," English said. "I'll read the head of that same person and tell you more and with greater accuracy. What's more, I'll do it blindfolded."

Eddy leaned back in his chair and smiled, his skepticism apparent and purposeful. English's study of medicine had concentrated on the science of phrenology, and phrenologists maintained that the brain was made up of numerous organs, each having a specific function and each developed more or less large in size, depending on the character and talent of the individual, and manifest in the conformation of the skull.

"You don't believe me, Poe," English said. "It's proven. As valid as chemistry or electricity."

"Well, what of Briggs's head?" Eddy asked, and they both turned to study the undulations of Briggs's bald spot, well defined in the morning sun. Briggs's jaw clenched; he refused to look up.

"Your forehead is more interesting," English said, turning back to Eddy. "In your case I don't have to feel your head to know much about you."

Not caring to have English analyze his character, Eddy broke the seal of the letter.

English persisted. "You see, just as the shell of a nautilus grows to accommodate the size of the creature inside, the skull expands to accommodate the organs beneath it. By feeling the shape of the skull, it's possible to determine which traits are well developed and which are not."

"Well," Eddy said, relenting, "what of my forehead?"

"This is the organ of comparison," English explained, tapping the tip of his forefinger to the center of his forehead and smiling as if he knew some secret about Eddy. "Most members of the European race have well-developed organs of comparison, but yours is monstrous. Your 'Murders in the Rue Morgue,' in which analysis is called into play, came directly from this organ. It's the one that enables us to analyze and compare. You also use it when you accuse people of plagiarizing. You are able to compare every poem you read to every poem you've ever read. You go too far, but no one can fault your ability to do it."

Eddy nodded and began opening the letter; he'd heard enough, but English would not be silenced. He leaned back in his chair, expansive now, his mustache seeming to float in air. He was like a man who had just made the lame walk, the blind see.

"Shall I read your head?" he asked.

Eddy was paralyzed by the notion of English's fingers probing his scalp for bumps and sinkholes.

"Compare your skull to that of the American Indian." English talked on, ignoring Eddy's reluctance. "Their sloping forehead indicates small organs of reason and perception. There are exceptions, of course, but by and large that's how God created them. Their skulls are not unlike the Hindus' and Africans'. Here, look at this."

With this, English turned to the bookcase behind him and took up a skull that sat atop a stack of books. It had been staring at Eddy for two months and made him uncomfortable, but he had avoided calling attention to it for fear English would make him touch it. English cradled the skull in the palm of one hand, and with the other he picked up his pencil and placed its point between the eye sockets.

"This is the skull of an orangutan," he explained. "Notice the absence of a forehead," and he traced the point of his pencil back along the slope of the ape's skull. "The skull recedes from just above the eye sockets, because there are no moral or intellectual organs to protect. The same is true of birds and reptiles. They have well-developed brains in other respects. They love their mates and care for their young. Some organs—adhesiveness, amativeness, philoprogenitiveness, vitativeness—can be as well developed in animals as in humans. But they have no organs of reason."

Briggs and Eddy stared as English pointed to spots on the skull, naming them with arcane facility and contemplating the orangutan with all the affection of Hamlet addressing Yorick.

"And take women," he continued. "They have more highly developed moral organs than men have. Differences in the shape of the skulls of the sexes prove the truth of phrenology. The organs of fondness and domesticity are so well developed in the brain of women that their size deforms the middle and back part of the skull. We don't notice it since it's covered with hair, but have you ever wondered why women don't go bald or why bonnets are designed with fullness at the back? On the other hand, men have larger organs of self-esteem and purpose. The reasoning organs and those controlling originality and power of thought are more highly developed in men. With this in mind, gentlemen, can you imagine anything more preposterous than giving women the vote?"

English paused, then placed the orangutan skull back on the shelf and folded his arms. Silence followed. Neither Briggs nor Eddy was about to prolong the discourse by asking questions or taking issue.

Eddy resisted the temptation to touch his forehead. Instead he unfolded the letter. Enclosed were two poems on expensive white paper. The street porter's mention of the Astor House led Eddy to suspect they were from Fanny Osgood, and he said as much to English, but he might have guessed her identity from the pen names alone: Violet Vane and Kate Carol. They seemed familiar; perhaps she had used them before.

He was grateful. The *Broadway Journal* did not yet receive many submissions, as they had not achieved a wide enough circulation to attract the multitude of women writers. The poems were quite good, he decided, and one of them, the one entitled "So Let It Be" and signed Violet Vane, was, without doubt, meant for him. It ended with a reference to Sissy.

> The fair, fond girl, who at your side,
>   Within your soul's dear light, doth live,
> Could hardly have the heart to chide
>   The ray that Friendship well might give.

But if you deem it right and just,
    Blessed as you are in your glad lot,
To greet me with that heartless tone,
    So let it be! I blame you not!

Eddy smiled. On the contrary, he thought, she blamed him much. He was being chastised for slighting Fanny at the theater. He passed the poem to English and read the second one, "The Rivulet's Dream," which spoke of a vision of love too bright to last. He guessed it was not new, and when he finished, he handed it to English also, deciding to publish them both. Like clover to the bee, they would invite other submissions.

"What did you do to her?" English asked.

"It was a misunderstanding."

"Whatever it was, it worked," English said, eyeing Eddy, a bemused smile on his face.

"What do you mean?"

"She's flirting with you, Poe. Can't you see?"

Eddy glared at English and took back the poems. As he read them again, English explained that Fanny and her husband were estranged and that Fanny was available. Eddy was not convinced that she was flirting; then he recalled the look on Fanny's face as he recited "The Raven" at Anne Lynch's. She had been sitting on the sofa with Sissy, and once he thought he perceived tears in her eyes.

Writers often received messages of affection from female readers. Willis got them all the time, and Eddy knew for a fact that he responded to some of them. Willis had that special talent for seeming to speak to one single reader instead of the mass of them, and Eddy had come to realize that some women considered Willis's columns their own private trove of love letters. Now it was Eddy's turn, and that the writer was Fanny made it all the more special. Her familiarity at their first meeting had made him somewhat uncomfortable, but as he reflected on it, something she said had kept resonating—"we are not all poets." It was as if she were saying that she understood him and that she felt the same way. What way, he wondered. On the surface she was just another writer, another fashionable New Yorker, pretty, rich, well-connected; but without consciously dwelling on it, he had imagined a different Fanny—a friend, someone he might come to cherish. And she was quite beautiful; in fact, he admitted to himself that her beauty and her probing questions had intimidated him. But her questions had conveyed an easy confidence unusual in a woman, an independence that was alluring. He hadn't expected that, and it had made him rather more reticent than normal.

He published both poems in the April 5 edition of the *Broadway Journal,* inserting a brief note of introduction to the first one, the circumscription of which was purposeful. He hoped the poems would invite more submissions.

The following Saturday night he attended another party at Anne Lynch's. It had been three weeks since the last one, and Eddy still felt uncomfortable. Sissy had refused to go, and he might just as well have saved horsecar fare. His suit looked as if he'd slept in it and, worse, he had nothing to read, having written nothing since January with the exception of magazine copy. He was not good with small talk; he listened and smiled, polite and proper. There was a crowd of about fifty people, more men than women, and Eddy recognized most of them. Cullen Bryant was there, an infrequent guest now that he had moved to Long Island. Eddy thanked him for attending his lecture, and Bryant was cordial, seeming to overlook whatever offense he might have taken. Eddy liked him better for that and decided it was time to cease his blasting of Longfellow. Much more of that sort of thing and he would wear out his welcome.

From the front hall he noticed Fanny at the far end of the parlor. She was staring at him, smiling, and he guessed she'd seen her poems in the *Broadway Journal.* He made his way to her.

"Your magazine must be selling well, Mr. Poe," she said. "Everyone is talking about the lovely poems, and they're wondering who the author is. Will you tell me?"

Amused by her banter, he wondered if she was always so coy. "Perhaps you could tell me, Mrs. Osgood," he said, knowing that, in truth, few present would have bothered to buy the magazine. "What are they saying?"

"That you have discovered a great new poet."

"Perhaps she's Elizabeth Ellet," Eddy blurted without thinking, referring to a young writer from South Carolina who had recently moved to the city and was beginning to make the rounds. Fanny was startled and apparently irritated by the suggestion.

"I thought we were on first-name basis, Mr. Poe?"

"Forgive me, Fanny," he said, cursing himself. After all, she had been paid nothing for her poems. "I should thank you. Your poems are first-rate, and I owe you an apology. That night at the Park—"

"No need to explain. I saw you with Willis, but you could have told me you were with him," and with this Fanny took his arm, indicating he was forgiven, and guided him into the dining room where Lynchie was ladling out cups of hot broth.

Eddy handed Fanny a cup and took one for himself. She wore a low-cut, gray satin evening gown and a thick silver necklace set with rubies. Her hair was parted in the middle and plaited into a diadem of braids, and her dark eyelashes made her eyes appear large and urgent. As she blew into her cup to cool her broth, she peered up at him such that she seemed a young girl. It wasn't only her small size; it was an ever-present expression of expectancy. She was like two different people, independent and strong-willed on the one hand, innocent and coy on the other, and it seemed that one never knew which Fanny one was talking to.

"Did Virginia not come?" she asked.

"No," he said. "She wouldn't hear of coming again."

Fanny's expression changed to concern. "Would she walk with me, do you think?"

"Would you, Fanny? She needs to get out. She won't make the effort for Muddy, but she would for you. Muddy is her mother; she lives with us."

"Tell her I'll come next week," Fanny said, "and we'll walk to the park. And we will talk about you, and I plan to tell her that you have agreed to be my mentor. I want to know your real opinion of my poems; I want to feel that tomahawk of yours. But I'll wager you're too *gallant*. Like all the other men; Willis too—especially Willis! Don't you see that your gallantry imprisons us? When will you learn that we're not teacups?"

She did not wait for his answer, as the recitals were about to begin. Eddy followed her through the crowded parlor and into the front hall, where several people were taking seats on the staircase. Fanny and Eddy made their way past them, and Fanny took a seat on the top step, above Eddy and just below the landing.

"Did Virginia see my poem?" she whispered, as announcements were being made.

Without looking at her, Eddy nodded and smiled at the recollection of Fanny's kind reference to Sissy: "The fair, fond girl, who at your side / Within your soul's dear light doth live." Sissy had seen it; she had been thrilled by it, thinking it a thoughtful invitation to friendship.

Though they could not see the speakers, they could hear well enough. At one point Park Benjamin, editor of the *New World,* gave a discourse on the art of literary criticism. Without mentioning names, he expressed disdain for the relentless attacks common in certain magazines. Eddy listened, thinking Benjamin might make reference to him in some specific way. He might use the word *tomahawk,* for instance, reminding the audience of those parts of Eddy's lecture best forgotten.

Just then Fanny put her hand on Eddy's shoulder and held it there. No one could see. It was just a touch, but one of such tenderness that he forgot about Benjamin and his troublesome discourse. He thought only of her hand on his shoulder and how much he missed being touched. Just before she took it away, she leaned down and whispered in his ear.

"What did you mean when you said 'let it be'?"

He did not respond. As Fanny was behind him, he could not turn to her and speak without being noticed; furthermore, he was reluctant to respond. Recalling certain lines of her poems, he decided perhaps she was conveying a message, and he wondered what that message might be. In truth he knew little about her, but just then, had he been able to respond, he might have let down his guard and said something about loneliness, about wanting someone to talk to. Instead he wondered about her—her gift of poems, her wanting to meet him, her saving a seat for him, her asking him to be her mentor. Perhaps she was lonely, too.

When the recitals ended, there was polite applause, and everyone gathered in the parlor to congratulate the speakers. As they all prepared to leave, Eddy lingered, watching Fanny as she put on her coat to go with friends in the carriage to the hotel. On the front steps, he watched her climb in; she looked back through the window, searching for him. When their eyes met, they smiled at each other.

He followed her carriage on foot as far as Washington Square. There he stopped to look up at a moon shaped like an egg, high over the city, midnight clouds floating beneath it. For perhaps twenty minutes he stood under the arch. The night was cold but not freezing. The air smelled of wood smoke, and in the far distance, he heard dogs barking. Once or twice a carriage descended Fifth Avenue and turned left to cross to Broadway. Recalling Fanny's touch, Eddy felt a rush of gratitude and affection. He needed a friend just then, a good friend, a better friend than the word implies—a confidant. And she felt the same way; he was certain of it. Savoring these feelings, he began to shiver; then he pulled up the lapels of his overcoat, crossed the park, and headed down Sullivan Street for the long walk home.

Sissy and Muddy were asleep when he got there. He stirred the coals, lit a candle, and tried to write, but his vision of Fanny would not go away.

THE NEXT WEEK a package arrived along with two more poems. The package contained a gold pocket watch. How did she know, he wondered, that his watch was broken? The truth was, the stem had been broken for years. He caressed the smooth gold case, wound it and set it, and put it to his ear. Aware that English was watching, Eddy looked over at him. "Had my watch fixed," he said, and put it in his watch pocket alongside his broken one; then, pretending to read the poems, he thought about Fanny's wonderful generosity and how fortunate it was that she had come into his life.

Turning his attention to the poems, he noticed that she had signed her name to the first one. Eddy suspected she had searched her portfolio of older work for something to convey a message. The poem told of a girl named Kate, one of Fanny's earlier pen names. Entitled "Love's Reply," it was written from the point of view of a man preparing for an ocean crossing. Before leaving he asked three "graceful girls" where in all of Europe they would like him to write from. The first girl chose Venice, "Queen-city of the Sea," the second chose "some proud palace, where the pomp / Of olden Honor shines," but the third girl, Kate, wished only that he "Write from your *heart* to *me*!"

The second poem, "Spring," signed "Violet Vane," suited a mid-April issue. A lament, it contrasted returning spring with the loneliness and despair of the poet, "'Neath thy blue eyes' careless smile!" There was that word *careless* again, a refrain of her first poem, "with that careless tone, / With those serene and silent eyes." His eyes were not blue; they were hazel, so he'd been told, though he thought they were really brown. Fanny was taking the flirtation a step further, and Eddy was enjoying the repartee immensely.

He must respond, he decided, a response "from his heart." He leaned back in his chair and smiled at the melodrama. English stared at him from across his desk, wanting to be told what Eddy found so amusing, but Eddy ignored him.

The following day, Fanny came to take Sissy to one of Margaret Fuller's ladies-only conversation circles. When Eddy quizzed Sissy about it that night, she said his ears must be burning.

"And what did Miss Fuller say?" he asked.

"She said, 'Men think woman is the poem, and man the poet, but it will not always be so.'"

This amused Eddy. "And what do you think she meant by that?"

"Fanny says she means to make women aware of their God-given rights." Sissy smiled; she almost laughed. "It was very exciting, and Fanny knows all about these things. When it was over she introduced me to Miss Fuller. They are friends and much alike, I think. I've never known a woman like Fanny. You should have heard her fuss at the driver when he took a wrong turn. She said he did it on purpose to pad his fare, and she refused to tip him."

The notion of Fanny and Sissy together made Eddy reconsider Fanny's poems. Had he let his imagination get the best of him? Fanny wanted to be a friend; that was all. And he was surprised at how disappointed that made him feel. It was as if he wanted Fanny to himself, and the impropriety of that vision burst his fantasy. He was being silly, he decided, so he published Fanny's poems without comment.

A week later Wiley & Putnam agreed to publish a collection of Eddy's tales. Despite the advance of one hundred thirty-five dollars, his financial situation remained strapped. On moving day, the first of May, the Poes moved into a cheaper boardinghouse on East Broadway. Sissy and Muddy hated leaving the Morrisons', but Eddy needed the two dollars a week the move would save them. Mrs. Morrison had taken to Sissy, just as the Brennans did. It seemed everyone loved Sissy. She was grateful for the least little kindness. Even the Morrisons' twelve-year-old serving girl adored her. She would come up after dark to make sure there was plenty of coal for the fire, so Sissy wouldn't get a chill. Sissy would make her sit on the floor beside the bed so she could brush her hair, telling her how pretty she was and how she'd be catching herself a beau any day now. Eddy watched, sitting at his desk, imagining that the serving girl was their own daughter and regretting that Sissy had never conceived.

Having neither the time nor the inspiration for new composition, Eddy began leaning on his old stuff to fill the pages of the *Broadway Journal*. He reprinted his "Berenice"; it was old and shopworn but filled four columns that needed filling. He tomahawked a performance of *Antigone* at Dinneford's with such sarcasm that Dinneford removed his name from the free-list. He was working twelve hours a day and attending the theater two or three nights a week.

Leafing through an old volume of the *Southern Literary Messenger,* searching for something to help fill the issue of April 26, he came across a poem he had written ten years earlier. Entitled "To Mary," he had composed it for Mary Starr, his sweetheart from his Baltimore days.

> Beloved! amid the earnest woes
> That crowd around my earthly path —

The first two lines brought Fanny to mind. He missed her. On an impulse he published it and renamed it "To F——." Addressing Fanny as "Beloved" was bold indeed, but the sentiment was from his heart, and hadn't she asked for that? As the poem fit the space available, he didn't think twice.

> My soul at least a solace hath
> In dreams of thee . . .

Fanny would be either mortified or thrilled, and if mortified, he could always deny that the poem was meant for her. But he did not stop there. As an afterthought he composed a four-line "Impromptu" which he inserted in "Miscellany" and addressed to Kate Carol.

> When from your gems of thought I turn
> To those pure orbs, your heart to learn,
> I scarce know which to prize most high —
> The bright *i-dea*, or bright *dear-eye*.

He had little time to consider the consequences, as the *Broadway Journal* also relocated on moving day, to Clinton Hall at the corner of Beekman and

Nassau, leaving Dunn English to fend for himself. Eddy figured the *Aristidean* was in its last throes. By contrast, the *Broadway Journal* now sold in excess of a thousand copies a week.

Eddy and Briggs had become openly hostile in part because Eddy had gotten drunk again. It had happened on a Thursday night in mid-April. His sold-out performance at the New-York Historical Society Library was to be repeated, and he was to get a percentage of the house, but the bottom had fallen out—rain, snow, and sleet. Only two dozen people showed up, half with tickets Eddy had given away. Too upset to lecture, he persuaded the curator to cancel it and return the ticket price. Eddy had hoped to clear fifty dollars. He went straight from the library to Sandy Welsh's Cellar and proceeded to get drunk, covering his bar bill by reciting "The Raven" for the crowd.

He tried laying off the whiskey after that, but the long workdays were taking their toll, so he fell into the habit of stopping at Sandy's for a few drinks after work and not arriving home until after Sissy and Muddy were asleep. To make matters worse, he began stopping for breakfast at a tavern on the corner of Franklin and East Broadway. Breakfast consisted of a pickled egg and a shot of gin. It was the only way to face Briggs alone.

He went from bad to worse.

One early May morning, Muddy poked Eddy awake with the handle of her broomstick. He turned over and looked at her through the fog of too much drink and too little sleep. He had no idea what time he'd gotten home; it must have been nearly sunup. It seemed Muddy didn't want to get too close, and Eddy resisted an impulse to snatch the broomstick out of her hand.

"You have a visitor," she said.

"Tell whoever it is to go away," Eddy said, and he rolled over, intending to go back to sleep, but as he did, Muddy started throwing his clothes at him. He turned back in a rage. "Leave me alone, you old bag."

"It's Mr. Willis and Mr. Lowell," Muddy said. "And I'm not going to tell them anything. No one can protect you from yourself."

"Lowell? What the hell is he doing here?"

Muddy went into the bedroom and came out with a clean shirt. Eddy studied her, wondering what he should do. He was in no mood to meet Lowell; they had never met, but Lowell had been kind enough to write a short sketch about Eddy for *Graham's* that appeared after publication of "The Raven," and they had exchanged letters. Eddy couldn't very well snub him.

"Go tell them I'm sick," he said.

"You tell them," she said, and left him to go into the bedroom.

She was furious, so he considered sending Sissy, then decided he'd best get dressed and go himself. When he stood, the room started spinning, and Eddy realized he was still drunk. He steadied himself, holding on to the bedpost and wondering how in the world he'd pull this off. He put on his shirt, steadied himself, buttoned it, steadied himself again, then pulled on his trousers, nearly tripping on the leg. He staggered to the washstand, took up his collar and struggled with the stays, finally giving up on the back stay, so that the collar rode up the back of his neck. He brushed his hair and mustache with his fingers, then glanced at himself in the mirror. He looked awful.

As he descended the stairs, Willis looked up from where he was waiting in the foyer.

"Sorry to bother you, Edgar," he said. "We went by your office, and Briggs told us you were ill, but Jamie wanted to meet you before he left to go back to Boston."

At the bottom of the stairs, Eddy stopped, afraid to let go of the banister, then turned to James Russell Lowell and extended his right hand.

"Mr. Lowell," he said, "what an honor."

Lowell shook hands and nodded. "I'm sorry you're ill, Mr. Poe."

"Call me Edgar, please. It's the ague; I'll survive. You know how it is. Come, sit with me in the parlor and tell me all about Boston. How is my friend Longfellow?"

Willis chuckled as they sat down. He appeared to comprehend the state of things, but Lowell seemed nervous and uncertain, sitting erect on the edge of the cushion as if he thought it might be infested. He had a pointy little beard that made him look like an elf, and Eddy took an immediate dislike to him, wondering how quickly he could conclude the interview. Lowell was considerably younger than he, not much older than Sissy. Willis sat back on the sofa beside Lowell, crossed his legs, and chatted, explaining Lowell's reason for being in the city and all that they had done together in the last two days. Eddy didn't listen; his eyelids were so heavy, he had to fight to stay awake, and Willis was making no sense at all. Lowell said little, but Eddy couldn't take his eyes off the sharp point of his beard. When Lowell did speak to punctuate something Willis had said, his accent irked Eddy, and he marked Lowell down as just another Frogpondian, his pet name for Walden, where the ducks could not be heard for all the croaking of the frogs—Emerson, Longfellow, and that bunch of sober, sniveling, snot-nosed, straight-laced, self-righteous Transcendentalists. Eddy started laughing, unnerving Lowell and Willis, but he couldn't make himself stop conjuring *S* words that might apply. He decided he must be the world's finest alliterationist, and thinking this, he doubled over laughing.

"Jamie," Willis said, "why don't we leave Edgar to convalesce," and the two men quickly rose to leave.

Eddy looked up from his chair, aware that he was chasing his guests away. "Must you?" he asked. "So soon?"

Willis smiled down at him. "Yes, I think we must," and he extended his hand as if to help Eddy up out of his chair, but Eddy stood on his own steam, taking care not to fall.

When they were gone, he climbed the stairs back to his room and collapsed on the bed, without bothering to remove his clothes. He slept until noon.

That was the last time Eddy saw Willis before Willis left town, his travel plans kept secret in order to protect Harriet Jacobs. Eddy was drinking so much and working at such a fevered pace that he failed to reconfirm their plans to pirate work from England, but even so, he assumed that in due time Willis would begin sending manuscripts for publication, thus relieving Eddy of having to fill his magazine with his own regurgitated tales.

Oddly, he heard nothing from Fanny regarding the poem "To F——." He had neither seen nor heard from her in almost a month, and she had not been to Anne Lynch's for three consecutive Saturday nights. Worried that she might have missed seeing the poem for some dire reason, he decided to try again. In the issue of May 10, following another of his old stories, "Three Sundays in a Week," he revised another old poem, renaming it "To One in Paradise." It echoed Fanny's earlier sentiment of a dream too bright to last, and he lopped off the final six lines.

Hearing nothing from her again, in the next issue he reprinted a short poem that had been published under Fanny's own name in *Graham's* June issue, a quatrain entitled "Forgive—forget." Perhaps she was sending her poems elsewhere, since he'd not offered to pay her, and he wondered what George Graham had paid her for four short lines. The sentiment of the poem was clearly not meant for him; Eddy suspected it might have been written with her husband in mind. He praised it, calling it "characteristic of the unpredictable and evanescent spirit that we have come to expect from the pen of so graceful a poetess." Surely this would elicit a response.

The following Tuesday morning he had a note from her. Brusque and hurried, it thanked him for publishing her poems. That was all. She did not mention "To F——" or his impromptu or "To One in Paradise" or his compliment of her quatrain. Nor did she include any new poems. Staring at her signature as if the note said good-bye, he felt a sense of loss. Had he gone too far by addressing her as Beloved? Or perhaps she had heard about his drinking. Feeling disheartened and abandoned, he could not bear the thought of her drifting away.

That evening, staring down at his desk and running his fingers along the smooth, stained surface, he recalled that English had said that Fanny and her husband were estranged, that she was available. What of it, he wondered? He was not available. The flirtation had been a silly illusion. It had nowhere to go, and perhaps that was not even Fanny's intent. She had asked him to be her mentor; that was really all. Probably she wanted honest criticism of her work and nothing more, but like a lovesick schoolboy he had responded with pledges of devotion, and now that he had failed in his promise, she was moving on, sending her poems to a magazine that could afford to pay her— *Graham's*.

How stupid not to perceive all this; he decided it was because of his drinking. He couldn't think clearly, had delusions of love and appeal, and he recalled his reflection in the mirror that morning: plain—ugly, even—his eyes puffy and bloodshot, his suit giving off the fishy smell of Sandy Welsh's Cellar. He pictured Fanny in her evening gown and ruby necklace, her eyes fresh and alive, her bare shoulders smooth and perfumed. She was rich; she had a husband despite what English said; and Eddy had a wife. If he'd taken time to sober up, he might have remembered that. He swallowed and exhaled a deep sigh of reality. He had to quit drinking or things would become unbearable.

He lit the lamp, took up a clean sheet of foolscap, and wrote a poem to Fanny.

> We both have found a life-long love
> Wherein our weary souls may rest

It came almost without his thinking to write it. He lost track of time.

> Yet may we not, my gentle friend,
> Be each to each the *second best?*

It was his first new piece in months. His spirits rose; perhaps he was not impotent after all. It was only a trifle, two eight-line stanzas, but just at midnight,
having polished it to the smoothness of a prism, he underlined the last two
words of the last stanza, an echo of the first, suggesting that he and Fanny
were "doubly blest,"

> With Love to rule our hearts supreme
> And Friendship to be *second best*.

He deemed it worthy of a friend and mentor and dismissed any notion of love.
He entitled it "To ——" and signed it "M," confident that she would make the
connection and hopeful that it would bring her back.

Chapter 11

❧ Fanny ❧

Graham's Lady's & Gentleman's Magazine

May 1845

FORGIVE—FORGET!
"Forgive—forget! I own the wrong!"
You fondly sigh'd when last I met you;
The task is neither hard nor long—
I *do* forgive—I *will* forget you!

Frances Sargent Locke Osgood

I DON'T PRETEND to tell you what to do," Ned Thomas said. "God knows you're the most independent woman I've ever known. Please understand that I'm only looking out for your interests, and I strongly advise you to keep this Poe at a distance."

Ned sat in one of the blue easy chairs in the ladies' parlor, his back to the window overlooking City Hall Park. They were alone. It was midmorning and sun warmed their little corner of the room, shining in Fanny's eyes, so that she could not see him clearly. Perhaps he thought she was squinting and blinking in an effort to fight back tears.

"I don't want to upset you," he continued. "I tried to warn you that night at the Park Theater. Your saving a seat for him was most improper. No doubt it was noticed by others, and it was embarrassing for me. And making me buy him a watch, for Christ's sake. But that's not the point."

He put his cigar in his mouth and blew smoke into rays of sunlight. Its odor filled the room. She did not object; Fanny rather liked the smell. He seemed so comfortable sitting there while she faced him from the edge of the sofa like a child called to her father's study for a reprimand. His legs were crossed, and he twirled a booted foot in slow counterclockwise circles as if he had no care in the world.

"The point is . . ." Ned hesitated. There was something he was not telling her, something he was reluctant to say, and she dreaded it. "The point is, the man is unstable. He's not to be trusted." Ned put his cigar in the ashtray, sat up, and leaned toward her, his elbows on his knees as if to impart a confidence. "I saw his little poem."

Fanny flinched, pulling away. She had said nothing to Ned about the poems, assuming he did not read the *Broadway Journal*. Now it seemed as though he'd been eavesdropping.

"'Beloved'?" He smiled, leaned back in his chair, and crossed his legs again. "'To F——' could only mean you."

She could not look at him. Dropping her eyes to her lap, she stared at her hands, which were clasped as if she were in prayer. Just then she recalled the time when, as a schoolgirl, she was caught cheating in the line, whispering the letters of the word to the boy next to her, so they would both go above the class. The word was *wharf*. She would never forget. The boy didn't even know what it meant. She did, of course; it was the only word that rhymed with dwarf. Fanny had such a crush on that little boy—bowl-cut red hair and a face full of freckles. Doubtless he was behind some plow. She would not have let him win, of course, but she wanted him to be second. She was always at the head of the class, and the others were happy to see her brought down a peg when the teacher caught her cheating. Did that boy ever think of her now? Did he ever wonder about the risk she took for him?

And now she had been caught whispering words to Edgar Poe only to see them in print in his magazine, and Ned made her feel sinful, as if she'd been cheating again. Did he think she belonged to him? What right did he have? He'd made no proposal.

"Fanny," Ned continued, making her look at him, "you can't let him do this. Do you fawn on him at those *soirées* of yours? I'd best go to Miss Lynch's with you from now on. I can only imagine what goes on with the two of you talking poetry. Do you think you're invisible? Fanny, you're the little sprite that everyone notices. Whenever I go out with you, people turn and look. They know who you are. If you're seen in the company of this man, people will talk. And if you don't know why, then I suppose I have to tell you."

Tell her what? It was something horrible and she didn't want to hear it, but she would. He wanted to tell her; he wanted to ruin it.

Again he sat up. "The man is a drunk," he said. "They say he can't hold his whiskey; one drink and he loses control, has no memory of where he's been or what he's done. One only arrives at that stage from years of drinking. How many times has he been fired from his job because of drinking?"

"I've never seen him take a drink," she blurted.

"And that's not all. I only wish it were." He took another puff of his cigar. "The man is a known forger," he added, exhaling a long stream of blue smoke.

Fanny stared at him as he shook his head in disgust.

"It's widely known, Fanny. He's poor as paint. I suppose he's had his share of hard times. I'm told his father was the richest man in Virginia. Disinherited him for being expelled from West Point. That sort of thing can drive a man to crime. But his misfortunes don't excuse him. I knew you felt sorry for him and wanted to help him, and that's admirable, but he's taking advantage of you. He's being entirely too familiar, and, if you don't put him off, I fear for your reputation."

She turned away, thinking Edgar could be a murderer and still she would forgive him. It surprised her to learn that his foster father was rich and had turned him out, but in light of his being an orphan, that only made the man all the more heartless. Ned would never understand, but she promised not to send more poems to Edgar, knowing that otherwise she might lose Ned.

SAM HAD COME and gone again. Fanny saw little of him. He kept to his studio on Sixteenth Street, though twice he came down to see Lily and May. They adored him and he was kind to them. May saw nothing strange in their arrangement, but Fanny could tell by looks from Lily that she knew they weren't a proper family. Fanny stopped short of asking Sam for money, and he offered none. And she made no secret of Ned. Later Ned told her that Sam had come to his office to borrow money, and Fanny could have killed Sam.

Though she stopped sending Edgar poems, he did not halt his public "correspondence" with her. On May 10, she saw his "To One in Paradise," and knew it was meant for her. A week later he reprinted and praised her "Forgive—forget!" for which George Graham had paid her three dollars—more money per line than she'd ever received. It was then she decided that she had to write to him, so she composed her note, telling him to stop without spelling it out. But then on the following Saturday, the 24th, she saw the new poem, "To——." It was Edgar's, no doubt about it. And he was writing to her—"M" could only mean Mentor. But *second best*? She understood what he meant, of course, and she thought the poem beautiful, but Fanny Osgood second best?

For the next few days she lived on pins and needles, fearing Ned would mention the new poems. She had not been to Lynchie's for a month and sent Anne apologetic excuses. She stayed away from temptation, spending every Saturday evening with Ned, following his commandments, being as proper as possible and wishing all the while that she were sitting in Lynchie's parlor. After seeing Edgar's poem, she had to go back. In some way, she had to convey her acceptance of his appeal for friendship, and she missed her world. Keeping her word to Ned did not entail abandoning all her friends. She persuaded him to escort her to Lynchie's on the 31st of May.

That evening as she soaked in the tub, lying almost completely submerged, she decided to read at the party. She had never read in the presence of Mr. Poe. Lynchie would let her, of course. Fanny thought no one wanted her married again more than Anne did, and she would remember Ned from the Ole Bull concert and understand. Sponging her arms for the umpteenth time, she wondered what poem she should read. Soon someone would knock on the door wanting in, or May would come crying that Lily was being mean to her. Fanny hated having to share a tub with half the fifth floor.

What poem would please Ned? she wondered. Then she sat up with a brilliant idea, a poem she had never dared publish. Did she have the nerve to read it? When she lay back in the sudsy water, she was wondering what Edgar Poe would think. Others might think it shocking, and she would rather enjoy that, but then she remembered Ned's dressing-down and put the idea out of her mind. She stood, shivering with cold, and reached for her bathrobe, all the while chiding herself for being so wicked; but before reaching her room, she had resolved to read it.

She selected two other poems, both short, from her *Casket of Fate,* published in London before she and Sam returned to America. She wrote out the one she had thought of in the bathtub and folded it between the pages. Then she dressed—another new dress. Ned was spoiling her beyond prudence. This one was made of light green moiré that the shop girl said went beautifully with her gray eyes. The sleeves were off her shoulders, and across the bodice a wide row of pintucks rose to her collarbone so that her bosom was covered. Ned would approve, but Fanny rather enjoyed the show of a pinch of cleavage, and a pinch was all she could muster though she corseted herself breathless.

They arrived early to alert Anne to Fanny's intention to read; then they moved to the dining room, where she and Ned chatted with Horace Greeley and his wife, in from Turtle Bay for the evening now that the weather was pleasant and the days were longer. The men talked politics while Fanny pointed out celebrities to Mary Greeley.

"And there is the author of 'The Raven,'" she said as Edgar came into the parlor, "the one with the high forehead and the new suit. What a handsome new suit!"

Mary Greeley turned to Fanny and smiled. "Will he read, do you think?" she asked.

"Go ask Anne," Fanny said. "Since you and Horace are not here often, I'm sure she'll agree." As Mary went off to find Lynchie, Fanny turned back to Ned and took his arm, thinking the familiarity would keep Edgar away.

With Willis gone, Anne chose General Morris as her moderator for the evening. He was not much taller than Fanny, and he had a little potbelly and long, bushy sideburns that were turning gray and made him appear haughty and gruff, though he was as sweet as molasses. On this occasion he began with a song he'd composed just that week, a song about Andy Jackson, who, as everyone knew, lay on his deathbed down in Tennessee. It was both rousing and sentimental, well received. During the applause, someone called for "Woodman, Spare that Tree," the general's ever-popular song memorized by every schoolchild in America by the third grade. The general refused, saying it suffered from too many rehearsals, and with that, he introduced Fanny.

She did not want to go first, but the women usually went first, as if their compositions were mere appetizers. She started with the poem Edgar had read the night of his lecture at the Society Library, "The Spirit of the Dance," but she hurried it, her heart racing in anticipation of the poem to follow. Feeling uncertainty rise like the tide, she almost lost heart, coming close to folding it back into her book and reading something safer. But she plucked up her courage, thinking, Fanny Osgood will give a reading they'll remember, and with only a brief pause to announce the title, she recited "He May Go—If He Can."

Let him see me once more for a moment or two;
Let him tell me himself of his purpose, dear, do!
Let him gaze in these eyes while he lays out his plan
To escape me, and then he may go—if he can!

Let me see him once more, let me give him one smile,
Let me breathe but one word of endearment the while;
I ask but that moment—my life on the man!
Does he think to forget me? He may—if he can!

There was an awkward silence when she finished. Several of the men cleared their throats. It was the custom to hold applause until after a reader finished, so Fanny did not look up. She paused again, introduced her next poem, one of moving sentiment, and recited it with fainting-heart emotion meant to blunt the edge of what had come before. The juxtaposition of the two poems was calculated to confuse the men. They would leave wondering if they had misunderstood, but the message would stick in their craw.

When she finished, there was polite applause as she joined Ned, who sat on the sofa facing the fireplace just in front of the speakers. Sitting on the arm of the sofa, Fanny hoped Edgar was behind her, staring at her. For a while she could pay no attention to the readers who followed. She willed her heartbeat to calm down and wondered how each person in the parlor reacted to her reading. Anne would be a little miffed, but she would say nothing unless Fanny brought it up, and she would, of course, and Anne would tell her she had been reckless to read such a poem. Horace and Mary Greeley and others would infer that the poem was addressed to Sam, and it was. Oh! that's what happened, they would think, and that was her intention. It was common knowledge that she and Sam were living apart. People talked and wondered; they would rather die than ask, and it was not polite to tell. She had never really thought she could hold Sam. The poem was written in a moment of injured pride, and though she hadn't wanted him to stay, she was devastated when he left. That had been unexpected. She almost came to tears thinking about it. How could Sam have left her?

Of course, Ned would think that she had read it to clear a path for him. If the world thought Sam left her pining away—hurt, proud, angry, determined—then they would welcome Ned.

As the recitals continued, Fanny gazed at the fire and composed herself. At the end of the evening, General Morris announced that there was a special request for Edgar Poe to recite "The Raven."

He made his way forward from the front hall, and Fanny was disappointed to learn that he had not been where he could see her. Anne motioned to several people to turn down the gas jets. The room grew hushed. Just then Ned turned to look at Fanny, and she turned to him, showing no emotion, though she feared it would come as soon as Edgar began to speak. And it did.

> Once upon a midnight dreary, while I pondered, weak and weary,
>   Over many a quaint and curious volume of forgotten lore—

The dim golden light of the room reflected in his eyes—fire and tears, both at the same time. More than once he looked at Fanny, and she did not turn away, his gaze so charged that she could feel its pressure on her skull. When he ended, his head bowed, as always there was an instant's silence, then the room erupted with applause and shouts of "Bravo!" Ned looked up at Fanny again, his eyes big with wonder, and she looked back at him with pride. Call him a forger; call him whatever you like; you must admit he's magnificent.

Afterward Edgar was surrounded by a swarm of well-wishers, and Fanny guided Ned away.

"I wanted to meet him," he said, when they were in the carriage.

"Perhaps another time," was all she said. She did not want them to meet. Edgar was hers.

Ned seemed pleased. He kissed Fanny repeatedly on the ride home, saying that the evening had not been what he expected and that he would like to go again. The idea was unsettling now; she found that she did not want him to go again. This was *her* world.

Her reading had been overshadowed by Edgar's recital. That was disappointing. Would Edgar even remember her poem? And if he did, what was he thinking? Dressed in his new suit, the creases in the sleeve revealing that it had only recently emerged from some dry goods store. And he had been in the front hall and not where she had wanted him to be, behind her, staring at her. At that moment she wondered whom he was with, and she imagined him standing in the hall beside the drop-leaf table that stood beneath the portrait of Anne Lynch's father. Perhaps he sipped a glass of lemonade. Whom was he talking to? Was it Lizzy Ellet? She would be starstruck, standing next to him, wanting him to tell her that her poems showed promise.

Indeed, had Edgar paid any attention to her reading at all? Did he not know that it contained a message for him, too? Fanny hardly knew what that message was. Intuition had told her to read it, that it was as apt for Edgar as for everyone else. And had he wondered who Ned was? Had he asked anyone? Perhaps he was asking Anne at that very moment.

"Is that her husband?" he would say.

"Just a friend," Anne would reply, offering no explanation, still upset with Fanny but careful of her reputation.

THE LAMP WAS ON. May was asleep, but Lily lay awake, staring at her mother as she removed her shawl. Fanny sat on the bed and caressed her daughter's hair.

"You look so pretty, Mama," Lily said.

"If only I were as pretty as you." Fanny smiled down into her daughter's eyes. Her face was losing its little-girl roundness, and as so often happened, her expression gave Fanny the reassuring sense that Lily understood her better than she understood herself. She will be taller than I, Fanny thought, tall like her father—thank goodness for that. "How would you like to go to Providence for the summer?"

"Oh, Mama, can we?" Lily asked. "And take the ferry? And stay at Aunt Sarah's?"

"I'll write John tonight," Fanny said. She needed to get away for a while and knew her brother would welcome a visit.

As Lily watched, Fanny undressed, put on her nightgown, and got out her paper and ink. Composing her letter to her brother, John, she thought perhaps they should also visit her sister, Anna in Albany, though Fanny didn't like her husband, Henry Harrington. A Methodist minister, he was too pedantic for Fanny; he considered her separation sinful and didn't approve of her living in a hotel. If he knew that Ned had been helping her with her bill at the Astor, he would be horrified. She laid down her pen and stared at the lamp flame. She hadn't given Ned's help a second thought so long as marriage was where it led, but now everything had changed, and the change scared her. Could she have fallen in love with Edgar Poe? Fanny, you've been playing with fire, she thought. She had to get away, get out from under Ned's thumb—go to Providence, stay with John and Sarah for a while, give herself time to think.

The following Friday, in the new issue of the *Broadway Journal,* Fanny read a story by Edgar, "The Assignation." She guessed it was not new, though she had not read it till now. It contained the same poem he'd published with revisions only a few weeks before, "To One in Paradise." That he republished it now, so soon afterward, made Fanny certain that it contained a message for her. There was a final stanza that had not appeared in the earlier version, and its message was blatant.

> Alas! for that accursed time
>   They bore thee o'er the billow
> From Love to titled age and crime,
>   And an unholy pillow—
> From me, and from our misty clime,
>   Where weeps the silver willow!

He was referring to Ned. Fanny decided that he *had* made inquiries at Anne's and someone had accused Fanny of being Ned's lover. That explained the "unholy pillow." Furthermore, it seemed Edgar was accusing her of being seduced by Ned Thomas's wealth with that word *titled*. There was also a subtle message implied by his reprinting the poem as he had originally written it. It was as if he were erasing the revisions he'd made for Fanny. It was a retraction. She was furious. Who was this person, spreading lies about her?

As soon as she asked herself the question, Lizzy Ellet popped into her mind. Lizzy had attached herself to Fanny since she'd arrived in New York in April, eager, it seemed, to become her best friend. At first Fanny had thought her pretty and charming, an aspiring young poet seeking help from someone she viewed as successful, but she soon learned that Lizzy talked too much. She had gone on and on about Edgar, begging Fanny for an introduction, but that wasn't all. She said things about other people that should not have been repeated, and Fanny concluded that Lizzy was a gossip. Thereafter she avoided her, and now she guessed Lizzy might be trying to get back at her by filling Edgar's ears with talk of Ned.

• • •

EARLY THE FOLLOWING WEEK Fanny received a letter from her brother, saying they were welcome in Providence for a visit, and she decided to take the noon ferry on Tuesday, the 17th of June. Ned agreed to fetch her and the girls at the hotel at eleven and take them, luggage and all, to the wharf. They'd been at the Astor for nearly six months, in which time Ned had showered all three of them with presents, all of which had to be packed for the trip or put into storage.

On the day before their trip, she composed a note to Edgar saying she was leaving the city the following day but would like to see him beforehand, at nine in the morning if that would be convenient. She sent it by private courier, to be delivered into his hands only, and she asked him to come alone. All the weekend before, she had rehearsed what she would say. She effected every pose imaginable, speaking in front of the mirror with such anger in her voice that Lily begged her to stop. She went from aloof and insulted to understanding but irrate to pained and confused to rejected and heartbroken.

He was prompt, his hat in his hand. She merely nodded as he entered the front door of the Astor. She then turned to the staircase and climbed to the second floor, trusting he would follow. Never once looking back, she entered the ladies' parlor, where other women were having their morning coffee and tea, and not wanting to start any rumors, she led him to a prominent corner of the room, the one where Ned had lectured her on the very things with which she now intended to confront Edgar. They sat down facing each other.

He wore the same new suit he had worn at Anne's. It was black, as was his waistcoat. He struck a proud pose, his head listing slightly to the left as always and his lips pursed in defiant anger.

She asked about Sissy and her mother, thinking a bit of polite conversation might ease the tension. His one-word responses indicated that he was in no mood for small talk.

"Edgar," she said, without whispering but not so loud as to be overheard, "to ensure that you have not misconstrued anything I may have done or said, I thought it proper before leaving the city to inform you that, though my husband has chosen to live apart from me, I am still a married woman. I assure you that I comport myself as befits my circumstance, though I have made friends here, including men friends, and I hope that I may include you among them. Please understand that by this I mean that friends are friends. Nothing more. I trust that you will not speak ill of me nor harbor any expectations that our relationship can be more than cordial, honorable, and professional."

"Fanny," he said, "of course." He seemed so undone that she saw at once the need to beat a retreat. They stared at each other for an instant. "If I have offended you, I apologize," he said.

"Edgar." She hesitated. She could feel her pulse racing as she worked up to the chore. "It has been reported to me that you have been guilty of forgery."

His eyes grew wide with shock. Fanny thought he would leap out of his chair, but he held himself back by the greatest effort of self-control.

"It is a lie, Fanny" he said, "a slander and a lie. Who told you this?"

She turned to look at the other women, fearing he would make a scene, then looked back at him and smiled, hoping her smile would reassure. "It was told to me by a friend," she said, "but he was only repeating what someone else had said."

Edgar looked down at the floor. How cruel, Fanny thought, that we cannot escape our past.

"It is not true, Fanny," he said again, defeat in his eyes, as if the injury were just another debt he could not pay. "You must tell me who told you. I have to stop this before it ruins me."

She should have known that the accusation would lead to this, and she dreaded the thought of Edgar's confronting Ned, who would know she was responsible for his finding out. She had been trapped as soon as Ned told her, and now she was doubly glad to be leaving the city.

"His name is Ned Thomas," she said. "His office is at 13 Broad Street. One hour from now he will take me and my daughters to catch the ferry to Providence. I shall spend the summer there. Please do not blame him. He bears you no ill will; he told me as a friend. If you like, I will tell him you wish to know and that you will inquire."

Edgar nodded, his reserve evident now, and his distance hurt Fanny. She had to reach out to him, not wanting to leave him like this.

"You may write to me," she said. "We will be staying at the City Hotel. I believe what you say, and my regard for you is no less than it was. Will you write to me?"

Without answering, he looked into her eyes, and she saw questions there.

"Promise me one thing more, Edgar."

"Yes?" he said, on his guard.

Fanny steeled herself for the final blow. "Promise you will not drink. Tell me you will take the temperance pledge for Sissy's sake and mine. You are all the world to her, and you promised to be my friend and mentor. Do you remember?"

"Did Sissy ask you to say this?" he said. He was angry now.

Fanny did not respond, only stared at him. In fact, Sissy had not asked her, but Fanny decided it might be best to let him think so.

Breathing a sigh of exasperation, he looked away. "I promise," he said, and he stood up to leave.

Fanny stood, too, but Edgar would not meet her gaze. At the door to the parlor he paused without looking back.

"I never had an opportunity to thank you for the watch," he said. "Thank you." It was as if he wished to conclude their lone remaining item of unfinished business.

CHAPTER 12
❧ Muddy ❧

WHEN SISSY COULDN'T sleep for coughing, Muddy brewed a special tea for her and sweetened it with honey or molasses. In the past she had gathered her own herbs, picking them when they flowered and before they went to seed. She dried them herself, keeping them out of the light and air. In the city, such herbs as Sissy needed had to be bought from an apothecary, and to Muddy's way of thinking, it was downright wasteful to pay good money for something that grew wild. The tea was made of mint, lungwort, and horseheal, and she let it steep for a quarter hour or more. Sissy found it disagreeable, but she drank it to please Muddy. It did help her cough and eased the night sweats.

Muddy put on the kettle; Sissy lay on the bed. She had started getting worse the day they moved into the city. As often as not, she just lay there staring into space and petting Catterina. *She's giving up*, Muddy thought, *and it's on account of Eddy*.

Muddy blamed Eddy's drinking in part on his being Irish and in part on his brother, William Henry, who was two years his senior. William Henry was Muddy's nephew, too, of course, and he had just come back from his second sea voyage when Eddy moved in with Muddy in Baltimore. That was in April 1831. Eddy was twenty-two, and they lived on Wilks Street, on the top floor of a two-story house with a large turkey oak in the side yard.

William Henry had grown up with Muddy's family in Baltimore. Her father, General Poe, took him in after his daughter-in-law died. Eddy had stayed in Richmond with the Allans, whereas Rosalie, their sister, went to another family in Richmond, the Mackenzies. So Eddy hardly knew his older brother. William Henry had been a shy child, kept to himself, seemed to grow up on his own with nobody really knowing what he was like or what he wanted out of life. He went off to sea the first time when he was fifteen. Sailed out on a merchant ship bound for South America and stayed gone three years. When he came back he was a grown-up, liquor-loving man. That summer Muddy's husband died, leaving her with Sissy and an ailing mother, Muddy's other two children by then, dead and buried. Those were hard times, so William Henry up and sailed out again. When he came back the second time, he settled in, lazy and worthless, with Sissy and Muddy doing his bidding. He kept a sea chest in his room, under his bed—told them not to touch it, said there was a shrunken head inside.

He was taller than Eddy, gaunt and with a wildness in his eyes, but he was strong, and when he'd been drinking, he could get awful mean. Most nights he'd come home drunk. Sissy would run to bed as soon as she heard him on the stairs. She was only eight years old and scared to death of him. While Muddy fixed his supper, he'd get a teacup from the sideboard and pour himself something. Didn't bother with a saucer. It wasn't tea in that cup.

Things got a little better when Eddy came. William Henry was in pretty bad shape by then, but it seemed Eddy gave him something to live for. They would talk for hours around the supper table. Talk about going to sea. Eddy would talk about the army and West Point and all the places he wanted to go. One day he'd be wanting to go to Russia; the next day, Greece. Sissy got big-eyed listening to the two of them. Sometimes they recited poetry—both of them dabbled in verse. William Henry surely took a liking to his little brother, but before long he was getting Eddy to join him on his romps. After supper they'd go down to the Widow Meagher's place to drink and gamble. Muddy got it in her head that William Henry had led Eddy astray. He made Eddy borrow money for him, a thing that nearly landed Eddy in jail for not paying his debts.

By summertime Eddy had become as leery of William Henry as Sissy and Muddy were. Seemed Eddy was more like Sissy than his own brother, and at the rate William Henry was going, he couldn't last long, and he didn't. Died the first day of August. Died in the middle of the night, out of his mind, raving like a lunatic, his whole body shaking so bad they thought they'd have to tie him to his bed. They buried him the next day in the graveyard beside the Presbyterian Church. Muddy made Eddy take the sea chest out to the side yard and go through it, hoping they'd find something to sell, but they didn't. Not even a shrunken head. Eddy burned every bit of it right there beside that turkey oak.

As Muddy stood over the stove waiting for the water to boil, she wondered why she was recollecting William Henry just then. Maybe it was because she'd come to believe that whatever demons had afflicted him were also inside Eddy. How was it a man could drink himself into the grave at age twenty-five? And him having spent most of his adult life cold sober on a sailing ship. Whatever it had been, she couldn't feel sorry for him. When he died, it seemed they all breathed a sigh of relief.

Eddy stopped drinking after that, but he was still a careless boy. Didn't know the meaning of the word *frugal*. Muddy knew that as soon as he moved in with them, and what was done was done. Economy is learned in childhood, and if it goes unlearned, no amount of discipline can teach it. Before Eddy had been in Baltimore a week, Muddy watched him ball up a brand new sheet of paper and throw it in the fire. She knew right then and there he was going to eat her out of house and home.

But it wasn't that Eddy ate too much; it was that he spent money on books, paper, ink—books, mostly. He read them through; Muddy gave him that. He didn't miss a word. But once he finished, he set them on the shelf. Muddy's daddy had books, and she thought the collecting of books was a fine thing for a man with the means to do it, but her family lived on a pension of twenty dollars a month. Eddy couldn't be counted on to help out. He couldn't find a decent job. Day labor was all, toting bricks for a levy an hour. His foster father sent him money if he wasn't mad about something, but he usually was. Their pension hardly covered food and rent, so, often as not, Muddy was buying on credit before the month was out.

Sissy turned nine that August. Skin white like biscuit dough and shy as a bluebird. Already she worked as hard as Muddy, helping her cook or nursing Muddy's mother or knitting stockings or picking blackberries to sell for a nickel a quart. She never complained. Never said no to a chore, never mind how cold or hard. Fetched firewood from the shed in the middle of the winter, lugging it up two flights of stairs. Eddy read to her, though Sissy was too young to grasp much of it. She'd be cutting squares for patchwork or weaving straw for a bonnet—smiling all the while. Didn't occur to her that he was worthless as a garden snake, not so long as he was reading to her. He told Muddy he was seeing to Sissy's education. Muddy told him he could earn some money to send her to school, if he was so intent on her having book learning.

Eddy tried to get a job teaching at a new school in Reisterstown. Said he was going to put part of his wages to pay tuition for Sissy so she could go to school there. She'd had some schooling; she could read and write, but it was looking like her school days were over. Muddy's mother was seventy-five and bedridden, and she couldn't afford for Sissy to go off to Reisterstown.

There was a rope swing hanging from that turkey oak, and Eddy would push Sissy with one hand, holding a book with the other, reciting verse in a put-on voice that sounded just like his daddy's. Muddy tried to tell him that, but Eddy didn't seem to want to know about his real daddy. Muddy's brother had left home when she was still a teenager. Ran off to marry Eliza Arnold, Eddy's mama, and become a stage actor. Broke General Poe's heart, it did; he'd wanted his son David to be a lawyer, but Eddy's daddy preferred drinking to reading law, and even as an actor he was a bumbling failure. Muddy didn't rightly know why Eddy was never curious about him. Seemed like some bitterness behind it, and she couldn't help but think John Allan had poisoned the boy's mind toward his natural father. John Allan was all the time jerking Eddy one way or the other. He was a selfish man if ever God created one. But Eddy did sound like his daddy. Pushing Sissy in the swing and reciting verse like a stage actor. Sissy hung on to that rope for dear life, twirling round at the top so she could watch him.

Those two became like brother and sister; he even started calling her Sissy. Eddy had a crush on a tall red-headed girl, a neighbor's daughter, Mary Starr. She was a pretty thing, seventeen and still going to school. He'd write her a poem or love letter, then signal to her by waving a handkerchief out his window so she'd know to meet Sissy on the front porch. Sissy would deliver it, then come tell Eddy what Mary said. But then Mary's mother decided Eddy was too old for her daughter and put a stop to his courting. He didn't pine away, not with Sissy fawning over him, and Muddy let her fawn. She was a lonely child, her brother and sister dead and gone, and her daddy in his grave when she was two years old and Muddy near about old enough to be Sissy's grandmother.

One night Eddy came home with a copy of the *Saturday Evening Visiter*. They were offering fifty dollars for the best original tale. That's when Eddy decided to become a writer. He stayed up night after night writing his tales, and he won that prize. He was so proud, it near about cured his drinking for good;

but just like his brother, Eddy had a weakness for it. Didn't happen often those first few years, but when it did, it seemed like William Henry Poe had risen from the grave. Eddy would come home, scaring Sissy and swearing at Muddy. Oh, he'd feel bad—next day he'd be waiting on them hand and foot. Then it would start all over.

Just like now. When he came home drunk in April that night his lecture at the library was canceled, it was sleeting outside. Sissy and Muddy blew out the candles and lay in bed listening to the wind and sleet against the window. Remembering the night when he failed to show up at the Brennans', in December, Muddy lay awake, worrying about him. Sissy couldn't sleep, either.

It happened again and again. One day the week before, he'd been so ill that he stayed in bed all day. Then late in the afternoon he remembered something he had to do, and he was off again. Didn't show up until after midnight. It didn't happen *all* the time—four, five times a week. He could make himself stop—and did—if he had something important to do, a deadline or one of Miss Lynch's parties. He never missed one of her parties anymore, said they were important to his career. Sissy stopped going, and God knew she wasn't up to it. Poor girl didn't eat enough to keep a butterfly alive.

One day shortly before they moved from the Morrisons' to East Broadway, Fanny Osgood showed up looking like a wedding cake. She was all pink and crinolines, curls and ribbons, smelling of perfume and wearing a bonnet covered with flowers. Muddy answered the door, and her first thought was that this poor creature was lost. Poor creature! She had wiles Sissy never dreamed of, but before Muddy could get a word out, Sissy saw her and came running to the door.

"Why, it's Fanny," she yelled, her eyes big as saucers.

Fanny hugged Sissy like as if they'd been toddlers together.

"Muddy, this is Mrs. Osgood," Sissy said, as Fanny removed her bonnet.

"Mrs. Clemm," Muddy inserted, to make a proper how-do-you-do, but nobody seemed to hear.

Sissy led Fanny to a chair next to the fireplace, and the two of them went to talking about Miss Lynch's party. All the while Fanny glanced at the door to the bedroom like she hoped Eddy would appear, but he had already gone to his office. When Sissy told her that, the disappointment in Fanny's eyes made it obvious to Muddy who she'd really come to see.

After tea Fanny took Sissy to some ladies' meeting, leaving Muddy and Catterina alone. While they were gone Muddy wondered, since she was "Mrs." Osgood, if there was a Mr. Osgood. She guessed he was dead, but later Eddy explained that Fanny and her husband were estranged. That was the word he used, but fancy words couldn't sugarcoat a thing like that. Muddy didn't hold with divorce; she would never sit still for such a thing in her own family, but she held her tongue, hard as it was. Fanny did seem to be fond of Sissy, and the poor girl didn't have a friend in the world.

That night, Sissy told Muddy that Fanny was on their side, that she could talk some sense into Eddy, and Muddy prayed that was true. She'd be grateful to Fanny for that and keep her mouth shut about her suspicions regarding Fanny's real intentions. But nothing happened; Eddy went right on drinking, and it seemed Fanny disappeared as suddenly as she had appeared.

One morning a few weeks later, after one of Eddy's late nights, Muddy and Sissy sat at the table having breakfast and watching Eddy pick his clothes up off the floor, where he'd dropped them the night before. He'll be late for work again, Muddy thought. What must his business partner think of him?

"You should eat something," she said, thinking what he really needed was a bath.

He turned and looked at her as he pulled suspenders over his bare shoulders. "Get me a clean shirt," he said.

"You know where your shirts are," Muddy said, pouring coffee through a strainer and into her cup.

"I said get me a Goddamned shirt, you old bag." And he started rifling through the papers on his desk.

Sissy got up and went into the bedroom. Returning to the doorway, she threw a clean shirt at him, turned, and slammed the door, leaving Muddy and Eddy alone in the outer room. He finished dressing and left without a word or a bite of breakfast.

For most of the morning Muddy worked on a bundle of piecework, sitting in the rocking chair near one of the windows that looked out on the rear of the house and the two privies near the back stoop. Occasionally their smell drifted up and through the opened windows. Sissy had remained in the bedroom. As she sewed, Muddy thought about Eddy and what it might take to get him to stop again. She had a notion that at the root of things was the fact that he and

Sissy weren't sleeping together. Of course, Sissy had always refused to sleep in the bed with him if he'd been drinking, but since moving to East Broadway, the sleeping arrangements seemed to have become permanent—Sissy and Muddy together on the bed in the bedroom and Eddy on the daybed in the outer room where he worked at home and where Sissy and Muddy spent most of their day. They would go downstairs to join the other boarders for lunch and supper, but as breakfast was not offered, they took that meal in their rooms. The fact that Sissy and Eddy no longer slept together had been preying on Muddy's mind. She tried not to pry in their marital affairs, but in her mind this thing had become a stain on their marriage and a dishonor to the family name. She couldn't live with it; she'd have no peace on her deathbed if she did, and Muddy gave great weight to her deathbed state of mind. That was the vision with which she measured all things, right and wrong, happiness and unhappiness—her deathbed, a four-poster, the linens pressed and neatly tucked in, a bed well made, a life rightly lived.

Just before noon Sissy came out of the bedroom, followed by Catterina, and took the chair facing Muddy. She had dressed, and brushed and pinned her hair. But for being too pale and thin, she would be lovely, Muddy thought. Put her in a dress like Fanny's and she would turn heads. Sissy picked up two cut pieces of a collar from atop Muddy's piecework bundles, threaded a needle, and started stitching them together. The two worked in silence for a while, Catterina curled on the scatter rug between them. Thinking that soon they would have to go down for lunch, Muddy decided now was the time, and she chose her words carefully.

"Sis, if you could just make a little effort, maybe he'd stop," she said, trying her best not to let her voice betray the tension she felt inside.

Sissy looked up at her mother, puzzled. "An effort to do what?"

"Be a wife to him." Muddy did not look up. Aware that Sissy was eyeing her, she kept right on sewing as if she'd been talking about nothing more important than pinking shears.

Sissy drew the sewing thread between her teeth and bit it in two; then she jabbed the needle back into the pincushion. Standing and shooing Catterina from the rug, she dropped the spool and the piecework to her chair. Before closing the bedroom door behind her, she stopped, not looking back.

"Why don't you sleep with him," she said. "He wouldn't know the difference."

CHAPTER 13

 Eddy

The Broadway Journal   Saturday, June 14, 1845

MUSICAL ITEMS

CASTLE GARDEN.—This popular summer resort will please those likely to visit the old fort, now a theatre. The price of admission has been lowered to twenty-five cents, and as a rule, the entertainments are first-rate though the upper reaches of the gallery should be avoided by the Hard of Hearing. Singing, dancing, and funny monologues fill up the passing hours; to say nothing of the vast area for promenading and refreshment, with the lovely walk which surrounds the whole, in full view of the Bay.

The Italian singers will, happily, *not* be re-engaged, which we think very fortunate for the Proprietors. Not only were they out of place, they were out of tune, and could not fail to take more from the treasury than bring to it.

FANNY'S LOVER NOW had a name—Ned Thomas—and for all Eddy cared, they could both go to hell. It was a slander, but perhaps not quite a lie, and he knew at once the source of it. There was a grain of truth, though an innocent grain. A dozen years earlier, while living in Baltimore, Eddy received a draft of twenty dollars by post from John Allan. By an oversight he had failed to sign the draft, and since Eddy was desperate for the funds, he signed John Allan's name. It was no forgery. The money was intended for him, and if he'd returned the draft for a signature, it would have been delayed two weeks, and there was always the chance that his foster father would change his mind. The bank caught the mistake, and John Allan was upset with Eddy for taking the liberty, talking it about Richmond that Eddy had forged his signature. If there was ever a basis for the charge, that was it.

Thirteen Broad Street was a mile from Beekman and Nassau, almost to the

Battery and just up from Water Street and near the wharfs, an area of brick warehouses and sail lofts. Ned Thomas's place of business was similar to the rest, a red brick, four-story warehouse with offices on the first floor. A clerk led Eddy past a row of desks.

"Mr. Poe," Thomas said as Eddy approached. "I've been expecting you."

He stood, and Eddy thought he intended to shake hands, but instead Thomas pulled a cigar from a case he carried in his coat pocket and lit it, puffing long and hard, then motioned Eddy to a chair beside his desk. Thomas's manner was cavalier and condescending, the conceit of the well-to-do, and there was no sign of remorse or even concern. He was taller than Eddy and heavier, prosperous-looking. A walking stick, that affectation of the Upper Ten, lay on one corner of his desk.

"Fanny said you'd be coming," Thomas said, thumping the ash from the business end of his cigar into a brass cuspidor on the floor at Eddy's feet. "As a friend, I deemed it my duty to tell her. Surely you understand."

He leaned back in his chair and smiled at Eddy.

"Mr. Thomas," Eddy began, "in doing your duty, as you call it, you have done me an injustice. You could have come to me. We have not met, but I've seen you, and you have seen me. We are both gentlemen, I presume. It would have been a simple and courteous thing to come to me instead of going to Mrs. Osgood. Or does your courtship of the lady require that my name be blackened?"

Thomas bristled and looked about to see which of his staff might have overheard. "You're out of line, Poe."

Eddy said nothing, but Thomas's use of his last name was satisfying in a way, the air cleared of the man's inflated self-esteem. Had Eddy implied that they were rivals? He hoped not. Fanny had toyed with him, pawed him the way Catterina pawed a bit of ribbon from Muddy's sewing basket. She cared no more for Eddy than any other New York editor artless enough to be taken in by her charms. Willis had fallen prey, but Eddy would not.

"You deny the charge, then," Thomas said, eyeing Eddy suspiciously.

"I do." Eddy said. "It is a lie and a slander."

Thomas looked away, considering the matter, and Eddy perceived that the incident was proving more troublesome than the man expected.

"I will make inquiries," Thomas said, "and let you know what I learn. If the charge is groundless as you say, then I'm sure you have nothing to worry about."

"I have rumor to worry about, Mr. Thomas, no thanks to you. Give me the name, and I will make my own inquiries. Can't you see the difficulty of my position? I have a family. I'm editor of a magazine. My business depends on my reputation."

"Perhaps I was indiscreet, Poe, in telling Mrs. Osgood," Thomas said, with a sigh, "and for that I apologize, but let's not drag others into this—people guilty of nothing more than repeating what they heard."

They stared at each other.

"Then you give me no choice but to await your response," Eddy said. "Perhaps it's trivial to you, but this charge could ruin me."

Eddy stood and proffered his card to Thomas, who stood also; then he made a slight bow and left. They did not shake hands.

ARRIVING AT HIS office two days later, Eddy noticed Briggs standing at the top of the steps just outside the door to their office. As Eddy climbed the stairs, he could see Briggs staring down from over his belly, anticipation in his eyes. He intends to say something, Eddy thought, something that will give him satisfaction. Eddy looked him in the eye as he approached. Briggs stepped aside to let him pass.

"Good morning," Eddy said, rather more cheerfully than he intended. It wasn't his usual greeting. Usually he said nothing at all.

"Good morning, Mr. Poe," Briggs said, and went to his desk.

It was a beautiful morning. The sashes were thrown up and the door was propped open. Already the flies were buzzing, and carriage wheels could be heard on the paving stones below. Eddy hadn't had a drink for four days and was feeling more energetic than usual. He dropped his papers on his desk, wondering what to do first and also sensing Briggs staring at him.

"I'm taking your name off the masthead," Briggs said.

What's he talking about? Eddy wondered, unable to suppress a smile. He and Briggs were partners, fifty-fifty. The man was not stupid. Something was amiss, but Eddy smiled anyway. "Why is that, Mr. Briggs?" he asked, trying to look him in the eye and not at the purple wen beside his nose.

"I had a letter from Lowell," Briggs said, rising and walking round his desk.

He was angry now, shaking; he'd been working up to this. His bald spot was red with rage. "Lowell said you were a little soggy the day he visited you. You've been drunk for a month. We're running a magazine here, Mr. Poe, not a tavern." He paused to let the words sink in, but it wasn't a wigging Eddy was getting. There was more. "I have a new partner," Briggs added, "and you, sir, can go to the devil."

Briggs turned, went to his desk, and pretended to attend to some business there.

Eddy stared at him. Their printer, John Douglas, had withdrawn a couple of weeks earlier. This signaled trouble, of course, but Eddy let Briggs handle those matters. And Eddy owned half of the *Broadway Journal,* by an agreement signed in December. How could Briggs fire him? He could not. Plus there was considerable unfinished business, and Eddy was due to be paid at the end of the month—pay he had earned and pay he needed.

"I think you have forgotten that I own half of this magazine," Eddy said.

"I've forgotten nothing," Briggs yelled, livid now, and Eddy guessed he'd been plotting this for weeks. "I put up the money; I pay the bills. Our agreement was that your share would be earned by literary contributions, but you have contributed nothing except those stupid letters attacking Longfellow and stuff lifted word-for-word from a magazine published ten years ago. Don't think for an instant that you've lived up to your part of the bargain. Our relationship is over. Clean out your desk and leave."

Eddy did not budge. Briggs, idiot though he was, had the nerve to attempt a *fait accompli,* and Eddy even felt a touch of admiration. But leaving would mean he tacitly agreed to Briggs's contention that he had not earned his share, and he would not only be out of a job, his interest in the magazine—which he had built with fourteen-hour days for six months at cut-rate pay—would be worthless. He resolved to stay, a squatter in his own company.

If Briggs ousted him, of course, Eddy would have no magazine in which to publish the manuscripts coming any day now from Willis. For an instant he considered letting Briggs in on the scheme, but he had promised Willis to keep their agreement a secret, and he couldn't go back on his word. Not to Willis.

The situation was absurd. Eddy hated Briggs; he would give anything to be rid of him, but in a sense, they were joined at the hip. He needed legal advice, but he had no money, and just then he recalled that among Dunn

English's mixed bag of careers was a brief stint as an advocate. That English hated Briggs as much as Eddy did might be helpful. He straightened the papers on his desk and grabbed up the review he was writing, tomahawking the performance of a troop of Italian singers who had recently appeared on the stage at Castle Garden. "I'll be back," he announced, scowling at Briggs. "Don't think that by my leaving I have agreed to anything."

"HE'S GOT YOU over a barrel," English said. "If you don't agree, he can always dissolve the partnership. You might get a little something in that case, but it would take months, and you would have legal expenses. Maybe you should refuse to leave. If he has a new partner, they might offer you something to be rid of the nuisance."

Eddy was demoralized by the idea that he was nothing more than a nuisance. But he had no money with which to start a new magazine, and he'd never make a go of it as a freelance writer—he couldn't write. And who would hire him if word got out that he was a forger? On an impulse he told English about the charge. "It's groundless, I assure you."

English started laughing. "How is it that you always get into such trouble?"

"Dammit, English, it's groundless I tell you."

"Then sue the bastard. You have a case for libel. You are an aggrieved party," he said, the legal jargon seeming to satisfy him. "I'll represent you for twenty-five percent of whatever we get, and I'll make him regret ever saying a word."

The idea of going to court unnerved Eddy. What if the truth came out? As trivial as it was, he couldn't prove innocence. Thomas would be vindicated, and Eddy would be ruined. "I should wait to hear from him," he said, and got up to go.

"Don't be a fool, Poe. This could ruin you. Scotch it now with a lawsuit," English said, thumping the table with his forefinger to press the point.

English was overreacting. Eddy had no choice but to wait to hear from Thomas; he couldn't sue, and not wanting to argue with English, he said nothing and left.

As it was nearly eleven, and Eddy did not want to return to his office, he resorted to Sandy Welsh's Cellar. Eddy and Sandy were on first-name basis. Sandy was a burly, fun-loving man with a thick black mustache, and he spoke with a heavy brogue. The eatery had a low, beamed ceiling and a dirt floor. Its subterranean situation kept it cool even in summer months and even with a fire going in the large brick fireplace that stood opposite the bar, which consisted of two four-by-eight beams resting on barrels and doing double duty as a chopping block. Sandy always stood at one end, opening oysters or gutting fish.

The appeal of Sandy's was a vaporous aroma of chowder that smoked its way up and along Ann Street, pulling in patrons despite the humble appearance of the place. Mrs. Sandy, as everyone called Sandy's stocky and sullen wife, stood over a stock pot that emitted the most savory aroma in all of Manhattan. With fists like a prize fighter's, she wielded a paring knife and a brass ladle the size of a spade and did not hesitate to poke it in the chest of a too-rowdy patron. Eddy had been on the receiving end of her threats, creamy soup splattered on his waistcoat.

Sandy had opened a million oysters in his day. His thick hands bore the scars of countless slips of the knife, and Eddy had never seen anyone open an oyster faster. He didn't need to advertise as long as he kept the door open to the street. Steam from that pot was curling up the stairs as Eddy descended. Mrs. Sandy stood over her kettle as Sandy cleaned fish at the bar, dropping heads and entrails into a pail. There was not another soul in the place.

"How 'bout an eye-opener, Sandy," Eddy said.

"Bar's not open," Mrs. Sandy replied, eyeing him suspiciously.

Sandy winked at him, and Eddy knew better than to ask him to overrule her. He'd have to wait.

He sat on a stool and pulled the review from his pocket, intending to finish it there and then and demand that Briggs pay him for it. Sandy related the news as Eddy worked. A steamship, the *Cambria,* had gone missing, and a fishing smack had picked up a bottle at sea with a piece of paper inside giving longitude and latitude and saying that the *Cambria* had ten feet of water in the hold. While Sandy talked, Eddy considered leaving the city and moving back to the Brennans'. Perhaps this break with Briggs was a blessing in disguise. He couldn't write in the city. He hadn't written a word since "The Raven," except for that poem to Fanny. Fanny! The thought of her was painful. On top of everything else crumbling around him, she had forsaken him. And he couldn't write, but why? If Dunn English's theories were right, he had the necessary facilities, or had those organs fallen into atrophy? He reached up, touched his forehead, and smiled, thinking about those pretentious phrenological theories.

An idea came. He turned his review over to the blank side, reached in his pocket for a pencil, and started writing. Deciding that there must be an organ that the phrenologists had overlooked, Eddy dubbed it the bump of perversity. He started a tale then and there. For an hour he was oblivious to Sandy and his wife and their preparations for lunch.

His inspiration was the question, Why did he, on certain occasions, become so argumentative? It happened with Dunn English. It happened with Briggs until Eddy stopped talking to Briggs altogether. For the sake of argument, Eddy often professed an opinion he did not hold. What was this if not perversity? He could almost feel the bump swell in his brain. Perhaps he could even isolate it if he remained in English's presence long enough. And what would make him accept a speaking engagement, as he had done the week before, for the purpose of delivering a new poem, when he knew he couldn't write one? What else but his organ of perversity? It was not unlike standing on the edge of a precipice, wanting to jump. It was madness, he thought, perhaps the very source of all madness, and he laughed out loud, thinking he had hit on something. Watching Sandy eviscerate a haddock, Eddy pictured a surgeon entering the brain with a paring knife, carving out a chunk of oversize muscle, removing the madness.

Deciding to call his story "New Revelations in Phrenology," he would give it such a ring of truth that people would confuse it for serious science. A year earlier he had done a similar thing with "The Balloon-Hoax." That had caused such a stir that a crowd blocked traffic in front of the *New York Sun,* waiting for an extra. Newsboys had made a fortune that morning. Eddy's spirits rose. Perhaps he could write the poem requested by New York University after all. It was due the last day of the month. They had offered twenty dollars, and he could sell this new tale for another twenty. Forty dollars was six weeks' room and board. To hell with Briggs.

Patrons began arriving, and Eddy ordered a drink. To hell with his pledge, too; he spent the afternoon and evening working on his story and sipping Sandy's whiskey. He gave neither Charles Briggs nor Ned Thomas another thought, ate a bowl of chowder, and staggered home to bed.

The next morning he had a letter from Tom Chivers, who wrote to say he was in the city to arrange for the publication of a new collection of his poems. Muddy tossed the letter on Eddy's bed as he grappled with his hangover.

Chivers wished to pay a call. It was a miraculous thing that at the bleakest hour, some means appeared to refloat the ship. Thomas Holly Chivers had the wherewithal to make Eddy's lifelong dream—*The Stylus*—come true. Or he would even call it *Chivers' Magazine* if that would dislodge the necessary funds. Chivers was from Georgia, the owner of an immense plantation with fountains and carriage houses and avenues lined with oaks dripping Spanish moss, an army of slaves, and cotton fields stretching to the horizon. The two had never met, but more than anything, Tom Chivers wished to be a poet. All his acres, his mansion, his julep life were nothing if he could not write verse, and some years back he had decided that the man to teach and guide him was Edgar Poe. "The Raven" had turned admiration into adoration. Chivers had written to say it was the greatest English-language poem ever conceived.

Eddy went to his desk and dashed off a note, inviting Chivers up to his East Broadway rooms. For obvious reasons, they could not meet at the *Broadway Journal* office, so Eddy pleaded illness. He had cultivated Chivers for years. On several occasions—usually when unemployed—he had proposed a new literary journal, promoting the venture as a way to bring Chivers's poetry before the public and not failing to point out that his poems would appear alongside Eddy's. Though Chivers was always interested, his distance had made it difficult for Eddy to land the fish.

Early the following Monday morning, Chivers arrived unexpectedly to pay a call. Muddy woke Eddy to say he had a visitor and that she was going down to bring him up. Before Eddy could get out of bed, Muddy reappeared, and Eddy could tell by the blush on her face that she had received some extravagant compliment. As it was hot and not a breath of a breeze, Eddy was lying undressed in the bed, covered only by a sheet up to his waist. His chamber pot had yet to be emptied and the room smelled faintly of urine. It sat under his bed, and Eddy needed to use it again, but here was Chivers standing before him.

"Poe," he said, "I am sorry to find you ill."

To Eddy's surprise, Chivers appeared to be the same age as he. By his letters and poems, which Eddy considered juvenile, he had pictured a much younger man. Chivers was clean-shaven; he carried a crooked-headed hickory walking stick, and his hair was dark, neatly parted, and shining with lacquer.

"Think nothing of it, Mr. Chivers," Eddy said. "A day or so in bed and I'll be 'fit as a fiddle' as you say down in Georgia."

Muddy returned with a shirt, and as Eddy put it on, he motioned Chivers to a chair near the window and instructed Muddy to hand him a recent copy of the *Broadway Journal* that led with Eddy's story "The Premature Burial." Just then Sissy came up with a cup of chamomile tea, Muddy's universal cure-all. Eddy introduced them as he buttoned his shirt. Sissy fluffed his pillows, helping Eddy to sit up; then she and Muddy went back downstairs.

Chivers perused the magazine, stopping at an article describing a new statue of Lord Byron. "Byron was a great poet, but not as great as Shelley," he said.

Eddy agreed immediately. He was eager for them to get on well. Sissy returned with a glass of lemonade for Chivers, and waiting for him to drink it down, she began coughing. When she left the room again, Chivers asked if she had a cold.

"It's not a cold," Eddy said. "Do you know Dr. Francis? The poet."

"I have heard of him," Chivers said.

"He says Sissy has bronchitis. She ruptured a blood vessel while singing when we lived in Philadelphia and hasn't been well since. And you were saying of Shelley?"

"That he is the greatest poet that ever lived," Chivers said.

"No poet has greater passion than Shelley," Eddy said, "but passion is misplaced in poetry. I think Tennyson is better."

"How can you say that?" Chivers argued. "The man is effeminate. His poems lack force. But Shelley!"

Not wanting to argue, Eddy took a book of poems by Horne from the nightstand and tossed it to Chivers. "You will enjoy this," he said. "Here is a work better even than *Paradise Lost,* yet no American bookseller will publish it. But show me a novel full of profanity and bad grammar, and New York publishers will jump at it. I met Lowell not long ago." Eddy was desperate to go to the privy. "I was disappointed in his appearance."

"He has written nothing remarkable," Chivers said.

"'Rosaline' is quite good, don't you think?" Eddy asked, then cursed himself for being so perverse.

"It is as palpable a plagiarism," Chivers said, "as has ever been palmed off."

Plagiarism! That's where they would agree. If Chivers thought Lowell a plagiarist, they would surely agree on Longfellow. "And what do you think of my articles on Longfellow?" Eddy asked.

"I enjoyed the debate," Chivers said smiling, "though I must say that I agreed as often with Outis as I did with you."

"And what if I told you that I was Outis, Mr. Chivers?"

Chivers's eyes grew large. Eddy revealed the hoax, explaining all the intricacies of the magazine business and how he had been persecuted for his opinions. "But one must stick to principle. What can I do but be faithful to the laws of versification? And to originality. And beauty. Beauty above all. It is the duty of the poet to create beauty. Won't you agree that beauty is the ultimate measure of a poem?"

Chivers smiled, and Eddy decided the time had come to bait the hook.

"Do you recall our discussions regarding the *Stylus*?" Eddy asked. "I had first thought to call it the *Penn Magazine*, but you correctly suggested that the title rendered it too regional. You were quite right. It was then I knew you to be a man of vision. I hit on the name *Stylus*, the writing pen used by the Greeks. What better title to express the precise nature of the magazine?"

With this Eddy reached for a bundle of letters that Sissy had fetched for him from the bureau and extended them to Chivers.

"Read the first one," Eddy suggested. "It's from a Mr. Tomlin of Jackson, Tennessee, who says he can obtain thirty paying subscribers. The other letters are similar, men from the South and West, all promising their assistance. I can get subscribers, Mr. Chivers. May I call you Tom? Please call me Edgar. The *Broadway Journal* has fifteen hundred subscribers. That's nothing. *Graham's* has fifty thousand at three dollars per year. The *Broadway Journal* is too political. Charles Briggs is in league with the abolitionists, so I have decided to resign my position."

"The abolitionists!" Chivers was shocked.

"Yes," Eddy said, "and I've been working fourteen hours a day. I can't do that and start a new magazine, too. I have manuscripts coming from London any day now, original work from England's greatest writers. I've made up my mind. If you're with me, I'll publish a new prospectus announcing our partnership. Your being from the South will have immense value. We cannot fail."

Chivers was silent for a moment, nodding and considering the proposition. "I could not join you until the first of the year," he said.

"If it's a matter of time, Tom, don't give it a thought. I'll lay the ground-work and arrange for a printer. Two thousand seed money is all we need. Give me the word, and I'll go to work on the prospectus."

Chivers rose from his chair in preparation to leave. "Let me think it over," he said. "I'll be in the city for a week or so, and we can discuss it further when you're feeling better."

Eddy claimed to be feeling better already. They shook hands, and Chivers descended the stairs as Eddy relieved himself in the chamber pot.

ON WEDNESDAY THE 25th of June, he left the East Broadway flat for the first time since his afternoon in Sandy Welsh's Cellar. He made straight for Wiley & Putnam bookseller's for copies of his *Tales* that went on sale that day. Then he went to his office to deliver the work he'd prepared for the issue of the 28th. He handed the work to Briggs and went to his desk, where he stayed for the remainder of the day, letting Briggs know he would not be dislodged without compensation. The two men said not a word, but Briggs fumed, revealing to Eddy that he had gotten the message.

He stayed home the next morning. He wrote a letter to Evert Duyckinck, offering his shares in the *Broadway Journal* for fifty dollars. He wrote Ann Lynch, sending her a copy of his *Tales* and pouring out his heart. He told her he was leaving the *Broadway Journal* and going away. To Briggs he sent an old essay, "How to Write a Blackwood Article," for the issue of July 5 with a note saying he was seeing to a matter of personal business and that he would return in a week to resume his duties. He wrote Ned Thomas. It had been over a week since their meeting, ample time, and Eddy decided to have Dunn English deliver the letter. Perhaps he should sue after all. Perhaps he had nothing left to lose.

At noon the post arrived, and among the letters was one from Providence. Eddy stuffed it in his pocket and invented an excuse to leave, worried that the letter might pertain to the forgery charge. He had said nothing to Muddy or Sissy about that. From the way they looked at him, it was apparent that they suspected he was going out to get drunk. He crossed Broadway and walked west on Chambers all the way to the Hudson River. Finding an unused bollard on the wharf, he sat down and read the letter.

Dearest Edgar,

How I have worried about you! You were in my thoughts all afternoon as we stood at the rail of the ferry, looking back at the city. After supper I put Lily and May to bed in the ladies' cabin, then returned to my vigil, listening to the paddle wheel, watching the stars, and thinking of you. You seemed so angry when you left that I fear I have driven you from me with that horrid accusation that, by your response, I know is untrue.

Leaving New York has helped me to perceive things as if from a high meridian. You know little of me, so I will tell you.

My husband left me. He rented a studio a year ago on the pretense of needing a place to paint his portraits. In truth it was a place for him to live. He does not love me—he doesn't know the meaning of the word—so I decided to make it convenient for him.

I met Ned Thomas at the Bartletts'. He is kind and generous, and I think he harbors dreams that we will someday marry. I, too, harbored such dreams until I met you. There! I've said it.

I pray you will forgive me. If, by my actions, I have lost whatever affection you held for me, then destroy this letter. My heart and my lips will be sealed forever. But if your heart bends as mine does, then come to me. Come to Providence. Come at once. I want to look into your eyes. I want to hear your voice.

Truly your devoted,
Fanny

PS. If you receive this letter, then you will know that I *did* have the courage to post it, though all the while, even now as I close, I know I will not.

Eddy read it again and again; then he paced the dock, looking up at the ships; then he sat back down and read it again. Finally, after an hour, having committed her words to memory, he walked to the end of the finger pier, tore the letter into tiny pieces, and watched the current carry them away.

He could not go home, not then. He went to Sandy's and ate a bowl of chowder. He watched Sandy pour, but he abstained. In bed that night, he lay awake wondering what to do. Yes, he would go. He could not resist.

In the morning he went to find English. Arriving too early, he waited. It was Friday, and English had a magazine to get out; he'd be along soon. When he arrived, Eddy explained that he had not heard from Ned Thomas. He handed English the letter he had composed the previous day, and asked him to deliver it and wait for a response. Eddy offered lunch and English agreed to meet at Sandy's at two.

Eddy was finishing up a plate of oysters when English arrived a half hour late.

"Well?" Eddy asked as English settled onto his stool.

English smiled—his smug, I-know-something-you-don't-know smile. He looked to his left and right as if to make sure he would not be overheard. "You can make money out of this," he whispered.

Eddy rolled his eyes. Not that again.

"Listen," English argued. "Thomas has money. And he's an arrogant son-of-a-bitch. Played right into my hands."

"What do you mean, played into your hands?" Eddy asked.

"I told him you would sue if you don't have a full, written apology within twenty-four hours plus the names of all others involved."

"And what did he say?" Eddy asked as Sandy set a bowl of chowder and a plate of soda crackers in front of English.

"He insulted me," English said, laughing and slurping his soup, his mustache fringed with white chowder. "Called me a 'jackleg shyster.' Threatened to throw me out. So I challenged him."

"You challenged him?" Eddy asked, incredulous. "To a duel?"

"'Jackleg shyster!'" English repeated. "I won't take that from anybody."

"Are you mad?" Eddy exclaimed, almost shouting.

English ignored him. Sandy gave Eddy a stern look. English sipped his soup, refusing to look up. Furious, Eddy ordered a whiskey. If English and Thomas fought a duel, the whole world would know about the forgery. He picked up a soda cracker and snapped it in half. "Do you think you're Aaron Burr?" he asked. "Well, did he say anything at all in response to my letter?"

"Said he needed more time," English said. "I warned him that one doesn't slander a man, then diddledaddle. Then he asked what right I had to tell him what to do, so I told him."

"Told him what?"

"I told him I had the right of a man who respects another man's wife." English turned to Eddy. "Everyone knows he's making love to Fanny Osgood. Was it Fanny who told you about the forgery?"

Eddy flushed. How could he have been so stupid as to send English on this errand? He ordered another whiskey. "I suppose that's when he insulted you."

English stood, reached in his pocket, and put a shilling on the bar. "My offer stands," he said. "I would sue for five hundred if I were you. He'll settle for two-fifty. You have him over a barrel. He can't drag Fanny's name through the muck. He'll settle out of court. Think about it."

Once English was gone, Eddy dismissed the idea, but the more he drank, the more he thought about it. He tried computing in his head three quarters of two hundred and fifty dollars, but the numbers kept flying away. Whatever the sum, it was more money than Eddy had ever seen at one time, and he warmed to the idea.

When at last he stood to leave, he realized he was drunker than he thought. Sandy saw him wobble and came round the bar to steady him. "Shall I recite 'The Raven,' Sandy?" Eddy asked, lightheaded now.

"Not today," Sandy said, leading him away. "Best go home and sleep it off. Let me help you up the stairs."

At the top, the sun was blinding, and he held on to Sandy's arm until his eyes grew accustomed to the light. Standing in the middle of Ann Street, he began reciting.

> Eagerly I wished the morrow;—vainly I had tried to borrow
> From my books surcease of sorrow—sorrow for the lost Lenore—
> For the rare and radiant maiden whom the angels name Lenore—
> > Nameless *here* for evermore.

"It's America's own Shakespeare," Sandy announced to the pedestrians.

Eddy staggered away, into the intersection, when who should he see coming up Nassau but Tom Chivers.

"By God," Eddy shouted. "It's Tom Chivers. The very man I was coming to see. Where are you going, my friend? Come. Go with me."

Poe!" Chivers exclaimed. "What in heaven's name?"

"Tom!" Eddy said, trying to stand erect. Feeling quite jovial, he turned and waved to Sandy; then he took Chivers by the arm and steered him up Nassau. "My friend," Eddy continued, "I shall now reveal the secret of my heart. I am in the damndest affair, and I am telling you as I would my own brother. I have a letter begging me to come to Providence. Begging me."

"And who is this lady in Providence?" Chivers asked.

"You must promise, Tom, to say nothing to my Sissy. It would break her heart, and I wouldn't hurt her for all the world." Eddy stopped talking, turned, and leaned in to Chivers, looking him in the eye. "She is the wife of an artist and a damned fool—always away painting portraits. I have to catch the four o'clock ferry." Then Eddy thought of money and reached in his pockets.

"Not now, Edgar," Chivers pleaded. "Let me walk you home. You can go tomorrow when you're more up to it."

"By God!" Eddy said, "you're right. Now that you're here, let's go home and begin work on the *Stylus*—the greatest literary journal in America. Chivers and Poe, editors. Has a fine ring, doesn't it, Tom?"

As they turned onto East Broadway, Eddy saw Sissy standing in the doorway. As soon as she saw him, she ran inside, and Eddy knew she would go squealing to Muddy. Sure enough, next minute, Muddy came running out into the street to meet them.

"Oh! Eddy. Eddy," she cried, grabbing him by the arm. "Let me put you to bed."

Eddy wished she'd take her hands off him, but he said nothing, careful not to make a scene in front of Chivers. She led them inside, up the stairs, and Eddy collapsed on the bed, telling her to pull up a chair for Chivers. By then she was spouting off to Chivers that she hadn't wanted Eddy drinking in front of him and that he was out of his head. Eddy wanted her to shut up with all this talk of drinking, but he gave up and passed out.

IT WAS DARK when he woke up. The windows were open and it was raining. Lying there, he tried to recall events, like sorting out a dream in that half-sleep state until images work their way into consciousness—English . . . Ned Thomas . . . Chivers . . . Fanny. He had told Chivers about Fanny! He sat up in bed, his head splitting. And Muddy had told Chivers he was deranged. How long had Chivers stayed, watching Eddy sleep it off, listening to Muddy rant and rave?

He closed his eyes and lay back on the pillow. He'd ruined it and his head hurt and he was dying of thirst. He tried going back to sleep but couldn't.

In the morning, without a word to Sissy or Muddy, he left the house, shoving several letters that had arrived the day before into his pocket. He walked down to City Hall Park and the horsecar terminal. He bought a copy of the *New-York Mirror* and a ticket to the end of the line at Twenty-third Street. It was Saturday. He intended to go out to the Brennans' to try and get their old rooms back.

Riding uptown, he leafed through the *Mirror* and there was a column by Willis.

Eddy's heart sank. It was a long, chatty one of Willis's pencilings about a carriage ride. Willis's traveling companion, an attractive young woman carrying a basket on her lap, kept talking to herself. Looking down at her cloth-covered basket, she whispered words of endearment as if rehearsing words she planned to say to an unseen lover. As this continued for an hour or more, Willis decided she was daft. Finally she fell asleep, her head on Willis's shoulder, and he didn't budge for fear of waking her. When she awoke, she pulled back the cloth covering her basket, and inside was a kitten. All along it was the kitten to whom she had whispered her words of affection.

It was vintage Willis. How overjoyed Willis's readers would be to have him back. He had no peer. But where were the articles he had promised? If Morris had heard from him, why hadn't Eddy?

He dropped the newspaper to his lap and stared out the window of the horsecar, thinking that if he didn't stop drinking, he was doomed. The trip to the Brennans' was for two purposes, to find a place to live and to mark the day—mark the day with ceremony. Instinct told him to do it. He would stand on Mount Tom and take a vow. Such solemnity was not easily annulled. Fifteen years earlier he had taken a similar vow as he closed the gate in front of John Allan's house in Richmond. After being dismissed from the Military Academy at West Point, he had decided to return home. Eddy had done well in his classes, but he wasn't a soldier. That life was not for him. So coming home was to be a time for taking stock and planning his future. His mother was dead, his foster mother had been dead two years, and John Allan had remarried. Eddy had never met the new Mrs. Allan.

When he arrived, he was greeted at the door by Toby, the butler. Eddy set his trunk down and embraced Toby. "Take my trunk to my room, will you, Toby?"

"New Mrs. Allan has redone your old room, Mr. Edgar," Toby said. "Your things have been moved to the end room."

The end room was above the kitchen, a servant's room. Toby eyed him cautiously.

"Is Mrs. Allan here?" Eddy asked.

"Yes, sir," Toby said.

"Then go tell her that I won't be staying in the end room. I'll be staying in my old room."

Toby started to say something, then stopped himself, turned, and went upstairs. Eddy left his trunk in the foyer and walked into the tea room. Parting the lace curtains, he looked down the lawn to the river. The sun was shining, but the ground was still wet with morning dew. He had forgotten how good Virginia smelled—the damp earth, the air perfumed like honeysuckle. Forsythia were in full, yellow bloom. He decided to saddle a horse when he finished unpacking and ride out to Duncan Lodge, see his sister, Rosalie, and the Mackenzies. It was good to be home.

"Edgar?"

He turned to see his father's new wife standing in the doorway. She was not much older than he and prettier than he had expected.

"Welcome home," she said, smiling. "Please don't think I'm pushing you out of your old room. You're a grown man, and we didn't expect you back. I have redecorated, as you can see, and your old room is a guest room now. Forgive me for saying this, but this is my home, too. Nevertheless you are welcome."

Eddy thought for a moment. Was he being unreasonable? Still, his feelings were hurt. The end room had been Frances Allan's maid's room. "I'm not here to stay," he said. "It's just a visit. That makes me a guest, doesn't it?"

She dropped her eyes to the floor. They were dueling.

"Mr. Allan has told me so much about you," she said, raising her eyes again. "You two have had . . ." She paused and stared at him. "It must be difficult for you," she continued, her voice soft and sympathetic. "When you left, your mother was alive. Now you come home, and someone else has taken her place. I'm very sorry for that, and I want to be your friend. Can't you see that your father and I are expecting a child?"

Her loose-fitting dress had concealed her pregnancy. Eddy had expected children, of course, but seeing her, he was suddenly disgusted by the idea of his father's hands on her, satisfying his lust with someone so young.

"I want to be a peacemaker," she continued, smiling. "But you must help me. You must remember that he *is* your father. Show some humility. Don't be so proud."

"Does that mean I'm to be a servant in his house?" Eddy asked.

"No." She bristled at his words. "It means making room for my family, too. For the children we hope to have."

They stared at each other. Eddy could see she was trying and decided he should relent, but then he heard his father at the door, asking Toby where he was.

"You sent for him," Eddy said, feeling betrayed.

"Edgar, he is your father."

John Allan appeared at the tea room door and looked Eddy up and down. There was scorn in his eyes. Eddy was not his son; he was an orphan, and he could feel it. John Allan was an old man, a stooped, stingy old man.

"You will stay in the end room," he said, "or you won't stay here at all."

Eddy looked back at the new Mrs. Allan. Despite what she had said, he was not welcome, and her eyes were cold and victorious.

He walked out of the room, picked up his trunk at the door, and left the house. He crossed the lawn and opened the gate, turned, and looked back. The front door was closed. He imagined John Allan saying, "Let him go; let him go."

He reached down and pulled the wrought-iron gate shut. Even now Eddy could hear the metal latch fasten into place. Intrigued by the finality of that sound, he had opened and shut the gate again, taking a vow as he did so, a vow to make his own way.

Now, on a Saturday morning, as he walked through the country along Bloomingdale Road to the Brennan farm, he wondered what might have happened had he stayed in the end room. Had he been too proud for his own good? Perhaps by now he'd be a prosperous Richmond merchant, running John Allan's sawmill or one of his plantations. Like Chivers, he'd compose his poems in the ease of a cushioned wicker chair on the front porch, looking down at the river and listening to the birds singing in the magnolias.

The Brennans had new boarders. And Mary Brennan wasn't as overjoyed to see him as he thought she'd be. Her sleeves were rolled up and her arms glistened with soap suds. She was too busy for a visit, but they chatted for a few moments on the porch. She asked about Sissy and Muddy. Mr. Brennan was somewhere out in the fields where the corn was chest high. Eddy told her how Sissy longed to come back and begged her to write if rooms came available, and he reminded her that he had written "The Raven" in their upstairs room. She smiled and nodded.

Afterward he climbed the rocky outcrop that they called Mount Tom, to sit on the rock and watch the river and the palisades beyond. He took out his letters and read them. He had one from Anne Lynch, sympathetic and reassuring; she invited him to her home that night. With Fanny gone he had no desire to go.

He took his vow. It was easy. On a hot summer day, what is difficult? Beyond the palisades were the green hills of New Jersey. Sunlight baked the rock, and he lay down and closed his eyes, letting his thoughts wander, and they settled on a vision of Fanny.

Later he walked all the way home, and it was evening when he arrived. Over supper he told Sissy and Muddy about the forgery charge, explaining that Fanny had warned him. He confessed to keeping it from them for fear of upsetting them, and he blamed his drinking on the distress it had caused. He swore to them that he had stopped. The forgery was untrue, but somehow he must resolve it, and for that purpose he needed to go to Providence to see Fanny. He needed to know the source of the rumor.

The next day Chivers called again to take Eddy for a carriage ride. Eddy put on his new suit and the collar and necktie that he'd bought for his lecture at the New-York Historical Society Library. In the carriage he explained everything, including the forgery accusation and John Allan's draft, just as he had to Sissy and Muddy. Chivers seemed to understand. They drove down to Battery Park and walked over the causeway to Castle Garden. Chivers preached, calling on Eddy to put his faith in God and foreswear forever the use of alcohol. Eddy swore. When Chivers pressed him about his boasting of a love affair, Eddy denied it, claiming he'd been out of his head. Chivers let the matter drop. He bought Eddy a crooked-headed walking stick like his own, saying he should carry one, that a walking stick was the mark of a gentleman. Late that afternoon, as the carriage dropped Eddy at East Broadway, Chivers promised to give the *Stylus* serious thought, and he consented to a final request, a loan of ten dollars. With this done, they said good-bye.

Eddy stayed in bed for the next two days, sending his regrets to New York University for being too ill to appear. It cost him twenty dollars. On Wednesday, the second day of July, having had nothing to drink for four days, he walked down to the Battery and took the four o'clock ferry to Providence.

CHAPTER 14

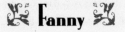 Fanny

Graham's Lady's & Gentleman's Magazine

Had we but met when both our hearts were beating
With the wild joy—the guileless love of youth—
Thou, a proud boy—with frank and ardent greeting—
And I, a timid girl, all trust and truth!

Frances S. Osgood
from "Ida Grey"

THE THOUGHT OF having posted that letter to Edgar Poe made Fanny positively contrite. She had been an absolute pox. Of course she told no one, but what if he came? She couldn't imagine what she would do with him. She would have to hide him in a steamer trunk or turn him into an airedale and put him on a leash. Or was he a fox terrier? Yes. He was rather too small for an airedale.

He would never come, of course. Perhaps she'd have a letter instead, and she would have been happy with that. She prayed for a letter. No, that was not true; she did not pray—she longed for a letter. Ned Thomas was to come on the sixth, just after Independence Day, to stay for a week, and it was only after Fanny had posted her letter to Edgar on June 19 that she realized Ned and Edgar might even arrive on the same ferry. What had she been thinking? Or had she done it on purpose, following some misguided impulse of which she was not fully conscious?

If he did come, she reasoned, he would come at once. That would put him in Providence a week before Ned. But of course he wouldn't come. She'd have a letter instead.

Fanny had burned at least a dozen drafts of her letter. She touched each one to the lamp, watched it flame, and dropped it onto the grate, making sure it turned to ash. But on that last revision, she hit on the word *meridian*: "Leaving New York has helped me to perceive things as if from a high meridian." She could not resist using such a bully word, dramatic though it was. Had she not thought of it, she might never have posted the letter. But in more serious moments, Fanny realized that she must write Edgar or risk losing him. No sooner had he walked out of the ladies' parlor at the Astor, than Fanny knew that she could not leave him that way, and in truth she had started composing her letter in her mind as she, Lily, and May descended the stairs following the porters carrying their trunks. Later when she had said good-bye to Ned at the ferry, it was as if she were saying good-bye for good. She didn't love him, but how to tell him?

Upon arriving in Providence, she rearranged the furniture in her hotel room so that the table stood just in front of the window and she could feel the sea air in her face. Her window looked across the roofs of several buildings on the hill that descended to the harbor. The view of water and ships inspired her. At night when they returned from supper at her brother's, she would put May to bed in their tiny room and get out her writing things. Lily stayed at John's, sleeping in the bed with his daughter. It was so pleasant there at the hotel, with Fanny's little May Vincent Osgood lying on the bed beside the writing table, her soft face lit by the lamp.

In the mornings she and May would breakfast at the hotel, then walk to John's to spend the day with his family. Fanny helped Sarah, John's wife, with the cooking and cleaning, making the beds and playing with the children. Sarah was a beauty and a joy. Seven years younger than Fanny, she was everything Fanny was not: a marvelous cook, an immaculate homemaker, a doting wife and devoted mother. Of course, Fanny was a devoted mother, too, but she came up wanting in those other areas. Sarah was taller than Fanny. Her hair was red-brown, almost the color of pine straw, and it was forever coming undone, since she was constantly in motion, never without a project. She painted one of the children's rooms, planted a kitchen garden, and hung new wallpaper and curtains in the dining room, all in the three weeks since Fanny had arrived. Every morning, she cleaned the stable and raked the yard before Fanny and May arrived from the hotel, and every afternoon, she bathed before

John got home so that the whole thing looked as effortless as if she had an army of servants. Sarah and John had three children, a girl and two boys, all under the age of seven, and after lunch, Sarah's three and Fanny's two were put down for a nap, while Sarah and Fanny sat on the porch, rocking in the rocking chairs, sharing gossip and sewing or shelling peas. It was small-town living, soothing after a year in New York City. Still, she left Fanny exhausted by the end of the day and looking forward to her quiet time at the hotel at night, when she would compose her poems and the story she was working on, "Ida Grey," the story of a woman in love with a penniless poet.

One day during nap time Fanny glanced up from her needlework, looked up the street toward the intersection of Benevolent and Hope—and walking toward the house was Edgar Poe. For an instant Fanny's breath caught in her throat, and she felt a tightening in her chest, her whole body constricted by the thrill of hopes fulfilled. Nothing else mattered now.

"Sarah," she said, "I think that's Edgar Poe." She had told Sarah about Edgar, of course, that she knew him and had heard him recite his "Raven," describing how amazing it was, but she had confided nothing of her personal feelings, and just then she could not imagine how to explain his being there. She set her needlepoint on the wicker table.

"Edgar Poe?" Sarah asked. "Why on earth?"

Seeing them, he turned at the walk and came right up to the porch as Fanny fixed the pins in her hair. She must look like a field hand, she thought. The sleeves of her dress were rolled above her elbows, and though she'd scrubbed them raw, her fingernails still showed the stains of the blackberries she'd picked the day before.

"Good afternoon," he said, removing his hat. He carried a walking stick, and his trousers were creased, his collar starched, and his boots shined. Fanny thought him magnificent.

"Why, Edgar, what brings you to Providence?" she asked, her heart racing, and she hoped his response would not sink her.

"I trust I'm not intruding," he said, and turned to Fanny. "I'm here on a matter of personal business, and I wonder if I might have a few moments of your time."

Fanny introduced them, and Sarah invited him onto the porch. As he took a chair, Sarah stood. "May I get you a glass of lemonade, Mr. Poe?" she asked.

"Yes. Do, Sarah," Fanny said, jumping at the opportunity of being alone with him for a moment. "And if I know Edgar, he hasn't eaten."

"What about a sandwich, Mr. Poe, and a piece of pie?" Sarah said.

"Perfect, Sarah, thank you," Fanny said, before Edgar could object, and Sarah left them and went into the house.

"Fanny, I . . ."

Fanny interrupted him, putting a forefinger to her lips and pointing to the upstairs rooms, the open windows. "Don't wake them," she said, almost whispering. "I'm glad you came. We'll take a walk and talk. Sarah will keep the children for a while. Where are you staying?"

"City Hotel," he said.

"Perfect," she said. "And you're not really here on business, are you?"

He took a deep breath and looked away, over the porch railing and out into the yard. "I went to see Ned Thomas," he said.

"Is that why you came?" Fanny asked, and for an instant her happiness turned to rejection—every word, every gesture seemed to convey life or death—but when he turned back to her, she perceived in his eyes an eagerness that matched her own, reassuring her that Ned was not the reason. She resisted the temptation to touch his hand.

Sarah returned carrying a tray with glasses, a pitcher of lemonade, and a plate of lunch for Edgar. Fanny stood and cleared a space on the table. Edgar pulled up his chair and ate cold beef, a salad of cresses, and a slice of blackberry pie while Fanny told Sarah about his recital at Anne Lynch's. Meanwhile, Edgar cleaned his plate, seeming to be ravenous, not even stopping to comment.

Fanny would have to tell Sarah not to mention Edgar to Ned Thomas when he came. Sarah and John knew about Ned, of course, knew he was coming for a visit. No doubt, they'd entertain him as if he were a new member of the family. Fanny thought John would do anything to be rid of Sam Osgood. She would have to tell them about the forgery charge; how else could she explain Edgar's coming to Providence? But she would not mention Ned in connection with it. She would say it was someone else. She would say it was Park Benjamin, and indeed, he was the person who had told Ned. Oh, what a muddle! And Park Benjamin wasn't the only one repeating the story. It was going the rounds; Fanny suspected that Lynchie knew. Needless to say, Fanny could tell Edgar none of this, and she would have to make sure that Sarah and John said nothing to Ned about Edgar or the forgery.

Edgar wiped his mouth on his napkin, folded it, and set it beside his plate. "Thank you, Mrs. Locke," he said. "I was hungrier than I thought. A sea voyage does that, I think."

"How long will you be in Providence, Mr. Poe?" Sarah asked.

"Just one night," he said. "I must get back."

"Oh, dear," Fanny said. "I think I hear the children."

Sarah turned her ear toward the upstairs windows. Five youngsters made for a houseful. Fanny had not heard the children, but it was almost time for their naps to end, and she had to change the subject. She knew where Sarah's question would lead.

"Sarah, darling, suppose I walk Mr. Poe back to his hotel? There is a matter about which we need to speak privately. Can you keep May for me? I'll be back in time to help with supper."

"Of course," Sarah said, and Fanny stood immediately. She and Edgar left Sarah standing on the porch, no doubt puzzled by their hurrying away. Fanny would have to get back before John came home from work, she was thinking. She must have been mad to invite Edgar to Providence, but his being there made her positively euphoric.

They walked down the hill toward the river, in the general direction of the hotel; then Fanny had a better idea; the Athenæum. The library would be more private, have less chance of seeing someone she knew. She took his arm to guide him there.

"What happened when you went to see Ned?" she asked as they walked.

Edgar started by telling her about his meeting with Ned, then about the letter he wrote and sending it by Dunn English and their quarrel. A torrent of words came pouring out of his mouth, a confusing jumble of confession, frustration, disappointment, and resolve. Fanny listened, eager to connect it all. The man was desperate to talk, and she guessed that he had not told these things to Sissy. Why, she wondered. He told her about his troubles at the *Broadway Journal* and about his not being able to write. He pulled a flattened scroll of a manuscript from his pocket, a new story, and gave it to her, saying it was sad evidence of his lost powers. He told her about Tom Chivers and his dreams for a new magazine and how he had probably ruined it by having too much to drink, which he did because he was so upset by the forgery charge, and he begged her to forgive him for breaking his promise to take the temperance pledge. He even confessed that he had feigned illness to avoid having to read the poem he could not write for New York University. It had cost him twenty dollars, he said, money he needed, and he confessed to having had to borrow money to come to Providence.

Fanny listened and reassured, listened further and reassured more, welcoming his confidence as the mark of intimacy but distressed by all his misfortunes.

They arrived at the Athenæum and climbed the steps.

Since the hot day made being inside uncomfortable, the library was nearly deserted. They wandered for a while among the rows of bookcases. The Athenæum was a fine library for a city the size of Providence, and the books seemed to take Edgar's mind off his litany of troubles. Fanny was not properly dressed for a visit to the library—she wore no corset, only a chemise under her dress—and she clasped her hands together to hide her blackberry-stained fingernails.

They climbed the stairs to the mezzanine and found a quiet corner with two green wing chairs. When they sat down, Fanny listened for any sound that might indicate someone else was on the mezzanine, and when satisfied that they were alone, she turned to him.

"You're here," she said, her voice giving vent to her emotions. "I hoped you'd come." The bones of his jaw clenched, and though he seemed grateful for her welcome, his eyes remained worried. A wrinkle had formed between his eyes, just at the top of his nose, a care wrinkle. "You are right not to sue Ned," she said, addressing the worry she saw. "Perhaps he's a little jealous of you," and she resolved to pressure Ned about this when he arrived.

Edgar dropped his eyes and nodded.

"Why don't you go see General Morris?" she suggested. "With Willis away he must need help at the *Mirror*. Perhaps he'll take you on at least until Willis gets back."

"I can't do that," Edgar said, shaking his head.

There were reasons for his refusal, and Fanny resisted the temptation to ask. He seemed desperate.

"I'll never get a job," he said. "People talk behind my back. No telling what else I'm being accused of. No magazine in New York would hire me now. I should never have been so hard on Longfellow. That's at the bottom of this. That and . . ."

"And what?"

He sighed deeply and would not look at her. "It's me, Fanny."

"Why do you say that?"

"I'm my own worst enemy," he said. "Sooner or later I write something too critical or I become argumentative for no reason but that others are so cock-sure of themselves. And I can be bought; I admit it; I'm corrupt. Willis bought my opinion, and I hate myself when I think that I'll write anything for ten dollars."

"You're not corrupt," Fanny said, and she took his hands and made him look her in the eye. "Don't you see? The very fact that you're so hard on your-self proves that you're not corrupt. There's not a writer in America who isn't guilty of the same thing, only their method is different. Do you think for a minute that they see themselves as corrupt? They flatter each other, thinking they're doing a good turn or that they're promoting American literature or helping the booksellers, but they do it for one reason only: to be flattered in return. It's a corrupt system, but only you are bothered by it. That makes you special, don't you see?"

He shook his head and smiled as if he'd heard that before but could put no faith in it. "I can't tell Sissy these things," he said. "I don't know why. Or maybe I do."

"I understand," Fanny said. "Really I do. But you can tell me."

They sat in silence for a moment.

"Why not write to Mr. Chivers?" she said. "Tell him you're ready to start your new magazine. Write the prospectus you were talking about, and send it to him. Let him know you're serious. Shall I write him, too? I could say that everyone in New York is excited about the new magazine."

Edgar seemed to consider the idea as he raked his mustache with his fingers. Fanny thought the gesture made him look weak, but before she could stop him, he dropped his hands to his lap as if giving up. "If only I'd hear from Willis," he said. "That would convince Chivers."

"What do you mean?" she asked.

Swearing Fanny to secrecy, Edgar told her of their plan to pirate work from England.

"But Willis is in Boston," she said. "He's not in England; didn't you know?"

"Boston?"

"He's spending the summer with Louise, his sister; he'll be back in New York in the fall."

Edgar stared at her, open-mouthed; the news seemed a severe blow.

"I have to get back," she said, putting on her bonnet and tying the ribbons.

"Why so soon?" he asked, startled by the suddenness of her movements.

"I have to help Sarah with supper, and I can't leave her alone all afternoon with five children."

"But will I see you again?"

"Does it matter so much?" she said, and stood up.

Edgar stood also. The wrinkle between his eyes had deepened. "Of course it matters."

"You haven't said a word about my letter," she said, "or about your feelings for me."

"Forgive me, Fanny," he begged. "Don't leave. Not just yet."

They sat back down, but Fanny kept her bonnet on. He was nervous now, his hands shaking.

"Your letter," he began, hesitant and refusing to look up, "made me happier than I have ever been. With all that's happened, I think, had I not received it, I would have gone mad. I wanted to come at once, but I had no money. I came as soon as I could."

Wanting more, Fanny waited, her hands in her lap, her bonnet tied.

"Your letter changed everything," he continued, looking at her now. "You haven't been out of my thoughts since I read it. It made me desperate to see you again." He swallowed and looked back down at his hands. He wants to say more, she thought, but perhaps he needs time.

She stood again, reached out, and touched his hair. "I'm in room 32," she said. "Third floor, almost at the end of the hall. Knock on my door at ten. My daughter will be asleep, so be very quiet."

• • •

AFTER SUPPER JOHN rocked in his chair on the porch, staring at Fanny as if he knew she was not telling him everything. She decided she was talking too much. John Locke was her younger brother, charged by their deceased father with responsibility for her modest inheritance. She was grateful for his concern, knowing she was careless in matters of money, but perhaps that resulted from being denied the responsibility for her own affairs. It was a rebelliousness of sorts. Her father had too little faith in women, and John had inherited that notion. She could have hated him for meddling in her life, but she didn't. She loved him too much to resent his dutiful fulfilling of their father's will. It was a man's world, and Fanny accepted that despite thinking it unfair. John loved her, too, but he would not approve of Edgar Poe. Disappointing as that was, it didn't change things.

"And where is he now?" John asked, rocking back and forth, cupping a teacup and saucer on his chest.

"Who?" Fanny asked, then cursed herself for thinking John would fall for such an innocent pretense.

"Mr. Poe, Fanny! Why didn't you invite him for supper?"

"He had other plans," Fanny said. "I don't know. He has to go back tomorrow. John, promise me you won't say anything to Ned when he comes."

"I'll promise if you'll tell me why."

"Because Ned is jealous of my literary friends. He doesn't like them, and he would be upset with me. Please. Promise me."

"I'll say nothing," John said, "if you promise not to get involved in any scandal."

Fanny stood up. "I suppose we should be getting back," she said.

John walked May and Fanny to the hotel while Sarah put the children to bed. Fanny stopped him at the door, not wanting him to come in. She hoped Edgar had better sense than to be waiting in the lobby, but she could not be certain. She kissed John on the cheek and sent him home.

He was not in the lobby, and Fanny and May climbed the stairs to their room. Fanny helped her daughter get undressed and into her nightgown, and she read to her for a while, wondering as she did if May could feel her heart pounding. Soon the child grew sleepy and Fanny pulled the sheet up over her and got out her paper, pen, and ink, as she always did. She could not write, of course; she was too excited. Watching her daughter until she saw evidence of sleep, she stood, went to the washstand, poured water into the bowl, and unbuttoned her dress and chemise to the waist, pulling her arms out of the sleeves so she could wash herself. Then she dried herself with the towel, brushed her teeth, and buttoned her dress. Looking at herself in the mirror, she repinned her hair. That was it. There was no time for more. She sat back down, doused the lamp, and waited.

A few minutes later she heard three light taps on her door and smiled, thinking, ". . . suddenly there came a tapping, / As of some one gently rapping, rapping at my chamber door—" It was the raven.

Fanny cracked the door and saw him there, turned back to check on May, and, satisfied that her daughter was asleep, slipped into the hallway and closed the door behind her. Turning to Edgar, she put her forefinger to her lips.

They embraced, the brief embrace of friends grown closer because of some new shared experience. When they parted, Fanny looked up at him, and in the dim hall light he appeared as he had at Lynchie's that first night she heard him recite: erect, unafraid, cocksure of his gift. The irregularity of his features—one eyebrow higher than the other, his too-long nose, his too-straight, too-serious, too-watchful mouth—made him unhandsome and handsome, both at once. And his eyes, as always, piercing, knowing, captivating, frightening,

"Will you walk with me?" he asked.

Fanny shook her head and smiled. "If May wakes up and I'm not here, she'll be frightened."

He seemed disappointed. They were alone. Gaslight sconces lit the blue floral wallpaper, a cabbage rose pattern. At each end the windows were open, and a light breeze blowing up from the bay inflated lace curtains at one end. Edgar looked up and down the hallway.

"We're quite alone," Fanny said. "If someone comes, we'll hear him on the stairs." They stared at each other for a moment. "I've been thinking about what we talked about in the library," she said. "And I realize that my image of a great writer has been all wrong. None of the others can compare to you—their comfortable lives, their easy ways, the praise they heap on one another. That's why you feel that you don't fit in—because those things hold nothing for you. And those men know that their soft lives sap their vitality. So they are jealous of you. You do easily what they can't do at all."

Skepticism showed in Edgar's eyes. Praise embarrassed him; it seemed he could not accept it just then. Fanny lifted her head, her eyes begging him to kiss her. When he did not, she reached up and touched the corner of his jaw with her fingers and nudged him down to her. They kissed and she lost herself there, lost all awareness, reason, care. Then she took his hands and moved them to the small of her back, drawing them together, and they kissed again, Fanny's knees trembling.

When it was over, she smiled up at him, caressing his cheek. "Whenever you look at me," she said, wanting now to tell him everything, every emotion, every reflection, every affectionate sensation she had felt since they'd met, "your eyes remind me that I've cheated myself, that I've done nothing but compromise all my life. My shame makes me want to turn away from you, but I can't. It would be cowardly to turn away; I won't do it. That's why I want you to be my mentor—because you make me realize that I've written nothing to compare to what I might have written. Marrying Ned would have been just another compromise, and I might have done it, but thankfully I met you, and you reminded me of what I was put on earth to do: to write, to be a great writer. I knew it that first night you recited 'The Raven' at Lynchie's. You looked at me with such intensity that I cringed. I started shaking. I was holding Sissy's hand; she must have noticed."

Edgar's smile ebbed. His eyes dropped to the floor, and Fanny cursed herself for mentioning Sissy. It would make it harder for him to say the things he hadn't said at the Athenæum, the things she needed to hear.

"I had to leave New York," she continued, to erase thoughts of Sissy, "and at the same time I didn't want to leave. And thinking you hated me for the things I said made it more difficult, but I had to tell you. I wanted you to know what people were saying so you could stop it. I told you because I care for you, and because I was furious that someone would want to hurt you."

"Why did you leave?"

Fanny searched his eyes for an instant. "Didn't my letter explain?"

"It explained half of it." He paused, and Fanny guessed he meant the Ned Thomas half.

"But don't think I ran away from you," she said, alarm in her eyes. "I'm coming back. I'm coming back in August, and I want you waiting at the wharf for me. And we can be together as often as you like."

She stared at him, starving for some expression, some word. She sensed it, and he had said that her letter had made him happy—happier than he had ever been—but she wanted more, some pledge, anything to keep her going during another month of separation.

"What do you think when you kiss me?" she asked, begging him now.

He looked away as if searching his mind. Then he smiled that broad, loss-of-restraint smile with which he was so stingy, and turning back to her, he shook his head. "I don't think I think at all."

It was the answer she wanted, and she would be satisfied with that alone and not ask for more. She could wait. For an hour more they talked, embraced, kissed. Fanny could have stood there all night. When someone came up the stairs, they separated to a discreet distance, then embraced as soon as they were alone again. Three times she looked in on May. They talked about missing each other and her return to New York in August when they would see each other often, every night if he wished. Fanny could not wait to be back.

Toward midnight the porter came up to turn down the jets. It was then Fanny told him that she would be unable to see him the next day except perhaps at breakfast, and if they saw each other then, they should not speak. As it was Independence Day, she and May would be spending the holiday with the Lockes.

"At breakfast," she said, after insisting for the third time that she must go to bed, "when our eyes meet, you must smile for me. Don't be morose; I want the vision of a smile to last me until I see you again."

Edgar seemed happier, life and hope in his eyes. After a final kiss she opened her door enough to squeeze in and left him standing in the hall. Once inside, in the dark, a wave of desire came over her again, and she leaned back against the door, crushed that it was over. She grabbed for the knob and peered into the corridor, hoping to find him there—but he was gone.

How long did they stand there kissing and talking? Two hours perhaps. Yet that time filled acres of Fanny's memory. She could recall the exact shape of one particular petal in the pattern of the wallpaper. She could see the billowing white lace curtains in the window at the end of the hallway. She could see the yellow flicker of the jets in the wall sconces and their orange and green shadows. She could smell the fabric of his lapel. How many poems would she write about this night? There was no law saying she could only write two or twelve or seventeen, and she resolved to write as many poems about this night as she wanted.

CHAPTER 15

 ## Eddy

The Broadway Journal   Saturday, July 5, 1845

OUR NEW VOLUME

TO THE PUBLIC.—The suspension of *The Broadway Journal* for one week, has been occasioned by the necessity for some arrangements in which the public has no interest, but which, beyond doubt, will give increased Value and Efficiency to the paper.

Henceforth the editorial conduct of *The Broadway Journal* shall be under the Sole Charge of

Edgar A. Poe

Editor & Proprietor

EDDY MISSED SEEING Fanny at breakfast. He had walked the streets of Providence until dawn. Four or five times he lost his way but kept going, not caring that he was lost, thinking only of her. Once, in the darkness, he saw a woman dressed in white and walking in a garden. He imagined it was Fanny and composed lines of a poem describing her in a garden in the middle of a summer night. Worn out, he overslept and nearly missed the ferry. From the deck he could hear the Independence Day celebrations starting up, a cacophony of musical exercises as the members of a band tuned their instruments. Somewhere firecrackers popped. By mid-afternoon the crowds had gathered, and passengers waved to people lining the harbor as the ferry pulled away from the dock and steamed out into Narragansett Bay.

Eddy tried to doze, sitting on a deck bench, but Fanny flitted in and out of his thoughts like a butterfly, and each time she landed there, he woke up, jolted by the memory of kissing her. Then he closed his eyes again and pictured her girlish figure, her gray eyes, her dark brown hair that smelled of soap and lemon. Again and again he recalled her kisses and the thrill of touching her through the fabric of her dress—the muscles of her back, her ribs, her shoulder blades, and the ridges of her spine. He had not touched her breasts, and now he imagined the sensation, intoxicated by it. He kept reminding himself that she had said her relationship with Ned Thomas was over. She had pledged herself to Eddy as surely as if she'd said so.

That night he could not sleep in the main cabin. Strewn with mattresses and sleeping bodies, it was stiflingly hot. Though exhausted, he paced the deck, savoring again every detail of the night before. In the morning there was fog in Long Island Sound, and he stood at the rail feeling the cool mist on his face, still reveling in his good fortune. He marveled at how bold Fanny had been, how unashamed of her emotions, and how exciting it had been to kiss a woman like that. He might never have kissed her had she not made the first move, hooking his jaw with her fingers and pulling him toward her. She was brave, brave and seductive.

By late morning the sun burned off the fog and with it Eddy's dreams of love. The bright sunshine illuminated a growing sense of guilt, and the closer the ferry came to New York, the more he thought of Sissy. By the time they landed, he felt dread.

Walking up Whitehall Street, his thoughts turned to Willis's being in Boston, not England. The news was devastating. Work from England had been the leverage he needed to find a new position. He had imagined poems by Tennyson, Hood, Carlyle, and others. He had imagined a serialized, chapter-by-chapter novel by Dickens that could sell magazines for months into the future. But now what? How would he live? Where would he go? Would he even be in New York in August when Fanny returned? Willis had done more than let him down, beginning with the Little Longfellow War that had made Eddy unpopular. Willis had duped him, but Eddy couldn't fault him. Mary's death had changed everything. It was bad luck, and indeed, bad luck seemed to dog him.

On the way home he walked through the terminal at City Hall Park to buy a copy of the *Broadway Journal*. He could find none for sale. Rushing to the office, he found it locked, no sign of Briggs. As it was getting late, he went on home, wondering what could have happened.

Sissy and Muddy were happy to see him. He was just in time for supper, and as they went down, Sissy asked all about Fanny. How did she look? Did she favor her brother? When was she coming back? Eddy could not avoid the subject, though he wanted to. In nine years of marriage, he had never kissed another woman. He avoided Sissy's eyes and deflected her questions with the news about the *Broadway Journal,* suggesting that Briggs had been unable to meet the deadline without him. His bragging fell flat. There were questions in Muddy's eyes, questions asking how they would pay room and board that had been due on the first of the month. They were late again.

When they went back upstairs, he went through the mail and found letters from Briggs and Ned Thomas. Thomas wrote to say that he had seen the person with whom the forgery charge originated—it was Park Benjamin. He said that Benjamin repudiated it *"in toto"*—that was his exact phrase—and claimed to have misunderstood some word spoken. Eddy suspected Thomas of lying and wondered if English had scared him off, but Thomas apologized, admitted the charge was groundless, and promised to tell Fanny very soon. He also said he was leaving the city, and Eddy wondered if he was on his way to Providence. Feeling a rush of jealousy, he realized that Thomas might be with Fanny at that very moment.

He passed the letter to Muddy, who read parts of it out loud to Sissy. Muddy smiled proudly, clasping the letter to her bosom as if Eddy had been pardoned from a death sentence.

As Eddy began reading Briggs's letter, he rose from his chair and walked to the window. The *Broadway Journal,* it began, had ceased to exist,

> . . . as you refuse to withdraw. Therefore, consider our partnership dissolved. Or, if you so choose, you may purchase my interest for two hundred dollars.

> Charles Francis Briggs

No doubt Briggs would refuse to pay him what he was due for the last two June issues—eighteen columns. And he had supplied another twelve columns for the aborted issue of July 5. Thirty dollars in all. On the other hand, if he could raise a few hundred dollars, he could be rid of Briggs and have enough money to keep the magazine afloat—his magazine—unencumbered by Briggs's politics. Edgar Poe, editor. Sole editor. Chivers was the obvious choice, but there might be others. His mind raced from option to option as he composed the announcement in his head. He would have to publish an issue that next week, missing two in a row could be fatal, but he could cobble together enough to fill sixteen pages.

He turned to Muddy, who was sewing in her chair beside the fireplace, and called Sissy from the bedroom. When she appeared, he explained what had happened or at least the gist of it. He didn't say that he was broke or that he would not be receiving his back pay. He said that Briggs was offering to sell his half of the magazine and that he was certain he could raise the money to buy it plus the seed money needed to keep it going.

"Don't you see," he said. "Finally I will have my own magazine." He would have engraved illustrations, expand to thirty-two pages, raise subscription prices. He cited *Graham's* and *Godey's,* claiming he would surpass them both. At present it would be too risky to change the name, but in time he would, and he would call it *The Stylus,* and it would be the finest literary journal in America.

Sissy listened, then turned to look at her mother, who seemed suddenly downcast.

"Oh, Eddy. Eddy," Muddy said. "We can't even pay the rent."

Eddy felt rage rush to his forehead. "It is the opportunity of a lifetime," he shouted, "and you want to talk about the *rent*? Don't you understand anything? Well, don't support me, then; I don't care."

He glared at them. Muddy dropped her gaze to the floor, but Sissy would not look away. She stared at him until he had to turn away, shamed by the memory of Providence.

"It's time to go to bed," he said at last. "I've got work to do."

"You won't go out, will you?" Muddy pleaded.

"I have work to do," he repeated. Reluctantly, Sissy and Muddy retired to their room.

EDDY SPENT THAT NIGHT and the whole weekend writing letters. There were letters to potential investors like Chivers and to those who might lend him the money to get started. He even wrote Neilson Poe and John Allan's widow. And there were letters to those who might serve as subscription agents: John Tomlin in Tennessee, Redding in Boston, Colon in Philadelphia, Hart in Charleston, Tom Pease in New Haven, George Jones in Albany, Peter Cooke in Hartford, J. C. Morgan in New Orleans. And he wrote to Charles Briggs to say he accepted his offer. He asked for a week to raise the money, saying he would oversee the production of an issue for the 12th and that there was no need for Briggs to return to the office but for his personal effects.

He abstained from drink, and though he'd been sober for a week, he did not sleep with Sissy. She might have allowed it, but even to broach the subject in light of what had happened in Providence seemed in one way sordid and in another a repudiation of Fanny, and Eddy could not do that. He could hate himself; he could suffer the guilt; but he could not turn his back on the one happy thing in his life. He refused to dwell on the possibility that he might never sleep with Sissy again.

He took time away from business long enough to compose a long letter to Fanny, telling her that she had been right in saying things would work out. She must be clairvoyant, he told her; no doubt she had charmed him, changed his luck. In truth Eddy had taken her words as nothing more than a woman's sympathetic consolation. He had not even believed that she believed what she said. He thought about asking her for money, but decided against it. Instead he asked her for submissions, praising her work and saying her poems would have inestimable value, though he stopped short of offering to pay her. Her poems would be as good as a loan.

He was not alone in writing Fanny. Sissy wrote her, too. Eddy could not object, of course, and he suspected Fanny would write her back. He went along with this charade, nervous of its implications and disconcerted by the memory of walking lovesick through the dark streets of Providence.

On the Monday after his return, he went to English's office. It was a fine day. Walking down Broadway, he decided New York was not such a bad place when things were going well. The bustle, which could be so irritating, suddenly energized him. He had kept the vow he made on Mount Tom, and he would continue to keep it. All it took was momentum, and momentum was on his side.

"Where have you been?" English asked as Eddy walked through the door.

"Away," he said. "I need to borrow twenty-five dollars."

"What for?"

"To pay Briggs. I'm buying him out and taking over the *Broadway Journal*. I'll pay you back inside two months."

"I was wondering what happened," English said. "Word on the street is that Briggs's new partners refused to put up the money. Maybe you scared them off. Did you ever hear from Ned Thomas? If it's money you need, that's where you'll find it."

"That's all over," Eddy replied. "I had a letter from him. He admitted it was a lie and apologized."

"Then deny you got the letter," English said. "You're a damn fool if you don't sue."

"Will you stop with that," Eddy snapped, irked by English's ridiculous persistence. "You're just looking for a fee to keep this stupid magazine afloat."

English stood, his chair falling back against the bookcase. "Then to hell with you," he said. "Get out of my office!"

Papers cluttered English's desk, so Eddy reached down to grab up a handful, intending to throw them, and knocked over the inkwell.

English's eyes flamed. He picked up the inkwell, then came around his desk to shove Eddy toward the door, smearing ink on Eddy's white shirt. Eddy shoved back and retreated toward the door, but English kept coming at him, his fists balled, his walrus mustache flaring. Eddy turned to flee, and as he did, English kicked him into the hall, then slammed the door and locked it.

Eddy stood on the landing, breathing hard and staring at the closed door. He heard English pick up his chair and set it back in place; then papers rattled. Eddy collected himself, thinking it would be just like English to keep the forgery rumor alive, bruiting it about just to get back at him. He needed a drink. The sudden craving scared him. It was palpable and sickening; fear swelled in his jugular. He swallowed hard, trying to choke it back down, but the urge remained. He descended the stairs, determined to resist.

Following a plan he had made over the weekend to spend the day raising the necessary funds, he made the rounds. He borrowed fifty dollars from Horace Greeley and another fifty from Fitz-Green Halleck; he borrowed twenty-five from Rufus Wilmot Griswold, who happened to be in town, and fifty from Elizabeth Ellet. She had been a long shot, but Eddy guessed she would be flattered by the request, and she seemed to be. He even asked her for submissions, all the while dreading the thought that he would have to publish her poems. Standing in her doorway on Broome Street, she batted her eyes so much that it made Eddy blink. He was scraping the bottom of the barrel. He begged pressing business and hurried away.

He thought of writing to Willis for money, thinking Willis might feel an obligation in light of their aborted pirating scheme and Eddy's battle scars from the Little Longfellow War, but he had no address and was reluctant to go to General Morris for it. He'd get it from Fanny when she came in August.

Certain that Chivers would come through, Eddy sent a note by courier to Briggs with a draft for a hundred dollars, saying he would pay another seventy-five in six months and that the missing twenty-five was due Eddy for work submitted in June.

On Tuesday he turned his attention to preparing a new issue. He went to the *Broadway Journal* office and started in on the mess. He opened the windows and sifted through the papers on Briggs's desk, planning to use whatever Briggs had prepared for the canceled issue of the week before, and he decided to reprint a review of his *Tales* that Evert Duyckinck had written for the July 5 *Morning News,* since it was very favorable and would save Eddy the trouble of puffing his own work. Beyond that, he'd have to lean on his old stuff again.

He went to Sandy's for lunch. When he ordered only coffee, Sandy smiled at him. One or two regulars greeted him, and Eddy chatted with them, trying not to think that they might be wondering why he wasn't drinking.

Back at the office, he went through Briggs's papers again and threw them in the trash. After emptying the drawers of Briggs's desk, he shoved it into a corner and moved his own desk to the window. Desperate for a drink and reasoning that he could begin fresh the next morning when he would be in better spirits, he decided to go back to Sandy's. He would have one glass of wine to calm his nerves, then go home. He locked the office, descended the stairs, and turned down Nassau, but at the corner of Ann Street, just a half block from Sandy's, he stopped. Standing in the middle of the street, he stared at the paving stones, shaking, his fists clenched, his heart pounding. He heard a door slam shut and turned to his right to see General Morris at the entrance of the *Mirror* office. Morris doffed his hat. Eddy straightened; he wore no hat, so he nodded, and the general walked away in the opposite direction toward Park Row. Eddy watched him go, swallowed, then returned to his office and worked until midnight.

On the 14th Briggs accepted his offer. Eddy now owned a magazine, though he was leveraged to the gills.

His twelve-hour days under Briggs turned into sixteen-hour days without him, and this not counting nights at the theater. Much was happening there.

He reviewed the dancing of Mademoiselle Desjardins at Castle Garden, a French troupe at the Park, and Anna Cora Mowatt, the author of *Fashion,* who had reappeared as a leading lady in the role of Pauline in *The Lady of Lyons.* The result was a sensation. Eddy realized now that acclaim for *Fashion* had eclipsed his "Raven." After that, he had no longer been the talk of the town. New Yorkers had someone new to marvel at. It was a bold move for a woman of Mowatt's reputation, and he wrote an article about the public's unfair bias toward actors and actresses. It was an opportunity to say more about his mother and his mother's mother, both actresses, and to juxtapose them alongside Mowatt, who was elevating New York theater with her presence. He wrote that his mother had played Ophelia in *Hamlet,* Cordelia in *King Lear,* Juliet in *Romeo and Juliet,* and won accolades for them all.

He led the August 2 issue with a review of Tom Chivers's new collection of poems, out from Edward Jenkins & Co. As Chivers had not yet responded to his appeals for money, Eddy heaped on praise, hoping the review would yield dividends. He claimed Chivers's verse belonged to the highest echelon, and—miracle of miracles—there was not a trace of plagiarism, not a hint of Byron, Shelley, Wordsworth, or Coleridge. It was a *rara avis,* and he gave Chivers credit for passion without decrying the need for passion.

All this he did and begged for work from others. By early August he had engaged agents in nine cities; still, subscriptions eked up at a snail's pace. He could not top two thousand in spite of his barrage of letters, the long days, and abstemious behavior. He had gone five weeks without a drink.

He had letters from Fanny three or four times a week, as often as not including a poem. The poems were not to be published, she warned, and he would not have published them anyway. They were too intimate. And they were so like Fanny—hurried, touches of brilliance, but needing polish. As her mentor, he wrote back, begging her to revise, but it seemed she had no patience for the task. She was always too excited about the new poem she was composing to go back and perfect an old one. Eddy saved her letters, tied them in a bundle, and put them in the bureau drawer. Muddy knew they were there and so did Sissy. His not hiding them, he reasoned, was proof that he had nothing to hide, and he rationalized that such was true.

"You have *another* letter from Mrs. Osgood," Muddy would say, and Eddy would glance at Sissy to see if she took notice, but she never seemed to care, never seemed angry or hurt. She had had one letter from Fanny, chatty and endearing, and Sissy hadn't written her back. Sissy knows, Eddy thought, but it was not something they would ever talk about, and he asked himself if he loved Fanny and if Sissy's knowing would make any difference. It would to Muddy. With menace in her eyes, she stared at him as he set Fanny's letters aside with others to be opened at the office.

Later, as he put the letter with the others in the bureau drawer, he would tell them Fanny's news; that was all. But mostly she wrote of missing him and their night together in Providence. It became Eddy's routine to pause from his work at seven each evening to reread Fanny's letter and compose his response. This became his favorite time of the day. He had no time to compose poems; instead he wrote letters telling her about his day and his most current frustrations. After a page or two of this, he inevitably turned the subject to her and how her letters made the pressures of the *Broadway Journal* bearable. Amazed by how many ways he could find to say essentially the same thing, he tried to vary the structure, but almost always it came down to the same message: "Hurry back; life is dreadful without you."

On the first day of August he had a letter informing him of her return. He was not to meet her at the ferry, she instructed. She would be leaving the children in Providence, she said, and in New York she'd be staying with John and Edith Bartlett, who planned to collect her at the ferry. She demanded that he call at the Bartletts on the night of her arrival, saying she could not go one day longer without seeing him.

On the day—Monday, August 4—eager and uneasy, he sat at his desk at the office, unable to concentrate. He took his watch from his pocket, the watch Fanny had given him; it was half past four. The ferry would be docking soon, and he pictured Fanny standing at the rail, one hand on her bonnet to keep it from flying off, her leather portmanteau sitting on the deck beside her. She would be wearing gloves and carrying a parasol. Yes, he loved her, he thought, as if his mental image of her confirmed it, and the thrill of knowing that she was little more than a mile from where he sat at that moment made him know that in the end desire would trump guilt. It shamed him to admit it, but he could not deny it.

He was not expected at the Bartletts' until nine—nearly five hours. He would go home, eat supper, and put on a clean shirt, saying he was going to the theater, and in the morning he would tell Sissy and Muddy that he had seen Fanny, that she was back. That was his plan. It was a lie, a small one, he reasoned, but still a lie. And later? How would he deal with later? More evasion; more lies. He stood, walked to the window, and stared up at gathering clouds, wondering if he would hate himself for this, wondering if the day would come when living with it would be unbearable. It no longer mattered, of course. Whatever price he'd pay, she would have been worth it. There might be regret, there might even be suffering, but those things couldn't stop him. Resigned to this, he straightened his papers, locked the office, and walked home.

Muddy thought it strange that he smelled of lavender and said so. Oddly, Sissy came to his defense, and Eddy wondered if she had read the letters. Did she know?

At nine o'clock he knocked on the Bartletts' front door. An evening thundershower had blown through Manhattan, so the umbrellas were out on Broadway, and the cobbles glistened with the last light of evening and reflection of the streetlamps. John Russell Bartlett, his wife, and Fanny were all in the parlor when a serving girl ushered Eddy in. The Bartletts doted on Fanny; she had often been their house guest. She sat with Mrs. Bartlett on a blue velvet sofa beneath a tall, gilt-framed mirror; an elaborate gilt and crystal chandelier hung from the ceiling. Mr. Bartlett stood with his brandy and cigar at the end of the room, in front of a window that looked down on Broadway. The drapes were open and the lamps were lit. A clock ticked. It seemed that they had just finished a formal supper, as both women were dressed in evening gowns, and John Bartlett wore a white tie and waistcoat.

Fanny's eyes widened with surprise at the sight of him. He guessed it was his having no mustache—he had shaved it—and the sideburns he was cultivating. She wore blue satin, her skin had the glow of sun, and seeing her made Eddy so nervous with excitement, he could hardly meet her gaze.

He presented Edith Bartlett with a personally inscribed copy of his *Tales* and the latest number of the *Broadway Journal*. He had met the Bartletts at Lynchie's, but knew them only slightly, and he found John Bartlett's presence intimidating. There followed an awkward silence once Eddy was seated and took his first sip of tea, having declined both brandy and cigar.

"Edith, you have not heard Edgar recite his 'Raven,'" Fanny said, turning to Eddy and smiling with pride. "You must promise them, Edgar. He is more amazing than anything at Barnum's or Castle Garden."

"It would be my pleasure," Eddy said, promising to recite it whenever they wished, and he told them about having recently judged a poetry contest at Rutgers Female Institute. "I do believe women will soon outdo us men when it comes to writing poetry. Their compositions were quite good. I read the winning one, by a Miss Louise Hunter. She is a great admirer of your poetry, Fanny; she told me she has worshiped you since childhood. And she was thrilled to have me read her poem, saying it sounded much better when I did it, so I urged her to practice reading aloud in front of a mirror."

"And do you do that, Poe?" John Bartlett asked.

Eddy smiled and blushed, which amused them all.

"Well, I know I do," Fanny said, as if coming to his defense.

They talked about Fanny's voyage from Providence; it had been delayed by low tide as the ferry approached Hellgate. They talked about the widening of Broadway that was imposing on the front stoops of some of the downtown mansions and about the dog days of summer, unanimously agreeing that the month of August should be spent in Saratoga Springs instead of New York City.

At length John Bartlett excused himself, said good night, and went upstairs. Edith remained and asked Eddy about his work, to which he explained his long hours and the lack of time to write anything other than magazine copy. All the while Fanny stared at him, seeming to burst with pride.

At ten-thirty Edith retired, inviting Eddy to return as often as he liked. He stood and bid her good night, and when she was gone, Fanny motioned him to the sofa beside her and took his hand. "Did you miss me" she asked, "as much as I missed you?

"Of course," he said, "but I felt your magic. The forgery thing disappeared and then Briggs disappeared. You said things would work out, and they did, but I need a little more magic now. I've not heard from Chivers; I think he's abandoned me. If only I could afford to pay for submissions, but I can't. I've never worked harder. Honestly, Fanny, I don't know how long I can keep this up. I'm running the *Broadway Journal* on a boot string. Three thousand subscribers would get me in the clear, but I'm woefully short of that."

"I'll write something for you," Fanny said, "and urge my friends to also. Be patient; it will end well. I have a story coming out in *Graham's*. It's called 'Ida

Grey? You used Grey as a pen name, remember? That's why I chose it. I would have sent it to you, but I couldn't. It's about us, you see."

They were silent for a while. Eddy hadn't wanted to complain, but his problems were too much on his mind. Despite his elation at seeing Fanny, he could feel a wave of disaster building.

"Sam is back," Fanny said, changing the subject and looking down at their clasped hands, caressing Eddy's. "I need to talk to him. That's one reason I came back, but not the main reason. You're the main reason." She looked back at him, a touch of sadness in her eyes. "You have complicated my life, Mr. Poe, but I forgive you," and she smiled again. "I want Sam to paint you. I want a portrait of you, and I like your new whiskers." She reached up and touched the short whiskers that ran along the line of his jaw, ending just short of his chin. "They are very *distingué*," she said. "Will you sit for him? It will only take a day or two."

Eddy stared at her in disbelief. He did not want to meet Sam Osgood. And where would Fanny hang a portrait of him?

"And I want you to escort me to Lynchie's Saturday night," she said. "We will all go. You can meet us here, and we will ride together. And you can recite 'The Raven' for Edith. I'll arrange everything with Anne."

He agreed to this, remembering that Ned Thomas had been her escort last time.

"Ned came to Providence," Fanny said as if she'd read his mind. "He was very put out with me for the forgery muddle. I'm glad it's over. Don't worry; nothing has changed. He doesn't know you came to Providence, but he does know that we are friends. I told him."

She sighed, seeming a little sad again.

"Tell me you love me, Edgar," and she peered into his eyes. "I need to hear you say it."

He looked down at their clasped hands. "I love you, Fanny," he said, but he could not bear her gaze just then. He wanted to tell her how much, and how much he needed her, too, but it was so hard to say.

They sat in silence for a few moments.

"I'm afraid it's time to leave," she said, at last.

They stood and faced each other. There seemed to be an invitation in Fanny's eyes, but the room was lit and the curtains were opened to the street and there must have been a servant nearby who would come in and douse the chandelier once he was gone. Eddy felt uneasy, but Fanny didn't budge, so he leaned down and kissed her on the mouth, and she put her arms around him and kissed him hard and long, refusing to let go. Afterward, she took him by the hand and led him to the door.

HE SAW HER AGAIN at the Bartletts' on Wednesday. On Thursday night they sat together at the Park Theater for the performance of a French opera, *La Muette de Portici,* and the following Saturday he met her at the Bartletts' and the four of them drove to Anne Lynch's party. Dunn English was there. Eddy caught his eye as they entered; upon seeing him with Fanny, English smiled as if he suspected something about them. The two men had not met since their altercation a month earlier, and Eddy decided to apologize. Perhaps he should ask for something of English's to publish in the *Broadway Journal,* and convenient for this purpose, English recited a poem that evening. Eddy praised it and asked for a copy.

He recited his "Raven" for Edith Bartlett. Fanny sat on a footstool near where Eddy stood in front of the fireplace. As he approached the ending, he looked down to see her eyes fixed on him, and then he noticed Dunn English staring at her, seeming to be disgusted by the whole display. Distracted by this, Eddy's ending was weaker than usual.

Fanny's story, "Ida Grey," appeared in *Graham's,* but Eddy couldn't be cross with her despite her transparent characters. Sitting together at Palmo's on the 13th for a performance of *The Four Sisters,* he chided her good-naturedly, then professed disbelief that the heroine of her story, Ida Grey—Fanny in disguise—would enter a nunnery because she could not marry her poet lover. It occurred to Eddy that others might see through the fiction just as he did, but he didn't care. Being with Fanny was all in the world that mattered now. He wrote to her every day, delivering the letters himself, and she did the same, letters and poems, and each new one was as eagerly awaited as the last. In his letters, when referring to the kisses of the night before, he described details that resonated in his memory: the way she was dressed, the softness of her lips, her delicate shoulders which he had caressed with his fingers one night when she wore a low-cut dress. He described how her eyes begged him to kiss her and how she refused to pull away from his kisses as if kissing could replace breathing, and he described her kisses as life-giving. And he would joke with her, pleading with her to find ways to convince the Bartletts to retire earlier so they would have more time alone. These letters often consumed three or four pages, and as often as not, he would have to hurry to finish in time to deliver them to her. As he watched the hot wax drip to form the seal, he could not help but think that if love letters were stories, he would be a wealthy man.

They didn't miss a single Saturday night at Lynchie's for that month, and at the end of each evening together, they kissed, long, parting kisses in the Bartletts' front parlor, kisses that provided both an outlet and a lid for their emotions. Had Fanny been staying at the hotel, there might have been more, and that thought occurred to Eddy, but he dismissed it, contenting himself with the kisses. It was as if they could not kiss enough.

On the rare nights on which he did not see her, he worked late, and for the entire month of August, he saw Sissy and Muddy only when he dressed in the mornings.

ON THE 22ND AND 23RD, he sat for a portrait by Sam Osgood. Fanny had insisted, overruling Eddy's protests and delays. They met in the Astor lobby at noon on the Friday, after Eddy had put to bed the latest issue of the *Broadway Journal,* and they took the horsecar to Osgood's studio. He was civil but aloof. Taller than Eddy and gaunt, he was Eddy's age but looked older. Graying, he had a wild and haggard look about his eyes. His studio was on the top floor of what had once been a warehouse. The room was large and, with the skylight propped open, sunny and filled with canvases leaning in stacks against the walls. Landscapes hung in haphazard arrangement. Osgood went straight to work. Shafts of dust-filled sunlight streamed in, lighting the artist's canvas and Fanny, who sat beside Osgood as he painted. The sun fell across their shoulders and onto Eddy's feet, while the rest of him was in shadow.

It appeared that Osgood was dutifully, even reluctantly, obliging Fanny, but she didn't behave as if she cared that she might be putting him out. She sat with her arms crossed and talked nonstop, telling Osgood what she wanted. He obeyed without comment.

"His eyes are hazel, Sam," she said, speaking as if Eddy weren't there. "But make them dark and give them highlight. I want them to flash the way they do when he recites. Oh, you should hear him."

Osgood came around his easel, took hold of Eddy's shoulders, and turned them slightly.

"Did you know Sam painted Henry Clay and John Calhoun?" she asked

Eddy, looking at Osgood with pride in her eyes. "He's the best portrait artist in New York, aren't you, Sam?"

Osgood said nothing. He worked rapidly. Eddy guessed he wanted to be done with this as soon as possible; he would make no money out of it. But Fanny was oblivious to Osgood's being ill at ease; it was as if she punished him still, and the tension was palpable. Eddy supposed it was guilt. He had even heard the name of Osgood's lover, Elizabeth Newcomb, from Boston. Dunn English had told him that the affair had caused the breakup of their marriage. Osgood had been in exile ever since, and Fanny's presence was probably an unwelcome reminder.

Eddy could not help but see himself in Sam Osgood—living alone, living with the shame of infidelity, an outcast.

Fanny left them, finally, and Eddy was relieved when she was gone. Thereafter the only sounds were of brushstrokes on the canvas and the clinking of a glass jar that held turpentine. Osgood would look at parts of Eddy as if he were a plate of fruit. Whenever he did that, Eddy tried to look him in the eye, tried to guess whether Osgood knew that he had kissed his wife, but Osgood never said a word, never offered him anything to drink, and when he finished, he covered the portrait and refused to let Eddy see. It was not done, he said.

When they parted later that night, Fanny handed Eddy a poem and told him to publish it in the next issue of the *Broadway Journal,* saying she would explain later. Entitled "Slander," its implications alarmed him.

He called on her again Monday night at the Bartletts', and late in the evening, as soon as they were alone, Eddy sat down beside her on the sofa and pulled the manuscript from his pocket.

"Fanny, I can't publish this," he said.

"Of course you can," she said. Her voice was adamant. "I want you to lead with it."

In disbelief he glanced back at the manuscript, scanning again the first stanza.

> A whisper woke the air—
> A soft light tone and low,
> Yet barbed with shame and woe;—
> Now, might it only perish there!
> Nor farther go.

Fanny stood and walked to the window, turned, and leaned back against the sill. "Lynchie has been preaching to me for weeks. I suppose I should have listened. Edith knows, too, of course, though she's a dear and says nothing. At any rate, someone is spreading rumors; I don't know who; we should have seen them coming."

"English," Eddy said, incensed by the thought of English's walrus mustache. "I'll go see him."

"Don't. It will only make it worse."

Eddy brandished the manuscript. "But this will make it worse, too. There's no reason to publicize the fact that people are talking about us."

"Publish it," Fanny snapped. "I demand that you publish it. I never asked for a cent for all the poems I sent to you. You owe me this. Or is it that you don't want Sissy to see it?"

Certainly he didn't.

"Talk to me, Edgar. Tell me what to do." She laughed. "I've stayed a week longer than I planned. My children are wondering where their mother is. My brother is furious. The Bartletts should be charging me room and board. What are we going to do?"

Eddy had no answers, had never even sought answers except in some vague, unthinkable way that had to do with Sissy's death. He would never speak such a thing; he hated himself for even having that thought in his head, but it was there. He could not purge it.

Fanny turned and looked out the window, exhaling a sigh of resignation. Or was it exasperation? And Eddy could only gaze into space, dreading what was coming. The clock chimed the half hour, ten-thirty, the time he normally left.

"I'm going to Providence," she said, without turning back to him. "I'm going for good."

Then this how it will end, Eddy thought; Providence might as well be Patagonia.

She turned around. "Have you nothing to say?"

What could he say? Don't? I'll be devastated if you leave? He said nothing.

"I've been back in New York for three weeks and in that time I've seen Ned once. It was awkward. He came here the night after I arrived, the night after you came. I was sitting just where you are now; the Bartletts had gone to bed.

It's not Ned's style to kneel and propose, but I thought that's what he intended, and so I stopped him. He said, 'I'm here to ask you to marry me, Fanny.'" She smiled and shook her head. "I said I couldn't, and I can't. How could I lie in bed with another man wishing he were you? He demanded to know why, and I told him—I told him I was in love with someone else. 'Poe,' he said; he knew it was you. You should have heard the way he shouted your name; I was afraid he'd wake the Bartletts. He preached to me for an hour—said I had deceived and betrayed him. I didn't knowingly deceive him. How was I to know that I would fall in love with you? I can't control my heart and wouldn't want to if I could. It's the truest part of me. It's the only part of me that's not . . ." She paused and looked back at Eddy.

"He was so angry," she continued. "Called me a fool. I haven't seen or heard from him since. My brother thought I came to New York to settle things with Sam and become engaged to Ned. He knows now that I turned Ned down. I wrote to tell him, and I'm afraid he's furious with me. I did come to see Sam, too, but not necessarily to settle things. I thought he might help and that with his help we might be able to stay in New York. He wants to be near the girls, but he can't afford his life and ours, too. I had hoped perhaps he could, but in truth I thought it was hopeless before I ever left Providence. Lily and May have to go to school; I can't afford to live here. Anyway my brother wouldn't allow it, and unfortunately, he holds my purse strings. I prefer Providence to Albany. Those are my choices, unless, of course, you have a better idea."

She paused again, perhaps hoping Eddy would say something.

"If only you were rich, Edgar," she said, when he did not, "but I don't care that you're not. I suppose I knew this would happen, but I didn't want to think it; all I wanted was to come to New York to see you—not Ned, not Sam. Just two weeks with you; that's all I could think about."

As she spoke, all the implications of what she said fell like lead. For an instant Eddy had a vision of his life without Fanny, and it was bleak: Sissy's illness, the failing magazine, the inability to write, drab boardinghouse rooms, debts. The debts would crush him; he could never repay the debts. The only bright spot was an invitation he had received just that day, wonderful news that he had planned to share with Fanny that very night, an invitation to deliver a new poem before the Boston Lyceum. They would pay him fifty dollars. It had thrilled him—Boston! His first book of poems had been published in Boston. He had been born in Boston, yet he had treated Longfellow dreadfully. It would be an opportunity to redeem himself, and he had thought to take Fanny with him when he went. More fantasy than plan, he had imagined being alone in the hotel with her. He had imagined making love to her there.

"When do you leave?" he asked.

The question made Fanny smile, and she rose from the window sill. From the table next to the sofa she picked up a porcelain figurine of a girl dressed in pink cradling a lamb in her arms, and she studied it. "We have our letters," she said, and turned to look at him. "Your letters mean the world to me. They will have to do."

"I need you, Fanny."

"Yes," she said, and with her finger she wiped dust from the figurine, then set it back on the side table. "We have that too."

IN THE MORNING Eddy was already waiting at the dock when Edith Bartlett and Fanny arrived in an open carriage. Though not surprised, he was disappointed to see Edith; her presence would mean he could not kiss Fanny good-bye. There was some confusion about the trunks and getting them aboard, and as Fanny did not want them lost, she almost hurried to board, rushing her adieus. She pressed a letter into his hand as she took her first step up the gangplank.

"Write me tonight," she said, and smiled at him. Her smile contained a sadness that was reassuring.

Then she was gone, and Eddy stood beside Edith looking up at the rail, thinking Fanny would reappear and that they would wave to each other; but she didn't reappear, and the workers threw the dock lines aboard and the ferry steamed out into the bay.

Edith turned to Eddy. "You must come for a visit soon. You're always welcomed."

Eddy thanked her and turned to walk up Fulton Street. Opening Fanny's letter as he walked, he found it contained another poem and a note saying he must publish it in the issue that followed the one that contained "Slander." Reading it, he felt a wave of despair. In predictable, defiant Fanny fashion, the poem provided a postscript to the rumors that had chased her away.

I know a noble heart that beats
　　For one it loves how wildly well!
I only know for *whom* it beats;
　　But I must never tell—
　　　　Never tell!

Eddy considered what had gone unsaid—what must go unsaid: that Fanny was going into exile, entering a nunnery, as she had put it in her story in *Graham's*. And what then? Would she wait for him, wait until Sissy died? He could not wish Sissy dead, and he closed his eyes and shook his head as if trying to rid his mind of the idea.

Just after Sissy's accident in Philadelphia, when Eddy and Muddy feared they would lose her, Eddy wrote a story for her. Lying on the sickbed, coughing, sweating, almost breathless, Sissy had insisted that he must marry again. To stop her worrying and bring her some peace, he wrote a fairy tale, "Eleonora." He didn't tell her it was for her; he maintained that it was just a story, but Sissy knew—he had conceived the fairy tale couple as cousins; he had even included Muddy. After Eleonora died, the protagonist remarried a maiden in service to the King of the Valley of the Many-Colored Grass, but he never forgot Eleonora. It was fanciful, but it had worked. Of all the tales he had written, "Eleonora" was still Sissy's favorite. Now, three years later, it was almost as if the king's maiden had appeared in the form of Fanny. Eddy thought that perhaps Sissy had drawn that connection, too, that perhaps it explained her affection for Fanny.

Later that night he lay on his back in bed staring into the darkness. He closed his eyes and slept, and in his dream he put on an overcoat. Holding the cuffs of his shirt with his fingertips, he slipped his arms into the sleeves, one and then the other. He could feel the woolen fabric, heavy when he hunched it onto his back, and when he looked up, as he buttoned the buttons, he saw Sissy lying on the bed, her arms crossed upon her breasts, so young, so peaceful in her repose—not old and wrinkled, but young; her breasts still firm; her face smooth; her skin taut and supple; the fingers of her hands long and graceful, not knotted and gnarled like Muddy's. How beautiful she appeared—only it wasn't a bed anymore, and the winter sky was dark, and standing about the garden between beds of lilacs were other men wearing overcoats, bareheaded, holding their top hats at their sides, their long faces bowed. They gazed upon Sissy as they might gaze at the portrait of a woman by a great artist, admiring her beauty and amazing pallor and stillness, following the line of her thin arms to the tips of her fingers, tracing the curve of her neck to her black, black hair.

Then from inside the coffin Eddy saw the lid closing down and heard the slow, gnarly twisting of screws tightening into wood. For an instant he could feel motion, like a rope swing, back and forth, until it bumped against the sides of the grave and came to rest at the bottom. Then shovelfuls of dirt fell on the lid, hollow at first; then as the dirt piled around, as his narrow cavern began to disappear, he heard the muted sound of earth falling on earth. It grew fainter, like someone churning butter or kneading dough in another room, downstairs, in the kitchen, until it became almost imperceptible, though he strained to hear, as if that sound of dirt on dirt was the last thread that bound him to the world. Then there was only silence until, by degrees, he became aware of a mustiness, and a clammy darkness, viscid and woolen like a river-bed, and a faint static pulsing like the distant roar of a furnace.

CHAPTER 16

❧ Muddy ❧

MUDDY COULDN'T HELP but smile as she wrapped her china in newspaper. The *Broadway Journal* was at least good for something. It was mid-September, and they were moving again, this time to Greenwich Village, Amity Street. It would be their second time living on that street, and Muddy was superstitious about that. Of all the streets in the world, they had to live on the same one twice. The first time was before Sissy got sick, and she had been so excited to be moving to New York. She was only fourteen at the time and grew a hand taller that year. Outgrew all her clothes. She turned into a beauty that year if Muddy said so herself.

"It's bad luck, moving back there," she told Sissy. Sissy paid her no mind. How could their luck get any worse?

It might have been a mistake letting Sissy marry so young, Muddy thought as she went back to her wrapping. That hadn't been her intention when she and Sissy moved to Richmond. Oh, Eddy had said he was going to marry her when she came of age, but that was just talk. Once she and Sissy arrived, they became a family again, just like in Baltimore. Eddy was so proud of them. He had not been included in John Allan's will, and him the richest man in all Virginia. It was a shame how he treated that boy, but John Allan was dead by then, and Eddy had made his peace with all that. He took them everywhere. Showed them where he had lived when he was a little boy. Took them to Shockoe Hill Cemetery where Jane Stanard was buried; the woman had been like a second mother to him. And he showed them the graves of his foster parents, explaining how he had taken their name as his middle name. He had done that on his own. He had wanted to be Edgar Poe Allan, but John Allan wouldn't adopt him. It sure was cruel to treat a child like that.

Sissy was too young to marry, but Eddy wasn't. Before Sissy and Muddy arrived in Richmond, he had been courting Eliza White, the daughter of his boss at the *Southern Literary Messenger*. Eliza would have been a fine match.

Her daddy was crazy about Eddy. Muddy decided that maybe his pledge to Sissy was getting in the way of his courtship, so she suggested that she and Sissy return to Baltimore and live with Neilson Poe. Eddy became frantic again. Poor boy had already lost two families, and she guessed he couldn't bear to lose another. He was so pitiful when his feelings got hurt. What Muddy hadn't realized was that Eddy was in love with Sissy.

So Eliza White faded from his life, and Eddy married Sissy in the parlor of the preacher's house on a Monday evening in the middle of May. He fibbed about Sissy's age; that was their little secret. She was thirteen. And he vowed to Muddy that he would not be a husband in the familiar sense until Sissy turned sixteen. She was to sleep with Muddy, while Eddy slept down the hall in Mrs. Yarrington's boardinghouse on the courthouse square right in the middle of Richmond. It was there that they had a little party after the ceremony. No one in the boardinghouse had known about the wedding plans, so when Muddy invited everyone up to her room for a celebration and the tea cakes she had baked that afternoon, there were a lot of surprised faces, including Martha Yarrington's. The party started out a little awkward, but soon enough everyone warmed to the idea and gave their congratulations to the happy couple.

Eddy became Sissy's teacher, giving her lessons to do during the day while he was at work. At night after supper, after Sissy had put on her nightgown, he required her to read aloud. She sat in a straight-back chair by the fireplace. Eddy made her sit up straight and hold her book with both hands while he sat opposite her, watching her every minute, smiling and patient, the proud teacher. When she stumbled over a word or mispronounced it, he laughed, charmed by her mispronunciation as if he'd never heard a more precious mistake, and her so embarrassed by it, she fled her chair, climbed into his lap, and hid her eyes in the crook of his neck.

"Now, now," he would say, stroking her black hair, "you don't get off that easily." And dutifully Sissy returned to her chair, picked up her book, and pronounced the word over and over until she got it right, searching Eddy's eyes each time until he nodded and smiled; then she continued on. Sometimes he made her memorize long passages from Shakespeare during the day; that night she would have to stand in front of the fireplace and recite while Eddy followed the passage in the book. When she finished he applauded her, and she blushed with pride, beaming at him like she worshiped him, and she did. And he deserved it; he was strict, but gentle and kind and always full of praise. He brought her out, gave her confidence, and anyone seeing them together could tell that he adored her.

Sometimes Eddy took Sissy to his own room to read. Muddy never asked any questions and never went into his room when he was there. Every now and again Muddy said something like "Be sure to leave the door open" or "Sissy shouldn't be going to your room in her nightgown." But sometimes Sissy disappeared, and how was Muddy to know if she was going to the privy or into Eddy's room? After a while she just stopped worrying about it.

That summer Eddy often took them into the country, to the James River, for picnics. He hired a rig for the day, and they rode out, south of town, through the tobacco plantations where slaves worked in the fields. Eddy was used to all that; he'd grown up with it; but slavery made Sissy and Muddy uncomfortable. One Saturday in July they drove to the river with Rosalie, Eddy's sister. Rose, as they called her, was good to Sissy too, often took her to the school where she worked as a cleaning lady so Sissy could play with the other children. Sissy and Eddy had been married two months to the day. Muddy remembered because all the way to the river, Sissy was begging him to buy her a present. She wanted a new dress. Her little body was just starting to sprout, and Rose teased her about wanting to show off her bosom.

When they got to the picnic ground, Eddy stripped down to his long johns and started splashing in the water, trying to coax Sissy in, too. Next thing they knew he started swimming out into the current, heading across the river. It was a long way across, and Muddy thought it a foolhardy thing to do. When he got to the other side, he climbed up on a rock and waved to them; then he jumped back in the water and swam back. While Rose and Muddy laid out the picnic, Sissy took off her shoes and waded into the water to watch him, never taking her eyes off of him, scared to death he wouldn't make it. But he was a fine swimmer, strong for someone so skinny. Afterward he walked around bare-chested, drying off in the sun, gnawing on a piece of fried chicken, his long johns wet and clinging to his privates. Sissy stared at him like he was some Greek god, and Eddy just posed for her. Muddy and Rose laughed at the thought that he might just bust right out of his britches.

They were as happy that summer as they had been in Baltimore after William

Henry died, leaving just the three of them. Only, in Richmond Sissy and Eddy were in love, and Muddy soon got over her concerns about their age difference and their being first cousins. Before they were married, Muddy had thought it was no more than puppy love, but they both proved her wrong. One night she watched Sissy kiss Eddy good night before he went to his room, and she was shocked by it. Where did Sissy learn to kiss that way? she wondered, thinking she'd never pull them apart. Apparently Sissy had conquered her shyness, and Muddy started worrying about what else was going on.

A crack in her cut-glass compote dish brought her back to the task of packing to move to Amity Street. She studied the crack, wondering if it was worse than the last time she looked. Then, out of the corner of her eye, she noticed Sissy drop her hands to her lap like she'd had bad news. While Muddy had been packing and daydreaming, Sissy had gone through the mail and found a letter addressed to her.

"What is it, Sis?" Muddy asked, setting the compote down.

Sissy said nothing, closed her eyes, and shook her head listlessly.

Muddy walked over to where she sat. The room was full of crates. They were nearly done. "Mind if I have a look?" she asked, taking the letter out of Sissy's hands.

It was short—"Dear Mrs. Poe"—and signed, "A Friend." It said people in New York were talking about Eddy and Mrs. Osgood. The writer thought Sissy would want to know. Muddy tore it into little pieces and threw it on the grate, thinking she'd strike a match to it before Eddy got home. Or maybe she'd do it now, she decided.

"Don't put no stock in this, Sis," she said, striking a sulphur match on one of the brick tiles and lighting each scrap. "Anybody won't sign their name to a letter is common and low-down."

Muddy was thinking if she could get her hands on the woman who wrote that letter, she'd wring her neck. Oh, it was a woman all right. And either she didn't know about Sissy's condition or she didn't care. Either way, Muddy wished she could jerk some manners into the witchy little so-and-so for poking her nose where it didn't belong.

After burning the letter, Muddy kneeled in front of Sissy, looking up at her, but Sissy refused to meet her eyes. She stared out the window.

"Sissy, listen to me," Muddy said. "There are hateful people everywhere and New York's no different. This don't mean nothing but spite."

"She never came to see me," Sissy said, still looking out the window. "She said she'd come, but she never did."

Startled, just then Muddy could have jerked some manners into Fanny, too. In her letter to Sissy she had promised to pay a visit when she returned to New York. But what scared Muddy was that Sissy seemed to be saying that she knew about Eddy and Fanny and that it didn't matter, that what hurt was being left out.

They hardly ever saw Eddy. He was gone early and home late. Mornings were the only time they saw him, but he never took his meals there, despite paying for them, and that was one of the reasons he wanted to move again. They hadn't talked privatelike in months. He may as well have been living somewhere else. He had stayed sober, and Muddy was thankful for that, and they had no reason to doubt what he told them, that he was doing the job of two men now that Mr. Briggs was gone.

Sometimes Muddy thought he had taken on airs. Bragged about being an owner now. He'd been an editor all his life, so she couldn't blame him for being proud, but he'd taken to carrying that walking stick Mr. Chivers gave him. Then he went and shaved his mustache and grew those chin whiskers. Muddy didn't like them one whit. If a man wanted hair on his face, then let him grow a proper mustache or beard and not pussyfoot around with muttonchops. Made him look stuffy.

Eddy kept telling them that Fanny would be paying a call any day. Muddy thought it odd she never came, and she wondered out loud about it, but Sissy insisted it was none of their business. Said Mrs. Osgood had demands on her time and that she would come when she could. Then Eddy had told them Fanny was gone, gone for good.

Anyway, it didn't take much to draw the wind right out of Sissy's sails, and that letter from "A Friend" did it. Seemed Sissy took the message to mean that Eddy and Fanny had turned their back on her. Next day, their last day at East Broadway, she wouldn't even come down for lunch.

Eddy hired a drayer to take their belongings out to Greenwich Village. Sissy, Muddy, and Catterina rode up front with the driver while Eddy sat on the back to make sure nothing fell off. They were moved in by nightfall, and Sissy hadn't uttered a word all day.

It was a third-floor apartment, two rooms above a butcher shop and across the street from a firehouse, and it was filthy. It would take Muddy a good three days of scrubbing on her hands and knees, and she refused to unpack until it was spotless. Though it was just one block from Washington Square, it was rundown. Worst place they'd ever lived.

That night Eddy built a fire and Muddy roasted potatoes and warmed up a loaf of bread. He began to take notice that Sissy wasn't talking. The three of them ate off their laps, him studying her like he was trying to read her mind. Finally he turned to Muddy.

"Is everything all right?" he asked. "Is something wrong with the apartment?"

"Only it's filthy," Muddy said. "And that fire bell will be waking us up at all hours. The mattresses have bugs, there's rat droppings everywhere, and it smells like a slaughterhouse. Other than that it's fine."

Eddy turned to Sissy again, but she avoided his eyes, staring down at her food, pushing it around her plate like it wasn't something to eat but something to help pass the time. "It faces south," he said. "It'll be warmer than East Broadway. Anyway, we can't afford board. We'll manage."

Sissy stood, put her plate on her chair, wiped her mouth, and left—went into the bedroom and slammed the door.

"What's wrong?" Eddy asked, turning to Muddy.

Muddy thought for a minute, trying to decide if she should tell him. "Sissy had a letter yesterday. Didn't sign a name. Said people were talking about you and Fanny. Judging by the stationery and the handwriting, it was a woman."

Eddy's eyes flashed and his jaw clenched like he was ready to murder somebody. Then he shook his head, looking downcast and too weary to deal with any more tribulation. "Where is it?"

"I burned it," Muddy said, "and I told Sissy to pay it no mind, but how's she going to ignore a thing like that when you're never home?"

He stared down at a half-eaten roasted potato and laid his fork on the plate. "I told you, Fanny's gone," he said at last. "She's moved to Providence. Anyway, the rumors aren't true."

"What rumors?" Muddy asked, thinking he wouldn't get off the hook that easy. "Exactly what are people saying about you and Fanny? And why didn't she come see Sissy while she was here like she said she would? What's gotten into her, hurting Sissy's feelings like that? Makes it seem Fanny's got something to hide, like maybe she's too embarrassed to pay a call on Sissy, like maybe the rumors are true."

"The rumors are not true." Eddy was furious. "Now go tell Sissy to come back to supper. She should eat something. Go on. I've got to go back to the office."

"You tell her," Muddy said, not giving an inch. "And what's so important that you have to walk all the way downtown at this hour of the night?"

"I have work to do," Eddy said, setting his plate down and putting on his coat. "Anyway, she won't listen to me. She hasn't said a word to me all day."

Muddy couldn't stop him. Sissy wouldn't listen to her, either, but she didn't bother telling that to Eddy as he was walking out the door. She just hoped he wasn't going to get drunk. When she went in for bed, the candle was out and Sissy was under the sheet, facing the wall. Catterina slept between them.

In the days that followed, Sissy maintained her silence. She sat at the window, staring out, rubbing Catterina, who sat in her lap. Muddy scrubbed the floors, washed the walls, leaned the mattresses out the window and tried to beat the bugs out of them. She turned the furniture upside down, washing it inside and out. Her face and hands black with soot, she even scrubbed the inside of the fireplace. When the two rooms were immaculate, she put their things away and carried the packing crates out to the street. Sissy refused to help even though Muddy was having to cook again on top of everything else. Muddy tried to carry on a conversation but ended up just talking to herself. Sissy didn't even seem to listen.

One day Muddy asked Sissy to baste a collar for a dress she was making for a lady who had been a neighbor at East Broadway. The work seemed to bring Sissy out of her daze.

"When I die," she said—right out of the blue, her voice as calm and natural as if she was talking about her thimble, "I don't want anyone to see me. I don't want people staring at me. Promise me, Muddy. Promise you won't let them. Nobody. Not even Eddy. Tell him it's what I wanted. Tell him you promised."

Muddy looked up as if to say they needn't be going on about that right now, but Sissy stared her down, as determined a look on her face as Muddy ever saw. If she agreed, she'd be admitting that Sissy was dying, and she couldn't do that. She'd be admitting that Sissy would go first, and that was the one thought she could not abide—the thought that she would outlive yet another child.

But Sissy's gaze was fixed. Wouldn't go away.

"I promise," Muddy said, blinking back tears. It was pitiful, Muddy's voice, timid and cracked. Sissy turned back to her sewing. Never said another word about it.

Up to that time, Muddy and Sissy had always maintained a little fantasy, like a child's game, pretending that Sissy would get well. It was almost like they were talking about what Sissy would do when she grew up. It seemed like Sissy never had a chance to grow up, like the consumption had taken hold of her at too early an age and her life had been suspended in late adolescence. Sometimes it seemed like Eddy and Muddy were father and mother instead of husband and mother. Sissy was twenty-two, but in most ways she was like a schoolgirl; Muddy still mothered her like she had the day Sissy was born, like there wasn't any need for her to grow up, so she never did. And now even Sissy had come to accept that she never would.

From that day forward—that day she brought up dying—they never talked about the future again. It was like Fanny had taken on the role of Sissy's future and wouldn't let Sissy be a part of it. One night, after Sissy had gone to bed, Muddy sat by the fire and cried for hours. Eddy wasn't home, and if he'd come in, she'd have gone straight to bed, praying Sissy wouldn't notice her bawling. But Muddy couldn't stop. The hem of her apron was soaked with tears. She was living in a family where no one spoke. They might as well be strangers. And Fanny Osgood might as well be sleeping in Eddy's bed.

That's what made Muddy certain something was up with Eddy and Fanny, but after agonizing over it for weeks, she concluded there wasn't a blessed thing she could do. Maybe they were in love, Fanny and Eddy. Could Muddy blame him? She thought about it and decided she could, and she did. She couldn't help it, though he and Sissy hadn't slept together in months. Even if they did, Sissy couldn't be a wife to him. Not now. She was so skinny, her face drawn, her little body pitiful to behold. Sissy kept complaining that the bed was lumpy, and Muddy didn't have the heart to tell her she was lying on bones.

Twice a week Muddy gave her a bath, and every time she preached to Sissy about keeping up her appetite. Little good it did.

What took Muddy's mind off Fanny was Eddy. He was drinking again.

During September the weather had been dry—no rain and hot. Eddy came home early one night. Muddy should have known right then. He sat there working at his desk. The windows were open, and a fire broke out somewhere. About eight o'clock the firehouse across the street came alive with clanging bells such that you couldn't hear yourself think. Eddy poked his head out the window and watched the fire wagons head east toward Broadway.

"I think I'll follow them," he said, pulling his head back in and grinning at Muddy and Sissy.

Muddy knew right then. His face was flushed with whiskey. She looked over at Sissy, and she saw it, too.

"You go to following fire wagons," Muddy said, "and you'll end up in Five Points. Better not go around there after dark."

"Oh, Muddy, don't be a spoilsport," he said, leaning back out the window so far, Muddy thought he'd fall if she didn't grab his suspenders. But she was ready to let him fall.

She looked over at Sissy, who was hurrying to put away her sewing things. She'll go straight to bed, Muddy thought. She'll get Catterina and shut the door. When he was on a drunk, she couldn't stand to be around him.

Later, when Muddy went in to bed, Sissy pretended to be asleep. It was like that all the time now. She shut Muddy out. Used to be, they could talk about things like this—worrying things, grieving things. It was that night, lying beside Sissy, listening to her muffle her coughs, that Muddy realized Sissy couldn't talk to her about Fanny. Not without talking about other things— things she was too proper and too sick to talk about. Things that were too private. And since she couldn't talk about Fanny, she didn't want to talk about anything.

My baby's too young to be agonizing like this, Muddy thought, but she couldn't do Sissy's agonizing for her. She could do her wash. She could cook her meals. She could bathe her, lecture her about eating, brush her hair. But Muddy couldn't be a wife to her husband; she couldn't be a rival to Eddy's lover. And she couldn't do Sissy's dying.

Chapter 17

❧ Fanny ❧

The Broadway Journal   Saturday, September 6, 1845

> TO F—.
> Thou wouldst be loved?—then let thy heart
> From its present pathway part not!
> Being everything which now thou art,
> Be nothing which thou art not.

HALFWAY TO THE FERRY, Fanny had started crying, just as the carriage passed the Astor House. She tried to laugh back her tears and turned to look at Edith Bartlett sitting beside her. Edith smiled and patted Fanny's hand as if to say she understood.

Later, standing at the port rail, she looked back at the city and wondered if she would ever return. That was too dramatic; of course she would; she was feeling sorry for herself. Before leaving, she had arranged for a collection of her poetry to be published late in the year by Clark & Austin, and she'd have to come back for that. She wouldn't have the patience to wait in Providence for her new book.

The sun was low, and the trees of upper Manhattan were just beginning to glow with color. As the ferry steamed between Turtle Bay and Blackwell's Island, Fanny could see black smoke from the Harlem train rise above the trees into a cloudless, orange, evening sky. Flocks of starlings crossed the river. She thought of herself as an outcast just then, which served to arouse the sense of injustice she felt. She and Edgar had been foolish. Their published verses were too transparent, including Edgar's latest, entitled "To F——." and published in the *Broadway Journal* the week before. Unsigned, it was inserted at the bottom of a column just below a signed article. How ironic that last line sounded now: "Be nothing which thou art not." That was the very thing she was leaving New York to do.

Her story in *Graham's* for August, "Ida Grey," was the most irresponsible thing she'd ever done. She knew it was a mistake the moment she saw it in print. It was more transparent than all the poems put together. She had even used a line from "The Raven": "Only that and nothing more." No one was deceived. "Ida Grey" was what started tongues to wagging, so she couldn't blame Edgar or anyone else. It was reckless—the same heedless impulse that had invited Edgar to come to Providence in June. Had Fanny penned the story in New York, she would never have published it, but in June in Providence, insulated as she was, so far away, it had seemed a thing of little risk or consequence.

"Ida Grey" was proving more autobiographic than Fanny ever imagined. At its end she banished Ida to a convent, since Ida could not marry the man she loved, the Poe-like poet. They could not marry, because he was already married to a wife who "is cold and does not love him." Why did she write that? It was cruel, unthinking, unforgivable. She reasoned that it hadn't been Sissy in her mind when she wrote it, but who would believe her when the main characters in the story were so obvious?

After she apologized, Edgar praised the story, calling it well written, but he couldn't hide his discomfort. She made him promise to keep it from Sissy, and she avoided Sissy altogether, guilty for having characterized her in such a mean-spirited way. It was as if only Fanny viewed the story as fictional, while everyone else saw it as fact. Anne was furious; she lectured Fanny no end. Sarah wrote from Providence to say that John was very upset; and, of course, there was no hiding it from Ned. In their one awkward and painful meeting at the Bartletts', Fanny found herself defending Edgar's character and, by doing so, only added insult to injury. To her surprise and to Ned's credit, he was understanding, saying he hoped to see her again when she came to her senses. He told her Sam had been around to borrow money again, as if Sam's debt would somehow accrue to Fanny. It was as if Ned refused to let her go, and oddly enough, she was grateful.

It was Anne who convinced her that she had been disgraceful. That was the word Anne used. Many people, Edgar included, had said of Fanny's poetry that it embodied *grace*. Was it not fitting, therefore, that in her wickedness she should be *disgraceful*? She played with the two words, *grace* and *disgrace,* in a poem that got no further than the morass of a portfolio in which she kept her unfinished scraps. She accepted the condemnation and its consequence; she deserved it. Exile would have come regardless, but the gossip could have been avoided, and since "Ida Grey" had sparked it, Fanny had no choice but to try and live it down.

The following afternoon, as the ferry approached the dock in Providence, she saw John, Sarah, and the children there to greet her. Just then she didn't feel exiled. Lily and May met her at the bottom of the gangplank with hugs and kisses, and Fanny realized how much she had missed them and how bleak Providence would have been without them. They all waited at the dock to ensure that the porter put all of Fanny's luggage onto the cart John had hired for carrying her luggage to the cottage he had rented for her.

"What's that?" he asked when he saw the crate.

"It's a painting," she said. "One of Sam's."

"Wasn't that nice of Sam?" Sarah said. "A painting will be just the thing to get you started decorating. You're going to like the cottage. Lily and May have seen it. They've already decided which room is theirs and where their beds will go."

As the gig jerked forward, Fanny resolved to abide banishment. She would be content to raise her girls, live humbly, and be penitent as befit her wickedness. Knowing full well that she was being melodramatic again, she took a deep breath and reminded herself that she could endure anything as long as she could write. Writing would be her refuge; she would devote herself to poetry. Surely John would not try to dissuade her from writing. He would know the futility of that.

He did suggest that she refrain from publishing for a while. That night after supper at his house, on the porch with her and Sarah, John said as much, and he berated her for her misbehavior, her lack of judgment, her wilfulness, her impulsiveness, her naiveté. She sat and listened, wanting to argue that it was her life, not his; but she said nothing, letting him have his say.

As he walked them home that night through the dark, quiet neighborhoods of Providence, Fanny realized how desperately she would miss New York. On that very night, all her friends were going to Palmo's Opera House to see the little Misses Kilmiste, the Singing Infant Sisters. She felt a sharp pang of loss. Had she stayed, she would have joined them, and of course they would all go to the Astor afterward for drinks and conversation and not get to bed until after two. They would all be at the Astor at this very moment, Fanny thought, but Edgar would not be there. He would have attended with her, but now that she was gone, she knew, he'd withdraw. He would stop going to Lynchie's; he would avoid her friends. She hoped he wouldn't resort to drinking again. It had not been easy to ask Edgar to take the temperance pledge. She reasoned she had done that for Sissy, too, not just for Edgar or herself. How could she have been so cruel to Sissy? Was she as heartless as all that? Fanny resolved to try and repair that damage; once they were settled, she would write to Sissy again, pledging to be a true friend and to love her.

The cottage John had rented for them was humble but quaint, in a middle-class section of Providence. Many of Fanny's new neighbors were the wives of merchant seamen whose husbands were always away. The cottage had a porch and a cozy kitchen with a red brick fireplace and a window looking out on weeds. Fanny resolved to turn the backyard into a sea of flowers come spring, but John suggested that raising chickens might be more practical.

THOUGH FANNY WAS determined to be a proper homemaker, her determination faded rapidly. She was a hopeless cook. Even Lily, who had turned nine in July, had better instincts when it came to building a proper stove-wood fire. She coached Fanny constantly for fear the cottage would burn to the ground. Just when Fanny thought she was getting the hang of the stove, she found the cellar infested with red ants and had to throw away a shoulder of mutton, five pounds of cheese, and three pounds of pork fat. By the end of September, desperate for help, she found a serving girl to come in twice a week to clean and cook. John agreed to most of her requests for aid. Though he pretended to be bothered, he seemed happy to have her nearby and under his thumb.

She hung Edgar's portrait in her bedroom, over the dresser behind the door. John would not come in her bedroom, she reasoned, and if Sarah saw it, Fanny would explain somehow and swear her to secrecy. Lily and May were puzzled by it.

"Who is he, Mama?" Lily asked as Fanny hammered the nail into the wall. An oval portrait, it was slightly taller than it was wide, the perfect size for hanging above the dresser. In it Edgar gazed off to Fanny's right as she faced it. He wore a high collar turned down over his black cravat, and a lock of hair fell across the top of his ear and another one curled at the top of his forehead.

Neither his mouth nor his eyes were quite right. Too pleasant and prosperous-looking, they failed to capture his turmoil and passion, things she loved about him. As it stood propped against the bed, Lily and May got down on all fours to examine it.

"He's a famous poet and a friend," Fanny explained, hoping that would suffice.

"Why don't we hang a picture of Daddy?" May asked.

"We don't have one," Fanny said, and she lifted the portrait, reached for the wire, and hooked it on the nail. "It's just something to decorate the wall," she said, straightening it. "That's all. Now let's go find something to decorate the walls in your room."

Fanny's beautiful gowns had to be stored in the Lockes' attic, as there was no room in the cottage, and there would be few occasions to wear them. A far cry from Broadway, Providence could boast of nothing so festive, entertaining, and stimulating as one of Lynchie's *soirées*. Instead there was church. John dragged her weekly—dare she say religiously—and Lily and May, too, though they were just as recalcitrant as Fanny when it came to being forced. To be shed of her keep, John would have liked to see Fanny bridled to a shopkeeper or a sea captain or some bureaucratic member of the state assembly who preferred his mare *and* his wife pretty and well broken. But she would have none of that and her brother knew it.

After getting the girls settled in school, Fanny threw herself into decorating their little cottage. John gave her an allowance with which to buy her necessaries—furniture and curtains. Sarah accompanied her on shopping trips for those things and the kitchen appurtenances. She introduced Fanny to the right butcher, baker, apothecary, greengrocer, and fishmonger, the best soap and candle maker, milliner, and dressmaker. They arranged to have milk, eggs, and butter delivered twice a week, and within a few days Fanny had a fair map of the town. Sarah promised to teach her how to make preserves, pickles, piecrust, doughnuts, bread pudding, and ginger beer.

The first few nights were spent at the Lockes' in an atmosphere so pleasant and reminiscent of June and July that Fanny was lulled into a false sense of her new life. Then, on her fourth day, with furniture arranged and everything put away, Fanny insisted on the Lockes' coming to her cottage for supper. She spent the day preparing a rump roast, roasted potatoes, cabbage, and as apples were in season, an apple pudding. It was the pudding that did her in. The recipe called for adding dumplings, but Fanny omitted the dumplings; she couldn't do everything—not on the first night. She pared the apples, cored them, filled up the holes with washed rice, and boiled them in a pudding bag for half an hour. Then she made her piecrust, rolled it out, filled it with quartered apples, returned it to the pudding bag, and boiled it for another hour. All this she did while basting the roast, washing the cabbage in preparation for boiling, and checking on the potatoes.

When the meal was over, and the children had excused themselves to swing on the porch, John turned to Sarah. "Have you ever tasted a better apple pudding?"

Sarah was about to profess that she had not, when Fanny laughed out loud, shaking her head, lamenting the prospect of spending the rest of her life standing over a hot stove.

John smiled sympathetically in lieu of saying "Of course you can, darling," and Sarah stroked Fanny's arm, looking earnestly into her eyes as if to say "You'll get used to it, dear." Lily and May will starve to death, was what Fanny was thinking. She was ready to give up and move to the City Hotel.

That night, after the Lockes were gone and the girls were in bed, Fanny got out her pen and ink. How could she write after such a day? She had not read a word or had a private thought; she had not seen the sun or thought of one bully word. Thank God for Lily and May. Recalling how, as an infant, May had tried to clutch spots of sunlight on the floor as if they were golden toys, she began composing a poem about her. The rhymes came and Fanny wrote, crossed out, wrote more, and sometime after midnight, she finished. She especially liked the final stanza.

> Ah, May! be still a child in this,
> Through life, amid its gloom and bliss:
> Though clouds of care be all about,
> Those eyes will find the sunshine out,
> Then pass the shade with Hope's delight,
> And stop to play where Joy is bright.

Yes, she could still write, even here. She put her writing things away, looked up at Edgar's portrait, and climbed into bed.

ON MONDAY THE 22nd of September, she had a letter from him. It was needy and desperate, and Fanny could not help but be thrilled by his wanting her. He could not write, he said, and the Boston Lyceum insisted on a new poem. Would she help? He praised her spontaneity and resourcefulness; she had vitality, he said, whereas, everything else in his life was falling into decay. He loved her and missed her intensely. He would come through Providence on his way to Boston, spend a night or two, on October 13 or 14.

Three weeks. In three weeks she would see him. Now the chores seemed less oppressive, and yes, she would help. She became preoccupied with ideas for a poem, a poem that would sound and feel like Edgar Poe. She reread everything she had of his, his collection of tales and the clippings of his poems that had appeared in the *Broadway Journal* and her treasured last two stanzas of "The Raven" that he had sent to her before they met.

She wrote him almost daily, sharing her latest ideas in her scrawling, hurried hand. He should write something different from "The Raven," she reasoned, because he should recite "The Raven" also, since the Boston audience would want to hear it. She suggested a ballad. She had an idea and wondered what he thought.

He did not write for two weeks. In the absence of a response, Fanny pursued the ballad idea and started composing. Each day, cleaning and cooking, sweating, her hands becoming raw and red, she kept pencil and paper at hand, scribbling thoughts, parts of lines, rhymes. At night when the girls were in bed, she went to work in earnest. The ballad was a manly form, and the subject not inconsistent with Edgar's fascination with the supernatural. She called her composition "The Diamond Fay," and she wrote it. She could not stop herself.

> Fair Lilith, listen, while I sing
> The legend of this diamond ring;
> And in its moral, maiden, heed
> A quiet 'hint, your heart may need.'
> In fairy archives, where 'tis told,
> I found the story quaint and old,
> Writ on a richly-blaxon'd page
> Of parchment, by some elfin sage.

It required only his touches of brilliance to transform it into a suitable presentation piece, and a week before he was due to arrive, she wrote him, saying not to worry.

The 13th came and went. Fanny was despondent. She had heard from him only once since his letter of the 22nd, and it said nothing about her ideas for the ballad. It expressed only more desperation—he was worried about the magazine and did she know someone in Providence who would act as his agent? It said nothing about his upcoming trip, and she wondered if he'd changed his mind.

Early the next afternoon, a messenger arrived at the cottage with a note: "Have just arrived. Am at the City Hotel. Can we meet? Where? When? Edgar."

Fanny wrote out a response for him to meet her on the mezzanine of the Athenæum at four that afternoon. That would give her time to dress and arrange for the serving girl to stay with Lily and May after school. Though she had already decided on a dress, she reconsidered, holding several up in front of the mirror. Blue was her best color, a medium blue, but it would have to be something appropriate for the library. She couldn't go there looking too formal. As she stared at herself in the mirror, she thought how brief this encounter would be. Why hadn't he come yesterday? One night and then what? He had to be in Boston tomorrow. When would she see him again?

Since the day was sunny and warm, she walked the seven blocks from her cottage, leaving early enough to arrive before Edgar. She wanted to be sitting in the same green wing chair where they'd sat in July. Her ballad, "The Diamond Fay," was folded into the pages of a book of poems by Shelley, one of her favorites, dark blue, leather bound. It matched the blue in the floral pattern of her dress, which was simple: full skirt, lace collar; oval broach set in gold; not a hint of bosom. She climbed the stairs to the mezzanine and found their spot unoccupied, so she sat down and arranged herself, removing her bonnet and spreading her skirts. Then she opened her book. When she heard him on the stairs, she looked up, then back down. It could be someone else, she reasoned, but let it please be Edgar.

His appearance shocked her. He was excessively pale. There were deep circles under his eyes, and she wondered whether he'd been drinking. He carried neither hat nor walking stick, and his hair was disheveled, blown by the wind into an odd pattern that needed a brushing.

They did not embrace. He bowed, avoiding her eyes, and took the chair beside her.

"Are you all right?" she asked.

"I got sick on the ferry," he said, attempting a laugh. "I've never been seasick before."

"Do you feel like eating?" she suggested. "Perhaps we should get you something."

"No. Please," he said. "I don't think I could eat anything just yet. I'll have something as soon as my stomach settles. Just now I'm still rolling with the swells."

He smiled, a sad, pitiful smile that worried Fanny.

They sat in silence for a moment. Yellow afternoon sunlight streamed through the windows. The room was quiet. Edgar bowed his head, and Fanny watched as he took deep breaths. At length he opened his eyes and gazed at her.

"I haven't written a word," he said, shaking his head and smiling hopelessly. "I even went to Dunn English for help. I must have been desperate to go to him, but you can't imagine the pressure. I had a letter from Chivers. Instead of offering to invest in the magazine, he accuses me of plagiarizing his work. Me? Plagiarize Chivers?"

He leaned down and put his face in his hands. "Tomorrow night is Boston," he said, "and I've written nothing. I'll be a laughingstock."

Fanny was incredulous. "Did you forget that you asked for my help? Did you not receive my letters?" He looked up at her, seeming to be surprised. "Or is it too preposterous to think that a woman could write a poem worthy of the Boston Lyceum?"

"You wrote something?" he asked, his expression guarded.

"You asked for my help, didn't you? Or perhaps you don't remember or don't care or don't consider that I'm good enough to write a man's poem. Maybe Dunn English is better qualified?" She slammed her book shut.

Edgar begged her to stay, fluffing her trampled feelings and professing not to have thought that she took him seriously. She handed over her composition, and he read it through twice. As she watched him read, Fanny sensed he was searching for a courteous rejection, and she wanted to snatch it out of his hands.

"May I read it tomorrow night?" he asked.

She was stunned. "Of course. That's why I wrote it. So you would have an original composition."

He smiled, shaking his head, then reached for her hand and squeezed it. "Fanny, you must be unique in all the world. If I read this poem, everyone would know it's yours. They'd accuse me of plagiarism. No one has your touch. It's truly a fine poem, and you couldn't possibly write a poem as ponderous and ghastly as one of mine."

"You are wrapping your tomahawk in flattery, Mr. Poe."

"It won't work, Fanny," he said. "Truly it's a brilliant poem. George Graham would pay you twenty dollars for it. I've decided to read my 'Al Aaraaf.' They won't recognize it. I wrote it at West Point." He laughed. "I'll pawn it off as something new and hope to redeem myself by ending with 'The Raven.'"

Fanny searched his eyes, unconvinced by what he said; then she relented. He might be right. "Perhaps you should read it for me," she said. "'Al Aaraaf,' I mean."

"Yes," he said, surprised. "It's at the hotel."

What he said was not true, of course. Fanny had never received as much as ten dollars for a poem, but Edgar seemed sincere, and his excuse plausible, now that she thought about it. He went on to tell her about the magazine problems; he had resigned himself to the fact that he was a writer, not a businessman. It's a vicious circle, he explained—no time to write; no money to pay contributors. He saw no way out.

He asked about her, and Fanny told him, lamenting her failed domestic efforts, bragging on Lily and May for keeping her upright, and praising Sarah Locke, a lifesaver, she said, admitting that they had supper three nights a week at the Lockes', plus Sunday lunch. She told him that John was urging her to sing in the church choir and asked him if he could imagine anything more absurd. She asked for news of Anne Lynch and her other New York friends and was disappointed that he knew so little. And she asked about Sissy and Muddy, promising to write to Sissy, which she still had not done, and she asked about the rumors.

"I don't hear the gossip," he said. "Since you've been gone, I don't see anyone except at the theater. I suppose the rumors have died down, but I would prefer being talked about to not having you in New York. Are you never coming back?"

Fanny smiled sadly, shaking her head.

"Then I will leave, too," he said. "New York is dismal without you."

"Where would you go?" she said.

"What if I came here?"

Fanny shook her head. "You cannot do that. New York is bad enough. Providence would be worse."

"Why, Fanny?"

"You know why," she said. "Follow me here and everyone in New York *and* Providence will know. I'll have no peace, nor will Sissy. In time, I think John can arrange for my divorce from Sam; he has friends in the state legislature. New York is too big; it's more difficult there. In a year or so, perhaps I'll be free."

She let it go at that. It was not necessary to remind Edgar that he was not free, but someday he might be. Yes, she thought, she must write Sissy at once; she had put it off too long.

"Then perhaps we'll move to the country," Edgar said; he told her about the Brennans and how happy Sissy had been there, and he talked about having the leisure to write again. "I wrote 'The Raven' in that house," he boasted.

"I believe your best work is ahead of you," Fanny said. "Your year in New York has not been wasted. You say you can't write, but think of all you've written. Think of the people you know. You say no one will hire you, but they will buy your stories and your poems. Your name sells magazines."

He reached up and brushed his hair with his fingers as if Fanny's compliment made him mindful of his appearance. "You are so wise," he said. "That's why I came. Instinct told me to come. 'Go see Fanny! She will work her magic.'"

"It's not magic, Edgar." She was adamant; she hated it when he seemed so helpless. Where was the man with the courage to blast Longfellow and defy the New York establishment? "I must go," she said, reaching for her bonnet. "I cannot have supper with you, but I will come to the hotel later. You can read me your poem and we can say good-bye properly."

She got up to go and bade him remain. She would have the serving girl stay on through supper and put Lily and May to bed. And she would go by Sarah's on the way home, on the pretext of borrowing something—a paper of pins?

ginger for a toothache? Oh well, she'd think of something—and tell Sarah that she and the girls had special plans. That would keep Sarah and John from paying an unexpected call. Oh, she was such a pox, but just this once; then he'd be gone. If caught, she'd agree to sing in the choir. No, maybe she wouldn't. The thought of choir practice was enough to make her vomit.

SHE LEFT THE HOUSE just at dark. It was late to be out unescorted, and she walked hurriedly, hoping she would not be recognized. Edgar was waiting for her, sitting alone on a sofa in a dark corner of the lobby, his manuscript in his hand. He had cleaned himself up: a clean shirt, his suit pressed, his hair brushed. He stood when she entered. Fanny felt uncomfortable, though there was no one in the lobby but the night clerk she'd encountered that summer. The clerk did, however, know John Locke was her brother. The safest place would be Edgar's room, so while the clerk was occupied, she made that suggestion, and they slipped upstairs.

They climbed to the third floor. Edgar unlocked the door to his room, and Fanny waited in the hall while he lit the lamp, standing very near where he'd kissed her in July. She went in and laid her shawl and bonnet on the writing table, as Edgar closed the door and pulled the chair out for her so that it faced the bed. As the pretense of their rendezvous was to hear Edgar read his presentation poem, he sat down on the bed so that he faced her, took a deep breath, and began reading. His hands shook. Reciting in a halting, uneven voice, he lost her. Hearing men's voices on the street below the opened window, Fanny stood and quietly closed it as Edgar read on, his voice a monotone. He could not concentrate, either. He stopped and stared down at the pages, and Fanny wondered if he had finished. She reached for his hands, which still held the manuscript, stood, and pulled him up off the bed; then she pressed his hands to her chest as if to stop their shaking.

"Put out the light," she whispered.

He pulled away and did as she asked; then, in the darkness, he found her and put his hands in hers again, wanting her to guide him. She opened his palms and placed them on her breasts. They kissed. For an instant, she wondered what to do. Should she make him stop here or guide his hands to the buttons at the back of her dress? Then she stopped thinking and kissed him again and pushed back the lapels of his coat. He pulled away long enough to remove it.

When he reached for her again, she guided his hands to the buttons of her dress. He hesitated, then began to unfasten the buttons, becoming more impatient the farther down he went. She slipped her arms out of the sleeves and let the dress fall to the floor.

There was a moment's pause. She turned back to him, her eyes now accustomed to the dark, and Edgar stood before her, facing the window, in his shirt-sleeves. She could hear his breathing.

"Hurry," she said.

He reached for his tie, and she began to unlace her corset. She turned away, put one foot on the chair, and reached under her chemise to take off her stockings. When she had removed them both, she turned back to find him removing his pants. When they came together again, everything rushed to her head. She kissed his chest, inhaling the smell of him, her body tingling with the feel of his hands touching her through the thin fabric of her chemise. They fell backward onto the bed, and—in a series of jerks and starts—before Fanny could get comfortable beneath him, still gasping and struggling for space, her arm here, her leg there, wanting to remove her chemise, wanting to take the pillow from beneath her head, wanting to take the pins out of her hair—he was inside her and it was over.

Edgar became a dead weight on top of her. Fanny had to push him off and aside. She could feel the wetness between her legs.

She groped for the washstand, found the pitcher, and poured water into the bowl. It was cold. She washed herself in the dark, wondering if it was possible to start again after all this housekeeping. How long had it been since she'd made love? Edgar seemed so frantic, and she wondered about him, too. If they were going to do this, would it not be possible to enjoy it?

When she turned back to him, he was sitting on the edge of the bed, his head in his hands. Fanny tried to pull his hands away, but he would not budge. He was short of breath, panting for air, almost crying. It seemed he couldn't speak. She brushed his hair with her hand, wanting to calm him.

"Fanny! I am so sorry," he blurted at last.

"Don't be sorry," she said, willing her voice to be calm. "Come, lie back down."

But he shook his head, pulling away, hiding his face in his palms.

She waited while he sat rigid on the edge of the bed, caressing his hair, still hoping. In this way they sat for a while until his breathing became even.

"I have done a horrible thing," he said, recovering his voice. "I can never forgive myself."

She took her hand away, giving up. Obviously he was thinking about Sissy, and Fanny wanted to be elsewhere. In the dark she found her corset. Not bothering with the stockings, she stuffed them down her bosom. She couldn't button all the buttons of her dress; he would have to help, but he seemed helpless. She wondered if he would even be up to walking her home, but he had no choice. Her bonnet would cover her hair, which she had not unpinned but which had been mashed about in that furious upheaval that could not have lasted more than a minute. She prayed the girls would be asleep.

"Light the lamp, Edgar, and get dressed," she said. She wondered whether she was presentable enough to cross the lobby without drawing attention. That was the challenge. Once outside in the dark, she'd be home free. "Edgar, get up; get dressed," she said, again. "Now!"

He pulled his hands away from his face, as Fanny struggled with the buttons of her dress. He stared at her across the dark as if he weren't sure who she was. She stared back. She had changed her life for this man, and he had called their love-making a horrible thing. As he lit the lamp, she supposed he'd get over it, but just then that didn't seem as important as crossing the lobby unnoticed.

They walked home in silence, arm in arm, Fanny guiding him. Edgar was mute and dazed. It was as if they had survived being struck by lightning.

When they reached the cottage gate, Edgar started to say something, but Fanny put her fingers to his lips.

"Don't say anything," she said. "We made love; we can't take it back. That's what it was. Love!" She forced a smile, reached up, and touched his lips. Even in the dark, she could see clouds of guilt and shame gathered in his eyes. As the girls' window faced the street, she could not risk kissing him. "Will you write to me?" she asked.

He nodded, and Fanny opened the gate. When she turned to say good-bye, he was already walking away.

"Edgar?" she whispered loudly.

He turned back, so that they looked at each other over the fence.

"Write to me!"

He nodded again and left her.

She watched him go, then went inside and closed the door. The parlor was dark. The girls were asleep, and by the light, Fanny knew that the serving girl was in the kitchen. She walked to the window and parted the lace curtains to see him in the distance, his head bowed, his shoulders stooped.

After the serving girl left, Fanny lit a candle. She was wide awake. She went to her desk and started a letter to Edgar, scratched through words, changed them, started again. Late in the night she finished, her desk covered with revised drafts. She took the drafts, balled each one up, took them to the fireplace, and with the candle, lit them one by one and let them fall to the grate. When she finished, she held the candle up to reread her final draft once again. Then she closed her eyes, opened them, and touched it to the candle, too, letting it burn with the others.

CHAPTER 18

 Willis

New-York Mirror   Wednesday, October 15, 1845

THE RETURN OF THE IDLER.—Readers, pardon our overflowing with delight in being back. We have not been absent these five months, only away, writing to you from the Hinterlands, indulging in little-or-nothings, and reveling in the hospitality of friends courageous enough to invite a spy for dinner and a fortnight.

We confess to *not* having missed the ledgers, the brown envelopes, the twine-balls and paste-pots, the piles of printers' proofs, and the poets and puff-seekers. *But we have missed you*—and we are bent on believing that the letters before us prove that you would never forsake us merely for our sloth and irresponsibility.

We have also missed the hubbub—the clang of horsecar bells, the chorus of newsboys, the salty taste of oysters, the inevitable crowds, the theatre, Castle Garden, Barnum's, Delmonicos, the Astor, and, of course, the Upper Ten whose *manifest destiny* (to borrow from O'Sullivan) is to surprise and amaze with unimaginable innovations, news of which must be disseminated to guard against fashion becoming the monopoly of Broadway. This, we hold self-evident, is *our* charge, and we *have* been derelict in our Duty, a failing we shall remedy forthwith. Rest assured that we are back and that we are back—for *good*.

One of the aforementioned letters greeting us from our receipts-box is from an Arkansas gentleman who writes to inform us of the recent death of his wife who, he claims, (with overmuch emphasis), was a devotee of this column and the possessor of virtues which he inventories and underpins with copious evidence. He begs us to coin a suitable epitaph and return it posthaste as the marble awaits. In a Perverse moment, we could not help but wonder what the lady's vices might have been, but as for the epitaph, no vice need apply. We are, of course, truly sorry that the lady is dead, and, though we cannot grieve the loss of every virtuous woman in America, we deplore the decline of the category in general.

Doubtless the Arkansas gentleman's sorrows are worthy of poetry, and, since we presume he is absorbed in grief, we forgive his forgetfulness in failing to enclose the price of return postage. Furthermore, as our nation is perennially negligent in matters of copyright, why should we contemplate even pecuniary compensation for a worthy turn-of-phrase? It seems universally expectant that poetry, like the Town pump, is free for all.

We are tempted, therefore, to hang a shingle on Ann Street announcing:—

Morris & Willis,
Epitaphs

—in an effort to prove that *bon mots* do possess great value and to determine what manner of profit might be gained from the venture. By way of an alternative, however, we suggest the work of our native poetesses—those authors of Sympathy and Sorrow—and within the pages of this very journal during this month alone, we have reviewed works by Miss Edmond, Miss Hewitt, Miss Hale, Miss Leslie, Mrs. Hentz, and Miss Fanny Forrester. Furthermore we understand that a new volume by Mrs. Osgood is in print and will soon be offered. Within this profusion of verse, no doubt, lie epitaphs aplenty.

———————

It may be of particular interest to our readers that Mr. Poe has gone to Boston to deliver an important new poem which we eagerly anticipate here. Will he surpass "The Raven"? we wonder—a wondering that begs another:—will anyone ever surpass "The Raven"?

T HE DOOR TO THE street slammed shut, and Willis watched as General Morris rose from his chair and walked to the window. He wants to make sure Stoddard has gone, Willis decided, so he waited. It was nearly seven, and dark except for the dim light of a sooty oil lamp, a time of evening that Willis normally spent in the nursery with Imogene before Harriet put her to bed. But that afternoon Morris had insisted that they must talk, and now, as Morris returned to his desk, certain they were alone, he wore a thoughtful scowl on his face. His side whiskers gave him the bullish bellicosity of a Boston terrier, and that plus the scowl gave Willis to know the gravity of what was to come. Morris sat down and looked at him.

"I don't trust Stoddard," the general began. "He's a hothead. I never liked his opinions in the first place, and I don't want them in my newspaper. Controversy is one thing; trying to pick a fight is something else. It's not our style. Taking him on as a partner was a mistake; perhaps we had no choice, but he's becoming more and more unruly, and I've decided the time has come to withdraw. I've been wanting to drop the daily, in any event. We should put our efforts into a weekly. I see the success of *Godey's* and *Graham's* and say to myself, that's more like what we should be doing, not struggling to compete with the penny press. I propose we offer to sell Stoddard the *Mirror* at a good price; let him have it if we must; he'll find new partners among that bunch he hangs out with. If he won't buy it, then we'll have to find a way to get rid of him, and after that we'll make a fresh start."

Though not surprised by this, Willis considered what the general said, thinking the move would cost him. If they withdrew, they would likely not get much for their interest in the *Mirror*, certainly not the necessary start-up capital needed for a new weekly magazine. He'd been dipping into his savings for five months, and the prospect of further depleting what was left unnerved him. Nevertheless, he shared Morris's opinion of Stoddard. They had taken him on as a partner in too much haste after Mary died, knowing Willis would require time away.

He knew also that Morris's motivation had to do with changes in postal regulations that negated the advantages of a daily.

Now it was Willis's turn to stand and look out the window. As he stared down toward the lights of Park Row and the horsecar terminal, he wondered if he really was glad to be back as he had said in his column. Unexpectedly, New York had become a lonely place, and though he'd been back only a week, he already felt restless. Rather than return, he had again considered going abroad to see Mary's family; in fact, he had gone so far as to send a threatening letter to Harriet Jacobs's owner, saying he would move permanently to England and take Harriet with him if his offer to purchase her freedom was not immediately accepted. His bluff had worked; they had agreed, and now he needed money for that too. Money had become a problem. For five months he'd done little. Since July he'd been sending Morris one or two columns a week, but mostly he had given in to distraction—anything to get his mind off Mary: hunting, fishing, long rides on horseback in the country, almost always alone. For two days in early June, he had visited Glenmary; the new owners had welcomed him back, and he had spent several midday hours sitting on his rock beside the bridge, shaded by the sycamore that grew there, reflecting on all that had happened and watching a hummingbird dart to and fro from her green thimble-nest. He couldn't write about it; it was still too painful to write about.

So what else could he do but go along with Morris's plan? Maybe the excitement of something new would do him good, jar him out of his depression. No doubt he'd be glad to be rid of the burdensome pace of a daily; by contrast, a weekly would seem almost leisurely. Willis would turn forty in January, and he resolved that the birthday would be auspicious and that he would look on Morris's proposal as the bellwether of his life's work, the *je ne sais quoi* that would put his stamp on posterity.

"Let's do it," he said, turning back to Morris. "What's next?"

Morris hesitated for an instant, then slapped the desk with the flat of his hand as if bringing down the gavel. "Supper, I think, and talk about the new magazine—not a copy of *Godey's*; I won't have that." He stood and walked to the coat rack. "And it must be fresh, unique. Let's take our time designing the thing, make all the preparations even down to office space and a printer's imp; then, when we're ready, we'll break the news to Stoddard—sometime after the first of the year, I should think."

Willis doused the lamp, and in the darkness they groped to find their way out the door, lock it, and descend the stairs.

"What of the *Broadway Journal*?" Willis asked once they reached Ann Street and turned toward Broadway. "I heard Poe bought out Briggs."

"Poe won't make it," Morris replied, matter-of-factly. "It's pitiful, really. I'm told he stayed drunk half the summer, and there was talk that he'd been charged with forgery. He owes money all over town, so people were ready to believe that he was guilty. Stoddard told me, and he seemed a little too eager to call Poe a rascal. I don't like Poe, as you know, but nor do I wish him harm. It's a fortunate thing for you that you weren't here when he bought Briggs's interest; he would have borrowed from you just as he did from everyone else, and you'd never see a penny of it. I suppose I have to give him credit for having better sense than to come to me. The forgery thing blew over, finally, I don't know how; but then in August rumors started floating around about him and Fanny Osgood."

"Fanny Osgood!"

"She was back in town in August," Morris continued. "I saw her at Lynchie's several times, always with Poe. And he was on his best behavior.

Then, when the rumors started flying, she disappeared and he did, too, for the most part; I see him at the theater once in a while. Fanny moved to Providence, so Anne Lynch told me. And it's a fortunate thing she did, if you ask me."

Willis laughed, shaking his head, as the two men turned up Broadway toward Florence's for supper, though neither had suggested the place; it was their usual. "What did the rumors say?" he asked.

"That they were having some kind of love affair."

"That's absurd," Willis said. "Poe and Fanny? Not in a million years. Did his wife die?"

"Not to my knowledge," Morris said, "but you might not have thought the rumors so absurd if you'd seen Fanny's story in *Graham's* in August. That didn't help matters."

"I saw it," Willis said. "Theatrical, if you ask me. I introduced the two of them. Did you know that? And I've met Poe's wife; she has the consumption. He seemed devoted to her." Just then Willis recalled his proposal to Poe in January that they pirate work from England, and he wondered if Poe had counted on that in buying out Briggs. Had he let Poe down? "I feel sorry for him, Morris," Willis continued. "He's a fine writer and an experienced editor. If his magazine fails, perhaps we should offer him a job."

Morris stopped and turned to Willis, who stood a head taller. They were at the entrance to Florence's. Other pedestrians walked around them, and the avenue was thick with carriages and horsecars. "You have a soft heart, my boy," Morris said, using the affectionate moniker he always used when he preached to Willis as he would to a son, which he often did despite the fact that he was only four years his elder. "And I have long believed that a soft heart is your finest trait and the chief cause of your popularity. Believe me, I would do nothing to harden it, so it's probably best that you leave the hirings and firings and all the other nasty little chores to me. Commission as many tales and poems and Little Longfellow Wars as you want from Poe; that's fine with me, but I'll not share an office with a man who is just as apt to show up drunk as sober."

"He never once came to work drunk last year," Willis pleaded. "Not once."

Morris stared up at him and shook his head. "I can't explain that," he said, "except to think that people change. I saw him one day back in June, early afternoon. I was leaving the office, going to lunch, and I saw him standing, dead still, in the middle of Nassau looking dazed, as if he didn't know where he was. I thought perhaps I should go pull him out of the street before he got himself run over, but then he saw me and nodded, and I decided he was all right. I didn't know if he was drunk or mad. He had the wildest look in his eyes — wild, I tell you. Then I would see him at Lynchie's with Fanny Osgood, and he was always neatly dressed, polite and cordial, an interesting fellow to talk to. You'd think he was two different people. There's something wrong there, my boy, something bad wrong. He frightens me."

Willis dropped his gaze to the sidewalk, remembering the bizarre scene almost a year ago when Poe had showed up drunk, wanting to borrow money, and raving like a lunatic about Briggs being a fool. Finally he nodded his agreement and the two men went in for supper.

CHAPTER 19

❧ Eddy ❧

Boston Daily Times   Thursday, October 16, 1845

TONIGHT AT THE ODEON THEATRE the Lyceum season begins with a lecture by the Hon. Caleb Cushing, Commissioner to China, and the recitation of a new, original poem by Mr. Edgar A. Poe, author of "The Raven." It is hoped that a full house will bear evidence of the public's appreciation for these distinguished visitors to our city.

FROGPONDIUM—EDDY'S DYSPHEMISM for Boston—was a set-up. He had railed against their favorite son, Henry Wadsworth Longfellow, too vociferously and for too long. Willis bore a share of the responsibility. It was Willis who started the war; then he disappeared, leaving Eddy bloodied and saddled with the blame. No doubt Willis would have advised Eddy to decline the invitation, but the Frogpondians baited the trap with fifty dollars. Hard up as he was, he could not turn it down. And no sooner did he accept than he suspected he was being flimflammed. Quite naturally, this suspicion pricked his organ of perversity, and he contrived the means to subvert it.

There was in that quarter of the United States that includes Boston a newspaper, the *Boston Evening Transcript,* that employed an editress, Cornelia Wells Walters. Miss Walters, a resident Frogpondian, a Transcendentalist, and a devotee of Mr. Longfellow, still smarting from Eddy's having called her a "pretty little witch" in response to one of her attacks, was ready with her cannonade before his train arrived at the station. Whatever he read as a new original poem, regardless of its merits, was to be fodder for her barrage. He would have been a fool, therefore, to labor over a new poem only to have it sunk by cannons that were packed with shot before he ever left New York.

On soberer days, however, he had thought to comply with their request for an original poem. Be forthright, honest, honorable, he told himself, and let the chips fall. Let their newspapers have their go at carving him up. It was on such days that he appealed to others for help. He had no time to write; what's more, he was boneless. Magazine copy was all he was good for anymore. Desperation drove him to Fanny and Dunn English, and the futility of that was evidenced by Fanny's fairy poem. Whatever made him think he could read someone else's poem, palming it off as his? That was first-class plagiarism.

After leaving Fanny, he had returned to the hotel and gotten drunk. On the train to Boston the following morning—trying to forget about Fanny and the transgressions of the night before, not to mention his splitting head and unsettled stomach—with no alternative, he resorted to the lure of perversity.

At the Odeon Theatre that night, emboldened by drinks at his hotel beforehand, Eddy perpetrated the deception. He prefaced his recitation with an apology for not reading a didactic poem and took a few minutes to explain that a didactic poem was no poem at all. This news, of course, was not calculated to be well received in Boston, but he judged it time they knew. With that said, he launched into the recitation of "Al Aaraaf"—written when he was twenty and renamed for the occasion.

The first stanza of "The Messenger Star," fifteen lines, sounded well enough, but the poem was too long, not to mention inaccessible and knotty, and there were remote mythological references that would drive the finest classical scholar to distraction. He let those names roll off his tongue with practiced fluidity and decided it was going better than expected, though he could perceive a rather large number of mystified faces.

At one point he found himself hurrying. More and more of the mystified looks turned to irritation. Someone near the back got up and walked out. Others followed. He thought to end it and go straight to "The Raven," but he wasn't half through.

When he paused to announce, "Part II," he saw a man in the third row throw back his head and catch the eye of a neighbor. Eddy glanced over at James Russell Lowell, who was sitting at one end of the stage with Caleb Cushing and the members of the Lyceum committee. Lowell's eyes were wide with fright, and his little elfin face so near tears that he scared Eddy. Quickly Eddy turned back to the audience and boldly read on, trying with the force of his voice and with gestures to enliven the piece, but his gestures only served to make it more ridiculous, and he couldn't contain a smile which infuriated the man who had rolled his eyes at his neighbor.

Twenty minutes later he came to the end.

There was not a sound.

Stepping back from the podium, he cleared his throat. Not having the nerve to ask that the gaslights be dimmed, he launched into "The Raven," giving it everything he had. It was a disaster nonetheless.

When the program was over, Eddy adjourned with fellow-speaker Caleb Cushing and members of the Lyceum committee, Messrs. Coffin, Whipple, Hudson, Field, and Lowell, to an eatery not two blocks from the Odeon, and there he sipped champagne knowing full well that his bluff was about to be called. It had not been his intent to divulge the deception until such revelation served his purpose in responding to the criticism that was sure to follow, and, since he had recited "The Raven," too, he had even thought it possible that the reviews might be favorable. Were that the case, Eddy planned to forever conceal the chicanery. He had even imagined that the high jinks would be a source of knee-slapping amusement for Willis when he returned, but such cheerful hopes were truly far-fetched.

"Might I have another glass of champagne?" he asked, rather too quickly upon being seated at the supper table.

As he poured, Mr. Whipple informed Eddy that his nemesis, Miss Cornelia Wells Walters, had been in attendance. "She doesn't like you, Poe," he said, and smiled. Whipple was a plump, jolly little man who seemed highly pleased that a dozen or more people had walked out during Eddy's recital, and as their meal was served, he did not fail to point that out to Eddy.

Jamie Lowell said little. He seemed exceedingly ill at ease and was not drinking. He addressed Eddy as Poe. For that reason, Eddy addressed him as "Mister Lowell," and Mr. Lowell didn't seem to notice the difference. He was ten years younger than Eddy and also shorter. His little clipped beard was so well pruned and so short that it seemed no beard at all, but simply the outline of his jaw, and it came to a sharp point just at his chin, giving his face an elfin shape. His hair was long, as if his mother could not bear to shear off his soft, childhood ringlets. His pointy chin and boyish curls made him seem a lad of twelve or thirteen. The others adored him; they thought of him as Longfellow's protégé.

Lowell and Eddy should have gotten on well. Two years earlier, Eddy had contributed his "Tell-Tale Heart" to Lowell's short-lived magazine, *The Pioneer,* and Lowell had written that favorable sketch of Eddy for *Graham's* after publication of "The Raven." Eddy had written to thank him—thanked him exuberantly, as he now recalled—but that had been before Eddy fell out with Briggs, who was Lowell's best friend in New York City. Briggs's enmity and Eddy's having been drunk when Lowell came through New York in June seemed to doom their relationship. At any rate, what good would it do for Eddy to ingratiate himself to Lowell now that he had insulted Boston intelligentsia with the recitation of a farcical poem?

"Regardless of what Miss Walters says," Caleb Cushing intoned, "'The Raven' is a fine poem, and hearing you recite it was the highlight of the evening."

Eddy thanked Cushing and heaped praise on his two-and-a-half-hour lecture on the continent of China that had preceded Eddy's recital. Doubtless, Eddy thought, the audience was half asleep before he was ever introduced. "Gentlemen," he added, his tongue being loosened by the champagne, "as you have been so gracious, I will share with you a secret. Though 'The Messenger Star' is indeed an original poem, it is, strictly speaking, not new. I wrote it when I was ten," he said, deciding that ten sounded better than twenty. "I knew that Miss Walters would condemn whatever I recited, so I deemed it fair to surprise her with a hoax," and he laughed as a cue for the others to join in the fun and slapped Mr. Coffin on the back.

Jolly Mr. Whipple, who had laughed all through the meat course, stopped laughing and stared. Eddy thought Jamie Lowell would weep. Mr. Coffin, Mr. Field, and Mr. Hudson got up to leave.

"Poe," Hudson said, "you are a scoundrel." And he threw down his napkin and walked out with the others.

Eddy couldn't help but smile at Cushing, Whipple, and Lowell. He felt ever so lightheaded. More champagne and the room would spin.

Lowell walked Eddy to the Pavilion where he was staying. Not a word was spoken. In spite of everything, perhaps Jamie Lowell still wanted to be his friend, and Eddy almost apologized, but he became lost in thoughts of Fanny. Why had he done it? He thought of her guiding his hands to the buttons of her dress, slipping her arms out, the feel of her breasts. Why hadn't he stopped there? They could have kissed and touched all night. He would feel guilty just as he had in July, but he wouldn't feel this way. This he could never live down.

It wasn't just that he had made love to her; it was also that he desired her still. The memory of her removing her stockings, her foot on the chair, made him short of breath.

At the steps to the Pavilion Hotel, Eddy shook Jamie Lowell's hand. It seemed that Lowell was lost for words. He turned and left.

In the morning, his head aching, Eddy caught the train back to New York. The jerking motion of the car and acrid, suffocating smoke from the engine made his stomach churn. Thoughts of the disaster at the Odeon were again overshadowed by thoughts of what had happened in Providence. How could he have done that to Sissy?

Eddy arrived at Amity Street late on Friday afternoon. He was exhausted and depressed, but Muddy had prepared a special supper, roasted pork with potatoes, carrots, and beets. It made for too cheerful a plate of food, and despite his mood, Eddy praised the meal above anything in the eateries of Boston or Providence. Sissy flinched at the mention of Providence, and Muddy let Eddy's compliment go by without comment.

"Is something wrong?" he asked.

Muddy went to the mantel and brought him a letter, a letter addressed to Sissy.

Eddy studied the envelope, sensing what it contained. "Is it the same handwriting?" he asked, afraid to open it.

"Same handwriting," Muddy said, defiant. "Are you going to read it or do I have to tell you what it says? It says you're making love to Fanny Osgood."

Eddy shot a glance at Muddy, shocked by her bluntness; then he looked back down at the envelope in his hand, thinking his mouth would betray his feelings of remorse. But it didn't matter now; it was out in the open. He almost felt relief. It was as if he'd been spared the painful duty of a confession.

Sissy stood and cleared the dishes, a thing Muddy usually did, and Muddy glared at Eddy, questions in her eyes. Sissy returned to the table with a dish of raisins and sat back down, her hands clasped in her lap.

Eddy studied her, screwing up his courage. "Fanny could never take your place," he said, feeling emotion rise inside him. "Or anyone. Ever." And he could feel the corners of his mouth give way as always happened when he was about to cry.

Sissy began to weep, and her tears brought his own.

He stood and walked around to her chair, took her by the shoulders, and squeezed her. She was so frail. He could feel sharp angles of bone. It shocked him to think that he must not have touched her in months. "I should not have gone to Providence," he said, wishing she would look up. "I needed help. I should never have accepted the invitation to Boston." As he said this, he glanced across the table at Muddy, whose jaw was clenched in anger.

After Sissy and Muddy had gone to bed, he read the letter and burned it. Leaning against the mantel, he looked about the room, feeling as impoverished in character as in fortune. Of the furniture only the bureau and his trunk and the portrait of General Poe belonged to them. In the cupboard was Muddy's china. These were their earthly possessions. The lot fit on a dray with room to spare. Over the years they had sold everything else of value. The bureau had belonged to Muddy's father, the general. They had lugged it along with Eddy's papers and the sentimental trinkets in its drawers from Baltimore to Richmond to New York to Philadelphia and back to New York. Its edges were bumped, its pulls broken and crudely repaired. These were their heirlooms, the bureau and the general's portrait.

Also inside the drawers, along with the bundles of newspapers, books, and letters, were Eddy's scrolled manuscripts—the production of a lifetime as worthless as the bureau itself. He imagined it being lugged out to the side yard, contents and all, like William Henry's sea chest, and burned, the ashes rising with the heat of the fire to be scattered by the wind. Such was the legacy of Edgar Poe. With little prompting he might have burned the contents himself, then and there. Should he give up the writing life and start afresh? Go back to Richmond and throw himself on the mercy of John Allan's widow? Perhaps that would give Sissy a little more time and some small measure of happiness.

On Sunday, flush with the fifty dollars earned in Boston—though the bulk of it he had given to Muddy to pay debts—Eddy rented a gig, and the three of them rode out to the Brennans' for a visit. It was a clear autumn day, and the smell of wet earth and dry leaves filled the air. Sissy hardly coughed at all. She and Tommy Brennan played checkers all afternoon. Muddy and Mary Brennan did their needlework in the parlor, and Eddy walked down to the river. Throwing stones in the water, counting the number of skips, he recited lines of verse, whole poems, thinking he could write again if he could leave the city and the burden of the *Broadway Journal*.

Their old rooms were still not available, but Mrs. Brennan loaded them up with a basketful of vegetables, fruit, and a ham hock. They were back in town before dark.

TEN DAYS LATER, on a Monday in late October, Eddy received by mail a sonnet from Elizabeth Ellet with a note: His reading of "The Raven" at Anne Lynch's had been the highlight of her stay in New York. The note gushed with sentiment. She added that she hoped to see him at Anne's again in the near future.

The handwriting gave her away. Though Eddy had burned the letter to Sissy and could make no comparison, he was certain of it.

He knew little about Lizzy Ellet, though it was apparent to everyone that she had money. He had published one of her stories when he worked for the *Mirror,* and he had seen her often at Lynchie's—girlish ringlets and batting eyes, a coquette. She was not much older than Sissy. When he had gone to borrow fifty dollars from her to buy out Briggs, she had been almost eager to make the loan.

Why would she do such a thing? Did she even care that he made the connection? Did she think she was doing something noble? Or did she want some hold over him, some means of getting her poetry in print and favorably reviewed? Her sonnet was knottier than a hickory, but what if he ignored her? More letters to Sissy? Had she been the source of the rumors that chased Fanny away? And did she somehow know about his trip to Providence? It was a frightening coincidence that her letter to Sissy arrived on the very day he returned. Perhaps the prudent thing was to publish her poem, but he would not praise it. He'd publish it and hope she would leave them alone.

He led with it in the issue of November 1. It was indeed embarrassing to lead with such doggerel, but Eddy was fast sinking to new lows. He would publish anything for a favor or for money. He was prostituting the *Broadway Journal*.

The following week, *The Raven and other Poems* went on sale at Wiley & Putnam on Broadway for thirty-one cents a copy. Since Eddy had already wrangled an advance of one hundred thirty-five dollars, he would derive little further benefit unless it sold better than expected.

Letters arrived from Providence, one or two a week, consoling and reassuring. Fanny became the solace to which he resorted when depressed; he wrote to her often. More than once, he asked her to forgive him, and she wrote back insisting that there was nothing to forgive, and she often included a poem. One cold and rainy afternoon in early November, Eddy stoked the coals into flame and tried to forget the ills plaguing his magazine by writing her a long letter. The dreary weather made him miss her all the more. He enclosed a copy of *The Raven and other Poems* and asked her to send him something to publish, saying he no longer cared about the rumors.

It was the longest letter he'd ever written to anyone, and she responded with new poems for him to publish. The first arrived in mid-November, "To——"; then another a week later, "To——." They were both to him. Not poems of love, but of praise, too lavish praise. She was propping up his flagging self-esteem, and though Eddy saw through her efforts, he was grateful. He published them both.

Fanny wrote to Sissy also, and Sissy shared her letters with Eddy and Muddy. Eddy felt awkward at first, but after the exchange of a few letters, though nothing more had been said since the night he returned from Boston, it seemed that Sissy had forgiven them both and that her attitude toward Fanny had reverted to its earlier affection. Muddy held her tongue.

The fusillade from Boston continued. Cornelia Wells Walters called Eddy every vile name and even invented a new one—"Poh." It became her favorite. Knowing it was meant to disparage and belittle, his defense consumed almost as many columns as had the Little Longfellow War. He called her the siren of Frogpondium. He claimed that Boston would have condemned him had he composed "Paradise Lost" or an even greater poem—"The Raven." But Boston, of course, considered "The Raven" no poem at all. Had not Emerson said as much? Hadn't he called Eddy the jingle poet?

The furor blew itself out by the end of November, as did Eddy's hopes for the *Broadway Journal*. The long days and lackluster results had taken their toll. How many late nights could he pace the floor? How many dark, early mornings could he leave the house and wander Washington Square cajoling, arguing, begging—as if the shrubs and trees were his agents and creditors? If only Chivers. If only Willis. If only.

The final straw came the day before Thanksgiving, when the landlord for the *Broadway Journal* office demanded the rent Eddy had failed to pay on time. When Eddy couldn't produce it, he was evicted on the spot. Despite the cold and rain, his landlord insisted that he vacate before nightfall. As Eddy was due at the printer's to get out the issue of the 29th, he became irate, and they argued, coming near to blows. When the landlord refused to relent, Eddy packed up—papers, books, magazines, everything—and carried them the four blocks to Dunn English's office. When Eddy walked in with the first load, dripping wet, his papers and manuscripts nearly ruined, English scowled at him, the waxed tips of his mustache looking like the horns of a bull.

"What are you doing?" he asked.

"I'm moving in," Eddy said. He set down the crate, then returned the four blocks for the next load. It took him five trips. His suit was soaked; he pulled off his boots and wrung out his stockings; his top hat looked like a wet puppy.

English had a new partner, Thomas Lane, who was absent that afternoon, and the office now contained a sofa covered in maroon corduroy, sun-faded and beginning to fray. The sofa stood on four claw-footed wooden legs. Books and newspapers were stacked on its cushions. As Eddy had no desk, he asked English to clear off the sofa while he went to the printer's—the *Broadway Journal* was now being printed by *The Farmer and Mechanic*'s press, inferior but cheap. English grumbled. At the printer's, Eddy inserted above the first column a notice that the *Broadway Journal* had returned to 153 Broadway, and beneath this notice was his leading piece, another sonnet by Lizzy Ellet. She had returned to haunt him; he was certain it was blackmail—one more reason to give up the ghost.

When he returned from the printer's, English had cleared the sofa, and as Eddy unpacked his things, English watched, awaiting an explanation.

"I'm giving it up," Eddy said at last. "The *Broadway Journal,* I mean. I can't do it all."

English laughed and twirled the ends of his mustache. "You're mad, Poe. Does anyone know you've moved?"

Eddy started laughing. He was so exhausted and everything was so absurd that he thought he must laugh or he would, indeed, go mad, and it was then he realized that the *Aristidean* would outlive the *Broadway Journal*. Here he sat, a sofa for a desk, squatting in the office of a man not half the writer he was, and hoping English would not ask for rent until the street receipts came in. Eddy pulled his papers into a pile, set his inkwell on the windowsill, bid English a happy Thanksgiving, and left.

On the ride uptown, through the rain-streaked windows of the horsecar, Eddy watched the crowds hurrying home, carrying parcels for the Thanksgiving feast, struggling under umbrellas against the rain and wind that blew down Broadway. Evening was coming on, and rain beat against the roof of the horsecar. A top hat went bounding into the street to be trampled by the crush of traffic. At Delancey the streetlamps were being lit, and Longfellow's poem came into his mind.

> I see the lights of the village
> Gleam through the rain and the mist,
> And a feeling of sadness comes o'er me
> That my soul cannot resist:

Before he died, Eddy resolved, he would tell Longfellow that his words were a comfort. They were *his* words, not Eddy's. A poet could pay no greater homage to another poet than to resort to his verse at times like these.

When he got home, there was a pumpkin pie covered with cheesecloth in the middle of the supper table. Sissy and Muddy were all smiles, the result of a visit from Lizzy Ellet.

"Now, *there's* a nice lady," Muddy said, setting the table.

Sissy sat by the fire, inking the worn seams of a pair of Eddy's trousers. He wondered whether he should reveal his suspicions.

"We'll have a nice Thanksgiving supper," Muddy said, "thanks to Mrs. Ellet. She's a pretty thing and sweet on you just like all the other ladies. It's no wonder folks are so jealous of Sissy."

"Lizzy Ellet is a frivolous, conniving woman," Eddy said, and he went to the bureau and took out the three letters he'd received from her, letters that had accompanied her poems. It could be said that they were flirtatious, more so than the usual flattering letters Eddy received from women who sought publication and praise for their poetry. He handed them to Sissy, wondering if she would recognize the handwriting and worried that if she did, it might dredge up things best forgotten. Either way, he could not let Lizzy Ellet get away with the gift of a pumpkin pie.

As she read them, Sissy smiled, then handed them back. "Why do you publish her poems, then?" she asked.

Eddy couldn't admit that he owed her money. Sissy and Muddy had no concept of the debts he'd incurred. Nor could he say that he was being blackmailed. He returned the letters to the bureau and sat down at the table.

When they finished the meat course, Muddy cleared the plates and brought out three dessert plates. She cut a wedge of pumpkin pie, set it on a plate, and offered it to Eddy. He shook his head.

Amused, Muddy and Sissy eyed him, but he was adamant.

SATURDAY NIGHT EDDY attended Anne Lynch's party, his first since Fanny's departure nearly three months earlier. It was a going-away party for Ole Bull, who was returning to Norway after more than a year of touring America. Anne had composed a farewell poem, and Eddy had published it for her in the *Broadway Journal*. She had insisted that he be on hand to read it aloud.

There was a large crowd. Eddy snaked his way through the parlor and into the dining room, where he was at once accosted by Lizzy Ellet.

"Mr. Poe, you flatter me," she said of the prominent placement of her sonnet in the *Broadway Journal*.

He was almost afraid to speak but forced himself to be civil; after all, he owed her fifty dollars. She was taller than Fanny and wore her blond hair long; the ringlets about her ears fell to her shoulders. Her nose was rather too prominent; her eyes were blue. She professed to have come north in the spring to escape the heat and humidity of South Carolina, but here it was November, and she was still in New York with no plans of returning. She had come to stay with her brother and visit her parents, who lived upstate on Lake Ontario.

Eddy listened, wishing the recitations would begin.

Lizzy went on to say that her father owned timberland and that his mills supplied lumber all over New York state via the Erie Canal. Her brother looked after the business at this end. She said little about her husband except that he was a college professor in Columbia, a chemist and highly respected.

She repeated "highly respected" several times. The drift of conversation led to odd and pointed questions. Had Eddy liked growing up in the south? Had his family owned Africans? Did he think them noble like the Polynesians?

As she spoke, Eddy had the impression that she was flirting with him. At one point she put her hand on his forearm and drew so close that he thought she might kiss him on the cheek.

"Is Miss Fuller not disgusting?" she whispered, cutting her eyes across the dining room table at Margaret Fuller. "She dresses like a woman, but everything about her is manly, don't you think?"

Eddy ignored her questions about Margaret Fuller, and, thankfully, the recitations began. When his reading was announced, Lizzy detained him momentarily, drawing him close again. "I am composing another poem for you," she whispered. "When it's finished, I will send you a note, and you can come to my house for it."

As he made his way to the fireplace, he realized that others had seen this exchange. It was as if she'd laid a trap for him, and it so unsettled him that he could not get into the spirit of his presentation.

On successive days not two weeks later, he had poems from Lizzy and Fanny. Lizzy's was a love poem. Fanny's poem, "A Shipwreck," shocked him. There was no letter enclosed, underscoring the message of the poem, which implied that their love was being cast away.

> And you, who should its pilot be—
> To whom in fear it flies—
> Forsake it, on a treacherous sea,
> To seek a prouder prize.

Lizzy Ellet, a prouder prize? Someone had written Fanny. Someone who had seen him with Lizzy at the party—perhaps Anne herself. He immediately wrote to Fanny and told her everything: that he suspected Lizzy of writing anonymous letters to Sissy accusing them of making love, that he suspected Lizzy was the source of the rumors that had driven Fanny away, that he suspected she was blackmailing him into publishing her poems, and that he had kept these suspicions to himself because of Sissy's condition and to spare

Fanny. He closed by reassuring her of his devotion, and he added a postscript meant to cheer her.

> P.S. I have your book. I went to Clark & Austin and demanded an advance copy. It is brilliant! You have no peer in Europe or America. I read it in the horsecar going home, but Sissy took it from me at the door, and I fear she will not give it back. She read it all through supper—some of it aloud. Yours—Edgar

During the first two weeks of December, Eddy began the work of disposing of the *Broadway Journal*. He was confident that he could sell it and wrote letters to every prospect he could think of, Duyckinck, Colton, even Chivers, but he avoided approaching those to whom he owed money. His payment to Briggs would come due in another month, and he hoped to get enough to pay off his debts and have a little something left over. In the meantime, he must keep the thing afloat.

As a sofa proved an awkward place to work and as English's presence was always disagreeable, Eddy started working out of the Amity Street apartment. He published anything that was handy, including the poems by Lizzy Ellet and Fanny, as controversial as they were. In subsequent issues he reprinted his "Tale of the Ragged Mountains" and "Oblong Box," but subscription sales all but ceased and street sales slowed to a crawl.

Then, on a Tuesday afternoon, ten days before Christmas, he returned home to find Sissy sitting with Fanny by the fire.

"Look who's here!" Sissy said, rising from her chair. "She brought macaroons."

"Fanny!" Despite Sissy's greeting, he sensed something was wrong. Why would Fanny be here? "We didn't know you were coming," he said. "Why didn't you tell us?" He was shocked to see her. Had she and Sissy been talking about him?

"I only decided on Sunday," Fanny said. "I came for my new book and to do some Christmas shopping." Her words belied the worry in her eyes. "May's list is as long as your arm, and Lily's, too."

Fanny turned back to Sissy as if expecting her to say something, but Sissy looked beyond Eddy toward the door to the apartment. Eddy didn't know what to say. Sissy was ill at ease, and it seemed Fanny did not want to look at him.

"Eddy, I have done a horrible thing," Sissy blurted.

Fanny stared at Sissy as if the two of them were conspirators.

"Where's Muddy?" Eddy asked, thinking her absence might explain things.

"I think she went after Mrs. Ellet."

"Mrs. Ellet? Lizzy Ellet was here?"

"Don't be mad," Sissy said. "You see, I showed Mrs. Ellet's letters to Fanny. It was all my fault. But we got tickled with all her cooing over you. I started reading one of them aloud. We were laughing. Muddy had been cleaning; she was in the bedroom. The door to the hallway was open, and we heard someone on the stairs but thought nothing of it. Oh, dear, Eddy! Next thing we knew, Mrs. Ellet was standing in the doorway. And she had overheard us."

Sissy studied him as if frightened of his reaction, and still Fanny would not look at him.

"What did she say?" he asked.

"Nothing," Sissy said. "She took the letter and left. I'm afraid she was upset. I think Muddy went after her."

Eddy laughed out loud; he couldn't contain himself. Upset is not the half of it, he thought; Lizzy must be livid. But the whole thing struck him as hilarious. Suddenly Lizzy Ellet was not so threatening as she had been before, and perhaps this was just the comeuppance she deserved. "Well, Fanny," he said, walking around to face her, "you will have to give me more poems. After this, I expect Lizzy will strike me off her list."

Fanny smiled but said nothing, and her smile seemed forced.

"Do you forgive me?" Sissy asked, concern and guilt still evident in her expression.

"Don't think a thing about it, Sissy," Eddy said. "Lizzy got what she deserved." Then he turned back to Fanny. "How long are you staying?"

"Just two nights."

"Well, since you're here, I have something for you," and he went to the bureau, took out a manuscript scroll, and untied the ribbon. "I shall prove," he said, rather formally and eager to show off, "by the length of this, our esteem for you. Sissy, help me."

Sissy stood, and, following Eddy's instructions, she took the end of the manuscript scroll and backed toward the far end of the parlor, unrolling it as she went.

"This," Eddy announced, "is my review of your new book—five full columns. It will appear this week. It was to be your Christmas present."

Fanny's smile was less than enthusiastic.

"Look at her, Sissy," he said. "As if her vain little heart didn't think she deserved it."

His teasing fell flat, and Eddy decided Fanny did not look well. Of course, he realized, she had been uneasy calling on Sissy, or perhaps Lizzy Ellet's visit was the reason or perhaps it was seeing him. She thanked him, stood and put on her coat, then kissed Sissy good-bye. Eddy went with her to the street. Before stepping into the carriage that awaited her, she handed him a poem and told him to publish it. When he closed the carriage door, she lowered the window.

"Wait," Eddy yelled up to the driver; then he turned to her. She leaned back in the seat, her eyes fixed on him, her very posture indicating something was wrong. This was not the Fanny he knew—eager, excitable, always on the edge of her seat. "Is it that you're upset about Lizzy?"

Fanny smiled, shook her head, and tears came into her eyes.

"What is it, Fanny?"

She fumbled in her purse for a handkerchief. "Nothing. Except perhaps that you and Sissy seemed so right for each other just now. You were kind to forgive her. It was probably my fault in any case. I shouldn't have come."

Eddy looked down at his hand clutching the window glass. What could he say in the way of consolation—that her presence had indeed produced that moment in which he and Sissy seemed content, right for each other?

"May I see you before you go back?"

She shook her head again. He could not. She was very definite.

"Fanny," he said, but she raised her hand to stop him.

"Thank you for your review," she said. "And your praise." She looked down at the handkerchief in her hand, then back up at him.

"When will I see you again?" he asked.

She composed herself and wiped her tears. "I don't know," she said, taking a deep breath, "but when you do, remember that I care for you no matter what happens."

"What do you mean, 'no matter what happens?'"

Fanny smiled, her tears wiped away. "As a poet-friend of mine once wrote, 'Only that and nothing more.'"

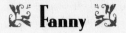 Fanny

The Broadway Journal   December 20, 1845

To "The Lady Geraldine."

I sought you not—you came to me—
    With words of friendly greeting:
Alas! how different now I see
    That ill-starred moment's meeting.

When others lightly named your name,
    My cordial praise I yielded;
While *you* would wound with woe and shame,
    The soul you should have shielded.

Was it so blest—my life's estate—
    That you with envy viewed me?
Ah, false one! could you dream my fate,
    You had not thus pursued me.
                Frances Sargent Osgood

FANNY HAD NOT COME to New York for her new book or for Christmas shopping or even to see Edgar. From the ferry she had gone directly to the Astor House to rent a room and drop off her trunk, then hired a brougham to take her out to Greenwich Village. She could not go to Edgar's office; the business district was off limits to a lady. Knowing he would likely not be home, she hoped Sissy would receive her, though she could not be certain. For this reason she had kept the brougham waiting in the street. If Edgar was not home, he would conclude she was staying at the Astor and would call on her that evening. Once she'd seen Sissy and made her peace with her, she could go about all her other chores, including seeing Sam and Lynchie. She dreaded seeing Sam, poor man. He was in town; that much she knew. Indeed, she had planned everything except what she would tell Edgar; she wouldn't know that until the time came.

Thankfully, Sissy had answered the door and seemed genuinely happy to see Fanny. They embraced as sisters. Mrs. Clemm stood at the door to the bedroom seeming wary and distrustful.

"Muddy, brew some tea," Sissy said, leading Fanny by the hand to a chair.

"May I help you with the tea, Mrs. Clemm?" Fanny asked, handing Sissy the parcel she carried so that she could unbutton her coat. "Tea will go with the macaroons I've brought. Sissy's favorite, I'm told. Am I right? They are fresh from the Astor kitchen, so they must be the best in New York."

There was no fire, and the room was cold, though the day was unseasonably warm. The gift of macaroons failed to thaw Mrs. Clemm's chilly reception, but Sissy ignored her. Now Fanny regretted saying that about macaroons being Sissy's favorite; it was Edgar who had told her. Leading Fanny to a chair beside the fireplace, Sissy knelt and placed several coals on the grate. Fanny watched as she tore pages from a copy of the *Broadway Journal* and crumpled them into balls for tinder; no doubt one of Fanny's poems went up in flames. Standing, Sissy brushed the coal dust from her fingers and smiled.

Still Mrs. Clemm said nothing. Noisily, she brewed the tea, then returned to her cleaning, leaving the parcel of macaroons unopened on the sideboard. Sissy brought them over to where she and Fanny sat by the fire, and they ate them out of the box.

Sissy asked about Lily and May, and Fanny described their adjustment to Providence, their school and new friends. It occurred to Fanny that she should bring Lily up to meet Sissy sometime, that they would get on well, and she realized that Sissy was almost as near Lily's age as her own. Yes, she decided, as soon as they moved back, she would bring Lily.

Meanwhile, Muddy grabbed up the rug in front of the fireplace, took it out to the landing, hung it over the banister, and beat the dust from it with her broom. Then she swept the floor of the apartment, even sweeping the hearth between Sissy and Fanny, sending Fanny the message that she was not a welcomed guest. Sweeping the debris onto the landing, Muddy left the door open so that there was a draft from the hallway below.

After a half hour of chatty talk, Muddy was out of earshot and Fanny seized the opportunity. "Edgar wrote me about the letters," she said. "The anonymous letters."

Sissy dropped her eyes, and Fanny wondered if Muddy could overhear from the bedroom.

"He suspects Lizzy Ellet," Fanny continued. "Did he tell you?"

Sissy looked up, surprise apparent in her eyes.

"He didn't, did he? Perhaps he's trying to protect you, Sissy. Let me tell you something about Lizzy. When she learned that Edgar was my friend, she wouldn't leave me alone. She wrote letters, paid visits—and compliments—until I thought she'd stop at nothing to be my best friend. I didn't mind at first. Really I didn't. It was charming, in a way. She is so young and seemed sincere. Young writers often fawn over those they view as successful. Little do they know the pittance paid to women for their poems. At any rate, she begged me to introduce her to Edgar. She came to Anne's every Saturday night, looking so lovely. It is I who should have been envious. Men flocked around her, but I could see that her eyes were always on the lookout for him—the author of 'The Raven.' She was starstruck, as is every woman who has heard him recite."

Sissy listened, apparently saddened by the revelation.

"But Lizzy became jealous of me," Fanny said. "Perhaps it was because Edgar praised my work or preferred my company, but at any rate, her attitude toward me had changed when I returned to New York in August. She avoided me, no more letters or visits, and I suspected she was talking about me behind my back. I think Edgar may be right that Lizzy was the author of those letters. Regardless, it was cruel and unkind, and I grieve now when I think that I was a cause of pain for you. I didn't know what to do. I didn't write to you because I thought you might hate me, but I have come to realize that I cannot be Edgar's friend if I can't be yours, too. And believe me when I say that I sincerely want to be your friend. Can you forgive me?"

Blushing, Sissy seemed almost embarrassed by the request. "There's nothing to forgive," she said.

Oh, yes there is, Fanny thought, but she couldn't confess it. That was impossible now even if she could muster the courage. Fanny told herself that she had not lied. She had chosen her words carefully. The affair—if that's what it was—was over, and she would be Sissy's steadfast friend to the end of her days.

As for Lizzy, Fanny had stopped short of accusing her positively, although she was positive.

"I think you're right," Sissy said. "I suspected it might be Mrs. Ellet after I read her letters. Eddy showed them to me. One is a love letter. There's another one written in German. Eddy pretends to know what it says. I don't think he does, but he's too proud to admit it. Do you read German, Fanny?"

Before Fanny could answer, Sissy turned to look for her mother. Not seeing her, she turned back to Fanny, a mischievous smile on her face. Rising from her chair, she went to the bureau and from the top drawer took three letters tied together with ribbon. She left the drawer ajar, intending, Fanny supposed, to replace them quickly if her mother reappeared, and she brought the letters to Fanny.

Fanny was reluctant to take them, so, kneeling before her, Sissy opened the first one and started reading.

"To the Raven," it began, and Sissy, oblivious to the possibility that her mother might overhear, started reading aloud, affecting a sentimental tone of voice that amused Fanny. "'When the blush has faded from my cheek—when my silken curls have turned to gray, I will hear your voice and see your flashing eyes as you recite to us in the parlor where I sit, one among the many who worship you. How many nights I have gone to that most amiable home on Waverly Place, praying you would notice me—one so shy and unimportant as I—because one glance from your eyes is a bolt of lightning to my soul.'"

Sissy giggled as she read, and Fanny, forgetting the purpose of her visit and the dread chore that had brought her back to New York, laughed also. She was sitting with her back to the door, Sissy kneeling before her. Muddy was in the bedroom. When Sissy finished reading, she offered the letter to Fanny, and as she did, she glanced beyond Fanny, a startled expression on her face.

Fanny turned to follow the line of Sissy's gaze, and there stood Lizzy Ellet. Fanny held her letter now. "Lizzy! my dear," she said.

"Mrs. Ellet!" Sissy said, rising from the floor, nervous and embarrassed. "Won't you come in?"

Muddy appeared at the bedroom door. Fanny turned to see her and could tell that she had been listening all the while.

Lizzy glared at Fanny, composed, her mouth tightly closed. She was dressed in a powder blue, woolen overcoat buttoned to the neck. Her perfect golden ringlets fell from beneath her bonnet. She carried a purse, an umbrella, and a book—a green case-bound book. Was it a gift, Fanny wondered?

Lizzy walked in, snatched the letter out of Fanny's hand, turned, and left.

Fanny and Sissy glanced at each other; then Sissy took the other two letters and put them back in the bureau, pausing before it as she closed the drawer.

"Oh, dear," Fanny said. Muddy reappeared, wearing her bonnet and coat, and left the apartment. The two of them remained silent for a moment, Sissy standing, facing the bureau, Fanny in the chair. I will pay for this, she thought; I will pay dearly for this.

When Edgar arrived and Sissy told him about Lizzy and the letters, Fanny avoided his eyes. He looked gaunt. He had shaved his sideburns and grown a mustache again. It made him look sadder, she thought, older and sadder. She decided her coming had been futile, and now she had insulted Lizzy Ellet, making things worse, much worse. She couldn't concentrate as Edgar read from his long review of her book. She wanted to be away and, remembering the brougham waiting in the street, used that as an excuse to go.

She didn't tell him while he stood beside the carriage. She couldn't.

THAT NIGHT, LYING in her bed in the dark, she again thought of ending her pregnancy. She knew that certain old New England cookbooks contained a particular recipe. It was the shared secret of schoolgirls who knew little about what they whispered. Fanny had some idea of the ingredients called for by that recipe, but surely there must be very specific measures and combinations that made it foolproof even in the hands of an indifferent cook such as Fanny. She wondered what it would be called, that recipe. Earlier, in Providence, she had thought to go searching for such a cookbook, but she never did. She had thought to go searching for a midwife who would know the recipe by heart, but she didn't do that, either. She came to New York instead, believing that if she looked into Edgar Poe's eyes, she would know what to do. It hadn't helped.

The next morning she was sick, heaving what little food she'd eaten the day before into the chamber pot. Choking back her nausea, she washed and dressed and went downstairs to inquire, in the privacy of the manager's office, about a doctor. She knew doctors in New York City, of course, but wanted none of them. There was a Dr. David Rogers within walking distance of the hotel, so she bundled up and went. His office was on Chambers Street, five blocks away, up one flight of stairs in a red brick building with ugly brown keystones. As she walked up, Fanny encountered two well-dressed women coming down. From their conversation, she guessed they were prostitutes, and she almost lost heart.

Dr. Rogers was in his forties. He wore a beard and pince-nez. Using her maiden name, she introduced herself as Mrs. Locke.

"I have been unwell," she said, having taken a chair beside his rolltop desk. "Nauseated."

The office smelled of carbolic acid, making her feel sick at her stomach again.

"How long?" he asked.

"Two or three weeks."

She hated his writing down everything she said.

"Do you have children, Mrs. Locke?" he asked.

"Yes," she said, irritated that he jumped to this conclusion so quickly. "Two daughters."

Dr. Rogers stopped writing, turned, and looked at her.

"Would you take off your bonnet, please?" he said, and, rising from his desk, he reached over and placed the palm of his hand on her forehead. "And your monthlies. Have they been regular?"

"No," she admitted, furious now, wishing she had not come. "Not since September."

Dr. Rogers sat back down and smiled at her. It sickened her, that smile, and she detested the man, so smug in his fine suit and silly eyeglasses.

"Can it be nothing else?" she asked. "Can you be so certain?"

"My dear madame, you are not ill," he said, then he turned back to his notebook. "Do you wish it were something else?"

What if she said yes, she wondered. She turned away and looked out the window. She could not hide her emotions even from this perfect stranger. Yes, damn it, she wished it were the blasted pox!

"I'm sorry," Dr. Rogers said. "Do you live nearby?"

"Thank you, doctor," Fanny said, standing, putting on her bonnet and pulling at her purse strings. She had to get out before the smell made her sick. "How much do I owe you?"

He put down his pencil and stood, removing his pince-nez. "There is no charge," he said, shaking his head.

Fanny supposed his waiver of a fee was her consolation. She swallowed to settle her stomach. "May I depend on your discretion, Dr. Rogers?"

"That goes without saying, Mrs. Locke," he said, clearly affronted by her question, though he tried to hide it. He will be intractable, she decided, and she thought better of him.

"Then please let me pay you," she said.

"There is no charge," he insisted, erect and proud.

Fanny hesitated, frustrated by his refusal, as if paying him would end it. She took a deep breath and put on her gloves.

"Are you all right?" he asked. "Shall I escort you home?"

"No. Thank you. That won't be necessary." She tied her bonnet strings, looked him in the eye, nodded, and left.

On the street her eyes burned from her tears and the cold wind that funneled down the side street. The smell of manure nearly made her vomit again. She swallowed back the churning and pushed her way toward Broadway, jostled and fretted by the crowd of men towering over her. They would have been a head taller than she even without their top hats. When she reached Broadway, she crossed to the park, desperate for fresh air. It was too cold to sit. No one was sitting on the park benches, and Fanny couldn't stay still even if she wanted to, so she paced the flagstones, up and down between the Croton Fountain and the steps of City Hall.

For a month she had thought of little else. Why she needed confirmation, she could not say. Perhaps it would help get her past the wondering and on to whatever came next. She had thought how simple it must be to brew a tea—send Lily and May off to school and put the kettle on. How it must smell up the house! She would have to lock the doors and draw the curtains—get out the slop bucket and the towels—drink it down—drink it quickly. And what happened next she could only imagine, a wrenching pain in her belly, no doubt—that would be her penance. She could even picture herself crawling on hands and knees from slop bucket to wash stand, her nightgown wet with sweat and blood. And afterward, despite the cold, she would have to open the windows if she could muster the strength. Perhaps she could do it; she had the courage. No, courage was not the word. What was the word that best described how much pain a woman would endure to preserve her good name? What a bully word that must be.

But she wouldn't do it. She could not take that life. And now she paced the flagstones from marble steps to fountain and back again. How to say the things she must say? She rehearsed her words, even put them into rhyme. She said them aloud, the brim of her bonnet hiding her face and the sound of her words from the passersby. She reasoned, debated, apologized.

Telling John would be the hardest. He would punish her by becoming more miserly with her money than he already was. Why did her father leave her in the hands of her brother? The answer, of course, was Sam; her father had hated Sam. If she hadn't ended up in the hands of her brother, she would have ended up at the mercy of Sam. Sarah would save her, she decided; Sarah Locke loved her. Fanny had not told her; she had told no one. She would have to write her sister, Anna, but if Sam took her back, perhaps she could spare Anna the truth; otherwise, Anna's husband, Henry, was apt to banish her from the family. Once, anticipating that Sam would take her back, she had nearly suggested to Lily and May that she might have another child, but just then they had started fighting over some trivial thing, and Fanny had lost her temper, shouted, and banished them to their room until supper was ready. Then, staring down at the pullet lying on the butcher block, she had started ripping the chicken apart with her bare hands, giving vent to her rage. It hadn't helped, and she cursed herself for taking her frustrations out on Lily and May. There was nothing she could do.

She reached the marble steps of City Hall once again, turned, and looked back toward the fountain. A man eyed her curiously. Had he been watching her walk up and down? Though the sun was behind him and she could not see his face clearly, she stared him down, indignant that he would gaze at her thus. When he turned and walked away, she felt a certain power. She resolved to assume that power and not be trampled by this, not hide somewhere, be meek; that was not Fanny Osgood. I will be myself, she resolved, and I will celebrate my child. I will even celebrate my child in verse.

She returned to the Astor. In the lobby she composed a note to Sam, saying she would pay a call at three that afternoon if that was convenient, and she asked him to respond by the bearer. She wanted to see his studio again, with thoughts of moving in.

After sending the note by a street porter, Fanny ordered lunch be sent up to her room and went there to wait. Her books had arrived. They were in a brown paper parcel on the bed. She had asked the publisher to deliver a dozen copies to the hotel, and here they were. Though it was her sixth book, there was still something miraculous about seeing her poems in print. Opening the parcel, she picked one of them up, caressing the green, embossed case boards. She opened it and, putting it to her nose, smelled its inky freshness. She had dedicated it to Edgar, though the dedication read simply "To Her Best Friend." She had conceived the dedication as a response to the poem Edgar wrote to her in May: "Yet may we not, my gentle friend / Be each to each the *second best*?" Had she the opportunity, she would change it now, but it was too late. He would know. If asked, Fanny might say it was dedicated to Anne Lynch. She would lie, but what of it? That lie would pale beside the ones to come.

While she waited for the messenger to return from Sam's, she opened the *Broadway Journal* one more time to read Lizzy Ellet's latest poem, "The Lady Geraldine." It had inspired a response, the poem Fanny had handed Edgar the day before as she left the Amity Street apartment. What Lizzy was doing to Sissy was no less than what she was doing to Fanny. Perhaps it had been a mistake to respond, but Fanny could not resist. She would expose Lizzy Ellet's duplicity and she would do it openly. She recited the last two lines to herself.

Ah, false one! could you dream my fate,
You had not thus pursued me.

How prescient those lines were.

SAM'S RESPONSE TO her note was warm and cordial. Yes, he was happy she was here and looked forward to her visit, and he hoped the children were along, as he had Christmas presents for them.

Perhaps her new life would not be so bad. At least she had New York to look forward to. Sam would travel, of course. They would live this pretense for a while, but how could she hope that they would achieve any sort of permanence? Sam was a nomad; there was no changing him. And then there was Ned Thomas. Ned would know it wasn't Sam's child; Fanny had confided too much, just as she had confided too much in Edgar. There would be no keeping it from him; it was hopeless to even try.

A waiter arrived with her lunch order. When he was gone, Fanny stared at the plate of food, wondering why she had bothered. She had no appetite. Thinking about the life inside her, however, she resolved to eat, sat at her table, and forced down bites of roast beef.

After lunch, standing in front of the mirror, she put on her bonnet and tied the strings. Poor Sam, she thought, staring at herself. He had so wanted to be free of her, and now this.

She left the hotel at two, taking a brougham up Broadway to Union Square and Sixteenth Street.

He greeted her at the door to his studio, led her in, offered tea, and asked about Lily and May. She answered his questions, brief answers, until he realized she was there for a purpose. When he paused, she blurted it.

"I'm pregnant, Sam."

Standing before her, he gazed at her for an instant, then looked down at the floor. Fanny sat in the same straight-backed chair from which she had watched him paint Edgar's portrait. Sam's hair was grayer than she'd remembered it, and he was thinner, too. She wondered if he'd been taking care of himself. Was he in love? She hadn't considered that possibility.

"I'm sorry," she continued, swallowing, deciding the little speech she'd rehearsed was too much, so she boiled it down to its essence. "It's two months now. You're the first to know. He's married. I have nowhere else to turn."

Sam listened, then turned to look up through the skylight. "I'd rather not know who he is."

"I wasn't going to tell you. It's not important now."

On the wall in front of her hung a landscape—a country lane, summer day, split rail fence, cows grazing.

"Poor Sam."

His back was still to her. She watched as his shoulders rose and fell with each breath he took. What was in his mind?

"I will be very happy to have you back," he said, without turning around. "I miss you. I miss the girls. It's my fault. I'm so sorry, Fanny. I'm sorry for everything."

She took a deep breath and closed her eyes tight to trap her emotions inside. She couldn't show him tears; not now. That would be too cruel. Poor Sam, was all she could think; poor, poor Sam.

 Eddy

---

The Broadway Journal   December 27, 1845

EDITORIAL MISCELLANY

We have a letter from Dr. Collier, the renowned Mesmerist, regarding the remarkable case of M. Valdemar, and we quote a portion of same:

> *Boston, December 16, 1845*
>
> DEAR SIR—Your account of M. Valdemar has created so great a sensation that it has been pirated by newspapers throughout New England. Everyone wishes to know if such a thing is indeed Possible.
>
> As one with considerable experience in the field, I am writing to confirm that it is. I, myself, by means of Animal Magnetism, restored to animation a person who had died of an excess of ardent spirits and had been laid out in his coffin for interment. He survives to this day.
>
> In order to satisfy the disbelievers of this city, I request by return post your assurance that the case of M. Valdemar is no fiction but a true and factual account of the suspension of death by means of mesmerism. Yours, most respectfully,
>
>   Robert H. Collyer.

Edgar A. Poe, Esq., New York

EDDY'S NEW TALE, "The Facts in the Case of M. Valdemar," was indeed causing a sensation. For a week after its publication he revealed nothing of the hoax. How many times had someone asked, "Is it true, Poe?" He would say only that mesmerism has been proven beyond doubt, and though he planned to admit the hoax in the upcoming issue of the *Broadway Journal,* he bragged of its veracity as he greeted the Christmas Eve crowd assembled in Sandy Welsh's Cellar for lunch. The place was packed; a roaring fire and the steaming cauldron of Manhattan clam chowder warmed the crowd. Sandy was serving up hot toddies, and at the far end of the bar three men were singing

"Joy to the World" in dreadful harmony. Eddy was popular with Sandy's regulars, and for the first time since "The Raven," his name was associated with something other than tomahawking criticism and doing battle with Boston. His new tale, therefore, was reason for boisterous celebration.

"Why is it not possible," he asked, shouting over the din, "to arrest any human condition with mesmerism? Why, I ask you, could not a drunken man be restored to sobriety? Though he would be in a state of physical suspension, he would be as sober as Mrs. Sandy."

The crowd roared with laughter and turned to see Mrs. Sandy by the fireplace holding her ladle like a trident. She glared at Eddy, so he raised his cup to indicate he was drinking to her health. He should have been at the printer's, but at that moment he would have given the *Broadway Journal*—keel, hull, and masthead—for coverage of his bar tab.

"Then you should see a mesmerist, Poe," someone shouted. "At the rate you're going, Christmas Eve will be short-lived."

There was more laughter, the joke on Eddy. "I don't need a mesmerist. I *am* a mesmerist," he retorted. "What I need is a volunteer."

Someone nearby turned a chair so that it faced Eddy, then turned to the crowd and called for a volunteer. There were shouts for Sandy, but he declined, citing sobriety. A young man was pushed forward, his eyes glassy, his tie untied, and his starched collar so unstayed that a strong breeze might have carried him aloft.

"Sit, my friend," Eddy said. "For this experiment I will require your pocket change."

The "volunteer" nodded, reaching into his pocket and producing an assortment of shillings and pennies. Eddy took them, slapped them on the bar, and motioned for Sandy to fill his glass.

"And a watch? Do you have a watch and chain?"

His subject produced the needed items and handed them over.

"Very good," Eddy declared. "Now. Do you admit . . . of your own free will . . . to this august assemblage of witnesses . . . that you are not only quite drunk . . . but that you are profoundly drunk?"

"I do," the man said.

"Don't say 'I do,'" Eddy shouted. "I'm not marrying you. I'm merely sobering you up, in which case you will not want to be married if you are a sane man. And if you're not a sane man, you must already be married. You must say instead, 'I profess to be profoundly, incontestably, and irrefutably drunk,' which, if enunciated without error, will be profound, incontestable, and irrefutable proof that you are not drunk at all, but that you must be an editor and, therefore, merely stupid."

The crowd grew restless listening to Eddy ramble. When sufficiently tippled, little-used words flowed to his brain. Under the influence, he admittedly became rather too garrulous—verbal to a fault.

"I profess," the volunteer said, in high, good spirits, "to be inconstrutably, irrefeasibly, and uncontrollably drunk."

Eddy turned to the crowd, held up his hand for silence, and announced that the subject had proven to be drunk and was, therefore, a suitable candidate for medical science. As he leaned down to look his subject in the eye, the crowd grew quiet and huddled around to see. After advising him to relax, Eddy held the watch by the chain and swung it slowly before his eyes just as Franz Mesmer prescribed.

His subject's head swayed from side to side with the motion of the watch, and Eddy perceived that his eyelids were growing heavy. The crowd grew quiet with anticipation. Finally the man closed his eyes altogether, a relief, as Eddy's arm was getting tired. Eddy stopped, turned to the bar, and took up his glass for another drink. When he turned back, he perceived his subject listing hard to starboard. Eddy feared, as did the crowd, judging from their absolute stillness, that the man would fall over onto the floor, but miraculously, after reaching a thirty-degree angle of list, he stopped, burped, and began breathing peacefully, his mouth lolling open.

"Who's buying?" Eddy asked, turning to the crowd, his glass empty again.

"Wait, Poe," someone said. "You haven't proved a thing. He's not sober; he's passed out."

"He has not passed out," Eddy insisted. "Can't you see he's mesmerized? And as such, he is neither drunk nor sober. In a sense, both conditions have been suspended. We could wait three days, rouse him from his mesmeric state, and he would resume his drunkenness as if no time had elapsed."

"Aren't you supposed to ask him questions?" someone said.

"Yes, of course," Eddy replied. "We can ask him whatever you like." Turning back to his subject, Eddy said, "My good man, can you hear me?"

"I can hear you," the man said, without opening his eyes and in a voice that was barely audible.

"Are you quite all right?" Eddy asked.

"A bit thirsty," the man replied, and, without moving, he opened his eyes to half mast and looked at Eddy. "And you picked my pocket, you blackguard."

Eddy clapped his hands in front of his subject's face to awaken him; then he turned to Sandy and ordered the man a drink.

"Gentlemen," he shouted, pulling the volunteer up by the lapels and putting his arm around his shoulders, "I rest my case. Before hypnotizing this fine, upstanding, highly inebriated, somewhat truncated, no doubt well-educated young man, I asked him for his pocket change. Being quite drunk, he gave it freely and required no explanation. In fact, in his drunken state, he was not aware of giving up his pocket change at all. Once mesmerized, however, he became perfectly aware of what had happened—that is to say, sober—and called me to task. The case is proven. Who's buying?"

Having thus entertained the crowd, Eddy's toddies were on the house, and he left Sandy's later than was prudent. He had no recollection of the ride uptown—presumably he took the horsecar—and he arrived home to a chilly reception. He collapsed on the bed and missed Christmas Eve supper altogether.

On Christmas morning, cold and overcast indoors and out, the Poes opened their presents before the fire. Muddy had baked a loaf of salt-rising bread the day before, and they breakfasted on that and strong coffee. Eddy's present for Sissy was an assortment of satin ribbons purchased at a little shop next to Bartlett & Welford's bookstore. After showing them off to Muddy, she fetched Catterina from the bedroom, set her on her lap, and fitted her with a red Christmas collar. She would not look at Eddy. She said not a word of thanks. In this way he suffered for the rest of the day—the silent treatment and a splitting headache. He swore off again.

By some miracle the *Broadway Journal* appeared on Friday, the day after Christmas, right on schedule. Eddy had never reached the printer's. He had left the layout incomplete. The thing could sink into the mire for all he cared. But there it was, being hawked by a newsboy wearing a cap too big for his head. Eddy bought a copy and thumbed through the pages with the fascination of a man reading his own obituary. There was his name beneath the masthead—Edgar A. Poe, Editor and Proprietor. There was his lead, a poem by Mrs. Ellet entitled "To——." He remembered it. He thought it vaguely a response to Fanny's poem that had run the week before. This was followed by an essay; three linked sonnets by a Mr. Richardson; Eddy's "Mystification," which he had revised and reprinted under a pseudonym; a poem by someone named Gallagher; reviews and notices, mostly by Eddy; a sonnet by Mary Hewitt; drama and fine arts reviews; a pirated *sonetto* by Giovanni Giudiecione; and lastly—ah! there was the answer to the riddle—in "Editorial Miscellany" a typographical error of a magnitude that could implicate only Dunn English. Here was the ghost editor revealed.

Reading further, Eddy saw that Dr. Collyer reported from Boston that Eddy's account of Monsieur Valdemar's case had been pirated throughout New England. In fact, to Eddy's amusement, one newspaper had even run an obituary of M. Ernest Valdemar of Harlem, N.Y., noted author and bibliophile. Dr. Collyer's letter and name were prominently printed just below English's short introductory in which he misspelled the man's name as Collier—a name correctly spelled a quarter column away. Any printer's devil in New York City would have seen the error from as far away as Hoboken, but not Dunn English. His usual errors belied a deficiency in basic grammar. How had he ever come by the name *English*? He was forever mixing plural nouns with singular verbs and vice versa, but his sensitivity on the subject of his own incompetence was too finely whetted for censure. Still, since English had been generous enough to see to publication of the magazine while Eddy partook of Sandy Welsh's Christmas cheer, he considered it best not to criticize the blunder.

It never occurred to him that English and his partner, Thomas Lane, intended to excuse him from the *Broadway Journal* altogether. They had in mind the merger of the two magazines, hoping to retain enough *Broadway Journal* subscribers to see the *Aristidean* emerge from the red ink that swamped its ledgers. As the *Aristidean* was a monthly and the *Broadway Journal* a weekly, the scheme was fraught with difficulties, but that was English's problem, not Eddy's. When asked to assist with the transition in exchange for their assumption of his debt to Charles Briggs, Eddy felt as much relief as indignation. Beyond that, they offered nothing for his ownership interest, though he pleaded, citing the debts he'd incurred to purchase the thing in the first place. In the end he agreed, deciding that the burden thus lifted from his shoulders was sufficient compensation. Yes, he would assist them, taking the month of January to find a place to live in the country and preparing a new series of sketches he had conceived that he planned to call "The Literati of New York City," and he believed nothing of the kind had been previously attempted— fair and honest essays on New York's most notable literary personages, including reviews of their works and items of human interest such as their habits and physical descriptions, as well as humorous anecdotes. He was certain that he could interest Willis in the series and thus provide a stream of income.

On New Year's Eve, as Eddy and Dunn English prepared the first collaborative edition of the *Broadway Journal,* he learned from English that Fanny was back in town. She was staying at the Astor House with her daughters. He had not heard from her since her brief visit before Christmas, and the news puzzled and worried him.

He saw her that very evening at a party given by Caroline Kirkland and her husband. As Eddy entered the parlor, he saw her across the room. Her back was to him, her hair pinned up, her dress cut low in the back, her head tilted in that unmistakable way of hers. He felt the inevitable tightness rise in his chest and thought to go to her immediately, but no sooner did he finish greeting the Kirklands than he was detained by Mary Gove. Mary had made a rather dubious name for herself in New England as a lecturer on female anatomy, and the resulting infamy had recently chased her to New York. She was a woman about Eddy's age, an advocate of the cold-water cure, and the prospects of mesmerism fascinated her. Thanking him for publishing one of her articles, she asked questions about his essay on M. Valdemar, but while he listened to to her talk, Eddy could think only of Fanny and the little wisps of hair that had pulled away from her diadem of braids and fell along the hollow of her neck.

At just that moment Willis arrived and chased those thoughts away. Eddy had seen him twice since his return, welcomed him back, but as yet he had not had the opportunity to speak privately with him.

"Willis," Eddy said. "I've been meaning to come around to see you. I have news."

Seeing that Eddy wished to speak with Willis, Mary Gove excused herself.

"I have sold my interest in the *Broadway Journal,*" Eddy continued, "and I have an idea for a series that might interest you."

"Edgar," Willis said. "Now is not a good time."

"What do you mean?"

"I can't say. Let's have lunch. Not next week, the following week. I'll have something to tell you then."

Eddy stared up at Willis for an instant. He had counted on an advance for the series, and a delay of two weeks would present problems. "I'm working on a story, too, quite unique, a surprise ending that will leave them amazed."

Willis smiled, seeming to understand Eddy's plight. "Send it to *Godey's*. Now is not a good time. Sorry."

Cullen Bryant walked up and pulled Willis into conversation. As they talked, Eddy noticed a tall man standing in a corner of the dining room, his back to Eddy. Was it Sam Osgood? Why would he be there? Eddy had never seen him at a party in New York, never once at Anne Lynch's. Then he noticed Lynchie standing at the entrance to the parlor and excused himself to make his way to her and ask for an explanation.

"Edgar, I have a favor to ask," Anne said as he approached. "I am having a party next Wednesday, a reception for Cassius Clay. Catherine Sedgwick will also be in town. I want you to send a note to Fitz-Green and Charles Lester asking them to come, and you must come, too."

Eddy agreed. Anne had gotten in the habit of asking for his help, and Eddy considered it a special honor. When he started to ask about Sam Osgood, he felt someone take his elbow and turned to see Fanny.

"Happy new year," she said, smiling up at him. She took his breath away. She wore a dress of the palest blue, cut low and off her shoulders. She seemed all porcelain and satin.

"Fanny! You're back," he exclaimed. "New York is whole again. It wasn't, without you."

She thanked him with her eyes and led him away from the crowd.

"Mary Gove says you are beautiful," she said. "I saw you with her and went to find you as soon as I could. She said you are like a marble pillar among wooden shafts. I wonder that women don't fall down in a swoon in your presence. I told her I must find you and see for myself. And here you are, as magnificent as she said."

"If anyone is beautiful, it is you," he said. "I have missed you."

"What are the rumors regarding the *Broadway Journal*?"

"I've sold my interest," he said. "To English. I'm out of it. Just today in fact."

"Oh, dear," she said. "Where will I send my poems?"

Eddy smiled at this. "Send them to Willis and I'll do the same."

"Then you haven't heard the rumors," she said. "It seems Morris and Willis have retired from the *Mirror.* Hiram Stoddard is to be the new editor."

Eddy was dumbstruck. Morris and Willis were a New York institution, and the *Mirror* had subscribers throughout the country—it must be profitable. "But I just saw him. He said nothing." And he wondered if what Fanny said might explain Willis's equivocation.

Fanny smiled. "It's all hush-hush, but rumor has it they will start a new weekly. Your experience would be of great value to them."

"No." Eddy shook his head. "I'm through with magazine work. I had thought of moving to the country, but that was before I knew you were back."

Fanny put her hand on his arm. "My coming back mustn't change your plans," she said. "How is Sissy? Tell her I'm bringing Lily up to see her. And for you, I have a new poem, so I will send it to the *Mirror* and hope that Hiram Stoddard will publish it."

"I don't think he would pay for one of mine," Eddy said, and he could have kicked himself for saying it. He had never paid Fanny a penny for all her poems.

She appeared to forgive his slip and leaned up to whisper in his ear. "Lizzy Ellet is here."

Then she was gone, melting into the crowd gathered in the Kirklands' parlor, dining room, and library, and Eddy did not see her again for the rest of the night. Nor did he see Sam again, and he wondered if he had been mistaken.

Rumors of his departure from the *Broadway Journal* were making the rounds, even as far away as Boston. No doubt English was bruiting it about. From the *Boston Evening Transcript* came a final salvo from the culverin of Cornelia Wells Walters.

> To trust in friends is but so so,
> Especially when cash is low;
> The *Broadway Journal's* proved *"no go"*—
> *Friends* would not pay the pen of Poh.

Since his battleship was sinking, Eddy could not return fire.

ANNE LYNCH'S PARTY ushered in the new season in festive, high fashion. Cassius Clay addressed the assemblage, but his abolitionist harangue fell flat. Among Lynchie's friends, he was preaching to the choir. Fitz-Green Halleck came, as did Cullen Bryant and all the rest of her regulars. Lizzy Ellet was there too. And Fanny, though this time there was no sign of Sam, and Eddy decided he had been mistaken, that it wasn't Sam at the Kirklands'. He thanked Fanny for her poem. It had appeared that same day in the *Mirror*. Addressed "To ——," she wrote of "worldly turmoil" and "troubled life," but Eddy assumed these phrases referred to everyday life and that nothing foreboding was implied. Nevertheless, there was an air of sad reflection about the poem, and he wondered if the demise of the *Broadway Journal* meant the end of something else. He recalled one particular verse.

> Like the memory of a fountain,
> Springing pure and falling free,
> In the midst of worldly turmoil,
> Is my silent thought of thee.

The following day, Thursday, Eddy worked at his desk in the apartment on Amity Street on his new story, "The Sphinx," an old idea that he was finally getting round to. It was unseasonably warm for January, and though they had a fire in the grate, Eddy opened the window to let in fresh air. The sun shone in his face such that he had to shield his eyes as he wrote, and when the post arrived he was thinking how pleasant the warm sunshine felt. He let Muddy go to the door, and she laid several letters on the corner of his desk. He glanced over at them and noticed Fanny's handwriting. He put down his pen and opened it.

Tuesday p.m.

Dearest Edgar,

    As you will hear soon enough, you may as well learn from me that Sam and I are reconciled. Since his studio is not suitable, Lily, May, and I will stay at the Astor until we find a place to live. He is doing well—more commissions than he can accept—so he is now able to cut back on his traveling and be a proper father to his daughters and to the new child that we are expecting. I have only just learned this joyful news. No doubt our child will be a poet, for never was a child conceived with so rich a vein of poetic sentiment. I have resolved that you will be a godfather to my child, though for now that must remain our secret. As Sam and I have not yet made the announcement, please tell no one.

Pray for me, as I require your prayers. Save for your love, they are all I ask.

I remain constant, as you said—each to each, the *second best,*

Fanny

A child! My child! Eddy felt numb. Though the window was opened, he could hardly breath. He grabbed his overcoat, shoved Fanny's letter into his pocket, said something about an errand, and left.

He walked over to Broadway and caught the horsecar downtown. Thinking to go straight to the Astor and see her, he rode to the end of the line. When he stepped down from the car, he turned and stared up at the Astor. The granite facade was somehow too formidable; then it occurred to him that her letter was intended to preclude his questions. He hesitated, then turned and began walking, going nowhere in particular. He crossed over Broadway, passed Trinity Church, and walked all the way downtown to the Battery. At the rail, he stared out on the water, Castle Garden off to his right and Staten Island in the distance.

"My God!" he whispered, over and over. "My God!" He held to the wrought iron and listened to the water lap the riprap, repeating the phrase—watchwords to keep from going mad.

Gradually he became aware of someone to his left, someone staring at him.

"You are Edgar Poe." she said. It was not a question. She was Muddy's age and seemed vaguely familiar.

"Yes." He turned back toward the bay, hoping she might see his distress and leave him alone.

"Forgive my interrupting. I'm Maria Child. We met, once."

"Oh, yes, Mrs. Child," he said, forcing himself to be polite. "I didn't recognize you."

"There's no reason you should," she said, approaching and turning to look out on the water. "We met only that once. You had just published 'The Raven,' and everyone wanted to meet you. I was one of many introduced to you that night. It was the night of the Ole Bull concert at the Park. Do you remember? Both of us reviewed that performance. It was magnificent."

Maria Child was short and stout like Muddy, the way some women in good health become as they approach old age. Her eyes were dark and perceptive, her mouth straight and forthright.

"Yes, I remember," he said. "I admire your work."

"It's kind of you to say that," she said. "To be honest, I'm not sure what *my work* is these days. You published two of my articles, and I always buy your magazine when it contains one of your stories. You're a wonderful storyteller, Mr. Poe."

"I'm not with the *Broadway Journal* anymore," he said, irritated that she would not leave him alone. "I've retired."

"Yes, I knew that," Maria Child said. "What will you do now?"

"I'm leaving New York. My wife is ill. The consumption. She needs fresh air, and I want to begin writing again—stories, I mean. And poetry, of course."

"I know about your wife. I will remember her in my prayers. But I'm heartened to hear you say that you will write again. Your genius lies in your ability to tell stories. They always contain the most amazing surprises. I think you waste your talent on magazine articles. You should write a novel. It seems that novels are what people want to read these days. Where will you go? You're from the South aren't you, Mr. Poe?"

"Richmond," he said, thinking of an excuse to leave.

"Richmond," she repeated. "I've never been south. I spent most of my youth just outside Boston; in fact, where we stand now is as far from home as I've ever been. I suppose that's why I like to come and watch the ships. A day like today is a gift. In the winter when the sun has gone south, it shines on the water as at no other time of the year. I live nearby and come here often. Every day if it's nice. In the summers I come at night. Oh, I don't go to Castle Garden, if that's what you're thinking, though I do love music. And I like to see the fireworks reflect on the water. But I don't have the wardrobe for society, and I don't like crowds. I come and stand here by the rail, watch the stars and the lights on the ships and wonder what sailors do when their day is done. Sometimes they sing, and it's comforting to hear their chanties. For some reason, when I hear them, I can imagine how big the world is, and I envy them. You wouldn't believe how often I've wished I were a man and could go round the world. It must be hard work, but, oh!—to see strange places!"

Her babble became a balm, reminding Eddy of his fantasies, his running-away fantasies—the world, three-quarters sea, a vast emptiness in which to be forgotten. No one thinks of you, longs for you, loves you, hates you, wishes you dead or alive, even knows your name. Such was his fate. He could see it clearly. It was the only way he could ever hope to live with himself. See Sissy safely in the ground, then run away—disappear forever.

"Don't go back to Richmond, Mr. Poe."

Eddy turned to her, startled.

"We have more in common than you might think," she continued. "I used to be a magazine editor. I resigned two years ago. People grew tired of hearing me rail against slavery. Their letters frightened me. They said hateful things. There was violence behind it. I am no coward, Mr. Poe, but I am a woman. Wars are fought by men. It was Cervantes who said 'the pen is preferable to the sword,' but I perceive that God gave us two hands—one for each." She paused, and for a moment they listened to the water break on the rocks below them. "Now I write about things I love," she continued, "music and all the things that happen in this city. I think on any given day there must be more to see in New York than any place on earth. I'm content writing about things I love, and you will be content writing stories."

For some time, without a word passing between them, they stared out onto the bay. Without thinking, Eddy reached in his pocket, and there was Fanny's letter. It brought him back, pulled him away from the sea and the ships and running away and writing again. Fanny!

"Don't go back to Richmond," Maria Child said, again. "I fear the day is coming when we must choose sides." She paused and turned to him. "But you didn't come here for advice from an old woman, did you? I don't see many people, Mr. Poe, so when I meet someone I know, I go on like an old biddy. But I hope you'll come again. On fine days I'll be here, and we can talk some more."

Eddy forced a smile.

"Very well, then," she said, "I will leave you to your thoughts."

She turned, and Eddy watched her walk away, across Battery Park toward Pearl Street, leaving him to thoughts he was loath to think. Maria Child, he thought. Fanny is going to have a child—my child.

CHAPTER 22

❧ Muddy ❧

WHENEVER EDDY RAN OUT like that, jumping up and mumbling about some errand, Sissy and Muddy feared the worst. And, sure enough, he stayed gone the rest of the day and most of that night. Muddy heard him come in, couldn't have been more than a couple of hours before sunup. Too drunk to light a candle, he made more commotion than a bucket brigade. Twice she thought he'd fallen to the floor, so she finally went in to see about him, hoping he wouldn't wake Sissy. But Sissy was already awake. Said next morning that she hadn't slept a wink till he came in.

When Sissy and Muddy went in to make breakfast, he was asleep on the daybed, grunting like a pig. His whiskey breath stank so bad they had to open a window. Muddy figured he'd be sleeping it off all day, so she made a fire and went about her chores. Sissy stayed in the bedroom with Catterina. There was no fireplace in the bedroom, but Sissy would suffer the cold before she'd watch him sleep off one of his drinking sprees.

Eddy had left a trail of clothing on the floor. He had missed the peg, and his overcoat lay just inside the door. His shirt collar, his socks, and his trousers, with the suspenders still attached, were heaped beside the bed. Muddy picked everything up, piece by piece, folding his pants so they wouldn't be so wrinkled when he went to put them on again. She hung his coat on the peg and checked the pockets. When he was drinking, there was a slim chance he'd get home with money left over, and if she found it, she kept it. Served him right, it did. She would take it straight to the landlord. She'd been doing it for years and didn't give it a second thought. Never told him, either. He was always too hungover to figure it out. Anything else she found, she put away. She knew where everything went. It wasn't like they had a ten-room mansion in Gramercy Park.

She found Fanny's letter.

It was just a one-page note folded in half. There was nothing else in his pockets; he was broke. Muddy studied it so she'd know where to put it. Eddy was fussy about his letters and papers. Kept his letters in little bundles tied with ribbon in the top two drawers of the bureau. If Muddy wasn't sure where it went, she'd leave it on his desk. If she was, she'd put it in the proper bundle. She never intended to read the letter, but the day before, she'd found an empty envelope and was thinking the two might go together. Sure enough, they did. That's all she was thinking, standing in front of the window, comparing the two—the handwriting, the stationery, the shade of ink.

She noticed Fanny's name at the bottom and, just above it, that phrase "Pray for me." It jumped right off the page. Oh, dear, Muddy thought. What's happened to Fanny? And she read the whole thing. At first it seemed to be happy news; then came that part about a poet and wanting Eddy to be the godfather and keeping the secret and needing his prayers, and they all added up to something dreadful. Dizzy suddenly, she had to sit down, still holding the note, her breath coming hard. She was shaking so bad she could hardly fit the note in the envelope, but she struggled with it like putting it back in would make the whole thing go away.

She turned and looked at Eddy, lying on the bed. It was no wonder he stayed out all night, she thought. No wonder he took to drinking again. Then she decided she was mistaken, and that sudden notion was a great comfort. She couldn't be sure what Fanny was saying—her words were kind of vague—but whatever it was scared the brass right out of Muddy, and she'd have to hide that letter from Sissy.

Putting it back in Eddy's coat pocket was the natural thing to do, but once he sobered up and went to thinking about it, he'd likely burn it. Before it went up in smoke, Muddy wanted some time to think.

Trouble was, Eddy let Sissy read his letters. He never chided her for going through his papers in the bureau. He didn't say a cross word to her after she and Fanny got caught reading Mrs. Ellet's letters. Muddy thought giving Sissy the right to read his letters was Eddy's way of saying he had nothing to hide. It was like he was telling her that all those lovey-dovey letters he got from women who drooled over his poems meant nothing to him. And Sissy could read them any time she wanted, and laugh at them, too, if she had a mind to.

But this one was different. He'd burn it. Muddy went to thinking if he didn't find it, he might decide he lost it. Maybe he'd ask her about it, but if she denied it—now mind you Muddy wasn't saying she could—he might decide it got lost in some barroom where he'd done his drinking.

So she hid it. She put it in the top bureau drawer—all the way at the back, behind all his packets of letters. Since she wasn't sure what to do, she'd keep it there for the time being, safe, until she could gather her thoughts. Maybe she'd never say another word. Or maybe if he asked for it, she'd fetch it for him—envelope and all, so he'd know she'd seen it. That would scare him off whiskey for a while. Or maybe she'd move it and put it with her own things for safe keeping, put it between the two bottom plates sitting on the sideboard. Or maybe she'd burn it. As she thought about all these possibilities, she wondered if burning it wouldn't be best. Seemed like Fanny was telling him good-bye, in a way. Maybe it was best to leave it be and try to forget about that last part. But two words kept plaguing her. Two words burned in her brain and wouldn't go away—"our child." Whose child did Fanny mean?

On Saturday Eddy stayed home all day. Muddy thought of such days as a sort of purgatory. Truth to tell, it was worse than purgatory. Sissy wouldn't speak to him and hardly spoke to Muddy. She was ailing, couldn't sleep—his binges always made her worse, and that in turn made Muddy so mad that she'd boss Eddy like a fishwife. When he wasn't doing Muddy's bidding, he sat at his desk, glancing over at the door to the bedroom every ten minutes, hoping Sissy'd come out and talk to him. Once she talked to him everything could get back to normal. It was no wonder that on such days Muddy liked to go out for a spell, and she did just that. She took her good time, too. She took the horsecar downtown and went to the factory in Maiden Lane to get a bundle of piecework. On the way back to the terminal, she stopped in Trinity Church. It wasn't their habit to attend church, and that transgression was heavy on her heart just then. She sat on one of the pews for an hour or more. Mostly she was thinking, but sometimes her thoughts turned into prayers.

"God, let Eddy quit drinking at least so long as Sissy's in this world. Give her a little time of peace and quiet and happiness before you call her home. Please, God. Amen."

And she'd go to thinking again. Eddy wanted to move to the country, and that was fine with Muddy. She would give anything if they could go back to the Brennans'.

"And let Eddy find us a nice home somewhere that we can afford and where there's plenty of fresh air for Sissy and space for a garden. Please, Lord. Thank You. Amen."

She thought about Fanny's note—truth was, that note was never out of her mind—and she felt guilty. Guilty for thinking maybe she took what Fanny said the wrong way. Guilty for hiding the note from Eddy. Guilty for the evil thoughts she had about the two of them.

"And, Lord, keep Mrs. Osgood safe and let her bear a healthy child and bless her family and forgive me for all my suspicions and conniving and mean thoughts. Amen."

As she left the church, she knew she'd have no forgiveness for her mean thoughts, because they wouldn't leave her head, and how could God forgive a sin that was still being sinned?

No one said a word that night at supper. At least Sissy came to the table. And she was dressed. But she hadn't taken two bites before she started coughing something awful. She couldn't swallow without coughing, and Muddy worried that she had put too much salt in the stew. Sissy's whole body shuddered with the fits. Muddy couldn't eat for watching her, and she decided to brew some of her special tea.

Eddy pretended it was nothing. That was the way he always reacted. He wasn't being mean. He did it to be polite, to keep Sissy from feeling she was spoiling supper. Talking like everything was fine, he announced that next morning he would go out to Turtle Bay and look for a place for them to live.

Good, Muddy thought. The sooner he got out of the house and did something useful, the sooner purgatory would end and they could all get back to normal.

He did go. It was Sunday, and he left right after breakfast, saying he intended to walk all the way. It must have been five or six miles out there, but he was broke, so he had no choice but to walk. It was a nice day, but cold. Maybe he'd get lucky and catch a ride.

Muddy brewed more of Sissy's tea. Sissy drank it down, and took a nap in the early afternoon. Poor girl hadn't slept for three nights. She cuddled up with Catterina, and Muddy covered her and closed the bedroom door so she could go about her housework without waking her.

At about two there was a knock on the door. It was Mrs. Ellet. Muddy was a little surprised to see her, and still embarrassed by what had happened two weeks before. Muddy invited her in, motioning to the bedroom door.

"Sissy's sleeping," she said. "She's had a hard time these last two days. We thought she'd never stop coughing last night. Eddy's not here. He's gone out to Turtle Bay."

"Why Turtle Bay?" Mrs. Ellet asked, removing her bonnet, concern evident on her face.

"It's a long story, Mrs. Ellet. Come in and have a seat by the fire. I've been working all afternoon. My hipbone's nagging at me, and I could sit a spell. Eddy stayed in bed all day yesterday, and I couldn't get a thing done around the house."

Muddy took Mrs. Ellet's coat and bonnet and hung them on the peg, then put two more pieces of coal on the grate.

"I do hope you'll find it in your heart to forgive Sissy," Muddy said, as she stoked the fire. "She shouldn't have done what she did last time you were here, but she didn't mean any harm by it. Eddy lets her read his letters. I thought it was sweet of you to write to him, and I know he appreciates it. I came running after you to apologize, but you were already gone."

Muddy was fibbing. At least about Eddy appreciating her letters. She had overheard Fanny accuse Mrs. Ellet of writing those anonymous letters, but Muddy wasn't so certain, and she had always liked Mrs. Ellet. Without proof, she gave her the benefit of the doubt. She didn't hold with people who wouldn't sign their name to a thing like that, for certain—but in light of Fanny's note, those anonymous letters didn't seem so evil after all. Fanny was a married woman, always had been, and ought to have been acting like one.

Mrs. Ellet gave a hint that she was still a little undone by what had happened, but she didn't say anything.

"I'm sorry Sissy is not well," she said, instead. "Is there anything I can do?"

"Best thing for her is rest and a special tea I brew," Muddy said. "It seems to ease the coughing and the night sweats. At the very least it helps her get some sleep."

"You must give me the recipe, Mrs. Clemm."

Maybe Mrs. Ellet was just being polite, but still . . .

"I'm sorry you're having such a hard time," she said.

"You don't know the half of it, Mrs. Ellet," Muddy said, wishing just then that she could be shed of this burden. "I've got a heavy heart, I have."

"Do you think Sissy is . . ." Mrs. Ellet couldn't bring herself to say it. Muddy could see tears well up in Lizzy's eyes, and she was sorry for giving her the wrong impression. Mrs. Ellet was ready to weep for her Sissy in spite of what had happened on her last visit.

"No. No," Muddy said, feeling her heart swell. "I don't mean Sissy. She's had bad spells like this before. It'll pass." She shut her eyes and realized she needed to talk to somebody so bad she could cry. Sissy wouldn't talk to her anymore, and now all these new suspicions were bottled up inside, and she was about to burst. The tears came. "If only he'd stop drinking!" she blurted, and she grabbed the skirt of her apron and covered her face. Not wanting to wake Sissy or embarrass Mrs. Ellet, she tried to muffle her sobs with the apron, but that only made it worse.

Next thing she knew Mrs. Ellet was on her knees, her arms around Muddy, inviting her to cry on her shoulder. And she did. She cried her tears out.

When she stopped, she pulled back, embarrassed, and found a dry spot on her apron to wipe her face. "I'm so sorry to burden you like this, Mrs. Ellet. It's just that I don't have anybody to talk to."

"You can talk to me," Mrs. Ellet said, seeming to be genuinely concerned. "I want to help. What can I do?"

Muddy looked her in the eye. If ever she saw a sincere spirit, she saw it then. They had misjudged her. She meant no harm; she was just trying to help. If she wrote those letters to Sissy, it must have been because she didn't know what to do and went about it the wrong way. "Eddy and Sissy call me Muddy," she said. "My real name is Maria. You can call me that, if you like. In fact, my maiden name is Poe. Did you know I was Eddy's aunty? He used to call me Aunty, before he married Sissy. He and Sissy are cousins, you know. First cousins."

"And call me Lizzy," Mrs. Ellet said, sitting back in her chair. She'd been kneeling all this time, wrinkling her skirts and probably soiling them, too. "Tell me more. I want to hear all about your family."

"Well, the Poes come from Ireland originally," Muddy said, taking up her invitation. "I was born a Poe; Eddy's father was my brother. Our ancestors had settled in Baltimore, and that's where I grew up. My own father was a general in the Revolutionary Army. He was a friend of General Lafayette, and he came to our house in Baltimore for a visit when I was a girl in my teens— I remember it like it was yesterday—he was a lot younger than my father, so grand, still wearing his French military uniform—that was the proudest day in my mother's life. You'd have thought General George Washington had come to pay a call. But Eddy grew up in Richmond. His daddy disappeared when he and Eddy's mama, Eliza, were living here in New York City. We never learned what happened to him. They were both stage actors. Eliza died a couple of years later in Richmond, died of the fever, and Eddy was taken in by a family there, the Allans. They raised him. His sister, Rosalie, went to another family in Richmond, the Mackenzies, and his brother lived with me. Sissy and I lived in Richmond for a spell. That's where Eddy and Sissy were married. She was too young, Mrs. Ellet . . . Lizzy. She was too young, and him being her first cousin. That has weighed down on me ever since. Did I do the right thing, letting her? I don't know." Tears came again, but Muddy wiped them off like they were grease stains. "You don't want to hear me go on like this."

"Yes I do," Lizzy said, then she turned to look out the window, seeming lost in her own thoughts. "I married an older man, too" she said at last, turning back to Muddy. Lizzy swallowed and shook her head as if to say it had been a mistake. "I was only seventeen, so I know what you mean. He's a fine man, but I realize now that I was too young. Sometimes I feel I hardly know him. I haven't been able to bear children, and that has been a great disappointment to Mr. Ellet."

Lizzy's confession brought tears to Muddy's eyes again. Perhaps it was the mention of children. "Mrs. Ellet—Lizzy, I mean—I'm suffering the trials of the damned," she said, and started bawling again. "I don't know what to do. I'm scared to death."

Lizzy was back on her knees, a handkerchief in her hand, dabbing at Muddy's tears. "What is it, Muddy?" she asked. "I'll help. I'll do anything."

"Eddy's had a note from Mrs. Osgood, and it frightens me. I don't want Sissy to find it. I don't know what to do."

Muddy sat for a long time, her face in her apron, hunched over in her chair with Lizzy caressing her arms. When she looked up, Lizzy was staring at her, sympathy in her eyes.

"What could Fanny possibly say that would frighten you so?" she asked.

Muddy hesitated. But it was out now, half of it, anyway. Her sixth sense told her she should have burned that note. Maybe she should burn it right now with Lizzy as a witness—not telling her a thing about what it said—and be done with it. But she couldn't see what good that would do. She had to get it all out. She had to set it free.

She went to the bureau and reached in the back of the upper left drawer and found the note right where she'd hidden it. Back in her chair, she stared at it for a minute, then handed it to Lizzy.

Muddy watched her read it. Lizzy's eyes grew large, and quickly she returned it to the envelope like she was worried someone would walk in and catch her. Then her eyes darted about like she was thinking what to do.

"I'll go see Fanny," she said, handing the letter back to Muddy. "She must ask for the return of her letters at once. Are there many others?"

"Oh, my, yes," Muddy said.

"Where?"

Muddy went to the bureau and searched among the bundles of letters. She was certain to find one belonging to Fanny, and she did, the biggest bundle. There must have been a hundred. Muddy turned and showed it to Lizzy, then returned it to the drawer.

"Have you read them?" she asked.

"No," Muddy said, returning to her chair and shaking her head positively. "I don't go reading his letters. Not unless he tells me to."

Lizzy thought for a minute. "I understand how this must trouble you. Trouble, indeed. It's no wonder you're so distraught. I will ask Fanny to see to the return of her letters at once. She has been careless. Can you hide the note until then? So Sissy won't see it."

There was another question in Lizzy's eyes, one she hesitated to ask, and Muddy didn't want to seem a snoop. "Eddy came home drunk Friday night," she said. "I think he was upset by this note, and whenever he gets upset, he takes to drinking. He's had so much on him lately, what with his magazine and all the hateful things people in Boston are saying about him. I was straightening up his clothes yesterday, and I found it in his pocket. I didn't know what to do with it, so I hid it."

"And he hasn't asked about it?"

"No. Maybe he thinks he lost it Friday night. He was out all night. No telling where he was. I thought about burning it."

"You mustn't," Lizzy said. "If it's not returned with the others, Fanny will wonder what happened to it. I think you must put it with the others and hope that Sissy doesn't see it."

"Then you must go straight to Fanny, Mrs. Ellet. You must go at once. If Eddy finds it there, he'll know it was my doing, and I hate to think what will happen."

"I'll go tomorrow. I promise."

Muddy heaved a sigh of relief. "Mrs. Ellet—Lizzy, I mean—you have taken a burden off my poor heart, but I won't get a wink of sleep so long as that note is in this house."

Lizzy Ellet smiled and put on her gloves. Muddy fetched her coat and bonnet off the peg, and before she left, they embraced.

EDDY RETURNED LATE Sunday afternoon, freezing cold and having had no luck finding a place to live in Turtle Bay. He was hopeful, though. Said he had the names of two farmers who took in boarders and that he'd go again when the weather improved.

He stayed in all the next day, sitting at his desk and doing Sissy's bidding. She was talking to him again, and he was staying sober. All afternoon, on pins and needles, Muddy looked for Fanny, but she didn't come. Nor did she come the next day. Or the next.

Muddy sent Eddy on errands, which he did cheerfully, but they had no money coming in. As a last resort, he went to Mr. Wiley and begged an advance for a new edition of his *Tales*. They put that toward the rent for the rest of January, saving enough out for food and for makings for a molasses cake, Eddy's thirty-seventh birthday was less than a week away.

It seemed to Muddy like Fanny's note was burning a hole in the bureau drawer. Aware of it every waking moment, she did her needlework in the parlor during the day while Eddy did his writing. He was into those drawers, going through his papers and such, but he didn't seem to notice anything amiss. Muddy thought if Fanny Osgood or Lizzy Ellet didn't come fetch those letters, she was going to have heart failure.

Saturday night he got dressed up to go to Miss Lynch's. He seemed nervous, and Muddy was nervous, too. Fanny and Lizzy Ellet were sure to be there.

Chapter 23

❧ Eddy ❧

The Broadway Journal   Saturday, January 17, 1846

VALEDICTORY

UNEXPECTED engagements demanding my whole attention, and
the objects being fulfilled, so far as regards myself personally, for which
The Broadway Journal was established, I now, as its Editor, bid farewell
—as cordially to foes as to friends.

   Mr. Thomas H. Lane is authorized to collect all money due the
Journal.

                              Edgar A. Poe.

SOMETHING WAS DIFFERENT. Eddy sensed it as soon as he arrived at
Anne Lynch's front door. Just at nightfall it had started raining, a
freezing rain. Since Anne's was only just up West Broadway and across
Washington Square, Eddy had walked, and his boots were wet and muddy.
As he wiped them on the stoop before going in, a carriage arrived bearing
Margaret Fuller and the Greeleys. Margaret came up first, climbing the steps
ahead of Horace and Mary. She noticed Eddy, met his gaze, then turned her
head, lifting her nose into the air, her nostrils flaring as if the mud on his
boots were manure. She passed without speaking. *What's gotten into her?*
Eddy wondered. Horace and Mary followed close behind. They were cordial and said hello.

   At the door to the parlor, he noticed several glances, but no one approached. Eddy had grown used to a small measure of celebrity. Lynchie was
always inviting new guests, and he was accustomed to someone rushing up to
introduce the author of "The Raven" to a new visitor in town. He enjoyed it.
It was reason enough for attending the literary *soirées*. Anne had never failed
to greet him when he arrived, give him a brief description of the agenda, and

often, ask him to take part. He saw her in the dining room, arranging glasses for punch into a pattern that pleased her. She was avoiding him, and he assumed she knew. Fanny would have told her. But Anne was his friend, too, and she had visited the Poes. They were near neighbors, and on several occasions she brought flowers or baked goods to Sissy and Muddy. She had always been kind to them; she knew that Sissy had the consumption.

Feeling awkward, he looked about for someone to talk to, some conversation to join. He looked for Fanny also, desperate to see her, and he wondered if she'd made the announcement. If so, Sam would be there, too, and Eddy had steeled himself for that encounter.

She was not there, and he wished he had not come. Seeing Fanny had been his only reason for attending.

Horace Greeley stood to Eddy's left. He had been polite coming in, but Eddy still owed him fifty dollars. No doubt Horace had heard that Eddy was out of the *Broadway Journal,* and he might be wondering about his money. In the group to Eddy's right he saw Lizzy Ellet, and, after what had happened, he wanted to avoid her. It was then he spotted Dunn English.

"Well, Poe," English said, smiling smugly as Eddy approached, "May the *Broadway Journal* rest in peace. As of next week she will be folded into the pages of the *Aristidean.*"

Eddy let the comment go by. "What about Willis?" he asked. "What do you know about his plans?"

"Morris and Willis are starting a new weekly; it's to be called the *Home Journal.* Now that postal rates have changed, they won't be saddled with the burden of a daily. Looks as though the *Herald* and the *Tribune* will own the penny press. Next Tuesday is Willis's birthday, by the way. Did you know that? He's forty. Anne plans to surprise him with a birthday cake tonight. With Morris and Willis behind a weekly, be glad you're out of the business. Wouldn't want to go head to head with them."

The notion startled Eddy. Willis was to have been his partner, not his competitor, and he was hurt that Anne seemed to have forgotten that his birthday was coming up, too.

He became aware of Margaret Fuller eyeing him. He decided to go and ask if he had offended her in some way, when Anne Lynch took him by the sleeve and led him away from Dunn English.

"Edgar, will you be at home tomorrow?" she asked.

"Yes, of course," he said. Tomorrow was Sunday, and as it was raining and cold, he would not be going out.

"I would like to pay a call tomorrow afternoon at two, if that will be convenient?" There was no smile on Anne's face. Her manner was austere. It seemed this would not be a social call.

"Perhaps I should come here," Eddy said, sensing that it had something to do with Fanny.

"No," Anne said. "I will come to you." She turned away and walked to the fireplace to introduce Horace Greeley, her master of ceremonies for the evening.

Undone by the gravity of Anne's tone, he wormed his way to the front hall, to the fringe of the crowd, where he'd be less obtrusive. On his way there, Lizzy Ellet appeared in his path and pressed close to speak.

"How is Mrs. Poe?" she whispered.

"She is very well," he said, as politely as he could. "Thank you. It's kind of you to ask."

"Did Mrs. Clemm tell you that I called?" Lizzy asked.

Eddy stared at her, puzzled. "Yes," he said, as if he had just remembered. She could not have been referring to her visit three weeks earlier. She must have come again, but neither Sissy nor Muddy had mentioned it. That was not like Sissy.

"Allow me," Lizzy continued, "to introduce my brother, Colonel William Lummis."

Eddy turned and shook hands with a stern, straight, and pugnacious man. He was half a head taller than Eddy, full-bearded and with a meaty hand that swallowed Eddy's. He was younger than Eddy by several years and had a heavy lotion smell about him. Visions of West Point ran through Eddy's mind. He had hated such men.

Lizzy turned back to him, again pressing close. "Your wife was not feeling well. She was sleeping. You had gone out to Turtle Bay, and I forgot to ask Mrs. Clemm why. Are you moving?"

Horace Greeley cleared his throat, and the room grew quiet.

"We'll talk later," Lizzy whispered, and let him go.

He went into the hall, got his coat, and left.

Sissy and Muddy were sewing by the fire when he got home. They were surprised to see him return so early.

"Why didn't you tell me Lizzy Ellet came last Sunday?" he said, before removing his overcoat, studying Sissy. Her surprise showed that she knew nothing of the visit.

"Muddy?" he asked, turning to her. Muddy's back was to him, and she did not turn around. When Eddy walked around to face her, she avoided his eyes.

"Oh, I forgot all about it, Sis," she said, looking at Sissy and avoiding Eddy. "She was only here for a few minutes. By the time you woke up, she'd been gone so long I plum forgot."

"What did she want?" Eddy asked. Sissy seemed confused.

"She was just paying a call," Muddy said. "She was right friendly. It was kind of her after the way she was treated the time before."

Eddy wanted to say that Lizzy Ellet was the author of the anonymous letters, but he didn't. He glared at Muddy instead, trying to find the logic in all that had happened. An uninvited visit from Lizzy Ellet made no sense after what had happened with Sissy and Fanny mocking her letter, and his cold treatment at Anne Lynch's was strange indeed. And there was Fanny's note, which he'd lost. He remembered fingering it in his pocket as he stood alongside Maria Child at the Battery. What happened to it? He had left Battery Park and walked along Front Street, along the wharfs. He'd wanted a drink, but didn't want to go to Sandy's, didn't want to see anyone he knew. He had walked all the way to John Street and gone into a tavern there, a place he did not know. Most of the rest was a blur. He had a vague recollection of walking home, and the next day when he searched for Fanny's note, it was gone. He suspected Muddy might have found it, since he couldn't find the envelope, either, though he searched his pockets and the papers on his desk a dozen times. Perhaps he had tossed the envelope on the coals as he left. He couldn't remember. He'd rather not know if Muddy read it, and he hoped she had better sense than to show it to Sissy.

Late that night, he lay awake in his bed. Unable to sleep, he got up and went through his papers again, searching in vain for Fanny's note. Why had Margaret Fuller acted the way she did? And Anne, too? And where was Fanny? She seldom missed one of Lynchie's parties. Were there new rumors, and did Lizzy Ellet have something to do with it? And why was Anne paying a call? It would definitely not be a social call; that much he knew.

• • •

THERE WAS A KNOCK on the door at exactly two o'clock the next afternoon. Eddy had told Sissy and Muddy that Anne was coming, so they were prepared for a visit. Muddy baked cookies and planned to serve tea, but Eddy had the uneasy feeling that refreshments would be refused.

Muddy answered the door, and Eddy was surprised to see Margaret Fuller with Anne.

"Miss Fuller, what a unexpected pleasure," Eddy said. "Sissy, please get another chair from the bedroom."

Margaret Fuller had never paid a call before, never met Sissy or Muddy. She lived in Turtle Bay with the Greeleys, so she must have stayed with Anne overnight. The two women stepped inside, and Muddy closed the door behind them. They did not remove their coats or bonnets. Anne said hello to Sissy and Muddy and introduced Margaret, who nodded politely but said nothing; then she turned to Eddy, who stood just behind one of the chairs beside the fireplace, which faced the door to the apartment.

"Edgar," she said, "we cannot stay. Mrs. Osgood has sent us to ask for the return of her letters."

"You mean Fanny?" he asked. So this was how it would be! They would close ranks around her. Shut him out. The men hated him; why not the women, too? It was Edgar Poe against the world. But surely Fanny had no part in this conspiracy. "Why didn't she come, herself? She has always been welcomed in this house."

Anne turned to Sissy and smiled, a smile meant to diffuse the tension. Margaret Fuller continued to stare at Eddy and he stared back. Did she know, too, he wondered. Did everyone know?

"Edgar, please," Anne said, turning back to him. She paused for a moment as if selecting her words. "You must understand Fanny's position. It would be improper for her to come, but she asked me to assure you that she remains a true friend to your family."

"I *don't* understand," he said, but he did, or at least he perceived the drift of things. Word was out. The rumors about them had resurfaced, and now Fanny was pregnant. This visit was an attempt to contain the damage. But why this humiliating confrontation? If Fanny wanted her letters, she had only to send a note for them.

"Does this," he asked, following his intuition, "have anything to do with Lizzy Ellet?"

Anne stiffened, and Eddy perceived the truth of it; Anne Lynch could not lie.

"Perhaps Fanny has been indiscreet," she said, avoiding his question. "You know how she is, Edgar. Her impetuousness is part of her charm. It's part of why we love her so. But now she is also vulnerable, and I think you know why. It would be best to return her letters."

Eddy heard little of Anne's speech. He was not a violent man. He had never killed anyone, nor could he, but had Lizzy Ellet been standing there, he might have torn her limb from limb.

"Lizzy Ellet," he said in a low, threatening voice, "had best look after her *own* letters."

Anne flinched. Margaret Fuller's eyes flashed.

Eddy went to the bureau and found the bundle that contained Fanny's letters, noticing the one on top—the one he'd lost. Here it was, in the most obvious place. He had looked everywhere—he, the author of "The Purloined Letter." The irony of it! He walked over to Anne, who was still standing in the doorway, and surrendered the letters. The two women curtsied and left.

He walked out to the landing and watched them descend the stairs, wanting them gone before he said anything. When he heard the door to the street slam shut, he went back inside. "Muddy," he said, "tell me you didn't show Fanny's letter to Lizzy Ellet."

Muddy neither spoke nor looked at him. In her hands was the plate that held the cookies. She'd been holding it all along.

"Do you know what you've done?" he demanded. The question was unfair, and immediately he regretted it. She glared back at him as if asking the same question, but she held her tongue.

He turned to Sissy, standing by the window, looking braced for bad news.

"Sissy," he said, composing himself, "Fanny and her husband are back together. They're looking for a place to live. That's why Fanny has returned to New York. They are also expecting a child. She wrote to tell me. She was confiding in me as a friend, and she asked that I tell no one. That is all. But now it seems that her news is out and that her confidence has been betrayed.

It's no wonder she didn't come, herself; she must hate me." He turned to Muddy, determination in his voice. "Lizzy Ellet is a gossip, a wicked, meddlesome bitch. She is the one who sent those anonymous letters to Sissy last fall, and she is never to be welcomed in our home again."

He went to the bureau and found Lizzy's letters. Returning to the door, he took his coat and hat off the peg and left.

He caught the downtown horsecar at Broadway. In spite of Lizzy's treachery, Eddy perceived his error in mentioning her letters to Anne and Margaret Fuller. He had implied that Lizzy's letters were love letters, and were she to hear of it—and it seemed that everyone knew everything in New York City these days—she had a perfect right to reproach him. But his main reason for returning her letters was to signal the end of their correspondence, a point he wished to make insultingly clear. Envisioning her consternation when she found the bundle at her front door gave him a degree of satisfaction. In truth, Lizzy had begun to frighten him. Thinking this, he decided to have a drink later.

At the Broome Street apartment where Lizzy lived, where Eddy had once borrowed fifty dollars, in a brass frame tacked to the door, he fingered the raised letters of an engraved calling card: "Colonel William M. Lummis." Beneath it was a mail slot. Rather than knock on the door, Eddy slipped the packet of letters through the slot and heard them strike the floor on the other side. Leaving quickly so as not to be observed, he headed to Sandy's. Now more than ever, he needed a drink.

He arrived home late. Drinking had not helped. He had kept asking himself if he and Sissy could live together with this thing in their midst—this child of Fanny's.

As he pulled the suspender straps off his shoulders, he wondered what Muddy's version of Mrs. Ellet's visit was. He did not want Sissy knowing the truth, and not only because he was guilty and ashamed. Pulling the covers over him, he expected Muddy had spun some fiction—her excessive talk perhaps evidence of his guilt—and he suspected Sissy would have seen through it. Once again, he could not sleep, nor had he eaten a bite all day.

AT THE BREAKFAST TABLE no one spoke a word. Eddy broke the silence by telling them he was going to Turtle Bay again to look for a place to live. He was desperate now to leave the city. He would be ostracized. No more invitations to Anne Lynch's. No more lectures, readings, judging contests. No more visits from women bringing cakes and flowers. No more letters. The isolation would be as painful for Sissy and Muddy as for him.

He walked to Third Avenue and turned north toward Eastern Post Road, looking back occasionally, hoping for a ride.

That night they celebrated Eddy's thirty-seventh birthday with a molasses cake. With a plate on his lap and his bare feet resting in a pail of warm water, he described Turtle Bay and the arrangements he'd made. He had walked all the way—six miles out and six back. They would move, the Monday after St. Valentine's Day, to live and board at a farmhouse owned by a widow, a Mrs. Miller. It was not an ideal situation, but once spring came, he would find them something better. No one said a word about Fanny's note or Anne Lynch's visit. Sissy made a special effort to talk to him, as if determined to hold things together. She asked if there were dogs—she feared dogs for Catterina's sake. Eddy reassured her. Muddy was still not speaking.

Two days later, Eddy had a letter from Lizzy Ellet's brother. It arrived at Amity Street, having been posted on Monday. Eddy knew it could only mean more trouble.

> Mr. Poe,
>
>   I am informed that you claim to have received letters from my sister, Mrs. Elizabeth Lummis Ellet. Sir, you are a liar. Produce such letters forthwith, or, if you cannot, I demand satisfaction on the field of honor. By insulting my sister, you have insulted me. I demand your immediate response.
>
> William M. Lummis, Lt. Col., Ret.

Eddy's mouth went dry. There must be some mistake, he thought. He snatched up a sheet of notepaper and began scribbling a letter to Colonel Lummis, but after two sentences he perceived the futility. Rage returned, and he felt a headache forming at his temples. His doing the honorable thing by returning Lizzy's letters had been answered with more treachery. Obviously Lizzy wasn't the only busybody in New York City. But Eddy couldn't think about that now. First was this ridiculous matter of pistols at ten paces.

He left the house and took the horsecar downtown, desperate to find Dunn

English. He would send English, he decided, to serve as his advocate—but not his second—to see Lummis and explain everything.

English's office was locked, so Eddy went to Sandy Welsh's Cellar, hoping to find him there; when he did not, he ordered a bowl of chowder and a glass of wine. He returned to English's office at about three. English was there with his partner, Thomas Lane, a young man in his early twenties, tall and tending to obesity, his mustache a poor copy of English's. Eddy had earlier decided that Lane must have inherited more money than good sense.

Standing before English's desk, Eddy pressed his fingers to his temples, where a vicious headache had settled in. "I think I'm going mad," he said.

"What is it this time, Poe?" English asked.

Eddy ignored the question and searched at the shelves behind English for the orangutan. The skull had become his touchstone, reassurance of his ability to reason. But reason had lost its sway. Here he was, groveling at the feet of Dunn English.

"I need your help," Eddy said, swallowing his pride. "Something so perverse has happened, it defies belief. I don't even know where to begin."

"Does it have anything to do with Fanny Osgood?" English asked, smiling up at him.

"What do you know about that?"

English shook his head and smiled—that infuriating, know-it-all smile—and he leaned back in his chair. "Fanny Osgood sits in Anne Lynch's parlor," he said, "playing the infantile, looking up at you with tears streaming down those lovely cheeks of hers, and you are taken in by it all. You write love poems to each other thinking no one notices, hoping everyone thinks it's merely an affair of the quill." He started laughing and Lane laughed, too, aping English. "You're a fool, Poe. Everybody knows you're making love to Fanny Osgood, and everybody knows she's going to have a baby. You call it perverse? I wouldn't disagree with that."

Eddy balled his fists ready to strike English. Surprised by this, English put his palms out to indicate he didn't want to fight.

"I'll have you know," Eddy said, "that Fanny and Sam are back together. How dare you blacken her name?"

"Okay," English said. "Okay! Calm down. I know about that, too. I like Fanny as much as anybody does."

"Then do you know about Lizzy Ellet's part in this?"

"Yes, I do," English said. "I think everyone in New York knows. And from what I hear, Sam Osgood is out for blood. Lizzy Ellet may be first on his list, but you can't be far behind. I wouldn't want him for an enemy."

Eddy hadn't considered that Sam Osgood might be out to get him, too, and the thought was doubly disheartening. Now there were two men who wanted to kill him. He sat down on the sofa, put his head in his hands for a moment, then looked back up at English. "Lizzy Ellet has hurt my family as much as Sam Osgood's," he said, as if defending himself in Osgood's presence, and he thought to add that Osgood had no quarrel with him, but how could he say that?

With a few discreet revisions, he related to English what had happened. He told him about Lizzy Ellet overhearing Fanny and Sissy reading her letters. He explained how Lizzy had, thereafter and by guile, become cozy with Muddy and used her for access to Eddy's letters from Fanny. He explained that as he and Fanny were friends—and he emphasized *friends*—they confided in each other. There was nothing perverse about that. He said Fanny had written to tell Eddy about Sam and the baby. By her snooping, Lizzy Ellet found out. Eddy told English about the visit from Anne Lynch and what he'd blurted regarding Lizzy's letters, and now there was this medieval challenge from her brother, no doubt a crack shot.

"Go to him," Eddy pleaded. "Tell him I returned Lizzy's letters Sunday afternoon. I wanted to do the honorable thing. There *were* letters. I can prove it. There were three of them. My wife saw them; Muddy saw them; Fanny saw them."

"And who else?" English asked, laughing. "No wonder Lummis is upset. You must have shown her letters to half of New York City."

"*But!*" Eddy yelled, jumping up from the sofa, "he claims there were *no* letters. Don't you see?" He stopped. What was the use? English was enjoying watching him squirm. "Will you go or not?" he asked, finally. "The man has challenged me, for Christ's sake. A duel! I refuse to fight a duel over Lizzy Ellet's honor. The woman's a meddlesome bitch. She'll ruin Fanny. Never mind me. For Christ's sake, English, do this for Fanny."

"I'll go," English said, condescension dripping from his voice. "I'll go."

"Today. Now. Please."

"I'll go," English said, affecting exasperation. "But I have a busy day. Come back in the morning, and I'll tell you what he says. Now go!"

Eddy stood, looked over at Lane and nodded, then turned back to English. "Thank you," he said, the words tasting bitter. "I'm indebted to you for this." He bowed and left.

So as not to be seen, he hurried down Cedar Street toward the Hudson River, his top hat pulled low over his forehead, his overcoat collar turned up. Then he took West Street and walked all the way back out to Greenwich Village.

He said nothing to Sissy and Muddy. Sissy's cough was back. Muddy made small talk, going on about Turtle Bay and how nice it would be to breathe country air again. Eddy paid little attention, preoccupied by the notion of Weehawken, of taking the ferry out to where Burr had killed Hamilton, where men still went for that grisly purpose. Were it not so frightening, it would have been laughable. Eddy had won a sharpshooter's badge while at West Point, but that was with a musket—and fifteen years ago. He had never fired a pistol in his life.

Thursday morning, on his way downtown he stopped at the pub he used to frequent for a fortifying shot of gin and a hard-boiled egg. He arrived early at English's office. Thomas Lane let him in. Fifteen minutes later, when English arrived, he announced a busy day as if Eddy's affairs were an annoyance.

"I have a magazine to publish," he said.

"What did he say?" Eddy asked.

"You mean Lummis?" English said, as if weeks had passed instead of twenty-four hours. "Lummis does not accept your apology. It was an apology, wasn't it? I wasn't sure."

"She denies the letters," Eddy said, giving up, looking down at the floorboards. He hadn't believed she would really lie if confronted, not when others had seen her letters. He had held to the hope that in the end she would acknowledge them.

"His sister never wrote you, Poe," English continued. "You made it up. Lummis says that if you won't meet him, he'll come looking for you. He probably suspects you're here. He could be waiting outside right now." English smiled, his enjoyment apparent.

"There *were* letters!" Eddy protested.

"You're a liar, Poe. What's worse, you believe your own lies."

"Give me your pistol," Eddy said, ignoring the insult. "I have no protection. The man is out to kill me. You have a pistol; I know you do. At least let me defend myself."

English started laughing. "Lend you a pistol?" he said. "Do you think I'm crazy? You'll kill somebody, Poe. You reek of whiskey. Do you drink every morning? Whiskey will be the death of you, unless, of course, Lummis gets to you first. Lizzy Ellet never wrote you. You're lying."

Eddy reached for him. He grabbed English by his lapels and tried pulling him across the desk. He intended to drag him to the floor and start punching him, but English fell on top of him. They wrestled, bumping up against Lane's desk. Lane was up and around his desk, aiming to pull Eddy off. Somehow, even with Lane pulling at him, Eddy and English got to their feet. English freed his right arm, pulled back, and delivered a punch. It glanced off. Eddy lunged at him, breaking free of Lane. He and English fell onto the sofa. Then English hit him again. It was not a well-thrown punch, but English wore a signet ring, and Eddy felt it hit his cheekbone. The intaglio stone popped out of its setting and rolled across the floor. Eddy was bleeding. He tried to free himself. He rolled off the sofa onto the floor. English kept coming at him, punching him in the face with the sharp edge of the setting. To escape, Eddy worked his way under the sofa. There was blood on the floor. English wrenched the sofa away, turning it upside down, and kicked Eddy in the side.

"You're mad, Poe," he yelled, kicking him again.

Eddy grabbed English's boot and twisted it, throwing him off balance and onto the floor. Now it was Eddy's turn. He jumped on top and let fly his fists. His knee pinned English's left arm to the floor, and he fended English's right with his left arm, all the while punching him in the face. Eddy could feel the punches landing on bone, and would have kept on beating him had not Lane grabbed him by the arm and pulled him off again.

English did not pursue. They stared at each other, panting. Lane held Eddy fast. English went to the washstand for a towel and threw it at Eddy. "You're bleeding," he said.

Eddy turned and looked in the mirror above the washstand, fingering the ridge of bone above his eye. He had a deep gash on his cheekbone that sent a stream of blood down his cheek. There were cuts over his eye and on his chin.

His collar and shirt were bloody. He wiped it off as best he could; then he turned, threw the towel at English, and walked out.

He headed home, covering his mouth with a handkerchief and searching the sea of pedestrians for Lummis. He tasted blood, tasting like rust. Running his tongue around the inside of his mouth, he felt a cut in his cheek and swallowed coppery-tasting mucus. His nose was clogged, and when he wiped it with his handkerchief, he saw crusted blood. His left eyebrow had begun to swell, and he had to blink constantly to keep his vision clear. Other men eyed him. He ignored them and kept walking, blinking, and searching for Lummis. His neck stiffened, and he worried that he might not make it home without help. Just let me get home, he thought; surely Lummis would not come to the house. Even someone like Lizzy Ellet would not permit that, knowing Sissy's condition. At Houston he had to stop, catch his breath, and wipe his face. He felt dizzy. He spat, swallowed, spat again, his spittle streaked with blood. He stared at it on the paving stone, took a deep breath, and walked on, thinking he could make it just a few more blocks.

At the apartment, Sissy spilled Catterina from her lap and screamed for Muddy. Eddy took off his coat, hung it on the peg, then removed his collar and shirt. "I'm all right," he said, collapsing on the bed. "It's only my face."

Muddy examined him while Sissy poured water into the bowl. She brought it over to the bed, and Muddy began dabbing at his cuts.

"I'll go get Dr. Francis," Muddy said. "Sissy?" She turned to look for Sissy, and Eddy raised his head to look, too. The bedroom door closed. He collapsed back onto the bed. "Lord help us," Muddy said, "I can't nurse the both of you."

"I'm all right," Eddy said, taking the wet cloth out of her hand. "Go see about her."

Muddy went into the bedroom, shut the door, and remained there for a while. When she came out, she wore her bonnet and coat. "I'm going for Dr. Francis," she said. "Sissy needs a doctor and so do you."

Eddy let her go. Though he worried about Sissy, he believed the sight of his face would do more harm than good. Better wait. John Francis was a friend. He had attended to Sissy several times. Though there was little he could do, he had always been willing to help. Poetry was his hobby, and he loved Eddy's work. Eddy had been a guest in his home; he had recited "The Raven" there.

About an hour later, Muddy returned with the doctor. Eddy had fallen asleep and let the fire die. It was quite cold.

"What happened?" Dr. Francis asked.

"I'm all right," Eddy said. "Best see to Sissy first."

Following Muddy, Dr. Francis went into the bedroom and remained there for fifteen or twenty minutes. When he returned, his distress was apparent, and it frightened Eddy. "Tell me what happened." he said, examining Eddy's cuts.

Eddy explained everything.

"Be still. This will sting," the doctor said, as he began stitching Eddy's cheek. "Virginia can't bear this, Edgar. She's having trouble breathing. If we don't calm her down, it could be serious."

"What can I do?" Eddy asked. "The man is roaming the streets with a pistol. I don't have the letters, and I can't protect myself."

"I'll go see him," Dr. Francis said, as he sewed Eddy up. "I'll explain Sissy's condition. You must write him a letter. Do it now. Apologize. Tell him whatever he wants to hear. I'll take the letter myself and demand that he cease, and if he doesn't I'll go to the police. Do it, Edgar, or I won't be responsible for what happens to Virginia."

When the suturing was done, Eddy went to his desk and wrote as instructed. How could he say that there were no letters? But he did. Dr. Francis told him what to write—that Eddy was temporarily deranged, that he was suffering cerebral congestion.

When he finished, Dr. Francis took the letter and left, his haste an indication that Sissy's condition was indeed critical. Eddy left Muddy alone with her. In the mirror he saw that his face was a mess. He had sutures in two places, his cheekbone and above his right eye, just at the edge of his eyebrow. The cut on his chin was less serious, but it was ringed by a purple bruise, and he was developing not one but two black eyes. He could not be seen in public for a month without attracting attention.

When Dr. Francis returned at four o'clock, he went straight in to see Sissy, who had fallen asleep, thanks to the laudanum he had given her.

"I did not see Lummis," the doctor told Eddy when he came out of the bedroom. "But I did see Mrs. Ellet. She accepts your apology and promises to rein in her brother. Consider the ordeal over. I told Virginia not to worry and to stay in bed for a few days. You should stay in bed, too. Whatever you do, you are not to upset her. If you do, you could endanger her life. I'll come back to-morrow."

Eddy agreed, of course. He remained at home thereafter, just as Dr. Francis prescribed. He could not go out looking as he did, in any case. He worried about Sissy and let her see his face, trying to make light of it. He told her almost everything—that English didn't believe the existence of Lizzy Ellet's letters; that he had called Eddy names, insulting him. Sissy sympathized but made Eddy promise never to fight again. Day by day she improved. Perhaps Eddy's constant attention helped. Muddy did the errands, even some for Eddy.

They were in desperate straits. As Eddy had made a deposit with Mrs. Miller at Turtle Bay, and Muddy had put something by for the mover, they had no money for food. He wrote a long letter to Willis, congratulating him on his new magazine and describing in detail the "Literati" series that he was working on, even including the first two installments—one on Horace Greeley and one on Evert Duyckinck. Eddy claimed his series would be just the thing to draw readership to Willis's new venture, promised three dozen sketches, and asked for an advance. When that produced no immediate response, he wrote letters to others asking for loans, letting Muddy deliver them, but they yielded nothing.

He imagined that rumors were rampant, but, as they had no visitors and al-most no mail, he could not know for certain. He was cut off; it seemed he had no friend in all of New York City, not Willis, not even Fanny. He felt such con-tempt for Lizzy Ellet that he was desperate to lash out at something, but there was nothing at which to lash out. He couldn't go out, and it was senseless to write any more letters. He could not prove the existence of Lizzy's letters, not even the anonymous ones. He tried writing Fanny, wanting to explain, but how could he explain without implicating Muddy, and doing that sounded self-serving. He did not expect to hear from her; still, he awaited the post eagerly each day.

A week passed. His eye turned black and purple, yellow at the fringes, the color of jaundice. Dr. Francis checked on them every day just as he had prom-ised. He took Eddy's stitches out. Sissy started coming to the table again. They talked about little things—their meals, Catterina, the upcoming move, the butcher downstairs, the firehouse across the street, the weather. The world seemed to be closing in on them.

EVERY YEAR ANNE LYNCH hosted a St. Valentine's Day party. It had become a tradition, and this year the 14th fell on a Saturday. She always insisted that her guests bring valentine poems and riddles. Eddy would not be expected to attend, of course, though Anne never issued formal invitations. He could not go; never mind his injuries, he was not wanted. Anyway, the Poes were moving to Turtle Bay on the Monday following, so they had packing to do. Eddy decided to compose a valentine regardless, a valentine for Fanny. He would post it to Anne, and perhaps she would allow it to be read. But if not, she might at least give it to Fanny. Anne would know it was his, but perhaps no one else would, since Eddy had conceived a cryptogram so cleverly crafted as to conceal the identities of both composer and recipient. Fanny would guess. She would know by the handwriting if nothing else, and perhaps she would decode it, find her name hidden among the letters. If he could not write to her openly, he would do it secretly.

He worked on the valentine for over a week. It proved the devil to write, but the exercise got his mind off his cuts and bruises and resentments and long confinement in the apartment. The first letter of the first line was the first letter of Fanny's first name; the second letter of the second line, the second letter of her name; and so forth.

One day while Muddy was out running errands, Sissy watched him at work. Neither of them had been out of the house for two weeks. She was sitting by the fire, her breathing improved, though she coughed constantly. She was finishing a letter to Fanny, having asked Eddy's permission to write her, which he had given. She did not show it to him, but she told him what it said, that Fanny had been wronged and Sissy wanted to apologize and wish her well.

"What are you writing?" she asked.

"I'm writing Fanny also," he said. "A poem." And he leaned back in his chair and smiled at her. "It's a cryptogram. The message is conveyed by the poem, but Fanny's name, her full name—Frances Sargent Osgood—is hidden among the letters, one in each line."

Sissy stared at him for an instant, puzzled, as if she wished to ask something. All she said was "Your eyes look better, but how in the world are we going to explain you to Mrs. Miller?"

They smiled at each other for the first time in a long time, and Eddy thought about how different their life would become. It would be peaceful in the country. They would get by somehow. Perhaps they would even be happy. He would forget about Fanny and the child. Perhaps whole days would pass without his thinking about them; in time, even a week, then a month. Did she love him enough to forgive him? Was it not possible that she might say to her child someday, "He was a fine man," even if she could not say "He was your father"? Eddy could never hope for that.

He posted the valentine in time to arrive at Waverly Place by Friday.

On Saturday night, he sat at his desk, thinking how gay and festive Lynchie's parlor must be—not three blocks away. Would he be missed? Would anyone ask "Where is Edgar Poe?" Was Fanny there? And Sam? And Lizzy Ellet? And Willis? Had all this not happened, Eddy would be delivering the valentine himself, standing in front of the fireplace, his head high, his audience in rapt attention.

> For her these lines are penned, whose luminous eyes,
> Bright and expressive as the twins of Læda,
> Shall find her own sweet name that, nestling, lies
> Upon the page, enwrapped from every reader.

The next morning Sissy, Muddy, and Eddy sat around the table finishing a spartan breakfast. Their trunks were nearly packed, and before nightfall they would finish filling the crates Muddy had rounded up for what of their possessions the trunks and the bureau would not hold. Eddy's injuries were healing and beginning to itch, but it would be another month before the black eyes disappeared.

As they sipped their coffee, Sissy handed him a piece of notepaper. He unfolded it and found a poem.

"It contains a riddle," she said, smiling proudly. He read it aloud.

> Ever with thee I wish to roam—
> Dearest my life is thine.

Give me a cottage for my home
And a rich old cypress vine,
Removed from the world with its sin and care
And the tattling of many tongues.
Love alone shall guide us when we are there—
Love shall heal my weakened lungs;
And Oh, the tranquil hours we'll spend,
Never wishing that others may see!
Perfect ease we'll enjoy, without thinking to lend
Ourselves to the world and its glee—
Ever peaceful and blissful we'll be.

He praised it through tears. He read it aloud again and again. He never gave "The Raven" better voice, though he stumbled several times, choked with emotion. He swore to find her a cypress vine if he had to walk to the ends of the earth, and he assured her that the country air would indeed heal her lungs, and time and again he expressed amazement that she had been so clever. He marveled that she was able to begin each line with a letter of his name and still maintain a perfect flow of logic with rhyme to boot.

Sissy beamed.

After she and Muddy went to bed that night, Eddy stared out the window giving vent to the emptiness he'd felt all day since reading her poem. He had no poem for her. He had spent his creativity on Fanny, and in all his poems and stories he had written nothing about Sissy's life, only her death— "Eleonora," "The Raven"—and he had betrayed her, as well. Tears came again, tears of recrimination. "Ever with thee . . . / Dearest, my life is thine." Over and over he repeated those words, thinking as he did so of all the words that described him—heartless, unthinking, contemptible, sorry. The list went on and on; it was endless. He made pledge after pledge: So long as Sissy lives, I will not drink, I will devote myself to her, I will write a poem to celebrate her life and it will be my greatest poem. It will make her immortal. And he raised his eyes to the night sky and took his vow just as he had on Mount Tom. This time he meant it.

The dray came at noon on Monday. The driver helped Eddy take down the bureau and the trunks and the crates and the portrait of General Poe. He was a small, jovial Irishman with a red nose and a salty sense of humor, very accommodating. He called Eddy Governor and stared curiously at his black eyes. It was cold and overcast. Eddy feared it might snow and urged everyone to hurry. With Catterina in her lap, Sissy sat on the seat between Muddy and the driver, who promised to cover them all with his oilskin if it started raining or snowing. Little did he know they had no tip for him—they were down to cheeseparings and candle ends.

Eddy rode on the back. He crawled up under the edge of the canvas tarpaulin that covered their belongings and sat, hugging his knees to his chest to keep warm. He took off his hat and held the edge of the canvas over his head to keep the wind out and to hide his face in the event someone looked as they drove by.

They crossed Broadway, turned left on the Bowery, then crossed over to Third Avenue and followed it north out of town.

At Mrs. Miller's they would have two rooms, with a wood-burning fireplace. She had promised Eddy a proper writing table. Muddy would arrange her teacups and her linens, and Sissy would reassure Catterina that there were no dogs.

Once they were on Eastern Post Road, it started sleeting. Not hard. The buildings and the fringing thicket of ships' masts that lined the East River to Fourteenth Street became hidden by woodland. Eddy looked up at the trees as they passed, bare, jagged limbs against a winter sky.

Pulling the canvas back over his head, he recalled that it had been nearly a year since he stood on the stage of the New-York Historical Society Library with Gulian Verplanck to accept the accolades of the finest literary assemblage in the history of New York. Eddy put that thought out of his mind. It was too painful. Perhaps Fanny would pay a price as painful, but they would keep her safe, hold her to their bosom. Not him, however. He was not one of them. Fanny's child would be one of them. He had always wanted a child. But, for Eddy, the child would be like the portrait Sam Osgood had painted—something of him that he would never see.

Hearing singing, he dropped the tarpaulin to look up ahead at Sissy and Muddy and the driver huddled beneath the oilskin. A crusty Irish tenor sang "Molly Malone," and Sissy and Muddy sang along. Eddy hadn't heard Sissy sing in years. He turned to look back at the landscape, searching for landmarks and judging that it wasn't far now.

The sleet was coming faster, and he covered himself again. He hoped Sissy was staying dry. And Catterina. He didn't worry about Muddy; no doubt she would outlive them all. Their new landlady would have a wood fire in the fireplace and a hot supper awaiting them. Eddy wondered if Turtle Bay would prove to be a good place to write, and writing put him in mind of all the scrolls of manuscripts in the bureau drawers. He resolved to go through them that evening, rerolling and pasting new ribbons on those that had come undone, for they were a treasure trove—to him, if to no one else.

🌿 Willis 🌿

THE GIFT BOOK.— Holiday gift books for the upcoming season are in press already. It is our contention that this innovation is native to America. We would even go so far—though modesty tugs at our elbow—as to say that we played a role in fashioning the custom. The English disagree. They have commandeered the gift book as their own invention, disavowing as they often do the notion that anything so clever can spring forth from their erstwhile Colonists. This bobbery aside, however, we must confess that the English are besting us in the art of binding, and nowhere are fine bindings so prized as in gift books. One need only browse the book shop of Bartlett & Welford under the Astor to make a fair comparison.

Some years ago while in England we had the pleasure of visiting one of England's finest bookbinders where we witnessed a level of craftsmanship that we in America must achieve or lose out to a flood of imports. Their ink is excellent; their types, beautiful; their paper, strong and white; their bindings, veritable works of art; and above all their press is next to *infallible for correctness*. By contrast our own paltry output is enough to make one wish we had chosen Chippewa as our national language instead of English.

Sadly, nonetheless, our tribe speaks English, and our bibliophiles prefer the import. Naturally and lamentably, gift books from England contain the literary output of that nation while our native poets suffer because the product of their pen is bound in inferior wrapping. We need bookbinders to match the quality of our literature and the quality of bookbinding in Europe. A clever bookbinder, willing to take a gamble, would profit by luring one or two craftsmen across the Atlantic and building an apprentice system to insure the future of this trade in America.

The gift book has been a particular boon to our female poets. Never has their output been greater nor their influence on society more profound. They are better than we men when it comes to expressing the sensibilities of the heart, the domestic affections, virtuousness, and benevolence. In making a Christmas gift of a book to a

WILLIS PUT DOWN his pen and picked up the very book that had inspired his column. It was a volume of poems by Thomas Hood, bound in fine-grained red leather over sturdy boards with ridges along the spine. Its gilt lettering was precise, its stitching tight. Placed alongside his own latest output, *Dashes at Life with a Free Pencil,* bound in embossed, pea green pasteboard and already showing wear along the edges, there was no comparison. His would likely not last out the decade.

With a frustrated sigh, he put his book aside and turned back to the *Morning Express.* Folding it in half, he stood, stuck it under his arm, and walked to one of the windows. It was nearly two o'clock. He wished Morris would return from the printer's; he was getting hungry. The *Express* contained a note about the Poes. Edgar Poe had been much on Willis's mind. He had not seen him since the family had left New York. No one had seen him. Willis had seen Mrs. Clemm once. She was making Poe's deliveries, coming in on the Harlem train from Fordham, where they were living now. On the occasion he saw her, she insisted that Poe considered him the best friend he had in the world. If such was true, the poor man was indeed impoverished, for Willis had been an insufficient friend, and he felt rather badly about it.

The *Home Journal* office faced Park Row, City Hall Park, and the Astor. Already the leaves of the maples in the park were turning pink and yellow, the first sign of autumn, and the white awnings of the shops under the Astor were bright with reflected sunlight. The Croton fountain sent its gush of water fifty feet into the air. It rose to the height of the windows of the Astor sky chambers and the flags atop the flagpoles in front of City Hall. To his left he could see the steeple of St. Paul's and a corner of Barnum's Museum, where the current draw was a genuine Fejee Mermaid. Willis decided to go see her; she would be good for a column. On Broadway, Anna Cora Mowatt was opening at the Park in *Much Ado About Nothing*—that would fill a column also—and a new display in the Minerva Room farther up was said to be drawing crowds. It was an exact scale model of New York City from Thirty-second Street all the way to the Battery, twenty feet long and twenty-four feet wide. It had taken over a year to construct and featured hundreds of thousands of miniature buildings, ships, trees, horsecars, pedestrians, street lamps, and a Croton water jet with actual running water. It, too, would fill a column.

But Willis's mind was on Poe and the note in the *Express*. Thankfully, Poe's series for *Godey's Lady's Book,* "The Literati of New York City," had come to an end with a final installment in the October issue just out. Willis had read them all and could not imagine what had gotten into Poe, and he wondered how Poe could have ever dreamed that he and Morris would be interested in publishing the series. No magazine in New York would touch it; Poe had to go as far away as Philadelphia to sell the thing.

He had left no one out; he had been thorough in his deprecation of New York City writers. His sketches were an assortment of backhanded compliments, damnation with faint praise, and unflattering physical descriptions. He had picked on Willis in the first installment, in May. Though Poe had been complimentary, calling Willis a "well-looking man," he added that neither Willis's nose nor his forehead could be defended and claimed the latter would puzzle phrenologists. Willis was amused at first, but Morris was livid. He called it unjust and disgraceful, dismissed the whole series as an insidious exposé, and accused Poe of biting the hand that fed him.

This hit rather too close to home. As a young man, Willis had been guilty of much the same thing, living off friends in England and then writing about them. He had seen nothing wrong with relating the table talk at Countess Blessington's or Gordon Castle, but the *haut monde* saw something wrong with it, and in the end Willis had been ostracized and labeled "the spy who came to dinner." In those circles he remained *persona non grata*.

In much the same way, Poe had burned his bridges; but Willis, for one, would not condemn him.

Poe had lacerated Briggs, called him "grossly uneducated," and he had as much as accused Gulian Verplanck of indolence and intemperance. He said Evert Duyckinck was simple, and his physical descriptions of women bordered on the grotesque. The whole thing was in poor taste. Philadelphia and Boston were having a hearty laugh at New York's expense.

The worst of the sketches was saved for Dunn English. While Willis was no admirer of English, he considered it a mistake to put one's quarrels in print as Poe had done. He accused the man of lacking the commonest school education and put his age at thirty-five, knowing full well he was still in his twenties. He even claimed not to be personally acquainted with English, which was pure rubbish.

For the most part, the sketches were a regurgitation of old stuff from reviews Poe had written for the *Mirror* and the *Broadway Journal*. It was clear he needed money, and it was money that reminded Willis just then of their scheme the preceding year, to pirate work from England for Poe's magazine. He recalled advising Poe to worm his way into the editor's chair. No doubt, he had let Poe down by not going to England.

This note in the *Express* was short. Willis needn't read it again, but he did. It said that Poe and his wife were ill, that they lived at times without the bare necessities of life, and suggested that Wiley & Putnam establish a fund for their relief. Willis recalled Mrs. Poe—Virginia—the day he had visited their boarding house on Greenwich Street. The vision of her was clear in his mind. She was otherworldly; her skin had the pallor of alabaster, yet her hair was black as jet. He had no doubt that she was dying.

It was then he understood. Precise contours of comprehension formed in his mind. Poe's wife was dying, and so to comfort her, he had burned his bridges the way one burns the few remaining sticks of furniture when it's cold and times are desperate and the firewood is all used up.

He returned to his desk and wrote out a postscript for his column.

We have learned by a recent notice in the *Express* that Mr. Edgar Poe, and his wife, are dangerously ill and suffering for want of the common necessaries of life. Here is one of our finest scholars, one of our most original men of genius, and one of the most industrious of the literary profession in our Nation, whose temporary suspension of labor from bodily illness, drops him immediately to a level with the common objects of public charity. A generous gift could hardly be better applied than to him, and the *Home Journal* offers to forward to Mr. and Mrs. Poe any gifts and tributes that come our way.

Though Morris had a low opinion of Poe, Willis felt certain he would not object to a small donation. It was not just Poe's intemperance that rankled Morris, nor this series of sketches in *Godey's;* it was also the ordeal of the previous winter, the rumors about Fanny Osgood and Lizzy Ellet that seemed to have their source in the Poe household. Willis dismissed it. This, too, he concluded, was much ado about nothing. Fortunately for all concerned, talk had died down after the Poes left town.

And speaking of Fanny, she had given birth to a daughter in June, or was it July? Mother and child were doing well, so Willis had heard, and remembering his own Mary and three daughters, he couldn't help but envy Sam Osgood—three girls and Fanny.

But that was in the past; Willis's thoughts turned to the future and his forthcoming nuptials, and his spirits rose. During the summer, while visiting Washington, he had met Cornelia Grinnell, daughter of a congressman from Massachusetts. She was half his age, lovely, well educated, and possessed a modest income—essential for a struggling, young magazinist such as himself. Yes, young! He didn't feel forty years old. Not in the least. He felt all the vigor of a twenty-year-old, and just then he set his pen in its cradle, stood, and searched for his reflection in the window glass. And there he was—a fortnight away from walking down the aisle—with a new beard and not a half stone heavier than the day he graduated Yale.

And he was famished. Where was Morris? He should have returned by now.

"Tell Morris I'm at Delmonico's," he said to the printer's imp as he reached for his hat and coat. "I'll wait lunch for him."

A beefsteak and potatoes was what he had in mind. And a walk through Battery Park on the way back. Perhaps they'd see a China clipper come sailing through the Narrows, and the bonnets would be out. A walk would aid the digestion, and the day was superb as only days can be in early autumn when the sky is cloudless and the air is clear.

"Tell Morris to hurry," he said, growing impatient and heading for the stairs. God knows Willis hated to dine alone.

Afterword

IN LATE APRIL of 2001 while researching this book, I traveled to New York to spend a weekend exploring those areas of the city where Edgar Allan Poe had lived and worked. I had read that the apartment building in which he lived in the fall and winter of 1845 was still standing, and the day after my arrival, a Saturday, I walked up West Broadway to Greenwich Village to see it. Spring had arrived, a warm, cloudless day. Patrons packed the sidewalk restaurants, and couples pushed strollers or walked their dogs. I was excited by the prospect of standing in the very room where certain letters had caused so much drama in the Poe household and among his circle of acquaintances in the winter of 1845–46. Recalling one of these letters years later, the poet Elizabeth Oakes Smith wrote

> A certain lady of my acquaintance fell in love with Poe and wrote a love-letter to him. Every letter he received he showed to his little wife. This lady went to his house one day; she heard Fanny Osgood and Mrs. Poe having a hearty laugh, they were fairly shouting, as they read over a letter. The lady listened, and found it was hers, when she walked into the room and snatched it from their hands. There would have been a scene with any other woman, but they were both very sweet and gentle, and there the matter ended.[1]

This letter and others known to have existed fascinated me. Their contents would unveil tantalizing secrets. No doubt they had all been destroyed, but my research provided some notion of what they said, and I hoped to re-create the drama surrounding them. The Poe apartment building at 85 Amity Street, now West Third Street, one block south of Washington Square, was the very

---

1. J. C. Derby. *Fifty Years among Authors, Books, and Publishers*. New York: G. W. Carleton, 1884, p. 548.

place where that "certain lady," Elizabeth Ellet, had snatched her love letter from the hands of Fanny Osgood and Virginia Poe, and I wanted to get a feel for the place, to see where the fireplace was situated and to imagine how furniture might have been arranged.

I turned left onto West Third and crossed the street, knowing the building faced south, and I walked all the way to where the street dead ends into Sixth Avenue without finding it. I walked back, going in and out of several buildings, all old, each a candidate; still I had no luck. Then, in front of an old fire station, I looked up to see a sky writer overhead, writing "I ♥ New York" in clear blue sky. I turned and went into the station and found a fireman there in a white T-shirt and black rubber boots, washing his fire engine. "Could you help me?" I asked. "I'm looking for the building where Edgar Allan Poe once lived."

He reached behind him to turn off the faucet and dropped his hose to the concrete, then squared around and pointed across the street to a vacant lot surrounded by chain-link fence and on which sat a yellow bulldozer. "They tore it down two weeks ago," he said.

I stared in the direction he pointed with deeper regret than I would have imagined possible. A hundred and fifty-five years, I thought, and I missed it by two weeks! It was as if I had missed seeing those lost letters. It was as if, by that narrow margin, I had missed Poe himself.

AFTER LEAVING NEW YORK CITY in February of 1846, the Poes lived for a few months at the farmhouse owned by Mrs. Miller in Turtle Bay, near where the United Nations building stands today. In May or June they moved out to the village of Fordham, where they rented a small cottage that is today a museum in Poe Park administered by the Bronx County Historical Society. Virginia Poe's health declined, and the Poes were, indeed, destitute. Aided by friends, notably Marie Louise Shew, a practical nurse, and Mary Starr Jennings, Edgar's old girlfriend from his Baltimore days who now lived in Hoboken, and by the generosity of N. P. Willis and others, they managed to eke out a living. Virginia died soon after the sun came up on Saturday, January 30, 1847, a bitter cold morning. At Edgar's request, Marie Louise Shew propped Virginia's lifeless body up on pillows and painted a watercolor portrait of her. It is the only extant likeness of Virginia Poe. A special horsecar carried New Yorkers out to Fordham for her funeral, and Willis was among the mourners.

I can find no evidence that Edgar Allan Poe took a drink of alcohol from the time he left New York City until after Virginia's death. The one extant letter Poe wrote to her, written on June 12, 1846, demonstrates his devotion and attentiveness during the last year of her life.

> My Dear Heart, My dear Virginia! our Mother will explain to you why I stay away from you this night. I trust the interview I am promised, will result in some *substantial good* for me, for your dear sake, and hers —Keep up your heart in all hopefulness, and trust a little longer—In my last great disappointment, I should have lost my courage *but for you*— my little darling wife you are my *greatest* and *only* stimulus now to battle with this uncongenial, unsatisfactory and ungrateful life — I shall be with you tomorrow P.M. and be assured until I see you, I will keep in *loving remembrance your last words* and your fervent prayer!
>
> Sleep well and may God grant you a peaceful summer, with your devoted
>
> Edgar[2]

He appears to have been on his best behavior as I imagined he might have vowed to be in the wake of all that had happened and especially after receiving Virginia's Valentine poem.

N. P. Willis lived to see his new magazine prosper, but in the early 1850s he became embroiled in what was labeled the Forrest Affair, a highly publicized divorce case involving the then famous actor Edwin Forrest, in which Willis was accused of having had an affair with Forrest's wife, Catherine. Then, in 1854, Willis's sister, Sara, writing under the pen name Fanny Fern, painted him in highly unfavorable colors in her novel *Ruth Hall*. The novel was a success and a great embarrassment to Willis. When the Civil War began, he went to Washington to report on the war for the *Home Journal,* later to become *Town & Country Magazine*. There he became a favorite of Mary Lincoln, frequently

---

2. John Ward Ostrom. *The Letters of Edgar Allan Poe,* vol. II. Cambridge: Harvard University Press, 1948, p. 318.

dining at the White House and accompanying Mary on rides around the capital in her barouche. He died January 20, 1867, his sixty-first birthday, at his home, Idewild, in the Hudson highlands. Among his pallbearers were Henry Wadsworth Longfellow, Oliver Wendell Holmes, James Russell Lowell, and Richard Henry Dana. Regarding Willis, William Makepeace Thackeray captured popular sentiment perfectly: "It is comfortable that there should have been a Willis."

In 1861 Harriet Jacobs published an autobiography, *Incidents in the Life of a Slave Girl*. Despite the fact that Willis had purchased her freedom, Harriet shied away from using her name, adopting the pen name Linda Brent. Her editor was Maria Child, and the book, a classic American slave narrative, has been through numerous editions and remains quite popular. Ironically, the poems and prose writings of her mentor and guardian, N. P. Willis, have long since been out of print.

Maria Clemm—Muddy—outlived her daughter and son-in-law. After Poe's death, on the very day she packed up to leave the cottage at Fordham for good, she found the black-and-orange tabby, Catterina, who had been such a faithful source of comfort to Virginia, dead in a corner of the loft. From Fordham, Muddy moved around the country as a house guest, going from one home to another, always begging for money and always pleading in vain to redeem her son-in-law's good name, as Poe had been unfavorably portrayed in a short posthumous biography by his literary executor, Rufus Wilmot Griswold. Muddy died in 1871 at the age of eighty. Had she lived a few more years, she would have seen her son-in-law rediscovered and two important and sympathetic biographies of his life published, propelling him into the forefront of American literature, there to stay.

As for Poe himself, his fate is well known. Returning from Richmond to Fordham in October of 1849, he stopped over in Baltimore for reasons unknown. In a tavern there he was recognized, though the clothes he wore were apparently not his own. He was drunk, delirious, and had not a penny to his name. He died two days later, on October 7, three months shy of his forty-first birthday.

I inquired of Sotheby's, the fine arts auction house, what a newly discovered, original Poe manuscript might sell for if auctioned today. Their response was three-quarters of a million to a million dollars, "with wind," meaning a strong market in auction parlance. But in his lifetime, from all of his poems and short stories, Poe earned just over six hundred dollars.

It was not Edgar Allan Poe, however, who drew me to this story. It was Fanny Osgood, whom Oakes Smith characterized as "sweet and gentle," the precocious, diminutive, and high-spirited "poetess." Though she was only thirty-three when she met Edgar Poe, already schoolgirls throughout America idolized her; no doubt Emily Dickinson grew up reading the poetry of Frances Sargent Locke Osgood; her influence on Dickinson is readily apparent. Both Poe and Griswold, the mid–nineteenth century's most prolific anthologist, hailed her as the finest living woman poet in America, though evidence suggests that both men may have been in love with her.

Fanny Osgood is, nevertheless, all but forgotten. There is no biography of her; no collection of her short stories was ever compiled; and her poetry has been out of print for one hundred twenty years. When I began my research, the university library where I do my work contained none of the eleven books that she wrote or edited. Presumably her poems are not worthy of the canon; their flashes of brilliance notwithstanding, many are occasional or sentimental or unpolished. Or perhaps her friends unwittingly sacrificed her place in literary history in their efforts to preserve her good name. The historical record is fraught with suggestion that she was more to Poe than a family friend as Elizabeth Oakes Smith's anecdote implies; nevertheless, Poe's early biographers make only passing reference to her. It's almost as if they were hiding something. It is impossible to know what really happened; one can only speculate, and speculation is fiction, a process of reading between the lines, not just of letters and memoirs, but also—perhaps most importantly—lines of verse.

In late June or early July of 1846 (the exact date is not known), Frances Osgood gave birth to a daughter, Fanny Fay Osgood. Little is known of this child. Whether or not Poe was the father, it is unlikely he ever saw her. Perhaps the engraving by Fanny's husband, Samuel Stillman Osgood, that adorns the frontispiece of the collection of Fanny's poems published in 1850 is a fanciful depiction of Fanny Fay. The child died in October of 1847, four months after her first birthday.

A few years later, in the spring of 1850, Sam Osgood prevailed upon Wilmot Griswold, who was Fanny's literary executor as well as Poe's, to tell her that she too was dying. Perhaps Sam could not bring himself to do the deed, and even Griswold had to write the message in a note, which he passed to her as he sat beside her bed in the Osgoods' apartment in New York City. According to Griswold,

> I wrote the terrible truth to her, in studiously gentle words, reminding her that in heaven there is richer and more delicious beauty, that there is no discord in the sweet sounds there, no poison in the perfume of the flowers there, and that they know not any sorrow who are with Our Father. She read the brief note almost to the end silently, and then turned upon her pillow like a child, and wept the last tears that were in a fountain which had flowed for every grief but hers she ever knew.[3]

Fanny had been suffering from tuberculosis for several years. Near the end, unable to speak, she was given a miniature slate by her family in order to communicate her wishes. On that slate she wrote her last word, scribbled in chalk and preserved to this day. The word was "Angel." She died at a quarter past three on the afternoon of Sunday, May 12, 1850, at the age of thirty-eight, seven months after Poe's death in Baltimore. Sadly, the following year tuberculosis also took the lives of Fanny's two surviving daughters, Ellen Frances Osgood, whom Fanny called Lily, and May Vincent Osgood. Lily was fifteen; May was eleven.

Despite all that had happened, one of Fanny's last poems reveals that her regard for Edgar Allan Poe remained steadfast to the very end of her life. It begins

> The hand that swept the sounding lyre
> With more than mortal skill,
> The lightning eye, the heart of fire,
> The fervent lip are still!
> No more, in rapture or in wo,
> With melody to thrill,
> Ah! nevermore!

---

3. Rufus Wilmont Griswold. "Frances Sargent Osgood," *Laurel Leaves: A Chaplet Woven by the Friends of the Late Mrs. Osgood,* Mary E. Hewitt, ed. New York: Lamport, Blakeman, & Law, 1854, p. 16.

THE POEMS

So Let It Be

TO ——

Perhaps you think it right and just,
   Since you are bound by nearer ties,
To greet me with that careless tone,
   With those serene and silent eyes

So let it be! I only know,
   If I were in your place to-night,
I would not grieve *your* spirit so,
   For all God's worlds of life and light!

I could not turn, as you have done,
   From every memory of the past;
I would not fling, from soul and brow,
   The shade that Feeling should have cast.

Oh! Think how it must deepen all
   The pangs of wild remorse and pride,
To feel, that *you* can coldly see
   The grief, *I* vainly strive to hide!

The happy star, who fills her urn
   With glory from the God of Day,
Can never miss the smile he lends
   The wild-flower withering fast away;

The fair, fond girl, who at your side,
   Within your soul's dear light, doth live,
Could hardly have the heart to chide
   The ray that Friendship well might give.

But if you deem it right and just,
   Blessed as you are in your glad lot,
To greet me with that heartless tone,
   So let it be! I blame you not!"

Violet Vane
The Broadway Journal
April 5, 1845

The Rivulet's Dream

FROM THE GERMAN OF — SOMEBODY

A careless rill was dreaming,
    One fragrant summer night;
It dreamed a star lay gleaming
    With heavenly looks of light,
Soft cradled on its own pure breast,
That rose and fell, and rocked to rest,
With lulling wave, its radiant guest,
    In silent beauty beaming;

And like a lute's low sighing,
    The rill sang to the star,
"Why camest thou, fondly flying,
    From those blue hills afar?
All calm and cold without thy ray
I slept the long dark night away—
Ah! child of heaven! Forever stay!"
    No sweet voice rose replying.

"Oh, glorious truant! listen!
    Wilt fold thy shining wings,
That softly glance and glisten
    The while the wavelet sings?
Wilt dwell with me? I'll give thee flowers,—
Our way shall be through balmy bowers,
And song and dance shall charm the hours:—
    My star-love! dost thou listen?

"No gorgeous garden-blossom,
    In regal grace and bloom,
May pour upon my bosom
    Its exquisite perfume;
But I may wreathe, with wild flowers rare,
That softly breathe, thy golden hair,—
The violet's tear shall tremble there,
    A fair though fragile blossom."

Alas! when morning slowly
    Stole o'er the distant hill,
From that sweet dream, so holy,
    It woke—the sorrowing rill!
No "child of heaven" lay smiling there,—
'Twas but a vision bright and rare,
That blessed, as passed the star in air,
    The rivulet lone and lowly.

Kate Carol
The Broadway Journal
April 5, 1845

Love's Reply

I'll tell you something chanced to me,
    (A quaint and simple story,)
Before I crossed, with beating heart,
    Old ocean's gloom and glory.

Around me came three graceful girls,
    Their farewell whisper breathing,—
Julie,—with light and lovely curls,
    Her snowy shoulders wreathing;

And proud Georgine,—with stately mien,
    And glance of calm hauteur,
Who moves—a Grace,—and looks—a queen,
    All passionless and pure;

And Kate, whose low, melodious tone
    Is tuned by Truth and Feeling,
Whose shy yet wistful *eyes* talk on,
    When *Fear* her lips is sealing.

"From what far country, shall I write?"
    I asked, with pride elated,
"From what rare monument of art
    Shall be my letters dated?"

Julie tossed back her locks of light,
    With girlish grace and glee,—
"To me from glorious Venice write,
    Queen-city of the Sea!"

"And thou, Georgine?" Her dark eyes flashed,—
    "Ah! date to me your lines
From some proud palace, where the pomp
    Of olden Honor shines!"

But Kate,—the darling of my soul,
    My bright, yet bashful flower,
In whose dear heart some new, pure leaf,
    Seems to unfold each hour,—

Kate turned her shy, sweet looks from mine,
    Lest I her blush should see,
And said—so only Love could hear—
    "Write from your *heart* to *me!*"

Frances S. Osgood
The Broadway Journal
April 12, 1845

Spring

She has come and brought her flowers,
    Loving, child-like, happy Spring!
Smiling out through sudden showers,
    Lo! the Peri plumes her wing!

She has come—the wood-bird, listening,
    Knows her step and warbles low;
Every cloud and wave is glistening,
    Where her light feet go.

Every leaf with love she blesses;
    Even the little violet's heart
Throbs beneath her dear caresses,
    While its purple petals part.

In the skies, a changeful glory,—
    In the woodlands, bloom and glee,—
All things tell a joyous story:—
    What has Spring brought *me*?

Hope—her promise-buds revealing?
    Joy, with light and dazzling wing?
Fresh and ardent founts of Feeling?
    These should come with sportive Spring.

When she came of old, she found me
    Gay as any bird she knew;
Hope her wild-flowers showered around me,
    Friends were fond and true.

Do not look so glad and bright,
    Loving, laughing, joyous Spring!
Weep awhile amid thy light,
    Frolic Ariel, fold thy wing!

Weep for *me!* my heart is breaking,
    'Neath thy blue eyes' careless smile!
Mine, with hidden tears are aching,—
    Weep with me awhile!

No! the winter of the spirit
    Melts not in the breath of Spring;
Birds and flowers her joy inherit:
    Let *them* gaily bloom and sing!

Sing and bloom for those who never
    Wronged their own hearts, pure and free:
Let her smile on field and river—
    Spring comes not to *me*!

Violet Vane
The Broadway Journal
April 12, 1845

To F——

Beloved! amid the earnest woes
    That crowd around my earthly path—
(Drear path, alas! where grows
Not even one lonely rose)—
    My soul at least a solace hath
In dreams of thee, and therein knows
An Eden of bland repose.

And thus thy memory is to me
    Like some enchanted far-off isle
In some tumultuous sea—
Some ocean throbbing far and free
    With storms—but where meanwhile
Serenest skies continually
    Just o'er that one bright island smile.

E
The Broadway Journal
April 26, 1845

Impromtu
TO KATE CAROL

When from your gems of thought I turn
To those pure orbs, your heart to learn,
I scarce know which to prize most high—
The bright *i-dea*, or bright *dear-eye*.

[Unsigned—Edgar Allan Poe]
The Broadway Journal
April 26, 1845

To One In Paradise

Thou wast all that to me, love,
　　For which my soul did pine—
A green isle in the sea, love,
　　A fountain and a shrine,
All wreathed with fairy fruits and flowers,
　　And all the flowers were mine.

Ah, dream too bright to last!
　　Ah, starry Hope! that didst arise
But to be overcast!
　　A voice from out the Future cries,
"On! on!"—but o'er the Past
　　(Dim gulf!) my spirit hovering lies
Mute, motionless, aghast!

For, alas! alas! with me
　　The light of Life is o'er!
　　"No more—no more—no more—"
(Such language holds the solemn sea
　　To the sands upon the shore)
Shall bloom the thunder-blasted tree,
　　Or the stricken eagle soar!

And all my days are trances,
　　And all my nightly dreams
Are where thy dark eye glances,
　　And where thy footstep gleams—
In what ethereal dances,
　　By what eternal streams.

Edgar A. Poe
The Broadway Journal
May 10, 1945

To ——

I would not lord it o'er thy heart,
    Alas! I cannot rule my own,
Nor would I rob one loyal thought,
    From him who there should reign alone;
We both have found a life-long love
    Wherein our weary souls must rest,
Yet may we not, my gentle friend
    Be each to each the *second best*?

A love which shall be passion-free,
    Fondness as pure as it is sweet,
A bond where all the dearest ties
    Of brother, friend and *cousin* meet,—
Such is the union I would frame,
    That thus we might be doubly blest,
With Love to rule our hearts supreme
    And friendship to be *second best*.

M.
The Broadway Journal
May 24, 1845

Poem From "The Assignation"

Thou wast that all to me, love,
    For which my soul did pine—
A green isle in the sea, love,
    A fountain and a shrine,
All wreathed with fairy fruits and flowers,
    And all the flowers were mine.

Ah, dream too bright to last!
    Ah, starry Hope that didst arise
But to be overcast!
    A voice from out the Future cries,
"Onward!"—but o'er the Past
    (Dim gulf!) my spirit hovering lies
Mute, motionless, aghast!

For, alas! alas! with me
   The light of Life is o'er!
   "No more—no more—no more—"
(Such language holds the solemn sea
   To the sands upon the shore)
Shall bloom the thunder-blasted tree,
   Or the stricken eagle soar!

Now all my days are trances;
   And all my nightly dreams
Are where thy dark eye glances,
   And where thy footstep gleams—
In what ethereal dances,
   By what Italian streams.

Alas! for that accursed time
   They bore thee o'er the billow,
From Love to titled age and crime,
   And an unholy pillow—
From me, and from our misty clime,
   Where weeps the silver willow!

Edgar A. Poe
The Broadway Journal
June 7, 1845

Had We But Met

Had we but met in life's delicious spring,
   When young romance made Eden of the world;
When bird-like Hope was ever on the wing,
   (In *thy* dear breast how soon had it been furl'd!)

Had we but met when both our hearts were beating
   With the wild joy—the guileless love of youth—
Thou a proud boy—with frank and ardent greeting—
   And I, a timid girl, all trust and truth!

Ere yet my pulse's light, elastic play
   Had learn'd the weary weight of grief to know,
Ere from these eyes had pass'd the morning ray,
   And from my cheek the early rose's glow;

Had we but met in life's delicious spring,
   Ere wrong and falsehood taught me doubt and fear,
Ere hope came back with worn and wounded wing,
   To die upon the heart she could not cheer;

Ere I love's precious pearl had vainly lavish'd,
   Pledging an idol deaf to my despair;
Ere one by one the buds and blooms were ravish'd
   From life's rich garland by the clasp of Care.

Ah! had we then but met!—I dare not listen
   To the wild whispers of my fancy now!
My full heart beats—my sad, droop'd lashes glisten—
   I hear the music of thy *boyhood's* vow!

I see thy dark eyes lustrous with love's meaning,
   I feel thy dear hand softly clasp mine own—
Thy noble form is fondly o'er me leaning—
   Love's radiant morn—but ah! the dream has flown!

How had I pour'd this passionate heart's devotion
   In voiceless rapture on thy manly breast!
How had I hush'd each sorrowful emotion,
   Lull'd by thy love to sweet, untroubled rest!

How had I knelt hour after hour beside thee,
   When from thy lips the rare, scholastic lore
Fell on the soul that all but deified thee,
   While at each pause, I, childlike pray'd for more.

How had I watch'd the shadow of each feeling
   That moved thy soul glance o'er that radiant face,
"Taming my wild heart" to that dear revealing,
   And glorying in thy genius and thy grace!

Then hadst thou loved me with a love abiding,
   And I had now been less unworthy thee,
For I was generous, guileless, and confiding,
   A frank enthusiast—buoyant, fresh, and free.

But *now,*—my loftiest aspirations perish'd,
   My holiest hopes a jest for lips profane,
The tenderest yearnings of my soul uncherish'd,
   A soul-worn slave in Custom's iron chain,—

Check'd by those ties that make my lightest sigh,
   My faintest blush, at thought of thee, a crime—
How must I still my heart, and school my eye,
   And count in vain the slow dull steps of Time.

Wilt thou come back? Ah! what avails to ask thee,
   Since honour, faith, forbid thee to return?
Yet to forgetfulness I dare not task thee,
   Lest thou too soon that *easy lesson* learn!

Ah! come not back, love! even through Memory's ear
   Thy tone's melodious murmur thrills my heart—
Come not with that fond smile, so frank, so dear;
   While yet we may, let us for ever part!

Frances S. Osgood
From "Ida Grey"
*Graham's Lady's and Gentleman's
   Magazine*
August 1845[1]

Slander

A whisper woke the air—
   A soft light tone and low,
Yet barbed with shame and woe;—
Now, might it only perish there!
   Nor farther go

---

1. *Graham's* for August would have appeared in mid-July.

Ah me! a quick and eager ear
   Caught up the little meaning sound!
Another voice has breathed it clear,
   And so it wanders round,
From ear to lip—from lip to ear—
Until it reached a gentle heart,
   And *that—it broke.*

It was the only heart it found,
The only heart 't was meant to find,
   When first its accents woke;—
It reached that tender heart at last,
   And *that—it broke.*

Low as it seemed to *other* ears,
It came—a thunder-crash to *hers,*—
   That fragile girl so fair and gay,—
   That guileless girl so pure and true!

'Tis said a lovely humming bird
   That in a fragrant lily lay,
   And dreamed the summer morn away,
   Was killed by but the gun's *report,*
   Some idle boy had fired in sport!
   The very *sound*—a death-blow came!

And thus her happy heart that beat,
With love and hope, so fast and sweet,
   (Shrined in its Lily too
For who the maid that knew
But owned the delicate flower-like grace
   Of her young form and face?)
   When first that word
   Her light heart heard,
   It fluttered like the frightened bird,
   Then shut its wings and sighed,
   And, with a silent shudder,—*died!*

Frances S. Osgood
The Broadway Journal
August 30, 1845

Echo-Song

I know a noble heart that beats
   For one it loves how "wildly well!"
I only know for *whom* it beats;
   But I must never tell!
      Never tell!
Hush! hark! how Echo soft repeats,—
     Ah! *never* tell!

I know a voice that falters low,
   Whene'er one little name 'twould say;
Full well that little name I know,
   But that I'll ne'er betray!
      Ne'er betray!
Hush! hark! how Echo murmurs low,—
     Ah! *ne'er* betray!

I know a smile that beaming flies
   From soul to lip, with rapturous glow,
And I can guess who bids it rise;
   But none—but none shall know!
      None shall know!
Hush! hark! how Echo faintly sighs,—
     But none shall know!

Frances S. Osgood
The Broadway Journal
September 6, 1845

To F——[2]

Thou wouldst be loved?—then let thy heart
    From its present pathway part not!
Being everything which now thou art,
    Be nothing which thou art not!
So with the world thy gentle ways,
    Thy grace, thy more than beauty,
Shall be an endless theme of praise
    And love—a simple duty.

[Unsigned—Edgar Allan Poe]
The Broadway Journal
September 13, 1845

The Divine Right of Kings

The only king by right divine
Is Ellen King, and were she mine
I'd strive for liberty no more,
But hug the glorious chains I wore.

Her bosom is an ivory throne,
Where tyrant virtue reigns alone;
No subject vice dare interfere,
To check the power that governs here.

O! would she deign to rule my fate,
I'd worship Kings and kingly state,
And hold this maxim all life long,
The King—*my* King—can do no wrong.

Edgar Allan Poe
Graham's Lady's and Gentleman's
Magazine
October 1845

---

2. *Broadway Journal* 148. Only the first four lines appeared on September 13, 1845.
The poem was evidently revised later and the title changed to "To F——S S. O——D."

Stanzas
[To F. S. O.]

Lady! I would that verse of mine
    Could fling, all lavishly and free,
Prophetic tones from every line,
    Of health, joy, peace, in store for thee.

Thine should be length of happy days,
    Enduring joys and fleeting cares,
Virtues that challenge envy's praise,
    By rivals loved, and mourned by heirs.

Thy life's free course should ever roam
    Beyond this bounded earthly clime,
Nor billow breaking into foam
    Upon the rock-girt shore of Time.

The gladness of a gentle heart,
    Pure as the wishes breathed in prayer,
Which has in others' joys a part,
    While in its own all others share.

The fullness of a cultured mind,
    Stored with the wealth of bard and sage,
Which Error's glitter cannot blind,
    Lustrous in youth, undimmed in age;

The grandeur of a guileless soul,
    With wisdom, virtue, feeling fraught,
Gliding serenely to its goal,
    Beneath the eternal sky of Thought:—

These should be thine, to guard and shield,
    And this the life thy spirit live,
Blest with all bliss that earth can yield,
    Bright with all hopes that Heaven can give.

E. A. Poe
Graham's Lady's and Gentleman's Magazine
December 1845[3]

---

3. *Graham's* for December would have appeared in mid-November.

To ——

Oh! they never can know that heart of thine,
    Who dare accuse thee of flirtation!
They might as well say that the stars, which shine
    In the light of their joy o'er Creation,—
Are flirting with every wild wave in which lies
One beam of the glory that kindles the skies.

Smile on then undimmed in your beauty and grace!
    Too well e'er to doubt, love, we know you;—
And shed, from your heaven, the light of your face,
    Where the waves chase each other below you;
For none can e'er deem it *your* shame or *your* sin,
That each wave holds your star-image smiling within.

Frances S. Osgood
The Broadway Journal
November 22, 1845

To ——
"In Heaven a spirit doth dwell,
Whose heart-strings are a lute."

I cannot tell *the world* how thrills my heart
To every touch that flies thy lyre along;
How the wild Nature and the wondrous Art,
Blend into Beauty in thy passionate song—

But this I *know*—in thine enchanted slumbers,
Heaven's poet, Israfel,—with minstrel fire—
Taught thee the music of his own sweet numbers,
And tuned—to chord with *his*—thy glorious lyre!

Frances S. Osgood
The Broadway Journal
November 29, 1845

A Shipwreck

I launched a bark on Fate's deep tide—
    A frail and fluttering toy,
But freighted with a thousand dreams
    Of beauty and of joy.

Ah me! it found no friend in them—
    The wave—the sky—the gale—
Though Love enraptured took the helm—
    And Hope unfurled the sail!

And you, who should its pilot be—
    To whom in fear it flies—
Forsake it, on a treacherous sea,
    To seek a prouder prize.

Alas for Love! bewildered child!
    He weeps the helm beside,
And Hope has furled her fairy sail,
    Nor longer tempts the tide.

Despair and Pride in silence fling
    Its rich freight to the wave,
And now an aimless wreck it floats,
    That none would stoop to save.

F. S. Osgood
The Broadway Journal
December 13, 1845

Lenore[4]

Oh! fragile and fair, as the delicate chalices,
    Wrought with so rare and so subtle a skill,
Bright relics, that tell of the pomp of those palaces,
    Venice—the sea-goddess—glories in still.

---

4. This poem was reprinted in the *Broadway Journal* within Poe's review of Osgood's *Poems,* published by Clark & Austin. The title implies a connection with Poe.

Whose exquisite texture, transparent and tender,
    A pure blush alone from the ruby *wine* takes;
Yet ah!If some false hand, profaning its splendor,
    Dares but to taint it with poison,—it breaks!

So when Love pour'd thro' thy pure heart his lightening,
    On thy pale cheek the soft rose-hues awoke,—
So when wild Passion, that timid heart frightening,
    Poison'd the treasure—it trembled and broke!

Frances S. Osgood
The Broadway Journal
December 13, 1845

To "The Lady Geraldine"

Though friends had warn'd me all the while,
    And blamed my willing blindness,
I did not once mistrust your smile,
    Or doubt your tones of kindness.

I sought you not—you came to me
    With words of friendly greeting:
Alas! how different now I see
    That ill-starr'd moment's meeting

When others lightly named your name,
    My cordial praise I yielded;
While *you* would wound with woe and shame
    The soul you should have shielded.

Was it so blest—my life's estate—
    That you with envy view'd me?
Ah, false one! could you dream my fate,
    You had not thus pursued me.

Perhaps when those who loved me once,
    Beguiled by you, have left me,
You'll grieve for all the hopes of which
    Your whisper'd words bereft me.

You'll think, perhaps, the laugh you raised
    Was hardly worth the anguish
With which it caused a deep, true heart,
    In silent pride to languish.

You'll think, perchance, the idle jest—
    The joy—will scarce reward you
For all the blame another's breast
    Must now, in scorn, accord you.

Yet go! 'tis but a darker cloud
    O'er one for-doom'd to sadness;
I would not change my grief so proud
    For all your guilty gladness.

Frances S. Osgood
The Broadway Journal
December 20, 1845

To——

Like the memory of a fountain,
    Springing pure and falling free,
In the midst of worldly turmoil,
    Is my silent thought of thee.

Like a soft and dewy wild-flower,
    Blushing 'mid exotics gay,
Far more dear in its shy sweetness,
    In its modest grace, than they.

Like a rainbow lightly bending,
    For a moment from the sky,
Weaving wings of heavenly beauty,
    Out of clouds that round it lie.

Weaving wings to fly and leave us,
    Out of mingled smiles and tears,
So thy pure and lovely presence,
    'Mid our troubled life appears.

Frances S. Osgood
New-York Mirror
January 10, 1846

To Her Whose Name Is Written Below

Valentine's Eve, 1846

For her these lines are penned, whose luminous eyes,
Bright and expressive as the twins of Læda,
Shall find her own sweet name that, nestling, lies
Upon the page, enwrapped from every reader.
Search narrowly these words, which hold a treasure
Divine—a talisman, an amulet
That must be worn *at heart*. Search well the measure—
The words—the letters themselves. Do not forget
The smallest point, or you may lose your labor.
And yet there is in this no Gordian knot
Which one might not undo without a sabre
If one could merely understand the plot.
Upon the open page on which are peering
Such sweet eyes now, there lies, I say, *perdu,*
A musical name oft uttered in the hearing
Of poets, by poets—for the name is a poet's too.
In common sequence set, the letters lying,
Compose a sound delighting all to hear—
Ah, this you'd have no trouble in descrying
Were you not something of a dunce, my dear—
And now I leave these riddles to their Seer.[5]

[Unsigned—Edgar A. Poe]
New-York Mirror
February 21, 1846

---

5. Note that Poe misspelled the name, spelling it Frances Sergeant [sic] Osgood instead of Frances Sargent Osgood.

To the Author of "The Raven"[6]

I asked the raven on his bust, above
    the chamber-door,
If that your fame would ever die—he answered
    "Nevermore."

[Author Unknown]
New-York Mirror
February 28, 1846

---

6. This poem was among nineteen valentine poems from Anne Lynch's Valentine *soirée* printed in the *New-York Mirror*. Poe's valentine poem to Frances Osgood was also among those printed in the *Mirror*.